The
WAR
ARTIST

The

WAR
ARTIST

JAN CASEY

An Aria Book

First published in the UK in 2024 by Head of Zeus,
part of Bloomsbury Publishing Plc

9 7 5 3 1 2 4 6 8

A catalogue record for this book is available from the British Library.

ISBN (PB): 9781803283876
ISBN (E): 9781803283852

Cover design: Simon Michele

Typeset by Siliconchips Services Ltd UK

Printed and bound in Great Britain by
CPI Group (UK) Ltd, Croydon CRO 4YY

Head of Zeus Ltd
First Floor East
5–8 Hardwick Street
London ECIR 4RG

WWW.HEADOFZEUS.COM

To my lovely aunt, Kathleen Casey. Thank you for all your support and encouragement. With all my love.

I

November 1940

If it wasn't for the rain, Sybil would have missed Dame Lily altogether. As she turned the corner and went to climb the steps into the Central School of Arts and Crafts, she peered through the fog and smoke at the older woman who tried to raise her umbrella three times. On the first attempt, a gust blew the black fabric inside out so violently it resembled a witch's broomstick. The second time, one of the ribs sprang loose from its tip and the freed sail flapped about with a mind of its own. Finally, on the third try, the umbrella stayed up but the portfolio the woman was carrying almost fell from her grasp. Watching all the fuss made Sybil hot and agitated.

'Bloody contraption,' Dame Lily grumbled as she tossed the ends of a blue and yellow scarf over her shoulder. It was then Sybil recognised her former tutor.

'Dame Lily.' Sybil rushed to help.

'Sybil.' Dame Lily touched her former student lightly on the arm.

'Come inside,' Sybil said. 'And we can get this umbrella sorted out.' She gathered everything together and they ducked into the school foyer.

'I thought you were well on your way, Dame Lily.' The doorman sounded surprised. 'Has something untoward happened?'

'I'm quite alright, thank you, Laurence. But my ridiculous umbrella is refusing to play ball.' She handed over the offending item to Laurence who studied the mechanism intently, then turned her full attention to Sybil. 'How lovely to see you, my dear,' she said. 'It's been ages since I've heard from you.' She offered her hand.

Taking off her gloves, Sybil felt caught between a bow and a curtsey. Although she took the outstretched hand and said, 'It's my pleasure, Dame Lily,' she was aware of her wet hair dripping from under her hat and the squelching noise her shoes made every time she moved. She twisted the simple wedding band on her finger, and as it caught the low light of a desk lamp, it twinkled for a split second.

'How are you holding up during this monstrous time?' Dame Lily gestured to the boarded windows, lack of artwork on the walls, the gas masks they were both carrying.

'I've been meaning to write.' Sybil coloured slightly. 'But I was waiting until there was good news to tell. Everything is so bleak, isn't it?'

'Ah, I see,' Dame Lily said. 'But I really want to hear any news from my students, good, bad or indifferent.'

'Thank you, Dame Lily,' Sybil said.

'That,' Dame Lily pointed to Sybil's ring, 'must have been good news.'

Sybil hesitated and gazed down at her hand. She managed to hold back the threatening tears, but there was nothing to be done about the swelling in her throat. In a hoarse voice she said, 'It was, until Graeme...'

'Mrs Paige.' A porter approached. 'The principal will see you now.'

Dame Lily raised her eyebrows.

'I want to talk to him about getting some hours as a tutor,' Sybil said under her breath.

'Good luck. Shall I wait for you? We can have a cup of tea together, or something stronger, and you can tell me the outcome of your chat.'

'I'd like that very much, if you can spare the time.'

'I have plenty of time for you, my dear,' Dame Lily said.

'I'll sit in the Queen's Larder. Do you know it?' She waved in the general direction of the pub, retrieved her umbrella from the doorman, took a firm grip on her portfolio and turned to face the filthy afternoon again.

On the few occasions Sybil had been in the principal's office during her time as a student, the room had been welcoming and warm, with astonishingly beautiful works of art hanging where light from the windows could show them to their best advantage. Now, as she sat in a rather shabby, green upholstered chair, the empty spaces on the walls and the gaps in the bookcases where paintings and leather-bound volumes had been removed to safety made her shiver. The only light came from the dwindling fire and a desk lamp.

'Mrs Paige, used to be Pickersgill?' The principal came towards her from a side door, a folder in his hand. 'Please don't get up.'

They shook hands and he took a chair across from her. 'Would you like anything? A drink perhaps?' He picked up a bell from the table next to him and held it out, ready to summon his assistant.

'No, thank you, Mr Warnsley,' Sybil said. 'I'm quite alright.'

The principal looked a bit disappointed, but he opened the file on his lap and whilst he shuffled through a few papers, Sybil studied his sparse hair and mottled scalp. He'd always been endearingly scatty, but now he looked as if he'd given up all attempts at organisation. A long thread hung from the hem of his trousers and what looked like a splat of porridge was glued to his tie. His eyes, too, when he gazed towards the boarded-up windows, were distant, as if he wanted more than anything to be holed up with the country's art treasures, wherever they might be.

'Thank you for seeing me,' Sybil said, hoping to start the conversation.

He stared at her as if he'd that minute become aware of her presence. 'Former students are always welcome,' he said. 'Would you like me to write a reference for you?'

'Not at the moment, Mr Warnsley, thank you. I was wondering if you had any hours as a tutor to offer?'

'Ah,' he said, taking a handkerchief from his pocket and wiping his face. 'I'm not sure.' He shook his head. 'What was your speciality?' He delved into the papers again. 'Yes, of course. Oils.'

'I've also been concentrating on charcoals recently,' Sybil said.

'Needs must. Paints are very expensive and bound to get more so.' The principal placed the folder on the table. 'I'm going to be honest with you. There are almost more tutors and potential tutors than students these days.'

Sybil wasn't surprised, but hearing the words caused tears of frustration to sting the backs of her eyes.

'I'm terribly sorry,' he went on. 'A lot of men and women who are too old to enlist have been taken on along with a glut of conscientious objectors who will hold on to their jobs like terriers for as long as possible. Have you had anything hanging in an exhibition or any reviews of your work?'

Humiliated that nothing of the sort had happened for her, Sybil answered in a thin voice. 'No, Mr Warnsley,' she said.

'Not yet, I think you mean.' He smiled at her. 'Have you tried the WAAC? You know, the War Artists' Advisory Committee.'

She hadn't because she was under the impression the WAAC commissioned artists rather than sought them out, so she answered with a no again.

'Well, I will put your name on my list and bear you in mind if and when a position becomes available.' The principal stood to signal the end of the interview.

'Thank you, Mr Warnsley,' Sybil said. 'I appreciate that. In the meantime, I'll probably sign up for war work as I'll no doubt be conscripted anyway.'

'That would be very noble of you,' he said. 'I'm afraid this war is putting paid to many an artist's ambition, much like the last one. But I refuse to be downhearted. It will end, also like the last one and there will be legacies left, old artists reborn and new ones, with fresh ideas, ready to take over.'

4

He shook her hand and as he turned, Sybil thought the slump of his shoulders made him look every inch a man who was trying desperately to convince himself that he didn't feel desolate about the current situation.

Dame Lily was sitting in a quiet corner of the pub and when Sybil walked in, she raised her hand in greeting.

Once upon a time, the pub would have been lit from within by soft lighting and from without by the glow of bright streetlamps through open curtains. It was too early for outdoor lights, but when the day ended, no comforting beacons would be ablaze anywhere in the land, and indoors there would be nothing other than low flickers casting their interesting but sinister maudlin shadows.

Night after night of atrocious, heartrending bombing raids sent swarms scuttling for shelter in the Underground or beneath tables or to huts in the garden. Everyone was so tired during the day, when it was business as usual, that they'd taken on the pallor of ghostly apparitions – herself included. Debris lay everywhere and what hadn't been incinerated was doused in water from burst mains or reeked of escaping gas. Evacuation meant there were few children anywhere and the absence of whooping and cheering and laughing and mewling rang loudly in her ears. It was all horrific. And not knowing what would hit them next gave living on one's nerves a whole new meaning.

Spread out on the table in front of Dame Lily was a small artist's pad and a piece of charcoal and as Sybil approached, she could see that her former tutor had been sketching the bookcase, the door and the row of unlit candles standing along the bar.

'Don't you have an umbrella or did my experience put you off?' Dame Lily said when Sybil stood in front of her, her teeth chattering and her lips blue.

'It's in here.' Sybil pointed to her canvas bag. 'I thought I'd be able to dodge the worst of it. But no such luck.'

'Well, there's certainly no harm done as far as your looks are concerned,' Dame Lily said. 'You're still as striking as ever. Sit, please. I ordered a gin for you.' She passed the glass to Sybil. 'How was your chat with Mr Warnsley?'

Sybil took a long draught from her glass before she answered. 'He said he'd bear me in mind, which everyone knows is a polite way of saying no thank you.'

'Have you tried the Slade?'

'I did before they evacuated to Oxford.' Sybil asked. 'And the outcome was the same. They said they'd keep me on their books.'

'I'm sorry, my dear. But something will come up, I'm sure.'

Sybil had no idea what that something could possibly be.

'I was about to give up on you,' Dame Lily said. 'And leave a note for us to meet another time. I try my best to avoid the Underground and time is getting on.'

'Would you prefer to postpone?' Sybil asked, concerned that she not do anything to impose on the revered Dame Lily.

'No, no, my dear,' Dame Lily said. 'Let's talk until the blackouts are drawn, then we'll make a run for it and hope for the best.'

'If you're sure,' Sybil said. 'I wouldn't want to cause you any discomfort.'

'Any hardship I have to endure is definitely not due to you,' Dame Lily said. 'We can plant that firmly at Hitler's feet.'

Sybil nodded and felt the ends of her damp hair, running her fingers through the strawberry blonde waves and trying to reset them with her hands. 'I spend most nights in the Tube,' she said, wrinkling her nose. 'It's not pleasant.'

'That, my dear, is an understatement. Personally, I would much rather be tucked up under the stairs with my sister and brother-in-law in Chelsea if I can't make it home to Norfolk.'

'I keep myself occupied whilst in the depths, though,' Sybil said.

'Probably much like me.' Dame Lily pointed to her sketchbook. 'I carry this with me wherever I go. Do you have your work with you? We could critique each other.'

Sybil felt herself redden. 'It would be an honour to see your sketches,' she said. 'But mine ...' She shook her head.

'Fair exchange is no robbery. Come along, don't make me click my fingers.'

Sybil shrank into herself when she recalled Dame Lily's method for getting an unwilling student to show their piece. She would ask them once, very courteously, and if that didn't have the desired effect, she'd ask again with a bit more force. If nothing was forthcoming from that, she would stand in front of them, snap her fingers and hold out her hand until the poor young man or woman handed over their work. It had happened once to Sybil and she'd hated being singled out in front of everyone else.

Reluctantly, Sybil passed her sketchbook across the table and swapped with Dame Lily.

'Another, my dear?' Dame Lily said before she opened Sybil's book.

'I'll get these,' Sybil said. 'Would you like the same again?'

Dame Lily hesitated, no doubt loath to let her pay for a round when the gulf in their circumstances was so wide. A fellow student had told her that tutors allowed their students to occasionally buy them one drink so they wouldn't be embarrassed and refuse to go out with them in the future.

'Yes, please,' Dame Lily smiled.

Waiting for their drinks, Sybil looked outside at the rain falling in grey sheets and the canopy of umbrellas dancing to the tune of the wind. If anything, she hoped it would get worse instead of better as poor visibility would make the Jerries' work much more difficult. Even supposing that were the case, if tonight was like every other since September – and there was no reason why it wouldn't be – the siren would soon start to wail and everyone would scurry to hide away.

A fresh drink in front of them, they opened each other's sketchbooks and turned the pages. As Sybil knew they would be, Dame Lily's drawings were wonderful. Despite being able to see where her former tutor had softened hard lines with the side of her hand, emphasised others with a bolder line and gone over sections to bring out one aspect or another, she was awestruck. There were a number of war-torn London and quite a few seascapes of the east coast, which was a large part of Dame Lily's body of work.

Looking up at Sybil, Dame Lily said, 'Those of the sea were drawn before the defences were put into place. Yet again.'

Confused, Sybil put down the sketchbook and was about to question Dame Lily further, but the older women carried on. 'During the first years of the Great War, coastlines were off-limits for artists. I adapted and concentrated on oils of military training, and whilst I welcome, in theory, having to adjust and diversify, I'm quite bitter because I reshaped my life and work during that war and the reality of doing so again is devastating.'

Sybil nodded, not wanting to say anything that would stop Dame Lily from continuing with this insight into her life. She couldn't believe that her former tutor – who had full membership of the Royal Academy – had founded an Artists' Colony, designed costumes for the Royal Ballet, etched prints for London Transport, won a Gold for painting at the Olympics, had her pictures of the circus on biscuit tins and had been created a dame – was talking to her as if they were equals. And yet, the conversation flowed, and Sybil no longer dwelled on whether what she said might be considered impertinent or above her station.

'After the war, there was Art Deco of course, and although I wasn't a part of the movement, I approved and admired the entire light, elegant style. Now its popularity has waned in favour of another round of dark, gloomy chiaroscuro war art that must speak for this terrible time. I was going along nicely, thank you, building up my portfolio of seascapes along with the ballet and chocolate box commissions, when here we go again.'

'I'm so sorry for you and anyone who's been through this before.'

'You'd think they'd learn, wouldn't you? Or that we'd learn.'

'I can't see what we could be doing differently at this stage,' Sybil said. 'None of it's up to us.'

'No,' Dame Lily agreed. 'Of course not. But we do need a

new philosophy or ethos or approach, although right now isn't the time to try to set that up. All we can do is ensure that art tells the story of the person or persons it's representing. You do remember that, I hope?'

Sybil nodded. There was no possibility that she would forget Dame Lily's edict that an artist must take a subject, render it dumb, inert and soulless, then give it back its movement and voice and spirit. 'Yes, Dame Lily, you drilled that into us and I try to live by it, as far as my art is concerned.'

'Well done. I'm glad I managed to teach you something tangible. And that is the role of the artist in this or any war. Terrible as it is.'

'Will you concentrate on war scenes from now on?'

'Inevitably,' Dame Lily said. She sounded drained. 'As will most of us. I'd rather not, but of course,' she leaned across the table towards Sybil, 'anything that artists produce that depicts this period of time will be a war scene. Even if it's a tranquil rural landscape or fishermen bringing in their catch or women knitting, it will be us during this bloody war. Does that sound logical?'

Sybil hadn't thought of the situation in that way, but now that she did, it made perfect sense. She nodded and said, 'So we're all war artists now?'

'Well, in theory. Practically and officially, though, we're not.'

Dame Lily opened the first page of Sybil's sketchbook and her breath caught in her throat. Sybil knew the drawing. It depicted a family of five lying underneath moth-eaten blankets pushed up against a tiled wall in the Underground. Around them were the nebulous shapes of other people sleeping or reading or sitting in poses that told of quiet resignation. The grandmother's eyes were closed, her jaw slack. Two small boys lay between her and their mother who faced away, pins falling out of her dishevelled hair. In the foreground, a little girl of about four leaned against her mother's back. She was wearing what must have once been a party dress and socks that had strayed down around her ankles. Wide awake and staring straight at the viewer with candour and innocence, the entire essence of the war had been captured in her eyes. The look on her face was at once knowing and uncomprehending and begged the viewer for an explanation of what was going on around her.

'My dear.' Dame Lily put a finger on the corner of the sketchbook. 'This is exquisite, and a perfect example of art speaking for those who have no voice.'

Sybil fidgeted with her wedding ring again and coloured from the collar up. 'Thank you,' she said.

'And this one,' Dame Lily exclaimed. 'These men peering over each other's shoulders to get a glimpse of the newspaper. Magnificent.'

The door opened to a laughing young couple who brought a squall in with them. Sybil shivered, tightened the belt on her jacket and watched their progress to the bar, the man's arm territorially around the woman's shoulders. That's how Graeme had claimed her for himself. An arm snaking around her waist. A hand on the small of her back. Fingers entwined in the space between them on the table. When she was with him, there had always been a high level of anticipation and excitement that bubbled away just beneath the surface. As if something wonderful were about to happen at any moment. She remembered when he'd left a trail of notes for her in five pubs across Haringey. On each one he'd written a clue about where to look for him next until she found him grinning behind a bouquet of flowers in The Finsbury.

Another time he'd booked them into a small hotel without giving her warning. Two endless days and nights had been spent seeking and finding each other's warm, slick bodies with eager hands and mouths and tongues. And that level of lust and love – which he couldn't possibly have contrived – hadn't stopped until a sudden, inexplicable change had come over him.

'I'm sorry, my dear.' Dame Lily's brow creased. 'I was so taken with your artwork I forgot to ask about your husband.'

Sybil shook her head. 'It's difficult for me to … talk about him.' She took a deep breath and sat up a bit straighter. 'His name is

Graeme Paige and we met at an exhibition at St Martin's,' she said.

'Were you exhibiting, or was he? Do you mind if I …?' Dame Lily produced a silver cigarette case and a lighter from her bag.

'Not at all,' Sybil said. 'The only exhibition I've been a part of was the leaving show at the Central, but Graeme was showing a watercolour. We got talking, then we met up and, well,' she shrugged, 'one thing led to another.'

Dame Lily waited for her to elaborate, but she was so lost in the vivid images of the early days with Graeme that she couldn't think of anything else to say about her husband. She saw again her own face when she'd found him clutching the flowers in the pub. Her eyes and smile had been wide, and she felt almost carefree when she'd thought about how he might save her from loneliness in her solitary bedsit. Now, she felt more alone than ever.

'He must be very special indeed,' Dame Lily said. 'Or just plain lucky, to get a young woman like you.'

Sybil felt heat burning her cheeks. 'He was … is very special. I thought about keeping my maiden name for my career, but now I'm glad I took his. It makes me feel as if he's still with me, being supportive and kind and generous. That's what he was like,' she said. 'And he will be again. I'm sure of it.'

'I'm afraid I was never as thoughtful with my dear Geoffrey. As you know, I kept my single name of Brampton rather than changing it to Fortescue. After all, I developed my skills and talent by study and hard work which was nothing to do with him. He can have his own name on his own work. But I don't quite understand, my dear,' Dame Lily said. She stubbed out her cigarette and put her hand over Sybil's. 'Whatever do you mean by saying he was like this or that? The silly man hasn't given you the heave-ho, has he?'

He might as well have, Sybil thought. *The way he left so abruptly*. But that must have been down to him wanting to do his duty. She was convinced it had no bearing on the way he felt about her. 'He's missing in action.' Sybil's voice cracked and she nearly pulled the ring off her finger before jamming it back down again.

'Oh, my dear,' Dame Lily said. 'I'm so terribly sorry for you.' Her face softened. 'You mustn't give up hope and you must keep busy.'

Sybil nodded, too miserable to reply.

'Did this happen recently, or have you had time to ... adjust?'

She felt rather taken aback. The thought had never occurred to her, although she was existing – eating, drinking, looking for work, smiling and laughing from time to time, experiencing whole minutes of thinking about other things – so she must have adapted and assimilated somewhat. But how, she wondered, could she possibly really do so when, for that short period of time when they were a couple, Graeme had meant everything to her. He'd obliterated her past, filled her present and embodied her future happiness. 'Seven months ago.' She looked down at her wedding ring. 'And I don't think I'll ever get used to it. Instead of being in hell, I'm in limbo and that's where I'll have to stay until I get news one way or the other, and God only knows how long that will be.'

'It's terribly cruel,' Dame Lily said. 'I'm sure people have told you many times that you're not the only one, and I'm equally sure it doesn't help.'

'No,' Sybil said. 'It doesn't. Although it stops me from feeling too sorry for myself.'

'For every door that opens, another one closes – and vice versa,' Dame Lily said. 'I don't suppose that's comforting either, is it?'

Sybil shook her head. 'All I seem to experience is the closing of doors behind me. Others never seem to open.' She wiped her eyes and took a deep breath.

Dame Lily sipped her gin and puffed on her cigarette. 'Let's talk about art, shall we?' she said.

Sybil nodded, then scrambled for something interesting to say. At last she offered, 'My biggest fear is that there won't be an art world left after this carry-on, let alone a world for it to circulate in. No doubt you've seen the denuded walls of the National?'

Dame Lily prised a beer mat off the tacky table, then stuck it back down in a different position. 'There will always be art, and consequently, an art world. I'm not sure how long it's been since you've peeped into the National?' She sat back in her chair. 'It was only closed for a few weeks after Hitler dropped one of his nasties on it in the hope it would collapse like a foldable easel. Anyway, it's open to the public again now.'

Sybil gasped and put her hand on her throat.

'Not to view the greats,' Dame Lily said. 'They're safe, my dear, and as we know, they wouldn't be if they'd been left on the walls of any building in London. No, the WAAC is displaying works in the galleries, so it's art at its defiant best. As it should be.'

Sybil looked disappointed and reached for her drink. 'I suppose you know where all those magnificent pieces of work are being stored, don't you?'

Dame Lily wouldn't be drawn, and Sybil understood the reasons why she couldn't say anything if she did know, so the conversation was steered back to Sybil's original statement. 'As far as your theory about this war annihilating art, why, no such thing could happen, and your notebook is a testimony to that. War cannot take away the urge artists have to create, but it will alter the finished product.'

Dame Lily held on so tightly to Sybil's portfolio that it seemed as if she were staking a claim on it. 'What do you intend to do with these pieces that speak so admirably for the subjects?'

Sybil drained the last of her gin and studied the empty glass for a moment. 'I think I'll put them away in a drawer and forget about them.'

Dame Lily looked appalled. 'I insist you send them to the WAAC for consideration.'

Sybil shook her head. 'The principal advised that, too, although he hadn't seen any of my work, so it must be a generic suggestion for struggling artists. Besides, I was under the impression the Committee approached the artist, not the other way around.'

'Yes, that is partly, but not wholly, the case. The Committee approaches artists with offers of short-term commissions based on a certain subject, or one can ask the Committee to view one's work with the hopes of gaining a commission, or an artist can tender a proposal. If stylised, the charcoal pieces in here,' she rapped lightly on the cardboard cover, 'would almost certainly be accepted.'

'I heard that you've been awarded a commission and a salary with the WAAC,' Sybil said.

'Yes, that's correct.'

'Very many congratulations. And the only woman, so I believe? Unless that's changed now.'

Dame Lily shook her head. 'Sadly, no,' she said. 'There are other women on board with short-term contracts, though believe me, I've tried to get the Committee to appoint a few more of us permanently. But no luck so far.'

'How many men have been engaged?'

'Full-time?' Dame Lily flapped her hand through the air and rolled her eyes. 'Dozens,' she said. 'Including Geoffrey.'

Sybil knew that Dame Lily's husband had an excellent reputation in the art world and deserved his commission from the War Artists' Advisory Committee, as did all of the other men, most probably. *But surely*, she thought, *there must be room for a few more women?*

'It's such a shame,' Dame Lily's voice rose with emotion. 'I do think the Committee is missing a trick. How they can fail to see the importance of documenting this period from a feminine point of view is beyond me. Who better to represent the Home Front, the Women's Land Army, the WVS, nurses, evacuation billeting officers, WAAFs, WRNS, motorcycle despatch riders, factory workers, women on the tools.' She threw her hands heavenward. 'The list goes on and on.'

'My thoughts exactly,' Sybil said. 'Most of the women's experiences are going to be recorded from a male perspective, and whilst that's not invaluable, think of how much more depth there would be to the artwork if the story were told by the women living it.'

'So, I repeat. You must put your work up for consideration.'

'I'm going to be called up anyway,' Sybil said. 'That's inevitable. And if I do then ...' She shrugged. 'I won't have access to materials or the time to draw or paint or offer my work to any organisation.'

'That would be a terrible pity,' Dame Lily said. 'Many men and women are going about their active duties and producing the most wonderful pieces – many eventually commissioned by the WAAC or the Recording Britain Project. Have you heard of that?'

'Vaguely,' Sybil said. 'Again, I presumed I would have to be petitioned.'

Dame Lily shook her head with the slightest tic of impatience. 'No one is going to commission your work if they've never seen it, are they?'

'I'd like to know a bit more about the Project, I must say,' Sybil said. 'Shall I get another round?'

'My turn,' said Dame Lily. 'Tell the barman to put it on my tab. Oh, bother, the bloody blackouts.'

Making his way from window to window, the landlord pulled the dark, dense curtaining across each pane of glass, causing what little light there was on such a bleak November afternoon to be drained from the pub pane by pane. His wife, a cloth under her arm, lit the candles which spluttered and sparked before they flamed and threw trembling patterns, like the children's game of shadow puppets, across the bar.

'I had no idea time had marched on so aggressively,' Dame Lily said, gathering her things together. 'I'm going back to Norfolk tomorrow, so I can write to you with details of the Project, and we can take it from there. You must make sure I have your current address.'

'Of course, Dame Lily. Thank you for showing an interest.' Sybil shrugged into her coat and pulled on her gloves. 'I'm in the same bedsit in Haringey. I'll jot down my particulars in case you've mislaid them.' She tore off a corner from a notepad and scribbled on it.

For a moment, Dame Lily narrowed her eyes and looked as if she were trying to dredge up a piece of information from the depths of her mind. Sybil was certain it wouldn't take her former tutor long to recall the time she'd found her sniffling at the end of a lesson. When pressed, Sybil had admitted that she was no longer able to keep on the flat she'd shared with her father after he'd died. She'd tried hard to be stoic, but the tiny bedsit she'd moved into was cold and functional, and hollow loneliness had engulfed her. Then Graeme had come along, and for a few months, he'd filled the dank, dark space with warmth and laughter and a reason to hurry home.

But the impending bombing raid put paid to further speculation on that subject from Dame Lily. Sybil handed her the scrap of paper. 'It seems as if the whole world – except me – is moving forward. I feel left behind or stuck in the same place at the very least.'

'You've got that completely wrong, my dear,' Dame Lily said. 'It's the world that's going backwards, not you. Goodnight,' she threw over her shoulder to the landlord. 'All the best.'

'Mind how you go, Dame Lily,' the man called out.

Much to Sybil's surprise, Dame Lily grabbed her elbow, pressed their arms together and marched them into the darkening drizzle. 'Have you a torch?' Sybil asked.

'There's always so much to think about,' Dame Lily said. 'I should have fished it out before we left the pub. Can you rummage in my bag and find it for me, there's a dear.' She raised her arm so Sybil could hunt around in her holdall.

Dragging out the flashlight, Sybil turned it on and played the beam, covered in tissue paper, towards the rain-streaked, grey pavement.

'I might just make it to Chelsea before the siren,' Dame Lily said. 'I hope you get home to Haringey in good time. Goodbye, my dear.'

Dame Lily turned to the left and Sybil to the right. There was little time to spare but for a moment, Sybil turned and watched her former tutor dart along the pavement with her head down, until she was no more than another opaque shadow in the darkening sky.

Sybil imagined Dame Lily fumbling for the key to her sister and brother-in-law's house and flinging herself into the hallway at the moment the siren wailed – at least she hoped that was the case. The Tube Sybil had jumped onto at Holborn terminated at King's Cross, and there was no point in trying to go any further. She had to admit she was rather glad of that because, although she would be uncomfortable, she would be surrounded by other people. There was a cup of tea from a steamy urn, the low hum of chatter and a corner where she settled herself on her coat. Taking out her sketchbook, she studied the drawing of the little girl leaning against her sleeping mother and tried to see what had made such an impact on Dame Lily so she could recreate it again and again.

Indistinguishable figures were caught like dark clouds in the background of the picture and the family she'd concentrated on had been captured in bold lines. Because of that technique, it seemed as though every aspect of the subjects' situation was painfully obvious. Consequently, the plight of all those down in the depths with them on that particular night became more apparent. Rather than focus on trying to bring emotion to everyone in a group scene, Sybil found that telling the story of one or two brought the other subjects to life. But she'd always thought of that as laziness or a failing on her part, something she needed to work on, not a characteristic that was worthy of positive comment.

Now, when she studied the picture again, she could see that she had told the story of the little girl's bewilderment as well as the comfort she found in being snuggled close to her mother. Perhaps rather than dismissing the style, which she seemed to be naturally drawn to, she should make more of it.

Consolidate and sharpen it into a skill that could be identified as her own.

She opened her tin of charcoals and drew, from memory, her former tutor sitting in the shadowy confines of the pub with a Gin and It at her elbow, a scarf wrapped around her neck and smoke curling from the cigarette between her fingers. Feathered lines of dark hair swept back off Dame Lily's face into a roll at the back of her head, with streaks of paper left white to represent grey strands. One side of the older woman's face was obscured, and on the other, Sybil traced faint lines around the eye and mouth with a light touch. Next to her subject, she added the shapes of the objects Dame Lily had been carrying, giving prominence to the portfolio of artwork and the gas mask. On the opposite side of the table, she drew her own hands, clasped together to give the impression that there was another person involved in the conversation.

Then she thought about turning her attention to two young women, who looked like twins, and the tiny babies they were trying desperately to rock to sleep. But instead, she opened a sketchbook that she kept secreted away and sketched a pastel image she'd been both longing to compose and fighting to forget. The subject was a young woman of about her own age, with the same pale strawberry blonde hair caught up in a clip similar to one sitting on her dresser. The girl was wearing a short-sleeved navy dress identical to one of her favourites, and she was slumped backwards in a chair with her eyes closed and a telegram identical to the one she'd received six months ago dangling from her hand. She thought she was ready to see the drawing through, but as she studied it, her tears soaked the paper, and the charcoal ran into rivers until it was no more than a muddy mess. Much like the field where she imagined Graeme had fallen.

2

Dame Lily Brampton, DBE RA ROI RWS,
Seagulls' Watch,
Cley-next-the-Sea,
Norfolk

Monday, 9th December 1940

Mrs S. Paige,
Flat 3,
47, Flowerpot Close,
Haringey,
London, N.15

My dear Sybil,

First of all, I do hope you made it home to Haringey after our drink in the Queen's Larder last month, although I got the distinct impression you preferred the Underground to toughing it out on your own in the bedsit.

I fell in the door of my sister and brother-in-law's house at the last possible moment to find them crammed into the understairs cupboard. I shone my torch on them and there was Catherine, with a funny old cloche hat on her head, and Desmond with a cloth cap on his. I couldn't help but burst out laughing. 'You do know that neither of those head coverings will provide you with any protection, don't you?' I asked. All they did was shrug and say it was better than nothing. Then my sister insisted I tie a knitted scarf tightly under my chin and join them. What a sight we must have looked. At least they agreed to let me sketch them, and the ensuing piece is both comical and poignant, and I think that, with a bit of work, it will speak to the viewer. Before I left the following morning, I put three saucepans at the ready in the cupboard for next time and my sister got a laugh out of that.

Secondly, I must apologise for taking such an inordinate amount of time to write to you. I am not one to make excuses for myself, but I have been extremely busy with things pertaining to art and to my personal life.

I'm not sure if you are aware, but Sir Geoffrey and I have three sons. Ignatius is thirty and an officer in the Army. He's the only one amongst our offspring who wants to follow in his parents' footsteps. Next is Dominic who is twenty-four and studying to be a doctor, and then there's Aloysius, twenty-two and in his last year at Oxford reading law. Despite Al and Dom being in reserved positions, they want to join up. Can you believe it? Perhaps you can as your Graeme must have been in the same situation.

We have had so many discussions with them but they keep saying they'll be called up eventually so they might as well go now, or they have a moral obligation that's much more worthy than finishing their studies, or that if they volunteer they can choose what they do which might prove to be safer in the long run. I think we may have convinced Dom to see sense by impressing on him how much more useful he'll be to the war effort as a fully qualified doctor, but Al will not have it. Geoffrey says if they want to go, we must let them, but I'm not ready to give up yet.

Despite this ****** bombardment night after night, much is happening in the art world. The WAAC continues to commission, and as we discussed, they're using the empty walls in the National Gallery to show some of the war art – your Underground sketches would be a wonderful addition. When members of the public walk through the building to listen to Myra Hess or one of the other distinguished musicians performing dauntlessly at a lunchtime recital, they can view the paintings and sketches which, so I understand, make them feel as though what they are experiencing day to day is being documented.

Besides that, I am continuing my seascapes with the addition of the ******** dotted all along the coast, so perhaps I could now answer your question about whether we are all war artists, no matter our subjects, with a resounding yes. The other afternoon, I left it a bit too late to pack up and found myself stumbling along in the pitch dark. When I peered out to sea, what I saw would have been the easiest of scenes to recreate, if I had dared waste the paper and charcoal – nothing but black. Stygian sea, with the sky and land as dark as ink. Not a pinprick of light anywhere. The stars and moon seemed to have heard the call for blackout and duly veiled themselves behind clouds. How I detest this control of light, although I absolutely understand the necessity for it.

Any more news from the Central's hallowed principal? I do hope he was able to give you a few teaching slots every week. I wonder if you've heard that the Marylebone has upped sticks and moved to a manor house in the wilds of Bedfordshire? Apparently, they're looking for a few tutors. The money will be a pittance, of course, but there will be board and lodgings and fresh air. If you're interested, I advise you to be quick with your application as many others will be pursuing the few posts up for grabs. Do say I highly recommend you.

Regardless of whether you teach or not, you will still have time for the WAAC or the Recording Britain Project, which is the main point of my letter.

Now, I don't want you to be discouraged when I tell you that the RBP was set up, in part, to employ those unlikely to be given a commission through the WAAC. I think you are extremely talented and more than capable but I, unfortunately, do not sit on the commissioning committee.

Sir Leonard Thwaites – you know who I mean, my dear, Director of the National, Chair of the WAAC, etc., etc. – is at the helm yet again and organising the whole thing with competence and aplomb, I must say. Apart from involving non-official war artists, the aims are somewhat different from those set down by the WAAC. Sir Leonard and the administrators want to preserve the characteristically British watercolour form, although drawings are also being considered. In addition, the Project is intended to boost morale by celebrating previously overlooked corners of London, the country's natural beauty and the heritage of our buildings. It is also hoped that the pieces will be a memorial to the war effort.

The most exciting news is that the Project is commissioning quite a few women, some of them straight from art school. I understand that you might consider the RBP a poor relation to the WAAC; however, if you don't think it worthwhile in its own right, it could certainly be a foot in the door to many other opportunities.

It is true that all of those involved so far have been commissioned, but artists are allowed to show the administrators their unsolicited work and from that, they could very well be appointed.

Please do think about it, Sybil. I truly believe you have so much to offer. If this letter doesn't convince you, I am speaking at the National Gallery on the 14th of January at 11 a.m., all being well, and this is your official invitation to attend. What an uncivilised hour for a lecture, but needs must when it comes to the so-called Blitz and the ******* blackout that goes with it.

Yours,

Lily

Mrs S. Paige,
Flat 3,
47, Flowerpot Close,
Haringey,
London, N.15

Thursday, 12th December 1940

Mr Edward Merton, Principal,
Marylebone School of Art,
Old Manor House,
Luton,
Beds

Dear Mr Merton,

I understand from Dame Lily Brampton, DBE RA ROI RWS, that you have a few positions for tutors at the Marylebone School of Art which has been relocated to Luton. On Dame Lily's recommendation, I would like to apply for one of the vacancies.

I am a graduate of the Central School of Art, where I specialised in oils, but I would be able and more than willing to teach any media required of me.

It would please me greatly to attend an interview and I am free to do so at your convenience. I would be happy to bring along my portfolio for scrutiny.

Yours sincerely,

Sybil Paige (Mrs)

Marylebone School of Art,
Old Manor House,
Luton,
Beds

Saturday, 14th December 1940

Mrs S. Paige,
Flat 3,
47, Flowerpot Close,
Haringey,
London, N.15

Dear Mrs Paige,

Mr Edward Merton would like to thank you for your letter of application to the Marylebone School of Art. We had a number of vacant posts for tutors as quite a few members of staff made the decision not to come with us when we evacuated to Luton.

I am pleased to tell you that, although most of those vacancies have been filled, there are three remaining positions, and Mr Merton would like to offer one to you without interview as you have been personally recommended by Dame Lily Brampton. You will be required to take classes of between six to eight students and you must be prepared to teach a number of different techniques.

If the above suits, a car will pick you up from Luton train station on Thursday, 2nd of January 1941 at 10:30 a.m.

Mr Merton, and the staff of the Marylebone School of Art, are very much looking forward to welcoming you.

Yours sincerely,

Abigail Rotherhyde (Miss),
For Mr Edward Merton

Mrs S. Paige,
Flat 3,
47, Flowerpot Close,
Haringey,
London, N.15

Tuesday, 17th December 1940

Dame Lily Brampton, DBE RA ROI RWS,
Seagulls' Watch,
Cley-next-the-Sea,
Norfolk

Dear Dame Lily,

Thank you for your letter dated Monday, 9th December 1940.

I cannot tell you how appreciative I am of your suggestion that I apply to the Marylebone School of Art, which I did immediately, and for allowing me to use your name as a recommendation. I am certain that the latter point is what swayed Mr Merton to offer me a position to start immediately after the New Year. I would have happily packed up and found my way to Luton the day of the principal's offer, but I will use the two weeks wisely to record Christmas in London during this time.

I'm so glad you made it to your sister's house after you left the pub last month. I spent the night in the underbelly of King's Cross tube station. However, it wasn't all bad news as, motivated by our talk, I was able to make a few reasonable sketches of the people around me which I have been refining. I think they could well speak for the subjects in time.

Thank you for the detailed information about the Recording Britain Project and I must say I understand the scheme much more than I did, but still doubt my work would make the grade. However, I gratefully accept your invitation to the National Gallery on the 14th of January and look forward to viewing the exhibition and hearing your speech, given, of course, that Mr Merton will grant me a day's absence.

With hope and best wishes for a peaceful Christmas,
Yours thankfully,

Sybil

Dame Lily Brampton, DBE RA ROI RWS,
Seagull's Watch,
Cley-next-the-Sea,
Norfolk

Thursday, 19th December 1940

Mrs S. Paige,
Flat 3,
47, Flowerpot Close,
Haringey,
London, N.15

Dear Sybil,

Very many congratulations on your appointment. I had no doubt you would be offered a position, and I hope it suits you and your circumstances. If nothing else, it will give you a different perspective to consider in your artwork whilst thinking about your next steps.

I am so glad you will be coming along to the exhibition. On arrival, please tell reception I have booked you in as my guest.

Do please bring along some of your drawings; as your mentor, I absolutely insist. Take this as me clicking my fingers in your direction.

I second your hope for a peaceful Christmas and add one of my own for an end to this ****** war soon in the New Year.

Yours,

Lily X

3

January 1941

Sybil's heart sank. She'd been looking forward to a trip in a motor and imagined herself in something sleek and sophisticated given Luton was home to Vauxhall, but the car that she'd been promised was no more than a farmyard heap. She felt downhearted and hoped this wasn't a bad omen for her new post in the art school. But she told herself to rally – the position would be what she made it, and she was determined to make it worthwhile.

Richard, the man who'd been sent to collect her, was wearing wellingtons encrusted in muck, dark green corduroy trousers, a heavy waxed coat and a sprig of hay or straw stuck to the hair in his ear, which he tried to bat away every few minutes. When he opened the passenger door of the vehicle, the stomach-churning stench of cabbages or cows or curdling milk hit her full-on. On the pretence of feeling the cold, she drew her woolly scarf up over her mouth and nose, but Richard was either unconcerned or his senses had been dulled to the stink, because he tossed her bags under a tarpaulin covering the back of the old wreck, climbed in next to her and started the engine on the fourth try.

Rattling along the streets of Luton, Sybil felt as if her bones were being knocked against each other and she wondered how it could feel colder inside the truck, if that's what it was, than it had outside. She tried to move her toes, but stopped after a couple of attempts because she was afraid they might snap off and she'd find them, white and bloodless, in her shoes when she took them off.

Then she saw the sliver of a wintry moon, hanging in the blue-blanched sky, and her breath stopped in her chest. With a jolt, she remembered that this was now where she lived, and she would have many opportunities to sketch the wonderful scene she could see through the windscreen. She inhaled deeply, and a sense of calm flooded her. She had a job that would allow her a certain amount of freedom to concentrate on her own art projects, there would be time to think about what to do next and she was free from that freezing, soul-destroying bedsit. If Dad had seen her in it, lonely and cold, he would have turned in his grave.

Tears filled her eyes as a picture of him hacking and coughing in his last months passed through her mind. His face had taken on an ashy sheen and an intricate tapestry of red veins laced the whites of his eyes.

Anger flared when the doctor visited for the final time and told her there was nothing else to be done. '*Keep him as warm and comfortable as possible,*' he'd said. Then he'd had the audacity to ask for his fee. She'd muddled about in her purse with shaking fingers and couldn't look at him whilst she dropped the coins into his open palm.

When she'd shut the door and turned back to Dad, she could see the shape of his skull through the tissue paper skin on his face and fear clawed at her. The one stable presence in her life would soon be gone, and she was afraid of being on her own. But she was also frightened of watching him linger for too long.

Poor Dad. He'd done his best after Mum had gone, when Sybil was too young to remember the face in the one photo they had of her propped up on the sideboard. He'd smoked and drunk and visited betting shops, but he'd worked hard so they always had food on the table and the flat to live in. But there was more to him – to them, as father and daughter – than that. She often wondered how such an undemonstrative father could have made her feel secure and surrounded by love. Was it the mere fact that he hadn't done a bunk and had stayed with her through what must have been one hard day followed by another? He'd understood little about school, but he made sure she attended. He'd polished her shoes and scrubbed the grime off her collars until she was able to do it herself. At bedtime, he'd never kissed her or tucked her in, although sometimes he smoothed a strand of her strawberry blonde hair, the same colour as her mother's, between his calloused fingers. But he would listen to her reading a bedtime story aloud, and he kept watch until she fell asleep before he crept out to the local. Those simple gestures had assured her that he'd loved and cared for her in his own way.

Sybil swiped at her tears and strained for the echo of her dad giving her a few encouraging words, but as time had gone on, his gruff voice had become more distant and less of a comfort.

Richard turned a corner, and they were faced with a row of terrace houses that lay as flat and flimsy as a fallen house of cards. Windows had been smashed, and from one frame a strip of lace curtain, probably some housewife's pride and joy not long ago, flapped about in the breeze.

'I know there ain't nowhere as bad as London,' Richard said, sending the dried stalk flying from his ear at last. 'But we've had our fair share, too. And it's a wonder there ain't been more, what with the ball bearings factory and the aerodrome and all the others.'

'I'm certainly not comparing,' Sybil said. 'It's all horrific as far as I'm concerned.'

They'd come to a stop at a set of traffic lights and waited whilst a few people hurried from one side of the road to the other. 'That empty shell over there.' Richard pointed to another bombed-out building. 'Was a hat factory not long ago. Luton's famous for hats and there used to be loads of them here. In fact, our football team is known as the Hatters,' he said with pride. 'Ain't so many of them left now. Factories, I mean. Not hats.'

Self-conscious, Sybil felt for her own battered beret, then

told herself not to be so silly as no one was sporting examples of millinery elegance. 'Oh dear,' she said, studying the razed building. 'What a shame. I hope no one was hurt.'

'Luckily, the factory were shut up for the night or there would have been quite a few women gone down with it. That,' he nodded towards a large, camouflaged area, 'is the motor works. It took a packet last August, and I'm afraid there was people caught up in that hit. But all power to them,' he said. 'They was up and running again in six days. Had to be, I suppose. We need them Churchill tanks.'

'I saw them and some trucks from the train window. Lined up and waiting to go.'

'It were a sight to see the nippers dodging convoys on their way to school.' The recollection made Richard laugh out loud. 'That's when we had little 'uns about the place,' he said in a softer voice.

He turned to her for a moment, a deep frown cutting into his forehead, then the lights changed and he forced the truck into gear with such a grating racket she was surprised pedestrians didn't run for cover.

Oblivious, Richard carried on. 'The night Vauxhall took it, I were closing the barn after settling the cows, when I looked up and there was six planes flying overhead in formation.' He took his hands off the wheel for a second to illustrate with his fingers in a V-shape. 'I knewed it weren't our boys, so I climbed up on the roof to have a good look, then – boom. The sound were deafening. I thought it were the end of the world – or the end of Luton, at any rate. My sister, who lives closer to town, told me she were fetching in her coal and were blown off her feet and onto her backside, which I'm pleased to say is well-padded, so not much damage there. See that pub – The Jolly Milliner?'

Sybil peered in the direction Richard indicated.

'I used to meet my mate, Bart, in there for a pint every Saturday lunchtime as regular as clockwork. After that bombing raid, I never saw him no more.' Richard's voice cracked and he coughed a couple of times into his elbow.

What had been said lay heavy in the cab of the truck. Sybil glanced at Richard's hands – large and gnarled and calloused – as they gripped the steering wheel. He came across as strong and capable and yet, he'd been reduced to tears by the passing away of his friend in a bomb incident that could easily have claimed his own life had it hit on a Saturday afternoon.

Staring out of the window, Sybil let the sight of townhouses giving way to the usual parade of shops wash over her. She felt like crying herself. Not for Richard in particular, but for all of them, wherever they were and whatever they were doing. How hard it must be for the commander of a ship to remain stoic when faced with the knowledge that the men in his charge could go down at any moment. A friend could step out to post a letter and never return; an aunt might ignore the warning siren for two minutes to put a teacup in the sideboard and poof – she would never be seen again; some poor lad on duty could look left instead of right, lift his hand for a fraction to wipe the sweat out of his eyes and have all his hopes blown skyward. Then there was Graeme. The telegram she'd received had brought her to her knees. She'd stumbled around and gone without proper food for days, disbelieving and bereft at the idea that everything he'd been – everything he was – might have vanished from the world forever.

Their first brief chat about his exhibition piece and watercolours in general had been interesting, but there hadn't been an immediate attraction, certainly not on her part. He'd asked if they could meet in a pub near the gallery, and when he'd helped her on with her coat after a couple of drinks, he'd brushed the bare skin on her neck. A shiver had run down her spine. 'Can I see you again?' he'd asked.

A blush had ignited her face when she'd said yes. Then she'd agreed to meet him another time and another again after that. During that period, the bedsit, along with her life, had been transformed. She would return on her own from seeing him and the walls that had previously closed in on her felt more spacious. The mildewed window opened without a creak. The icy bathroom behind the tattered curtain was cosier. Of course, she knew logically it was nothing more than her imagination and the knowledge that Graeme was lifting her out of the lonely slump she'd been living in.

She would lie awake some nights and wonder what it was about him that gave her such hope. There had been other young men who'd thought a lot of her and some she'd been attracted to in return. But none of them made her feel like Graeme did – as if the light he brought with him would last forever. He wasn't very tall, but she loved the square set of his shoulders and his thick, dark hair that refused to do as his comb dictated. She loved how the strong contours of his jaws tensed when he threw back his head with laughter. But what drew her to him more than that was his capacity to make ordinary, everyday things almost magical.

There had been a picnic that he'd prepared himself. The bread was a bit stale and the boiled eggs rubbery, but they'd snuggled up on a threadbare rug and eaten with relish. He'd lain back, his hands behind his head, and closed his eyes to the bright light. 'Are you happy?' he asked.

She'd traced a blade of grass over the contours of his face. 'Never been happier,' she replied.

He opened one eye and grinned. 'That's what I like to hear.'

Sybil had moved a bit closer, put her head on his chest and put her arm around him. 'And you?' she asked, peering up at him.

He hadn't hesitated to say he felt the same, but he'd looked away – or at a point beyond her – when he said it as he always did when he talked about his own feelings. For a moment it made her feel cold, as if she were transparent and he was looking through her for something, or someone, she couldn't see. That was the only thing about him that nagged at the back of her mind, but she dismissed it as an endearing trait of shyness or reserve. Besides, what mattered was what he did. He'd asked her to marry him, and he'd moved into the bedsit – bringing the sunshine with him. Five months later she'd felt something in him shift and the next thing she knew he was gone.

At the time she couldn't fathom how he could bear to leave the bliss she thought they were living in. Then the doubts had intruded and she wondered if she'd imagined the intensity of the whole episode. Or the part he'd played in it. Whilst she'd been blanketed in excitement, devotion and security, perhaps he'd been suffocated by her fevered devotion. Or maybe his happiness, which she thought mirrored hers, was nothing more than a perceived fantasy on her part and that was the reason he'd taken the first opportunity to prise himself out of the situation. Then again, it was possible she'd completely misread the signs and he had never been as devoted to her as she'd craved him to be. After all, if the most rudimentary of acts had made Dad a loving hero in her eyes, perhaps she'd been as delusory about Graeme. Whatever the reason, she could see now that as she'd been moving closer to him, he'd been pulling away from her.

The news that came with the telegram had seemed final and yet, it wasn't, so she dared to hope he would come home. Despite her reflections and ruminations and despair, she longed to have the chance to put things right with him. To start over and have him fill her life with light again.

For now, she was doing all she could to hold herself together – everyone was.

In the distance, fields speckled with farm workers, cottages and animals grazing provided a lovely, bucolic backdrop to the town. Yet more chances to catalogue the war from a different point of view.

'The place is crawling with Land Army girls,' Richard said. 'That's them up there.' He pointed in the direction they were driving. 'Not that I'm complaining. It could be a lot worse. On their days off, they like to come into the town to have a look around and sometimes they go into one or other of the pubs for a drink.' He scratched under his cap and looked bewildered. 'I've never known anything like it. Bart used to say it were all the rage in London, women going out on their own for a drink. But it almost puts me off me pint, I can tell you.'

Sybil thought about the few drinks she'd had in the Queen's Larder with Dame Lily and had no intention of sitting in her room with nothing except a cup of tea for company.

The built-up area came to an end, and as they wound their way down narrow country lanes that were no more than dirt tracks in some places, Sybil wondered how on earth the Land Girls made their way into town and back, especially on dark evenings.

'Have we got much farther to go?' Sybil asked, beginning to feel bruised and battered.

'About three miles,' Richard said. 'We have to pass through a village, then we'll come to the Old Manor House.'

They meandered past a brick-built general store, a bright red pillar box standing to attention next to the post office, an icy pond teeming with ducks, a pub, a school and a quintessentially English church. They veered off the road and crunched along a gravel driveway. Sybil's heart pounded as she bobbed down, straining to take in the façade of what was to be both her new home and place of work.

'Right you are then, Miss.' Richard cut the engine.

For a moment, Sybil wondered if the rasping racket that continued to resound in her ears would become a permanent fixture of her hearing, then it stopped and the quiet overwhelmed her. Before Richard could walk around to her door, she jumped down from the cab and stood, her arms and legs jangling from the drive and took in the grand, rather foreboding house, covered in the barren leftovers of what must have been a glorious Virginia Creeper a couple of months earlier. A sudden rush of nausea washed over her, and she steadied herself with a hand on the side of the truck. Nerves, she thought, as her fingers found her wedding ring, although it could be motion sickness or the repellent petrol fumes that seemed to be lingering in the air. Then a flash of light across an attic window made her squint and, as she began to think about how she might capture the moment on paper, any anxiety she'd been feeling melted away and left excitement in its place.

A tall, dapper gentleman in a tweed three-piece suit hurried down the steps towards her and held out his hand. 'Mrs Paige,' he said. 'I'm Edward Merton, the principal.'

'Pleased to meet you,' Sybil said.

'I trust all was well with your journey?' he asked.

'Yes, thank you. And thank you, Richard,' she called out to her driver who was about to hop back into his farm vehicle.

He raised his hand and said, 'Good luck to you, Miss.'

'Let me take your things,' Mr Merton said, reaching down to gather up her bags as if it were a commonplace occurrence for the principal of a renowned art school to fetch and carry for his tutors. She couldn't imagine Mr Warnsley ever allowing such a thing to happen.

'I'm sure I can manage,' she said. 'I did so all the way from London, after all.'

'No need now.' He turned to her and smiled, then smoothed his hand around his neatly trimmed white beard. 'I'm going to give you a whistle-stop tour of the school, show you to your room, then leave you in the capable hands of Miss Ellen Hewitt, another of our tutors. Does that sound reasonable?' he asked.

'Absolutely, thank you,' she answered.

Sybil followed the principal into what looked like it had once been a spacious reception room but was now crowded with all manner of chairs and small tables, books and ashtrays and lamps. A lone man sat in the corner, a pipe in his mouth and a newspaper in front of him. 'Ah,' Mr Merton said. 'Let me introduce you to Morgan Langley. Langley,' he called out, 'please meet our newest recruit, Mrs Paige.'

Morgan Langley sauntered over and stood beside them on a large Turkish rug.

'Pleased to meet you,' Sybil said.

'The pleasure's all mine.' Langley shook her hand with the virility of a wet fish, which made ants dance along Sybil's spine.

'This is our lounge or common room,' Mr Merton explained. 'We pile in here after our evening meal and on days off to discuss art or anything else that captures our imaginations.'

'Yes, indeed,' Langley said. 'It's for staff and students alike.'

'Or anyone at all who's involved with the school,' Mr Merton added.

It sounded like a bohemian attitude, which Sybil admired, but she found it difficult to imagine Richard joining in after his tea.

'No class?' Mr Merton turned his attention to Morgan Langley.

'I've sent them out with instructions,' Langley said, not in the least bothered to be questioned by his employer.

'Ah, well,' the principal said. 'I look forward to viewing the fruit of their labour. Mrs Paige, shall we?' As they left the lounge through a different door, Mr Merton said, 'Langley is one of our conchies. There are quite a few biding their time here.'

He sounded like Switzerland about the matter – completely neutral. She wasn't surprised as she knew the art world attracted a number of conscientious objectors, or conchies as they were known, and plenty of people were quick to air the opinion that the arts provided a cover and a haven for the cowardly. A row had ensued between her and Graeme when he'd announced that he wasn't going to wait to be conscripted – he was joining up. It had ended half an hour later with a fierce accusation from her. 'You're only doing this so gossips won't harangue you for dragging your heels like so many other artists.'

'You might have a point,' he'd conceded.

How she wished now she'd talked about what was really bothering her. Why things had become so awkward between them and why it seemed he couldn't wait to get away. A feeling of deep sadness pressed down on her when she thought about that evening. On the surface they'd made up almost immediately, but her worries had rumbled on and now it might well be too late to ask him to put her mind at rest.

Mr Merton walked her through the dining hall where the aroma of something warm and earthy met them. 'I think it might be one of my favourites today – vegetable and oatmeal goulash.' He rubbed his hands together in anticipation. 'We have dinner at 1 p.m., and Miss Hewitt will show you the ropes.'

They passed through the library, down a corridor where Mr Merton introduced her to his assistant and pointed out his own office. 'There are two studios down here,' he said. 'But yours is on the first floor with the majority of the others. Let me show you.'

The staircase was airy and wide and the walls were covered in drawings and sketches and paintings torn from notebooks. 'We ask students to pin up examples of their work and encourage tutors to write comments and suggestions on them that will help to better their skills.'

'What a lovely idea,' Sybil said.

'Well, the walls looked so bare, and we thought we'd make the most of the space. When the staircases are covered, we plan to start on the dining room walls. Ah, here's your studio,' he said, opening a door and letting her go ahead of him into the room.

'And my classroom, also?' she asked.

'Of course,' he said.

For a few seconds, Sybil was speechless. She could not believe that the space belonged to her. 'It's beautiful,' she murmured at last. The windows overlooked the outhouses, and she could see Richard and another man shovelling feed into a trough. A woman with a basket was picking through vegetables in a walled plot and beyond that, a formal rose garden was laid out with paths and seats. Inside, stools stood ready at tables, and a scant amount of artist's equipment was waiting near the tutor's desk – her desk – at the front of the room.

'How many students will I have?' Sybil spun around to look at Mr Merton.

'Seven initially. But there is a bit of drifting around.'

'I beg your pardon,' she said. 'I don't think I understand.'

'We're very unconventional,' Mr Merton said. 'So we allow students to wander into a different class for a day or week if they so choose. I find it broadens them and gives them a different outlook. Some in the art world wouldn't approve, but ...' He shrugged.

Sybil thought it sounded wonderfully stimulating after the stuffiness she'd come across in other schools. 'I'm not one of those,' Sybil assured him, but wondered how she would be able to keep tabs on the students she was responsible for. That was probably a question best left for Miss Hewitt.

'We'll continue heavenwards to your room,' Mr Merton said, leading the way up staircases that became chillier, creakier, darker, and more narrow the higher they climbed. 'This is yours,' he said, coming to a stop in front of an attic room. He produced a key that he handed to her after he unlocked the door and stood back. The room was tiny with one single camp bed, an upright chair, a lopsided cupboard and a chipped washstand crammed into the space. 'Miss Hewitt and Miss Northcutt share next door which is slightly bigger,' he said, as if he thought she needed an apology for her limited domain. But she was used to living in cramped conditions and it was lovely to think two other women would be close by.

Handing in her bags, Mr Merton said that he would see her again in the dining room and that Miss Hewitt would knock as soon as she returned from teaching. 'I do hope you'll be pleased with your situation here,' he said, looking at her earnestly again.

'Thank you, Mr Merton,' she smiled. 'I have a feeling I'll enjoy my post very much.'

As he closed the door behind him, Sybil took two steps to the window, opened it and let a deep breath of country air course through her. The light was soft and tinged with pastel pinks and purples; a few billowing clouds scudded across the sky; the moving figures of Land Army girls dotted the fields and art students were making their way back to the manor house, portfolios and folding chairs and paintbrushes under their arms. From what she understood, they were allowed to ramble for the sake of their studies, but it couldn't be that easy; they couldn't learn entirely by being left to their own devices and a few scribbled words of feedback on sketches hung around the walls. There would have to be some hours of tuition and research and guidance – she had quite a few questions for Miss Hewitt when she made her acquaintance.

If she pushed her face up against the glass and contorted herself into a corner of the pane, she could peer down onto the driveway where she'd stood earlier. This must be the window that caught the flare of light so beautifully. She thought it might make a lovely study to draw it from both inside and out.

Opening one of her bags, she started to hang her clothes in the cupboard and set out her makeup and toiletries when the slamming of a door made her start. Then she heard Miss Hewitt and Miss Northcutt's voices from next door, as plain as if she were in the room with them.

Although she reminded herself she wasn't eavesdropping, she felt the sting of a blush across her cheeks. She tried to occupy herself with arranging her belongings but was so distracted she couldn't think where to put the vest she held in her hands. In the end, she gave in to the inevitable and listened as if she'd been invited to participate in the conversation.

'For goodness' sake, Ellen,' a woman Sybil presumed to be Miss Northcutt said between clenched teeth. 'Must you make such a dreadful racket every time you come in? Didn't your parents ever tell you off for behaviour like that?'

Sybil imagined Ellen trying to tiptoe across the threshold in an attempt to make up for her clamour, then heard her slam the door shut, knock something against the wardrobe, flop onto a bed and send her shoes flying as she kicked them off.

'Sorry, sorry, sorry,' Ellen said. 'And I've told you before, I was brought up by my gran and she did nothing but tell me off. What are you looking at?'

'The vegetable plots, the crops, the light.' The window creaked when Miss Northcutt must have closed it.

Then there was a burst of enthusiasm from Ellen. 'Look what I did today.'

Sybil could hear the rustle of paper then all was quiet for a few moments. 'Any comments?' she asked eventually. 'Please tell the truth.'

'I'm always honest about your work,' Miss Northcutt said. 'About anyone's for that matter. You know that.'

Sybil, twisting her wedding ring, looked down at the vest waiting to be put away and thought Miss Northcutt sounded middle-aged and very practical, and Ellen, in her late teens and rather flighty.

'My arms ache from holding this up.'

'Oh, stop whinging, Ellen. No part of you ever hurts. Wait till you get to my age.'

'Now who's whining, Blanche. You're always telling me you're only in your fifties.'

'Very early fifties,' Miss Northcutt, or rather Blanche, corrected her.

Aware that if she could hear them, they could hear her, Sybil stuffed the vest into her mouth to stop herself from laughing out loud. She wiped the tears from her eyes and felt pleased she'd gauged their ages correctly.

'You can put it down now and nurse your shoulders,' Blanche said. 'Good job you're not a Land Girl yourself, then you'd really have something to complain about.'

So, the drawing must be of the Land Army girls at work.

'Well?' Ellen asked. 'You're making me wait a long time so it must be a load of old rubbish. Perhaps I should forget about art and join the nursing auxiliaries right away.'

'For goodness' sake.' Sybil could hear the smile in Blanche's voice. 'If I had a shilling for every time you've threatened that, I'd be quids in. Anyway, I think they're wonderful.'

Ellen gasped, then there was the rhythmic sound of quick feet on the floorboards, as if the younger girl was dancing around in her stockings. 'Are they realistic?' she asked. 'You know I'm not one for impressionism.'

'They're definitely not impressionistic,' Blanche said. 'How long did they take you to produce?'

'All morning in the field.'

'What happened to your students during that time?' Blanche sounded tight-lipped.

'I set them up on a task,' Ellen said in a chastened voice. 'Don't look at me like that, all the tutors do the same. You should try it. Some of my students ended up in the fields, drawing the same subjects as me. They all produced something,' she carried on. 'You can have a look at their work if you're so bothered.'

'No,' Blanche said. 'I have enough to worry about with my own students.'

'There you are then,' Ellen said sulkily.

'Ellen,' Blanche said to the backdrop of a chair being dragged across the floor. 'They're not perfect, but you are going to refine them in the studio, aren't you?'

Silence from Ellen.

'Ellen, we've talked about this before. You must get into the habit of developing and reworking your compositions. You'll regret it if you don't.'

Sybil imagined a shrug from Ellen.

'With a bit of work on these, I think you could show them.'

'In the school exhibition?' Ellen said. 'I'm working on a watercolour for that.'

'You know what I'm going to say,' Blanche said wearily.

'Oh yes.' Ellen sounded short-tempered and cross. 'The War Artists' Advisory Committee or whatever it's called,' she said with sarcasm. 'And what about you? You should take your own advice.'

The WAAC again, Sybil thought. There was no getting away from it.

'Don't do that to your drawing,' Blanche's voice rose. 'You'll ruin it. For goodness' sake, stop being so hot-headed. We've been over this many times. The clue is in the word war. I create paintings and drawings of country gardens and houses with thatched roofs and Labradors snuggled together after their morning walk around the farm. The WAAC does not want those.'

Sybil knew that wasn't the entire truth about the WAAC and certainly not for the Recording Britain Project.

'Officially,' Ellen drew out the word. 'The WAAC is supposed to be concentrating on commissioning artists for propaganda posters. Not buying works that depict Land Army Girls or thatched cottages.'

'I'm trying to help you and your career,' Blanche said, more softly. 'And this country. Not only do we need the record of pictures such as these right now. But they will be crucial for generations to come.' Sybil had heard that argument before. 'At least say you'll think about it. Please?'

'Alright,' Ellen said reluctantly. 'And perhaps you should reconsider your subject matter,' she said. 'If you believe so passionately in leaving a legacy.'

There was a bit of shuffling, the opening and closing of drawers, a polite cough. Then Blanche said, 'Ellen, aren't you supposed to be next door with …'

'Oh no.' Sybil imagined Ellen covering her mouth with her hands. 'Mrs Paige,' she said. 'I'll go now.'

Sybil quickly shoved the vest she'd been nursing into the cupboard, smoothed her hair and skirt and waited for a knock which, when it came, was more of a hammering with a blunt instrument.

Ellen's face was red and her breath ragged as she apologised to Sybil for keeping her waiting. She was young, but in her early twenties rather than her teens. Her thick, dark hair was tied up in a knot with a ribbon around it, and although it was freezing, her arms were bare. 'I must apologise, Mrs Paige,' she said. 'I should have called and introduced myself right away.' She held out her hand. 'I'm Ellen Hewitt.'

'Please don't worry, Miss Hewitt,' Sybil said. 'I've been busy putting my things away and getting my bearings.'

'I'm to show you around for the first couple of days, starting with dinner which should be any minute now,' Ellen said in a rush. 'Would you like to come and meet Blanche, the woman I share with?'

Sybil thought it a good time to tell Ellen she could hear every sound distinctly through the flimsy wall. 'I feel as if I know her already,' she said. 'Both of you.'

For a moment, Ellen looked puzzled, then she smiled. 'Oh, because you can hear us. I don't know why Mr Merton didn't warn you about that.' Ellen strode past Sybil, raised her fist, and as she knocked on the dividing wall, it rippled and rattled as if it were attached to Richard's farm truck.

An answering tap came from the other side and Sybil raised her eyebrows in alarm. 'It's about to come down,' she said. 'That wouldn't stand up in an air raid.'

'It used to be all one room, but a partition was put in to gain space and yes, it would collapse if we took a hit, but the wall on its own wouldn't do much damage. Feel how light it is.'

Sybil touched her finger to the chipboard and withdrew it quickly when the whole thing shivered again. 'I think that was one of the reasons Miss Carrington before you left so suddenly, she liked her quiet and couldn't get used to being able to hear what was said from our side. We'll try to tone it down, but it's not always easy.' Ellen's features fell and she looked self-conscious, as if she was sorry for being a nuisance. 'On the other hand.' She brightened up. 'We told Miss Carrington and we'll tell you. You are welcome in our room whenever you want company or feel you can't bite your tongue any longer and have to join in.'

Sybil laughed. 'Well, I would so like to have a look at the drawing you showed to Miss Northcutt.'

'Blanche. And I'm Ellen.'

'Then I'm Sybil.'

'Come on, I'll show it to you now.' Ellen bashed her way past the door and led Sybil to the adjoining room.

Blanche was quite prim and proper in a tartan skirt, white blouse and black cardigan. Despite needing spectacles as thick as chunks of ice, she moved about gracefully, so it was no wonder Ellen's boisterous movements rankled her. She pulled the only chair out for Sybil and reiterated that she must come and sit with them any time she liked.

Ellen pulled her drawing from her portfolio and handed it to Sybil. It consisted of a series of sketches rather than one large drawing and depicted members of the Women's Land Army at work in the fields behind the school. Turning for a moment, Sybil took in the scene from the perspective of the tiny window and noted that Ellen had captured the softly undulating land, ripe with potatoes and cabbages and carrots but, because the time of day differed, so did the light. Steely grey blanketed the charcoal scenes and an icy mist swirled close to the ground. The watery sun was partially covered by thin streaks of cloud, and it was difficult to tell whether they would scatter and leave the day to warm up or band together and bring an icy rain.

It could have been an idyllic English countryside scene, except there were the Land Army girls in their green jerseys, brown breeches, long socks and khaki overcoats that blended into the crops and foliage, trees and fences surrounding them.

Brandishing spades and pitchforks, they were digging into the ground and throwing the winter's food into a huge cart pulled by a tractor. The sketches showed the farming implements in the women's hands moving incrementally as they went about their work, like one of those children's illustrated flip books that tell a fast-paced story. And in the corner of two of the sketches, three girls were catching the rats that plagued farms, incongruous smiles on their faces. Ellen's drawings were so realistic that Sybil could picture every detail of the figures working in the fields.

'These are very good.' Sybil gave her verdict. She agreed with Blanche about Ellen spending time to refine them but didn't think she was in a position to say so. 'I'm an ex-student of Dame Lily Brampton and ...'

Both women breathed out a sigh of admiration.

'... she says art must speak, if you like, for subjects that don't have a voice. And these most certainly fulfil that criterion.'

Ellen smiled and said thank you, pressing the paper lightly to her chest before placing it back in her portfolio. 'I thought that tomorrow we could amalgamate our two classes and take them out to the fields again, unless you'd like to stay indoors with your lot. It will be a chance to see one of the ways in which you and your students can take advantage of the landscape.'

'I'd like that very much,' Sybil said. 'Will you do the same, Blanche?'

After a few moments of deep thought, Blanche said, 'I haven't done so yet and I'm torn. My conscience finds it difficult to be so ... I don't know. Free and easy and liberal? I've been tutoring on and off for a long time and have always been more structured in my approach.'

'We've talked about this on numerous occasions, Sybil,' Ellen said. 'I admire Blanche's fastidiousness, but also think we should try different approaches whilst working here. After all,' she looked at Blanche, 'none of us knows how much longer we'll be able to stay cocooned in this situation.'

Sybil looked from one to the other of her fellow tutors, following the conversation that had taken a turn towards the serious. She had enjoyed listening to their frivolous banter earlier, which must be the result of living together in such cramped quarters. But she thought she'd find their deeper talks interesting, too, and could happily imagine herself spending a good deal of time squashed up with them. 'I know, I know,' Blanche said. She pushed a stray corkscrew of hair behind her ear. 'It's just that leaving my charges for an entire day to pursue my own artwork so goes against the grain and makes me feel irresponsible. To me, it's the brink of anarchy and mayhem.'

Sybil recalled Morgan Langley relaxing with his paper and pipe and thought that at least Ellen wasn't suggesting they go that far.

'Everyone does it,' Ellen said.

'Yes, but that doesn't mean I can live with myself if I follow suit.'

Sybil was aware of being the new girl, and she didn't want to put any noses out of joint by saying too much too soon or by telling tall tales, so when she spoke it was with caution. 'Whilst I was being shown around earlier, something Mr Merton said made me think he was all for sending students off for a time to get on with their own pieces. So, if he approves, then I suppose the practice must be alright to pursue?'

'Yes.' Ellen was enthusiastic. 'He's all for it, but Blanche is still not convinced.'

Blanche sighed heavily and stood up with determination as if she'd come to a decision. 'Alright then,' she said. 'I'll give it a go for the morning session.'

'Well done, Blanche.' Ellen looked delighted and patted her colleague on the back.

'But,' Blanche carried on, 'I'm going to lay down some strict rules. I will be telling my students that they must all report to me at least once – if not twice – during the time they're allowed to roam free.'

'I think that's fair,' Sybil said, daring to be more forthright with her opinion.

Ellen turned to the chipped mirror on top of the chest of drawers and began to retie the ribbon in her hair. Her reflection raised its eyebrows at Sybil then she sought out Blanche with her gaze. 'That's what I do each and every time I take my class out. I've told you that more than once.'

'Oh.' Blanche was taken aback then she narrowed her eyes. 'I don't remember you saying any such thing.'

'That's because, Blanche Northcutt,' Ellen said with a touch of arrogance. 'You don't always listen. You merely hear what you want to hear.'

Blanche opened her mouth to reply, but the sound of the dinner gong reverberated through the school and Ellen turned to Sybil. 'Stick with me,' she said. 'I'll make the introductions and show you the ropes. Coming, Blanche?'

'Not until you cover your arms.'

Ellen coloured, shrugged on a jacket she hauled out of the closet and shut the door behind her with a bang.

'For goodness' sake, must you,' Blanche said. 'Every time you come in or go out?'

Following behind them, Sybil smiled to herself and thought that, as well as the room, the light, the opportunity to teach and the liberation from her solitary way of life, Ellen and Blanche were two more advantages to this post and she was determined to make the most of their company whilst she could.

4

January 1941

The following morning, Sybil went about her preparations for the day without hearing much from Ellen and Blanche except a yawn, the splashing of water, a squeak from the wardrobe door and Blanche asking for a towel to be handed to her.

When she was ready, she sat on the end of the bed, eased on her black brogues, straightened her stockings and opened the blackouts to take in the view. Instead of the ice-blue sky of yesterday, a heavy hoar frost covered the garden and sparkled on the fields in the distance. It looked magical, as if a mythical creature had touched everything with a white wand, and Sybil thought she'd like to draw the intricate, feathery crystals in close-up. She imagined that the Land Girls, who had to start work at the crack of dawn no matter the weather, were not as enchanted with the scene as she was.

Then she was faced with a dilemma. She could call for Ellen and Blanche, wait for them to knock on her door or make her own way down to the refectory. None of those made her feel particularly comfortable and she stood, twisting her ring around and around her finger. She craved company and wanted to pursue a friendship with the two disparate flatmates, each of whom fascinated her in their own ways, but didn't want them to think of her as a nuisance. Eventually, she decided to make her way down and gauge their reactions to that.

Moving quietly, as Ellen and Blanche had been doing, Sybil

pocketed her key and strode down the stairs. She hadn't paid much attention to the pictures tacked on the walls yesterday but this morning, in a different light, one or two caught her eye. As interested in the comments as she was in the sketches, she stopped and angled her head to read as many as she could. '*Needs more definition between dark and light,*' one read. '*Think about perspective,*' another said. '*There's a reason it's called background.*'

'*Hands are notoriously difficult to get right ...*' she mumbled under her breath.

'*... it might help if you made a study of hands on their own,*' a deep voice behind her finished the sentence.

She turned and found Morgan Langley at her elbow.

'That last comment was mine,' he said.

'Oh, and has the student undertaken the task?'

'No idea.' He peered at the name scribbled in the bottom right-hand corner. 'I wouldn't know W. Burroughs if he passed us right now. It's all wrong.' He retrieved a mechanical pencil from his pocket and wrote, '*Skewwhiff. Bin it and start again.*'

Sybil was stunned. What a way to communicate with a student. She narrowed her eyes at Mr Langley and wondered if he'd be quite so bold if he had to put his name to his comment. Studying the drawing of a smoke-fuelled sunset in London, buildings demolished to little more than crumbs in the foreground, she agreed that it wasn't very good, but nor did it warrant such harsh criticism.

'Going down to breakfast?' Morgan asked.

Sybil looked up towards the attic and wished she'd waited for Ellen and Blanche. She hardly knew her fellow tutor and didn't want to be unfair, but what she'd seen and heard of him so far didn't give her the impression she'd enjoy his company. There wasn't an excuse she could give, though, so they made their way to the refectory together.

Despite the small fire in the grate, the gas oven and the bubbling urn, the room was bitterly cold. She and Morgan both plumped for the omelette surprise with bread and margarine, and as they sat opposite each other, Sybil quickly realised that his overinflated opinions, smug self-belief and judgemental attitude would ensure the two spare chairs at the table remained empty. The grime under his fingernails and the white flakes he brushed off his shoulders didn't help either.

Blanche appeared with Ellen close behind, pulling down the sleeves of her jumper until they covered her hands. The younger woman nodded in greeting then tapped Blanche on the shoulder and surreptitiously pointed to Sybil. When Blanche turned, she raised her eyes skywards and Sybil hoped the gesture was aimed at Morgan and not at her for coming down to breakfast without them. Thankfully, they plonked their trays down on the table and began to chat away, not giving Morgan a chance to get a word in edgeways.

'Probably not a good day for drawing in the middle of a field,' Blanche said, blowing on her hands.

Ellen shook her head. 'I'm determined to get out regardless. If those Land Girls can do it, so can we.'

'They're moving around,' Blanche said. 'That makes a big difference.'

'I'll tell my students they can get up, stamp their feet, clap their hands as many times as they choose, and I'll do the same.' Sybil thought Ellen sounded less convinced than she felt.

'I opted for the porridge,' Ellen carried on without a pause. 'As I couldn't be sure what the surprise element of the omelette would be.'

'Perhaps there isn't any egg in the dish at all,' Sybil offered.

The other two women laughed, but Morgan Langley's features were pulled down with sulky despondency.

'Or maybe there's a crunch provided by bits of shell,' Sybil said.

'That's horrid.' Ellen devoured her porridge with relish. 'You've put me right off.'

'I doubt that would be possible,' Blanche said.

'Oh, here it is. Look.' Sybil held up the tiniest sprig of parsley imaginable before popping it into her mouth.

'You must give your compliments to the chef,' said Ellen.

Sybil considered Cook, standing at the door to the kitchen with her arms crossed over a stained apron, a look on her face that dared anyone to complain. She gulped dramatically and said, 'It's quite alright, Ellen. I'll leave that for another time.'

Around the room, students and tutors began clattering crockery and trailing from the refectory to begin their classes. Morgan stood, picked up his tray, bowed towards the three women in a fawning manner and joined the exodus.

'He's a bit of a bore,' Blanche dropped her voice to a whisper. 'Harmless enough, but a pest nevertheless.'

'Yes,' Ellen added. 'He tries to curry favour with all the new girls, but he's too full of his own importance to be charming, I'm afraid. Not that he's got much to be cocky about.'

Sybil watched Morgan's back as he walked down the corridor by himself. *Perhaps he's lonely and just wants a chat*, she thought, feeling rather sorry for him. She knew what that was like, so she couldn't blame him. Not everyone would be as lucky as her in finding such amenable companions from the start. His decision to declare himself a conchie must detach him from others, too, although he would be more sheltered in this environment than out in the normal run of society where he would be treated like carrion for vultures. Then she remembered his handshake and the unfeeling note he'd written on W. Burroughs' composition, and any pity she'd felt for him vanished.

'Now I can show you this.' Blanche beckoned for Ellen and Sybil to move in closer. She produced an envelope from her pocket and smoothed it down on the table with her thin hands. Triumphantly, she held up an invitation card for Ellen and Sybil to read. 'It's taken quite a while to arrive.' She blinked at them. 'What with Christmas and New Year, I suppose.'

Dear Miss Northcutt,

As an Olympic Bronze Medallist, you are cordially invited to attend a lecture and an exhibition of works that have been commissioned by the War Artists' Advisory Committee and the Recording Britain Project on the 14th of January 1941 from 10 a.m. onwards at the National Gallery.

The keynote speaker will be Dame Lily Brampton, DBE RA ROI RWS, who will address the audience at 11 a.m. Refreshments will follow. Please feel free to bring one guest.

RSVP to Miss Jane Butterworth at the above address by the 6th of January.

Yours sincerely,

J. Butterworth (Miss),
Personal Assistant to Sir Leonard Thwaites, CH KOB FB

'An Olympic medallist,' Sybil enthused. 'You're a dark horse.'

'And she's had umpteen landscapes hanging in exhibitions, but she wouldn't have told you herself, would you, Blanche? She's much too unassuming.'

'That's wonderful,' Sybil said. 'Very many congratulations.'

Although Blanche lowered her eyes, she was smiling broadly.

'I've been invited, too,' Sybil said. 'We can travel together if you like.'

'I'd like that very much, and you're welcome to stay with me and Auntie Myrtle in Wandsworth afterwards. I like to check on the dear old girl every chance I get. We'll no doubt have to spend at least part of the night in the Anderson, but she's managed to make that cosy, too.'

Sybil twiddled and twisted her ring. The sound of an Auntie Myrtle was comforting, and she imagined there would be toast and a fire waiting for them. 'If you're sure it won't be too much,' Sybil said.

'Of course not, Auntie Myrtle would love to meet you. Ellen, would you like to come along as my guest?' Blanche looked at the younger girl.

'I was waiting for that.' Ellen jumped up and threw her arms around Blanche's neck.

'But there's a proviso,' Blanche said sternly.

Ellen bumped back down, the stuffing knocked out of her. 'I should have known it wouldn't just be a nice day out.'

'You must bring some of your work in case there's an opportunity to show it to members of the committee.'

'It doesn't say anything about that on the invitation so I wouldn't want to assume.'

'Is that your Dame Lily, Sybil? What do you think?'

The thought that Dame Lily belonged to anyone other than herself made Sybil laugh. 'She did mention that I should bring along some of my work, so I think we can safely presume that will pertain to everyone. And if we don't get to show it, there's no harm done, is there.'

'Agreed,' said Blanche. 'Now.' She peered closely through her spectacles at the invitation once again, then put it back into the envelope with great care. 'I'm going to direct my students to the fields. I'll probably see you there. Good luck with your lot, both of you.'

Ellen's students had joined Sybil's, who peered around each other to get a good look at the woman who was to be their new teacher. It didn't seem long ago that she had been in a similar studio at the Central, waiting to be introduced to Dame Lily. Sybil's chest tightened as she looked from one to the other of them, taking in their trusting, admiring expressions, and knew that, although she could never hope to live up to the influence bestowed by Dame Lily, she would do her best for them.

After Ellen introduced her, Sybil clasped her hands together and felt for her wedding ring. 'I'm so pleased to meet you,' she said, her voice shaking slightly. 'And I hope to get to know all of you through your artwork. I'm assured that, for you to be students at the Marylebone, your talents and skills must be exemplary, but by working together, we will turn your excellent pieces into extraordinary works of art.'

Some of the students smiled at her, others nodded towards each other with a look of anticipation on their faces.

'For this week, we will all be working under the guidance of Miss Hewitt.' She turned to Ellen. 'I believe we'll be drawing the Land Girls in the fields, but I'll let her give you the details.' She stood aside, happy with how her first talk had gone.

'Absolutely correct,' Ellen said. 'It's up the hill to Hightop Farm for us. Mrs Paige and I will station ourselves near the farm vehicles, and you must all come to see us at least once during the morning. And, as always, each of you must produce something to work on in the studio when we return.'

'That includes me,' Sybil added. 'An artist has never finished his or her education.' She glanced at Ellen pointedly, remembering the discussion yesterday when Blanche had admonished her roommate for failing to refine her own work.

But Ellen ignored the statement, although it seemed to please the students. When they'd gone on their way, Ellen said, 'That was a lovely introduction. You made it sound as if there was no them and us. You know, "we will work on this and that". "We will be under the guidance of Miss Hewitt." I'd like to adopt that approach myself.'

Sybil breathed deeply; she felt as if she'd got off to a good start.

Bundled in an array of thick clothes and carrying their sketchbooks, charcoals, pencils, rugs and shooting sticks, they trundled through the village and up the hill towards Hightop Farm with Ellen, the ends of her hair ribbon slipping out from under her woollen hat, leading the way. The morning hadn't warmed up, and their breath went in as frost and came out as puffs of white mist. Again, Sybil's feet were rigidly numb, and she wondered how any of them would be able to hold a pencil or stub of charcoal in their hands. Despite that, the students began to point out aspects of the landscape they found interesting and talk about what scenes they were looking forward to recreating.

They passed a forlorn-looking coppice, the branches that

looked to be riddled with arthritis dripping with frost. A very small pond was completely iced over and one of the few young men in the group broke the surface with a stone. Some of the girls giggled and for a moment, Sybil thought Ellen was going to join in, until she made a show of coughing behind her hand instead. 'Stop anywhere that gives you inspiration and get started,' she said through frozen, rubbery lips. 'But please don't forget to come and find us at some point. Is that all okay?'

There were various murmurs of understanding, and the lad who'd thrown the stone and two girls tramped closer to the pond to study the potential of the setting. When the rest of them reached the highest point, there were only three students left.

Some of the Land Girls waved but didn't stop their work. 'Come to draw us again?' A young woman in a felt hat, her sleeves rolled up to her elbows, called out. She turned for a moment as she threw a spadeful of potatoes onto the back of a lorry and Sybil could see that her cheeks were red raw.

The young woman shrugged. 'Makes no difference to me,' she said. 'I used to do a bit of sketching myself.'

'Did you?' Sybil was interested so stepped closer to continue the conversation. The ground was thick with shards of ice and sticky mud and no matter how she tried, she couldn't avoid the mess.

'You need a pair of these,' the Land Girl said, pointing to her sturdy brown boots. 'Especially if you're going to make a habit of tramping through fields to find your subjects.'

Sybil laughed. 'This is my first day at the art school, and I should have asked to borrow a pair of wellies. Was sketching a hobby or did you hope to make a career of it?'

Now it was the young woman's turn to laugh out loud, her chapped cheeks round and glowing. 'The likes of me don't get to think about art as a career,' she said. 'Barely a hobby, really. Just something I liked to do when I had five minutes between helping Mum with the washing, shopping and looking after the little ones. If there happened to be the stump of a pencil and a scrap of paper around.'

Sybil felt shame redden her cheeks and she was grateful the weather could be blamed for the blossoming blush. The art world was dominated by the middle classes and those who had the time and means to dabble in music or painting, literature or philosophy because they were certain where the next meal was coming from.

'What about school, did any of your teachers encourage you?'

The Land Army girl leaned on the handle of her spade and eyed Sybil as if she felt sorry for her. 'I missed a lot of school and when I did go in, I was stuck in the corner and made to catch up with reading and arithmetic on my own, so I wasn't allowed to sit in on lessons like games and drawing and singing. 'This war and this job,' she said enthusiastically, 'are the best things that have ever happened to me. If I wasn't so bloody tired every evening and if I had a pencil and paper lying around, I might send in a couple of drawings to *The Land Girl* magazine.'

'I had no idea there was such a publication.' Sybil was intrigued. 'Can you buy a copy in the newsagents?'

'No,' the young woman said. 'It's only distributed amongst us. But I've finished with last month's copy, if you're interested.'

'Thank you,' Sybil said, thinking it might be an outlet for her or Ellen's artwork.

The young girl fished around in her satchel and handed a well-thumbed, rather sparse booklet to Sybil.

'I've something for you,' Sybil said. 'Back in a minute.' She clumped to her bag for a small sketchbook, a pencil and piece of charcoal. When Sybil handed them to her, the young woman's eyes widened with disbelief.

'Are you sure you can spare them?' she asked.

'I'm sure,' Sybil said. 'Good luck with your submission to the magazine.'

Beaming, the young woman picked up her spade and posed with it mid-air, her arms taut with strength. 'Do you want to draw me like this?' she asked.

Sybil smiled. 'Oh, please don't put on any postures,' she said. 'We like to sketch you naturally, as you go about your work.'

'Of course,' the girl laughed again. 'I was only ribbing you.' She sent a few pounds worth of potatoes flying into the back of the lorry.

'Thanks for the chat,' Sybil said.

The girl tipped the rim of her hat, and Sybil realised that, despite their talk and the exchange of tokens, she'd probably come across as nothing more than a privileged woman who was in a position to indulge her creative leanings. But that wasn't the whole story, although she would never have justified herself to anyone, let alone to someone who had experienced a much harder life than she had.

The teacher who'd recognised her flair for art had spurred her on to apply for a scholarship, and although she was thrilled when it was granted, it hadn't been easy. At the Central, scholarship students were often singled out because of their functional, well-mended clothing and lack of personal belongings like hand mirrors and silk stockings, but Sybil had worked hard and proven herself to her tutors – Dame Lily, in particular. And at least she'd had the opportunity, unlike the Land Girl and countless others.

She set up her seat next to Ellen and Blanche, produced her sketchbook and pencils and began to draw the young woman with the sore cheeks as she rested for a moment on her spade. Using a variety of long and short strokes, she worked quickly, paying attention to the shadows in the dark earth, the light streaking the sky, the subject's mucky boots as they sank into the mire. The girl didn't take her eyes off her work as she swung her head in time to the rhythm of the shovel's movements, and Sybil captured the beads of sweat that flattened a few strands of hair across her forehead.

Next, she turned her attention to two young women in the distance, laughing and chatting as they ploughed a harvested field with the help of a huge, steadily lumbering shire horse. When that sketch was completed, she drew four girls digging a ditch between the coppice and the potato field, their hands and faces splattered with mud.

The students showed up in small groups, and Sybil leaned over their shoulders to give them advice or suggestions. On the whole, they were polite and appreciative if a bit diffident, and she thought she would have to work hard to get to know them properly. Momentarily caught off guard when one girl introduced herself as Winifred Burroughs, Sybil gave a lot of time and attention to every little detail the young student had captured well.

When they'd had enough cold as they could take, the students asked to be allowed to walk back to the school and get on with refining their compositions there. Sybil said she would find them in her studio after the dinner break.

Freezing, too, she stood every few minutes and tried to thaw her hands by beating them against her coat, but to no avail. Under any other circumstance, she would have been moderately pleased with her drawings, but she was faced with having to show them to her students later – which was only fair. Perhaps, she thought, smudging a line with her fingertip, that would help to harbour an ethos of honesty and openness so the students would share their work safe in the knowledge that it would be critiqued fairly. Either that, or she'd have to resort to clicking her fingers at them, and Dame Lily was the only tutor she knew who could get away with that.

Taking a deep breath, she decided to practise on Blanche and Ellen and asked them if they could spare a minute to have a look at her drawing.

'Of course,' Ellen said. 'Let's view each other's masterpieces.'

Ellen had come up with a sketch of the field, a Land Army girl chipping encrusted mud and chunks of ice off the wheel of a cart. Although the subject faced away with her collar turned up against the cold, there was no doubt from the slump of her shoulders that she felt frustrated and dejected. The sun was watery, and she had perfectly captured the white fuzz of frost on the hedgerows. 'What do you think?' she asked. 'Should I join the nursing auxiliaries now and be done with it?'

'It's beautifully detailed,' Sybil said. 'I feel I could reach out and touch the icicles.'

Ellen beamed around chattering teeth.

'Dame Lily says we should be the voice of our subjects, and this certainly speaks loud and clear for how that girl feels about her work.' She looked sideways at Blanche. 'But you can easily do that in the studio when you put some further work into it. You are going to do that, aren't you, Ellen?'

Sybil and Blanche waited for Ellen's reply.

'I know I should,' Ellen said, sounding disheartened. 'It's what I tell my students to do. But when I look at my own work again, I feel quite fed-up with it and want to get on with the next composition.'

'For goodness' sake, force yourself,' Blanche said. 'Once you see the benefit of making it a habit, you'll be glad you did.'

'I agree,' Sybil offered. 'Your work is excellent, but you're doing yourself an injustice if you don't make yourself revisit your work in order to improve it. I don't know of any artist who can produce masterpieces in one sitting. Not even Dame Lily.'

Ellen sighed. 'Let's see yours, then,' she said to Blanche.

Although she'd been persuaded to take her students to the site of the Land Army's activity, Blanche hadn't been convinced to draw the girls herself. 'I've made it quite clear on many occasions that I won't be coerced into producing pictures of the war. I want to stick to the bucolic.'

'It's all to do with the war now,' Ellen said. 'Isn't that what Dame Lily said, Sybil?'

'That's right. Like it or not, anything we draw depicts the country during this time.'

Blanche swept her hand in front of her sketch of the coppice where some of the students had stopped earlier. 'How can this be a war picture?' she asked.

Sybil and Ellen studied the piece of work. 'I don't suppose it is specifically,' Sybil said. 'But I don't think Dame Lily meant that every scene had to have the hard evidence of bombs and destruction in it. If you were to put the location and date in the corner, everyone would know what this little woods and pond near Luton looked like on this day during the war. Tomorrow might be a different matter.'

'That makes more sense,' Blanche said slowly. 'And if I were to display it next to one of the Land Girls at work, the bigger picture becomes more apparent.' She nudged her piece of paper next to Ellen's.

'Or, if you sketched the girls at work yourself and hung them together, that would be very striking. But, oh no.' Ellen shook her head. 'I almost forgot. You refuse to draw anything other than pastoral scenes.'

'Excuse me,' Blanche said. 'But landscapes are what I'm known for.'

'None of us are known for war pictures,' Ellen's voice rose in frustration. 'Or wanted to be. Until bloody Hitler came along.'

'Swearing doesn't become you, Ellen.' Blanche began to pack up her equipment.

'Well, I was never known for being a lady,' Ellen retorted. 'War or no war. Your turn, Sybil.'

Sybil held up her drawing so she could hide behind it and waited.

There was silence for a few beats, then Blanche said quietly, 'It most definitely speaks for the girl and the time and place. I'm very impressed.'

'Beautiful,' Ellen said. 'It's breathtaking.'

Sybil felt herself redden behind the picture. 'You're being kind because I'm the new girl.'

'We're always honest about artwork, aren't we, Ellen?'

'Yes, I can promise you that.'

'What can I work on to make it better?'

Nothing but silence again. Sybil dropped the paper and peered over it to make sure Blanche and Ellen hadn't crept off.

'Maybe you could make the sky more dramatic by defining the darkening clouds?' Ellen said tentatively.

'I was going to say the same,' Blanche said.

Ellen tutted in the older woman's direction. 'It's really very good. It's excellent. You must take that one with you to the exhibition.'

'Do you think so?' Sybil had decided on the one of the family in the Underground, but perhaps she should think again. 'Have you decided which of yours to present?'

'No,' Blanche said, suddenly sounding lost. 'I'm not convinced my work is right for this period of time.' She shook her head slowly. 'I'm getting left behind, aren't I?' she asked, looking directly at Ellen.

'Never,' Ellen said. 'Your work is brilliant and would be perfect for the Recording Britain Project. The one Sybil was telling us about. Anyway, why don't we help each other choose which pieces to take with us?'

'I'd like that,' Sybil said. 'We could spread everything out in one of the studios and have a good look through all of it.'

The Land Girls started to unwrap sandwiches, take the tops off flasks and rest for a while on the mudguard of the truck or any piece of ground that was marginally less boggy than the rest. Sybil had read somewhere that when they finished in the fields, the evening wasn't their own. They had to bundle hay and fodder in barns, feed the animals, clean out the pens and stables. She was grateful that she could go back to the manor, as cold as it might be, and have time to work on her passion.

She returned a wave to the girl she'd spoken with and started to pack up her things. After a few moments of silence, Sybil related her conversation with the Land Army girl about the magazine. 'It might be an avenue into having our work recognised, Ellen,' she said. 'And yours, Blanche, although I know you're already renowned.'

'I'm not at all, or I wouldn't be here now,' Blanche said with a touch of bitterness. 'The art world is very fickle. You can be the bee's knees one minute and the next, no one knows your name.'

They stomped their way past the phone box next to the pub,

the post office, the haberdasher's and the general store. An air of sad resignation about a potentially unfulfilled future hung over them.

'How about this,' Sybil said. 'I know we've agreed to take at least one example of our work along to the WAAC exhibition. Am I right?'

Blanche and Ellen agreed that was what they had decided.

'Let's make another pact. One piece of artwork each to *The Land Girl* publication for consideration. By March. What do you think?'

'I'm game,' Ellen said, her whole manner brightening. 'Blanche?

'I don't think there's any point for me. But I'm not going to be left out.'

'If my hands weren't frozen to the bone,' Ellen said. 'I'd say we should shake on it.'

'Consider that having happened,' Sybil said.

The women picked their way through the garden that was cloaked in shadows and reached the school in time to hear the dinner gong.

'I hope it's vegetable and oatmeal goulash,' Blanche said.

'Mr Merton told me that was one of his favourites,' Sybil said.

'I don't really mind what it is,' Ellen said. 'As long as it's not that vile liver and heart hotpot.' She shuddered.

'For goodness' sake,' Blanche snapped in frustration. 'You ate it last time.'

'I was hungry,' Ellen's voice rose. 'And there was nothing else.'

'Can you save me a place at your table?' Sybil asked. 'I want to go and wash my hands.' She held them out for Blanche and Ellen to inspect.

Rushing upstairs, she paused on a step and tore down the sketch by Winifred Burroughs that had offended Morgan Langley so deeply. No one was going to treat one of her students with anything but the utmost respect. She would see to that.

5

January 1941

Not a word was spoken by any of them as they made their way across Trafalgar Square towards the National Gallery. They hadn't fallen out or had cross words, but the ground was as slippery as an ice rink and the pavements so rutted and ragged that it was all they could do to keep themselves upright. Holding onto their portfolios and overnight bags, they picked their way around piles of bricks and potholes and lengths of splintered timber that appeared no sturdier than twigs. When Sybil felt her feet go out from under her, she made a grab for one of the others, then it was Blanche's turn to skid, followed by Ellen taking a slide.

Chancing a look up, nausea washed over Sybil. From the heaps of debris, smoke drifted upwards in ghostly vapours until it was difficult to distinguish from the freezing fog. The fountains were turned off, but there was more than enough water, frozen or otherwise, lying around in huge puddles or bubbling up from under the pavements. A brickwork air raid shelter had been constructed against the perimeter wall of the historic quadrant; the crumpled side of the Royal College of Physicians and Surgeons looked as if it needed to be tended by its namesakes; windows that hadn't been boarded had been blown out leaving gaping holes in complex shapes that resembled the hoar frost crystals she'd wanted to draw; the crater that had been carved deep into the earth by an incendiary last October had been roped off and workmen buzzed around it.

A mere two weeks in the relative quiet of Luton had rendered her scarcely able to believe they were living in the thick of such an awful situation. Despite reading the papers and listening to the wireless, observing the Land Army girls at work and pulling down the blackouts every night, the war had begun to seem unreal to Sybil. She'd felt as though she were watching it unfold from afar or that it was someone else's reality that she was learning about second-hand. Being in London again put paid to that nonsense as the stark evidence of the cold facts were more than right in front of her – she was walking through them. Shivering violently, she asked herself how long London could continue to take hit after nightly hit? And her next question was how could art do justice to the heartbreak and devastation? She would have liked to get out her sketchbook and charcoals, draw the scene and send it around the world so that everyone could feel the emotions she was experiencing – alarm, fright, apprehension, dread, a deep disquiet and pride that they were all fighting back with such determination and tenacity.

Guilt, too, for having it so easy in the country, teaching eager students and capturing the light as it hit the window of her attic room. Looking at Blanche and Ellen from the corner of her eye, she wondered if they or any of the other artists invited to the exhibition today, had the same misgivings.

'I forgot,' Sybil said. 'You haven't been to London for quite a while, have you?'

'No.' Ellen shook her head. 'Not since we were ousted out of Marylebone. Blanche comes more regularly, to visit Auntie Mrytle.'

There was no reply from Blanche, who hadn't taken her eyes off her feet. With her fragile build, wiry hair and thick spectacles, she gave the impression of being frail and older than her fifty-one years. Yet, during the past couple of weeks, Sybil had come to learn that she was in fact as robust as steel. But to someone as young as Ellen, the age gap probably seemed huge.

'Let me take your portfolio.' Ellen tried to prise the folder from Blanche. 'Your fingers are so numb you can hardly keep a grip on it. You are quite a bit older, after all.'

'For goodness' sake, Ellen,' Blanche said. 'You can barely manage to carry your own. And given that I am your elder, you should be a bit more respectful. Anyway, we're almost there.'

'Well, you say that ...'

'Another cordon.' Sybil sighed on a puff of condensation. She stopped and studied the changed layout of the road and wondered which way around would be the quickest and safest.

'Look.' Ellen pointed. 'There are quite a few people making their way to the Portico entrance.'

'Best we try to get around that way, then. Ready?'

'Ready,' Blanche said, putting her foot down firmly as they started off again.

They converged with a queue snaking up the side steps to the entrance, a good number of them holding on tightly to portfolios. Sybil thought about the pictures they'd chosen to bring and hoped they would have the courage to show them if the opportunity arose. Stamping their feet to keep warm, they inched their way forward to a makeshift reception area where a woman ticked names off a list. Her dark red lips and nails were so artfully applied that she looked, at first glance, much younger that she was.

'Blanche Northcutt and guest,' Blanche announced when it was their turn.

'And your guest's name?' the woman asked in a clipped voice.

'Ellen Hewitt,' Blanche answered. Sybil saw Ellen squeeze Blanche's arm and hoped she wouldn't start to jig around like she did when she was excited.

'There's a cloakroom halfway down the corridor on your left. When you come out, continue in the same direction and you will arrive at the exhibition. You'll be told when and where to assemble for Dame Lily's address at 11 a.m.'

'And I bet she'll do the telling,' Ellen whispered to Blanche as they moved to the side to wait for Sybil. 'She's wasted here. She should be a sergeant major in the Army.'

'Stop your nonsense right away,' Blanche hissed. 'If you can't say anything nice, don't say anything at all.'

Sybil smiled to herself as she gave her details to the woman behind the desk. She'd read about love-hate relationships, but never imagined they could be as entertaining as Blanche and Ellen's.

They checked in their coats and cases and found their way along the corridor, its windows cut off from outside light. In the exhibition hall, a hum of rather troubled, low voices greeted them, as though what was on view was something illicit that had nevertheless caused a fevered flurry.

Sybil and Blanche followed the crowd to the left whilst Ellen veered off to the right and had to be hauled back by a tug from Blanche. 'This way round,' Blanche said. She indicated towards Sybil with a tilt of her head.

'But there was something over there that caught my eye,' Ellen protested.

'We can view it when we get there,' Blanche said between gritted teeth. 'Why can't you do what everyone else is doing, for once.'

For a split-second Ellen's mouth turned down and Sybil felt sorry for her. 'I don't know,' Ellen said. 'I think I get carried away.'

Sybil was surprised there was any answer at all to what she'd thought was a rhetorical question, so she grabbed Ellen's arm and manoeuvred her round. 'Come on,' she said. 'Stick with me.'

The exhibition space wasn't large, but panel after panel was filled with pieces that portrayed some aspect of the war. People lingered around each picture as they discussed and analysed the scenes they viewed. They compared one technique with another and took notes of the titles and artists' names. The day was cold, yet the air in the gallery was warm and damp and shot through with tension.

The first picture they viewed was an oil of Trafalgar Square, painted soon after that immense abyss had been ripped into the ground. Sybil, who'd felt compelled to take out her equipment and paint the same scene, thought she would never be able to reproduce anything that could tell the story so vividly. The Square and the surrounds were a blur of washed colour that portrayed the idea that the day had been shrouded in a fine drizzle of cold rain. Despite that, the setting was unmistakable with Nelson's Column and the iconic lions easily decipherable. And in the foreground, as plain and bold as possible, was that deep, dark, vulgar hole. A rope was being laced around the open wound by men whose backs and arms and shoulders looked so weary, she could feel their heaviness.

'The pigeons are missing,' Blanche said. 'It's eerie without them.'

Ellen nodded. 'It's so realistic and yet …'

'You can't see anyone's face properly.'

'That's right,' Sybil said. 'But you can feel their emotions so deeply that they almost punch you between the eyes.'

'Jonathan Akerman-Frankham,' Sybil read out from the ticket next to the picture. 'And it's called *Trafalgar Square October 1940*.'

'Not very imaginative,' Ellen said. 'Perhaps Jonathan used up all his creativity producing the painting. He probably didn't have enough energy left to think up a fancy name.'

'It says it all.' Blanche led them towards the next panel. 'What would you have called it?'

'Oh, I don't know.' Ellen thought about it. '*Nelson's Near Miss*. Or *Nelson Doesn't Like What He Can See with His One Good Eye*, something witty like that.'

The occasion was not light-hearted, so Sybil tried to stifle her laughter behind her hand.

Blanche shook her head and giggled. 'You're too much, Ellen,' she said. 'Those ideas are sacrilegious and not at all witty. Please run titles for your pieces by me before you commit to them. Oh, look at these.'

They stood in front of a board on which hung a number of works drawn in a hospital. In shades of black, white and grey, they depicted nurses calmly and diligently attending to injured men who lay on expertly made beds. His broken leg in a sling, one man was having his blood pressure monitored; another, with an arm amputated below the elbow, had a thermometer in his mouth and was turned towards the viewer, an accusatory look of bitter betrayal on his face; the third showed a young man reading a newspaper with his bandaged head resting on a pile of pillows. They peered closer to take in the details and when they scrutinised the fourth, of a nurse sitting next to a patient tucked up in bed, they frowned, then stared at each other with alarm on their faces and turned back to the picture again.

'Is he dead?' Ellen said in a low voice. 'He looks so pale.'

'Yes, I know,' Sybil answered. 'His stillness suggests that.'

'Perhaps he's in a coma.' Blanche studied the picture again. 'It's really rather shocking, isn't it?'

'Andrew Anderson,' Blanche read aloud. 'And it's called *On the Ward*.'

'Oh, I studied with him under Dame Lily at the Central,' Sybil said.

'Well, Dame Lily definitely instilled her ethos about art speaking for the subject in him. Wouldn't you agree?'

'Yes, I do,' Sybil said. 'They definitely speak for the injured men and the nurses. This one in particular.' She pointed to the picture of the motionless man. 'His peacefulness is palpable.'

'And the nurse's calm, quiet acceptance of the situation is too,' Ellen said.

'Although if you look very carefully,' Sybil said. 'You can see that she's lacing her hands so tightly together that I wouldn't be surprised if some of the bones in her fingers were about to snap. So, there's a lot going on under her outward serenity.'

Blanche and Ellen inspected the picture again and stared at each other as if stunned when they took in that tiny element that amounted to a huge revelation. 'I don't think I would have noticed that detail if you hadn't picked it out,' Blanche said.

'Nor me,' Ellen agreed. 'And I'm very cross for that oversight. I think it's nursing for me.'

'I wouldn't necessarily have noticed it either,' Sybil said. 'But subtlety was a technique of the artist's that caused him and Dame Lily to disagree quite often. She used to say that his touch was much too light, but he insisted that eventually the trait would make him well known. Time will tell, I suppose. He's done better than me, at any rate.'

They found themselves in front of a watercolour of a village post office, a glossy red pillar box next to it. The small brick building was covered in an orange and crimson creeping plant and a pram was nestled next to the door.

'That could be our village,' Ellen said. 'And it's just the sort of subject matter you like to paint, Blanche. Although yours are much better.'

'Thank you, Ellen,' Blanche said. 'But keep your voice down. The artist might be standing next to us.'

Ellen stared without shame at the people nearby, then seemed to come to a conclusion about them as she shook her head and was about to pass a remark when an announcement was made. 'Ladies and gentlemen, may I have your attention, please.'

The receptionist stood in the doorway holding up a bell that, despite the crowd waiting with hushed anticipation, she couldn't help but tinkle. 'Please take your seats in the hall through that door.' She pointed behind her. 'Dame Lily will begin her speech in five minutes. There will be time for you to further view the artwork on display afterwards.' Then she stood aside and considered each of them in turn as they filed past her.

They found three seats towards the front of the hall, Sybil between Blanche and Ellen, and rummaged in their bags for books and pens to jot down notes.

'Ladies and gentlemen.' It was the ubiquitous receptionist again, standing behind the lectern with a rather haughty look on her face. 'I am pleased to introduce Dame Lily Brampton, DBE RA ROI RWS, keynote speaker at our gathering today.'

A hearty round of applause greeted Dame Lily as the receptionist stepped aside and the older woman took the platform.

Sybil thought her mentor looked striking in a burgundy suit and soft white blouse, with a vibrant scarf in blues, greens and reds wound around her neck. The colours looked magnificent amongst the dull and dingy shades of grey in the audience and singled her out as being part of the creative world. Perhaps that was what Ellen was trying to achieve, in a much less sophisticated way, with the ribbons she wore in her hair. Sybil wondered what she could adopt in the way of style to make a statement about herself, then thought she'd be better off putting her energy into having her pieces shown.

Sitting up as straight and tall as possible, she hoped Dame Lily would pick her out and give her some small indication that she'd seen her, but she didn't get any more recognition than a share of the welcoming smile imparted to the audience as a whole.

'Thank you, fellow artists,' Dame Lily began. 'I don't intend to take up much of your time as I know that the exhibition and tea are the real stars of the show today.

I would like to say that it is heartwarming to see so many of you here during a time when our very way of life, which most definitely includes art, is under such a terrible threat. I have said many times and will continue to say, art will not die. It simply cannot. It will change, both in the way it is created and viewed, and we must take it upon ourselves to be the eyes, ears and senses of the world during this heinous time. I, for one, believe that as a body we should accept the role we have to play in telling the story of the subjects we draw, paint, sculpt, lithograph and sketch willingly and seriously, and that brings me to the main point of my talk today – the WAAC and the Recording Britain Project.'

Sybil nudged Ellen on one side and Blanche on the other and stealthily touched her ears to indicate they should listen closely.

'As most of you are probably aware, the WAAC commissions war artists on a full-time and short-term basis. In addition, it commissions for individual works. These commissions might come about after pieces have been brought to the attention of the Committee or when the Committee thinks that a particular artist would be best suited to a specific subject.

On the other hand, the Recording Britain Project is dedicated to preserving the very British tradition of watercolour and portraying our heritage from the Highlands to Cornwall, Wales to East Anglia and every point in between – the very places we are fighting to protect. The importance of British life has come into sharp focus, and this scheme will ensure that our heritage is preserved forever.

As a consequence, and this is very important to me, the RBP will be looking to commission a good number of works by women whose view of the war will be very much home-based.'

An electric murmur buzzed around the room. Although women artists must have been delighted with that outcome and the men perhaps a bit disappointed, it was considered rather audacious to speak the words aloud so brazenly.

'Very brave,' Sybil whispered to Blanche. 'She's always been outspoken.'

'Good for her,' Blanche said.

Dame Lily held up her hand and carried on. 'Of course, I'm not saying that men are excluded from the scheme, far from it. It is open to everyone. But vast swathes of our men are fighting overseas where some of them have continued to draw and paint, and there are a number of official male war artists moving along with the troops. No women have been appointed to that role, so that leaves a plethora of us ladies to record what is happening here at home.'

An unsure round of applause started a few rows behind them and increased in intensity until the entire audience was clapping wholeheartedly. Sybil looked to the back of the hall and glimpsed Sir Leonard Thwaites joining in with the appreciation.

'Now,' Dame Lily continued. 'I believe that many of you have brought examples of your work with you. I, and Sir Leonard,' she gestured towards the director of the WAAC, 'would love to view as many pieces as we can today.'

This time most of those in the hall turned with Sybil to stare at the great man, who looked momentarily surprised, but gathered himself together quickly and nodded to various points around the room.

'Please don't be worried if you don't have watercolour works to show us,' Dame Lily said. 'The RBP is also commissioning drawings and we can advise you whether any piece you've created can be reworked into other mediums. Now, Miss Butterworth,' Dame Lily turned to the receptionist, 'can you please arrange to set us up at the front of the room? Then anyone interested can line up and Sir Leonard and I will view as many pieces as time permits.'

Another muffled murmur of excitement ran through the audience and a few people began to reach for their bags.

'In conclusion,' Dame Lily said, and everyone was quiet again. 'I would like to reiterate that this is a great opportunity for you, as artists, and for the country, which will benefit, both now and in the future, from your talents and skills in telling the story of this war. May I also congratulate those of you who have already had pieces commissioned, and to those whose war work is in a different area from the arts, I would like to tell you that I am eternally grateful to you for everything you are doing. God bless and keep all of you safe.'

Applause loud enough to rival a bombing raid rebounded around the room. Miss Butterworth jumped onto the stage and began gesticulating to where Dame Lily intended to set up camp. Sir Leonard Thwaites followed closely behind, his face creased with concern – he probably hadn't been expecting this.

'Please form two lines behind these tables,' Miss Butterworth was giving out orders again. 'And if you are not interested in showing work to Dame Lily or Sir Leonard, please continue to view the exhibition or make your way to the room set aside for tea.'

'Well,' Blanche said. 'That was a rousing talk, especially for us girls.'

'Ladies,' Ellen corrected her. 'Dame Lily called us ladies.'

'Her interest in championing women artists is nothing new,'

Sybil said. 'She has long made it her mission to get women artists the recognition they deserve. Let's join the queue, we don't want to miss out. I don't think I'll be accepted but nevertheless, we owe it to Dame Lily for giving us such encouragement.' She stood, smoothed the front of her jacket and picked up her portfolio.

The atmosphere in the hall was different now. A number of people had returned to the exhibition or were desperate for a cup of tea and slice of cake or had to make their way home to avoid whatever the Jerries had in mind for the long, dark night ahead, and the frisson of excitement had gone out the door with them.

'You've got the right idea, Sybil,' Blanche said. 'Come along, Ellen. This is too good an opportunity to miss.'

'Are we going for Dame Lily or Sir Leonard?' Ellen was agitated.

Blanche gave her a withering look and rolled her eyes to the heavens. 'You really do take the cake,' she said. 'Dame Lily, obviously. Now get in that line.'

Sybil was finding it difficult to quell the waves of anxiety coursing through her arms and legs. She felt sure that Blanche and Ellen's portfolios would be kept to one side with the others that were worthy of a second scrutiny, but she thought she'd have hers thrust back and be sent away with a flea in her ear. She could almost feel the leather branding her hands with humiliation when she had to carry her portfolio back through the exhibition hall to the tearooms.

Ellen, behind her, was shuffling from foot to foot. She turned a number of times and gazed longingly at the door, but Blanche placed her hand on her shoulder and kept her firmly in position. 'Look, only three in front of you now. No, two,' she said as a young man sauntered past, a bogus look of nonchalance on his face and his rejected artwork under his arm.

Peering ahead, Sybil caught Dame Lily nodding towards Sir Leonard. 'Me?' She mouthed the word, her finger digging into her chest.

Dame Lily widened her eyes and whispered, 'You must.'

Sybil sighed, turned to the two women behind her and said, 'Out of fairness, I suppose, Dame Lily wants Sir Leonard to look at my work, so that's me done for.'

'No.' Blanche was adamant. 'Don't think like that. I'm sure you'll do very well. We'll meet you in the tearoom afterwards.'

Sybil moved across and suddenly Ellen had nowhere to run.

'Hello, my dear,' Dame Lily said. 'Your name?'

'Ellen Hewitt,' Sybil heard Ellen falter, her mouth dry.

The luminous scarf still draped beautifully around her neck, Dame Lily smiled as if she and Ellen were old friends. 'I'm afraid there isn't enough time for me to enquire about your background, but perhaps we can exchange information about each other some other time.'

Ellen nodded and swallowed hard.

'Let's have a look at what you've brought along today, shall we?'

Ellen spread out two charcoals of Land Girls hard at work, put her hands behind her back and waited.

'Ah,' Dame Lily said. 'The Land Girls. I have a soft spot for them. I was commissioned to create a recruitment poster for the WLA.'

That will give her hope, Sybil thought, and she could almost hear the thump in Ellen's chest.

'You've captured the light with such poignancy. Oh,' Dame Lily's face crumpled, 'I do hate all this messing about with our light.' She held out the pieces at arms' length, then brought them closer to her face, and put them down on the table again. She seemed to be wavering and Sybil thought Ellen might snatch up her portfolio and bolt for the door if a decision wasn't made soon.

After what seemed an eon, Dame Lily smiled and said, 'Is your name and address in your portfolio, my dear?'

Was Dame Lily accepting her works for consideration? Ellen seemed to be so overawed she could barely speak. 'Yes,' she said on an exhale.

'Then we'll be in touch in due course. Thank you, Miss Hewitt, for bringing your pieces to our attention.'

As quickly as that, Ellen was dismissed. She turned, pale and incredulous, her feet shuffling as if she might start a jig again. But Blanche touched her arm softly, smiled and stepped forward for her own few minutes with Dame Lily.

Taking a deep breath, Blanche passed Dame Lily a charcoal of ducks on a village pond and three others depicting scenes which looked as if they'd captured the heart, soul and lifeblood of Britain.

'This is rather lovely.' Dame Lily held up the piece of the ducks on the water. 'Very idyllic. As are these. Where is the setting?'

'Near Luton, Dame Lily,' Blanche said. 'I'm a tutor at the relocated Marylebone.'

Dame Lily studied Blanche for a beat then cast a look in Sybil's direction. 'So, you probably know Mrs Paige?'

'We've become firm friends.'

Studying the pieces again, Dame Lily asked if Blanche created artworks of bomb destruction or women at work in various jobs they'd undertaken in lieu of men.

At this point, Sybil would have begun to sweat and stammer, but Blanche pushed up her spectacles, remained cool and stuck to her guns. 'So far I've managed to avoid that and remain loyal to my landscapes and arcadian scenes.'

'Ah,' Dame Lily smiled. 'I, too, have been doing my utmost to sketch as many seascapes as possible, despite the view of them having changed. However, I also draw scenes of devastation and human suffering. Tell me.' She looked Blanche straight in the eyes. 'Do you refuse to do so because it offends your sensibilities or because you can't bear to believe the reality?'

Ouch, Sybil thought. *What a hard-hitting question.* She stared down at the floor, too embarrassed on Blanche's behalf to look up.

'That's a good question,' Blanche answered slowly. 'And one I should give myself time to think about. But as a quick reply, I think the reason is probably a bit of both. And also habit. I have been moderately successful in the past, and perhaps it's easier to stick with what works.'

Very courageous, Sybil thought and looked up in time to hear Dame Lily tell Blanche that she admired her honesty.

'Besides,' Blanche carried on. 'Everything we create now is a record of Britain at war. So I believe.'

Sybil quickly averted her eyes to a corner of the hall, but she felt Dame Lily staring at her. When she chanced a peek, Dame Lily was smiling wryly. 'What I'd like to do, my dear, with your approval, is keep the ducks and one of the village scenes and show them to the Recording Britain Project. In my opinion, you would be eminently suited to join their ranks.'

'Thank you very much for your time, Dame Lily,' Blanche said, a relieved tone to her voice.

'You'll hear from us soon, my dear,' Dame Lily said by way of dismissal.

Blanche turned, widened her eyes towards Sybil and blew a huff of breath towards her top lip. Sybil nodded her congratulations and Blanche crossed her fingers in her direction.

The woman in front of Sybil turned, her shoulders slumped and her portfolio hanging listlessly from her hand. Sir Leonard, she thought, would not be as forgiving as Dame Lily.

'Your name?' he asked without looking up.

'Sybil Paige.' Sybil felt for the comfort of her wedding ring.

The director scribbled in a notebook. 'What would you like to show me today, Mrs Paige,' he said.

Sybil placed the charcoal of the family in the Underground in front of him and watched his eyes take in the detail, then he looked up to appraise her. She felt a thin patina of sweat coat her face but tried to maintain her composure as Blanche had done.

Without giving away an inkling of his thoughts or feelings, he asked if she had any others to offer.

With a slight tremor in her fingers, Sybil passed him the drawing of the men peering over each other's shoulders to read the paper and the sketch of the four Land Girls digging a ditch.

'Are all your pieces directly associated with the war?' Sir Leonard asked.

'The only one that isn't is this.' She took out the drawings of her attic window from outside and in and placed them on the table.

Sir Leonard spent a long time studying them without comment or criticism, then said, 'Please place them carefully back into your portfolio, Mrs Paige.'

That's it, Sybil thought, her spirits sinking. *I can say goodbye to my hopes of a career in art and hello to the delights of war work in a factory or on a building site.*

'Your details are inside, I take it?'

'Why, yes,' Sybil stuttered. 'But …'

'We'll be in touch in due course. Next, please.'

It felt as if her feet were stuck to the floor, and when at last she managed to move, Dame Lily was smiling broadly in her direction.

'I cannot believe it,' she said to Blanche and Ellen in the tea room. 'I knew you'd both be in, but me …' She tried to picture the proud but bemused look on Dad's face if she could tell him. As for Graeme, she ached to send him a letter with the news, but there was no known address to post it to.

'We all made it,' Ellen said, tucking into a carrot and beetroot sandwich. 'It would have been horrid if one of us was still holding their portfolio.'

'In case you hadn't noticed.' Blanche held up her leather folder.

'You know what I mean,' Ellen said.

'Rarely,' Blanche quipped.

Ellen snorted then said, 'Dame Lily did ask you to leave some examples of your work.'

'Yes, she did, which is very exciting. But may I remind you of two things,' Blanche said. 'One – none of us has made it just yet. They've only taken our offerings with a promise of looking at them in more detail.'

'Such a killjoy.' Ellen shook her head. 'Shall I get us another cup of tea?'

'And two,' Blanche carried on undaunted. 'I knew yours would be selected in this round. I told you so, didn't I?'

Ellen grabbed Blanche's arm and gave it a squeeze. 'I suppose I ought to say thank you,' she said. 'For having faith in me.'

'Yes, you ought,' Blanche said. 'But I don't think you will.'

'Not now at any rate,' Ellen said. 'Not if this is how it's going to be from now on, with you constantly reminding me that the WAAC and RBP wouldn't be having another look at my work if it wasn't for you.'

Blanche closed her eyes for a moment and nodded. 'Yes,' she said at last. 'This is how it's going to be.'

Ellen laughed. 'I'd do the same if the roles were reversed.'

Blanche turned to Sybil and said, 'Sharing a room with her must be a punishment for something terrible I did in a former life.'

'I think it must be very difficult for both of you,' Sybil joined in the banter.

Ellen smiled at Blanche. 'That is a huge understatement,' she said.

Around them, others drained the dregs from their cups and the tea room began to feel chilly. 'The exhibition remains open to anyone who would like to peruse the works of art again.' Miss Butterworth stood next to the door, a cup and saucer in her hand.

'Shall we?' Sybil turned in that direction.

'All I want to do is get to Auntie Myrtle's,' Blanche said.

Ellen tightened the length of ribbon in her chestnut waves. 'Yes, I can't wait to see Auntie Myrtle, too,' she said. 'But I could do with a gin.'

'I second that,' Sybil said.

'There's sure to be a bottle or two of homemade sloe gin, Ellen. You know that.' She turned to Sybil. 'There's a blackthorn in the front garden and Auntie Myrtle makes the most of it.'

Ellen raised her eyebrows. 'But you never know, Auntie Myrtle might have drained the last bottle,' she said. 'Then we'd be disappointed.'

'Oh, for goodness' sake, Ellen,' Blanche said suddenly. 'You're right for once. Let's find a pub and have a drink.'

'Make it two, at least.' Ellen said.

They redeemed their cases and coats, hats and gloves and stood at the Portico entrance for a moment, looking out at the pouring rain that had thawed the snow in a matter of hours. Sybil thought it would have been wonderful if the obscene hole, the concrete shelter, the rubble that stood in mountains on every corner and the air raid warnings could be dealt with as quickly and with so little fuss. But the buoyancy she felt after the success of the day, along with the promise of gin and a night with Blanche's aunt, lifted her spirits to a giddier altitude than they'd reached for a long time. Since before the telegram about Graeme, to be precise.

6

The Land Girl Magazine,
6, Chesham Street,
London, S.W.1

Monday, 3rd March 1941

Miss Ellen Hewitt,
Marylebone School of Art,
Old Manor House,
Luton,
Beds

Dear Miss Hewitt,

Thank you very much for your interest in *The Land Girl* magazine and for sending two charming pieces of art for consideration.

We have been exclusively publishing artwork submitted by working members of the WLA as we believe they are best suited to represent the roles they undertake. In addition, we hope seeing their contributions in print will encourage them in what everyone knows to be a demanding job. However, in this case we are happy to make an exception and would like to reproduce your compositions on the covers of two of our magazines.

The jolly charcoal of one of our girls festooning a shire horse with a Christmas wreath will, of course, have to wait until our December issue, but we are going to use the series of girls hurling potatoes into the back of a lorry, which you entitled, *Mash, Chips, Roast!*, in the April issue. May I remind you that should the Allies be victorious and the WLA disbanded before either of those dates, the magazine will happily cease publication.

There is no fee attached for using your work, but your name will be cited as the artist, and the pieces will remain your property; to that end, we will return the originals to you in due course.

I do hope this meets with your satisfaction. Do not hesitate to contact me with any further queries.

Yours sincerely,

Maisie Atkins (Mrs),
Editor, *The Land Girl* Magazine

War Artists' Advisory Committee,
Ministry of Information,
The National Gallery,
Trafalgar Square,
London, W.C.2

Tuesday, 4th March 1941

Mrs S. Paige,
Marylebone School of Art,
Old Manor House,
Luton,
Beds

Dear Mrs Paige,

The Committee would like to sincerely thank you for allowing them to scrutinise your portfolio. As a result of discussions following your meeting with Sir Leonard Thwaites, the Committee is happy to offer you a short-term commission. Initially, the contract will be for six months and is for works of women performing various services across the length and breadth of Great Britain.

You are invited to meet with me on Friday, 14th of March at 11 a.m. to sign your contract and receive written instructions. At that time, I will also requisition your stipend, permits to restricted areas, rations for materials and sketching permits to draw and paint in public. Please confirm this appointment by Monday, 10th of March.

On behalf of Sir Leonard and the War Artists' Advisory Committee, I would like to congratulate you on your appointment.

Yours sincerely,

J. Butterworth (Miss),
Personal Assistant to Sir Leonard Thwaites, CH KOB FB

The Land Girl Magazine,
6, Chesham Street,
London, S.W.1

Wednesday, 5th March 1941

Mrs S. Paige,
Marylebone School of Art,
Old Manor House,
Luton,
Beds

Dear Mrs Paige,

Thank you very much for sending two examples of your work to *The Land Girl* magazine for consideration. Both pieces are evocative, and we particularly liked the one of the girls enjoying a well-deserved rest under the branches of a tree.

Unfortunately, we have decided that your pictures are not quite right for us at this time, but please do feel free to submit again.

I have enclosed your originals and wish you the best of luck in your career.

Yours sincerely,

Maisie Atkins (Mrs),
Editor, *The Land Girl* Magazine
(Encs)

The Land Girl Magazine,
6, Chesham Street,
London, S.W.1

Wednesday, 5th March 1941

Miss Blanche Northcutt,
Marylebone School of Art,
Old Manor House,
Luton,
Beds

Dear Miss Northcutt,

Thank you for submitting your beautiful drawing of a coppice in the thick of winter. We did so enjoy the depiction of hoar frost clinging to barren branches and the sheet of ice on the pond.

However, the pieces we select for publication always portray WLA workers somewhere in the picture so if you would like to send in more for consideration, please bear that in mind.

Yours sincerely,

Maisie Atkins (Mrs),
Editor, *The Land Girl* Magazine
(Encs)

War Artists' Advisory Committee,
Ministry of Information,
The National Gallery,
Trafalgar Square,
London, W.C.2

Thursday, 6th March 1941

Miss Blanche Northcutt,
Marylebone School of Art,
Old Manor House,
Luton,
Beds

Dear Miss Northcutt,

On behalf of the Committee, I would like to thank you for allowing them to consider a selection of your compositions.

Whilst not quite the work Sir Leonard and the Committee is commissioning at the moment, your pieces were passed to the Recording Britain Project, and they would like to offer you a commission. The contract will involve you travelling widely throughout Bedfordshire, and possibly the surrounding counties, to record the natural beauty and architectural heritage of the area. For this, you will receive expenses for travel, board and lodgings, and a small fee will be forthcoming for each piece of work accepted by the Project.

Please meet with me on Friday, 14th of March at 10:30 a.m. with a view to signing your contract and receiving additional information. Please confirm this appointment by Monday, 10th of March.

May I congratulate you on behalf of Sir Leonard and the Recording Britain Project.

Yours sincerely,

J. Butterworth (Miss),
Personal Assistant to Sir Leonard Thwaites, CH KOB FB

War Artists' Advisory Committee,
Ministry of Information,
The National Gallery,
Trafalgar Square,
London, W.C.2

Friday, 7th March 1941

Miss Ellen Hewitt,
Marylebone School of Art,
Old Manor House,
Luton,
Beds

Dear Miss Hewitt,

Sir Leonard Thwaites and the Committee have asked me to convey their appreciation to you for allowing them to view your portfolio.

Whilst they agreed that your work shows great promise, they feel that it has not yet reached the standard of artistic maturity they are seeking at this time. The ideas are excellent, and the compositions show that you have talent, but the completed pictures lack refinement and appear to have been rushed. The Committee has asked me to convey the message that you should take more time and care in the final stages of production and use your initial sketches as the basis to work from, not as the end product.

The Committee will gladly view examples of your work in the future and would like me to give you their best wishes for your success.

Please feel free to collect your portfolio from my office at your convenience.

Yours sincerely,

J. Butterworth (Miss),
Personal Assistant to Sir Leonard Thwaites, CH KOB FB

Dame Lily Brampton, DBE RA ROI RWS,
Seagulls' Watch,
Cley-next-the-Sea,
Norfolk

Saturday, 8th March 1941

Mrs S. Paige,
Marylebone School of Art,
Old Manor House,
Luton,
Beds

My dear Sybil,

Very many congratulations! I am so pleased for you and so very proud. Well done on your commission – you must be delighted.

I understand that you are to meet with Miss Butterworth on Monday to go through the yawn-worthy administrative process after which I hope you will meet me for a glass or two at The Marquis in Chandos Place, to celebrate. I will be in situ from noon. If either of your friends from Luton would like to join us, it would be lovely to meet them properly.

If by any chance you're unable to meet me once Miss Butterworth has dismissed you, please leave a note for me at reception.

Yours etc.,

Lily X

7

March 1941

The Rose Garden in late afternoon was a pallet of yellows, pinks and reds. Daffodils, narcissus, pale primroses and tulips strained towards the light from half-hidden corners and amassed around the unused fountain. Sybil sat on her favourite stone bench, an unopened sketchbook in her lap. She closed her eyes and inhaled deeply. When she'd had her fill of the earthy aroma, she took in the details of the dainty furling petals and tender green stems that looked so vulnerable but must have been made of stern stuff to appear now, in such glory, after the hard, cold winter. *I hope that's how we appear to the Jerries*, she thought.

Richard had told her that the rose buds wouldn't unravel until the end of the month and would be at their majestic best during the summer. He'd laughed when she'd asked if she could sketch him pruning the barren branches a couple of weeks earlier, then reddened and hid his face from view when she'd gone about the task. 'You won't want to be out here drawing when I put the horse manure down,' he said.

'When will that be?'

'May time. The stink is overpowering but it brings on the roses something beautiful.'

Sybil thought it would be lovely to see the garden when it was in full bloom, but she'd be gone long before then. When she thought about that her stomach somersaulted, but not entirely with excitement. A nauseous sense of apprehension had weaselled its way into her consciousness, and it stemmed from one thought – where would she live? When she was travelling she'd pay for lodgings from her stipend, but she needed a base. Somewhere to store her things, kick off her shoes and call her own.

Damp made its way up from the stone bench and Sybil's bottom soaked up the clammy cold. Complete darkness painted the sky, and from under hedges she heard the soft shufflings of night creatures. A bird flapped around in a nearby tree as it settled in its nest and the aroma of vegetable and oatmeal goulash wafted towards her from the kitchen.

Then there was a kerfuffle on the path – a few heavy footsteps followed by the sound of someone missing their step and a 'bloody paving slab,' from Ellen. Sybil smiled and covered her mouth to stop herself from laughing.

She remembered admonishing the younger woman that she would regret it if she didn't present her sketches to Dame Lily and now the poor girl was full of remorse because she hadn't refined her work as she and Blanche had advised her to do. It was hard not to see the tell-tale signs of deep disappointment in her eyes or hear her muffled sniffles through the makeshift wall when she was alone in her room. She played with the food on her plate and had forgotten her hair ribbon on a couple of occasions. The repartee with Blanche had waned, too, and talk of joining up as a nursing auxiliary had escalated. Whilst the promise of publication in *The Land Girl* magazine was lovely, it was no real compensation.

Sybil stood and gathered her things. 'Ellen,' she called out. 'Have you hurt yourself?'

'Only a bit.' Ellen hobbled through a gap in the hedge. 'Whatever are you doing out here so late? We were beginning to think you'd left for your new post without saying goodbye.'

'No, of course not.' Sybil threaded her arm through Ellen's. 'I was just thinking about … how much I'm looking forward to seeing Dame Lily in the pub after I sign my contract. She's invited you and Blanche to meet with her, too.'

Ellen breathed in on a gasp and moved to start a little dance, but Sybil held her back, worried she might rick her ankle again.

'Let's go and tell Blanche,' Ellen said. 'I can't wait to see her face.'

Blanche was indeed beside herself with excitement when Sybil passed on the invitation from Dame Lily. Her face took on a glow, her eyes behind the thick glasses blinked in surprise and the corners of her mouth turned up, but she'd gone straight back to organising her life to make way for the Recording Britain Project. 'I've had a talk with Mr Merton and he was most kind,' she reported to Sybil and Ellen.

'What did he say?' Ellen was lying on her bed, a pillow behind her head and her stockinged legs crossed at the ankles.

'He said he was very pleased for me and also relieved that I wouldn't be resigning my post.'

'You've got the best of both worlds,' Ellen said. There was heartache in her voice, but not a trace of envy. 'Working here during the week then gallivanting all over the county during the weekends. Drawing and getting paid for it.'

No one said anything for a few moments. 'Neither of us will get paid anything until our work's accepted.' Sybil filled the silence.

'Yes, I know but chances are …' Ellen said. 'Have you made an appointment with Mr Merton, Sybil?'

Sybil looked out of the window at the rain falling in large, lazy drops from a stony grey sky. It was so heavy she could barely make out the Land Girls working in the fields.

'Yes,' Sybil said. 'In fact, I'm seeing him in half an hour's time, but I don't suppose Mr Merton will be quite so happy with me.' She turned back to Blanche and Ellen. 'I'll have to give up my job and I've only been here five minutes.'

'He must be used to teachers coming and going,' Blanche said. 'Younger people in particular.'

'I agree,' Ellen said. 'And he'll probably use it to lure in his next set of tutors.' She mimed reeling in a fish. 'I can hear him now – "*Do you know, two of my tutors have gone on to be commissioned by the WAAC and the RBP? The relocated Marylebone School of Art is obviously a hotbed of up-and-coming talent.*"'

Sybil smiled at the perfect impersonation. She leaned against the windowsill and said, 'It's all going to get very awkward when I ask him to store my worldly goods until I can find some sort of lodgings to stay in when I return from wherever.'

'How about asking Dame Lily?'

Sybil shook her head. 'I wouldn't have the audacity,' she said. 'Besides, she lives in Norfolk and things would be easier if I were as close to the WAAC as possible.'

'Could you rent a place in London again?'

She shivered when she thought of the dingy bedsit she'd recently managed to escape from. 'That would be a complete waste of money as there would be weeks at a time when I wouldn't be using it. I suppose that leaves me with no choice but to go into a different small hotel every time I come back.'

The deluge hammered an offbeat rhythm against the window and the three women listened to it intently as the reality of Sybil's situation filled the room.

'I would hate that,' Ellen faltered. 'But might it help if you use the same hotel each time? One you quite like that you could become familiar with and call home ... some kind of home ... or substitute for your own ...'

Blanche put her arm around Sybil's shoulder and pulled her close. 'I have every sympathy,' she said. 'My nerves jangle and my stomach turns over every time I round the corner into Auntie Myrtle's road. I don't know what I'd do if she or the house weren't there and I had no place to call my refuge. But that's it – the solution.' Blanche moved so abruptly she almost knocked Sybil off her feet. 'I don't know why it didn't occur to me before.' She turned and grabbed Sybil's hands in hers. 'It's perfect,' she said, beaming.

'What is?' Ellen said. 'Tell us, then.'

Blanche looked from one to the other and said, 'Auntie Myrtle,' as if that were explanation enough.

'Yes, we know Auntie Myrtle,' Ellen said. 'She's lovely, but what about her?'

'You can live with Auntie Myrtle.'

'I couldn't possibly be such an imposition.' Alarm spiked through Sybil at the thought.

'Yes, you could. Auntie Myrtle would love to have you, there's no question of that. There's a spare room surplus to mine.' Blanche's words continued to tumble out. 'Why, just last week she told me she was toying with the idea of taking in a lady lodger. It might as well be you.'

Sybil shook her head slowly. 'I don't think I could do that. Wouldn't it be strange for you?'

Blanche stared at Sybil for a few moments. 'What's so strange about a friend lodging with one's aunt?'

Sybil couldn't come up with an answer.

'Nothing,' said Ellen. 'I think it's the perfect solution. And we would get to see you when our visits coincide.'

'Exactly. And you'd be helping me enormously by keeping an eye on Auntie Myrtle when I'm not able to get to London as often because of having my own commission to think about.'

Sybil pictured Auntie Myrtle who moved about with the same agile, purposeful step as her niece. Spectacles, too, that mirrored Blanche's were rooted to her nose. Then she saw herself established in Auntie Myrtle's house – a hot stone between the sheets before she got into bed; a bottomless pot of tea brewing despite rations, her things close by in what would become known as 'Sybil's Room'; her soap and talc and hairbrush in the bathroom where she'd left them until next she came home; the pair of them sitting in comfortable companionship in the Anderson.

'It seems too easy,' Sybil said.

'All the best things are simple. Cooking, artwork, acting, fashion. Simplicity is extremely effective.'

'Well,' Sybil said, warming to the idea. 'If you're sure, then please write and ask on my behalf. But you must impress on her that I won't mind at all if it's not possible, for any reason.'

'For goodness' sake, no need to write.' Blanche was blasé. 'You can take it as given that she'll agree. Besides we're going to see her on Monday when we can tell her all about it. I know she'll insist that her house should be your home.'

So that was that and everything returned to how it had been. Ellen threaded a ribbon through her hair, Blanche went back to organising herself and Sybil headed down the stairs to meet with Mr Merton.

Despite his face being dragged down with disappointment, Mr Merton was gracious about Sybil handing in her notice. He congratulated her and said if the school had to lose her, it might as well be to an organisation as worthy as the WAAC.

He sat facing her and crossed his legs. 'We all have to make sacrifices,' he said.

Sybil wasn't sure who he considered the sacrificial lamb to be. She thought the commission was a step up for her.

'The school will miss you,' he said.

'It's certainly the same for me. You've made me very welcome.'

'Your students will find it difficult. They hold you in high regard. I have nothing but excellent reports about you from them.'

Sybil hadn't thought too deeply about saying goodbye to her charges. She didn't know what she'd thought would happen, but she couldn't do a moonlight flit so knew she'd have to face them with the news fairly soon. 'Thank you, Mr Merton,' she said. 'They're a fantastic bunch. And very talented. I'm sure they'll do well.'

'Not as well as they could have done with your continued tutelage. How long can you give me?'

Sybil hadn't thought about that, either. Why was everything

so complicated? 'I've a meeting with the WAAC on Monday, so I'll know more after that. But ...' She hesitated, not wanting to commit herself to a timescale she couldn't fulfil. 'I presume I can start whenever it's convenient – within reason. So, if I say I'll stay until the end of the month, would that be helpful?'

Mr Merton rubbed his hands together. 'More than I can tell you, Mrs Paige. Thank you for being so considerate.'

The simple sentiment made her blush. She cleared her throat and turned away.

Besides their own cases for an overnight stay with Auntie Myrtle, Blanche insisted that each of them should carry one of Sybil's extra bags to save her having to manage the whole lot by herself at the end of the month. Sybil hadn't been sure it was a good idea. She'd protested that she'd been more than capable of managing her bags on her initial journey to the school and would be again when she moved out. More importantly, she wondered what Auntie Myrtle's reaction would be when she opened her front door to see the three of them standing on the step as if they'd found their way from the workhouse – bedraggled and surrounded by a motley array of belongings.

When they turned the corner into Broxash Road and saw that number 78 was still standing behind the blackthorn tree, the sigh of relief from Blanche clawed at Sybil's heart.

When the door opened, Auntie Myrtle smiled cheerfully then looked down and took a step backwards. 'My goodness,' she said. 'How long are you girls staying? Or,' she looked at them closely, 'has the school turned you out en masse?'

'Hello, Auntie Myrtle.' Blanche put her arms around her aunt. 'We haven't been chucked out, but Sybil's going to be living with you from the end of the month.'

Auntie Myrtle turned her attention to Sybil and peered at her through her glasses. 'Oh,' she said, pressing her hands together. 'How lovely.'

Sybil let go of the breath she'd been holding. 'I'm so sorry, Myrtle. There is a story behind all this. Shall I explain now?'

'Auntie Myrtle, if you please. And I love stories. Tell me when I've made a pot of tea. And don't leave out the smallest of details.'

Ellen and Blanche followed Auntie Myrtle, but Sybil stood quite still, taking in the fact that this was going to be her home, at least for a while. Warmth and contentment and solace enveloped her like a soothing balm. She hung her coat on the rack, took off her shoes and padded into the kitchen.

'Shortbread!' Ellen pounced on a plate of biscuits. 'May I?' she asked, stuffing one in her mouth.

'Of course,' Auntie Myrtle said. 'I didn't have the correct ingredients, no one has these days, but I did the best I could.' She nudged the plate towards Blanche then Sybil.

'They're mouth-watering,' Ellen said. 'If I were you, I'd never go back to the old recipe.'

'Come along now.' Auntie Myrtle picked up the teapot and went into the sitting room. 'You girls bring the other things and sit in here with me.'

A slice of sunshine carved the room in two. Michelangelo, the ginger tom, could not be enticed from his place on the windowsill. A potted plant shed a leaf and it floated languidly to the floor between the sideboard and the fireplace. Auntie Myrtle took up position in her favourite armchair, poured the tea, then put her feet on a battered leather pouffe. 'You two,' she nodded towards Blanche and Ellen, 'can keep quiet. I want to hear all about it from Sybil.'

They sipped their tea as Sybil spun her wedding ring around her finger and related the news to Auntie Myrtle. Blanche managed not to interrupt, but Ellen couldn't stop herself from blurting out her version of events once or twice. When Sybil announced Blanche's commission from the Recording Britain Project and hers from the WAAC, Auntie Myrtle hugged them both. Ellen got two, one because she hadn't been accepted and another for the promise of a cover on the Land Girl magazine.

'I don't want you to think I took your agreement for granted,' Sybil said, giving Auntie Myrtle one last chance to back out. 'But Blanche said there was no need to write in advance as you were sure to say yes. However, if for any reason you'd rather not have me here, do please …'

Auntie Myrtle laughed with delight. 'My niece knows me too well,' she said. 'But if I'd had notice I could have aired your room and cleared the shelves and set out towels. I'll do that now.'

'No need just yet,' Blanche said. 'Sybil's teaching at the manor until the end of the month. Besides, when the time comes, we can sort everything out together.'

'Lovely,' Auntie Myrtle said. 'It's all settled then. Oh, I must tell you. Abington Avenue took a packet two nights ago.'

Blanche gasped and put her hand to her throat.

'I'm guessing that's close by?' Ellen said.

'Two streets over.'

'How frightening for you – for everyone.' Ellen put her arm around Auntie Myrtle.

Sybil thought it was insensitive for anyone to say, 'Thank goodness it wasn't my grandmother or my uncle or my younger sister, cat, flat or best friend,' as that would denigrate the suffering of the people who had lost their home or loved ones. But this time, the fact that it had been someone else's Auntie Grace or Auntie Lydia instead of Auntie Myrtle flooded her being and left her arms and legs weak. And she knew that from now on she would, like Blanche, breathe out a sigh of relief every time she came home and saw that 78 Broxash Road and its owner were standing.

Miss Butterworth was at her organisational best, which was just as well as Ellen was eager to get to The Marquis and meet Dame Lily. She was handed her portfolio with a curt thank you, then dismissed to sit in an anteroom and wait.

Blanche was next up and came out of the office clutching a bloated buff envelope and looking confident.

Then it was Sybil's turn and she was told to take a seat across from Miss Butterworth who said, 'I have all the necessary paperwork to hand.' Sybil expected nothing less. 'Do take the time to read through your contract before you sign – here.' She pointed to a dotted line.

Sybil sat tall and read every word of the three-page document. It all made sense and there was nothing that took her by surprise. The term was for six months; she would be given a list of appropriate subjects and the places where they could be found; she would have a weekly stipend but was to keep a note of her expenses; she could show her work to the Committee as she accrued each piece or wait until the completion of her tenure; there was no guarantee that her work would be approved and accepted.

Miss Butterworth was ready to pounce with the pen. 'Any questions?' she asked.

'Yes, please,' Sybil said. 'When am I expected to start? I've told the Marylebone I'll work notice until the end of the month. After which my address will be care of Miss Myrtle Ashcroft at 78 Broxash Road, Wandsworth, S.W.11.'

'That will be adequate. I'll fill in Tuesday, 1st of April as your starting date. You're not superstitious about April Fools' Day are you?' Miss Butterworth studied her.

'Not a bit.'

'Good.' She consulted a calendar on her desk. 'And the end date of the contract will be Tuesday 30th September. I'll also change your address on our files.'

'In here,' Miss Butterworth pushed an envelope exactly like Blanche's towards her across the polished wooden desk, 'is everything you will need to get started. Please don't hesitate to contact me if you have any further queries.' She stood to draw the meeting to a close.

'There are two more things,' Sybil said. 'I'm very sorry.'

Miss Butterworth sat back down and looked as if she were making a monumental effort to remain patient. Sybil wondered how many others she had to meet with that morning.

'I don't have access to ...' Sybil was embarrassed and didn't know how to word her question.

'Money? That's the same for so many people.' Sybil didn't know if that were the case for Miss Butterworth with her perfectly manicured nails and well-heeled shoes, but the little lines around her mouth and eyes softened and her demeanour was more compassionate. 'And bound to get worse. It certainly is a big problem for our artists.' She smiled. 'But you'll find your first month's allowance in your package, and as per instructions, you must inform me of your whereabouts so I can telegram each stipend. If you fall short, let me know immediately and I will sort it out. We'll not have you stuck. And the other?'

'I ... my ...' It was so hard to get the words past the tight knot in her throat that threatened to strangle her every time she talked about Graeme. Miss Butterworth sat, her hands folded on her desk, concern lining her face. 'My husband is missing in action, so may I give your address to the authorities in case he ... for when he ... That way I can be notified right away instead of having to wait until I'm back in London to hear the news.' She took a deep breath but couldn't look at Miss Butterworth for fear that any kindness or sympathy would cause her tears to break the floodgates.

'Of course you may,' Miss Butterworth said. 'My long-term manfriend is in the RAF and I dread the same kind of terrible notification. You may be assured that I will inform you immediately when there is news of your husband's return.'

Sybil was pleased with how the secretary had referred to Graeme as if he were alive, although she wished there had been more conviction in her voice.

Miss Butterworth stood and offered her hand. 'Good luck,' she said, resorting to her usual manner.

'Thank you,' Sybil said. Then added, 'And the same to you,' because all of them needed it.

Happily, the meeting with Dame Lily was not so intense. A gin was waiting for each of them, and they sat around a table sandwiched in a corner away from the hubbub but within warming distance of the open fire. Blanche and Sybil produced their documents and Dame Lily said they were all standard.

'My dear Sybil.' Dame Lily wound her black and white scarf around her neck. 'I am so pleased for you.'

'Thank you, Dame Lily. I couldn't have done it without your help.'

'Nonsense. All I did was prod you in the right direction. Do you mind if I ...' She produced her cigarettes. Without waiting for a reply, she lit up and said, 'Would anyone else ...'

'No, thank you, I don't,' said Blanche.

'And I know that Sybil doesn't partake. Ellen?'

Much to Sybil's surprise, Ellen took one and allowed Dame Lily to light it for her. The tip flamed orange and Ellen sat back, her eyes half-mast with bliss. Then she doubled over with a fit of coughing. Blanche glared at her and shook her head.

'Now, Sybil, my dear, I insist you keep me informed about where you are and what you're drawing, and if our times in London coincide, we will, of course, meet up. With either of you, too.' Dame Lily gestured towards Blanche and Ellen. 'You'll find many different destinations on your list, including Norfolk,' she said. 'So if you decide to venture east, you must stay with us in Seagulls' Watch.'

'Thank you, Dame Lily, I would be most appreciative.'

'Another round?'

'I'll pay for these, although I'll need a hand carrying the glasses,' Blanche said.

'Let me help,' Sybil offered.

'And when you've finished that cigarette, Ellen, you can show me your portfolio and perhaps I can give you some guidance.'

When Blanche and Sybil returned to the table, Dame Lily was in full flow about Ellen's work. She thought it was excellent, but only half finished. Refinement was what was needed. Blanche raised her eyebrows at Sybil and the two of them sat in silence, not wanting to interrupt. Hopefully, Ellen would take the chastisement from Dame Lily and learn from it.

Sybil took a sip from her glass, twirled her ring a few times and thought about the first of April. She still could not imagine how the commission would work. Thoughts of walking into a room full of Women's Voluntary Service members, following them around and sketching them filled her with a mixture of excitement and dread. Then catching a train to Scunthorpe or Cardiff and drawing women working in factories and on building sites. She couldn't quite fathom how or why her lifelong dream of being an artist had come true, but it had, and it would be her at the end of that pencil or piece of charcoal. What she did know was that she would do her utmost to ensure that her pieces spoke for the subjects during this terrible time. She would do that for Dame Lily, for art, for the WAAC, for Graeme and for everyone now and in the future.

8

April 1941

Although she felt some apprehension about being far from home on her own, Sybil had talked herself out of beginning her commission in Norfolk and into starting in Darlington.

Leaning her head against the train window, she let the glass cool her face and thought about her last week in Luton, which had been a boiling cauldron of emotions. Saying goodbye to everyone, including Morgan Langley, had been more difficult than she'd imagined, but moving in with Auntie Myrtle had made up for the wrench in terms of comfort and reassurance. Blanche and Ellen had stayed with them until Sunday afternoon and the house in Wandsworth had been full of chitchat and sketchbooks, broken biscuits and hot drinks. They'd ventured on a few reconnaissance missions to familiarise Sybil with the area, and it had been decided that she would give all her food and fuel rations to Auntie Myrtle when she was at home. The payment of rent, though, was dismissed without discussion and that made Sybil feel awkward, so she decided she would leave a few shillings behind the mantelpiece clock for every week she lived there and not have any arguments about it.

To get used to brandishing her permits and drawing in public, she'd given herself a few days to sketch scenes of London, now disappearing behind the train like the dwindling trajectory of a path in a painting. So she'd roamed the entire city, getting on and off tubes and buses, spending a couple of nights in the

Underground, taking diversions, joining queues for essentials, listening to sing-songs in local pubs before the blackout descended.

At first, she'd felt embarrassed as she shyly took out her supplies and charted the heartbreak around her. It was as if she were forging a name for herself on the back of everyone else's misery. But she channelled her concentration into telling the subjects' stories and she became more confident. Two older men sitting on bricks next to a demolished building squinted at her through narrowed eyes but when she showed them her permit, they nodded and let her get on with her work.

She'd drawn them dragging on cigarettes and looking beyond her, one of them pointing towards something in the distance. When she turned to see what had caught their attention, she was greeted with the same catastrophic scene. When she'd finished, she asked them if they wanted to look at her work, to approve the way she'd drawn them.

'No, love,' one said. 'We know only too well what all this looks like.' Then they'd stamped on their cigarettes and started to haul bricks into a pile with their bare hands.

She'd hurried away, that last statement going over and over in her mind. There had been an edge to it that made her feel small and inconsequential as if what they were experiencing cut deeper, the tasks they had to undertake more onerous, their efforts more valiant and their understanding more poignant than hers.

And perhaps they're right, she thought. She pictured herself through their eyes and in front of her, she saw a smartly dressed young woman with nothing better to do than walk around with a notebook and art supplies drawing whatever took her fancy. It had crossed her mind to try to explain that art wasn't an indulgent hobby – she'd been commissioned, and the compositions were for posterity, as well as for now. But she was glad she hadn't raised the subject on a whim, as the men might have been trying to uncover the bodies of their wives or grandchildren, or desperately wondering where they would sleep that night, or weeping inwardly at the loss of every possession they'd worked for lying broken under the rubble. If that were the case, they had every right to think of her war work as trivial.

Auntie Myrtle had listened when Sybil related the story to her. 'It made me feel as if … I don't know. What I'm doing isn't valid. Or as valuable as the things other people have to do.'

'How awkward for you.' Auntie Myrtle's cup rattled as she placed it in the saucer. 'And my guess is you'll get those sorts of looks and sarcastic remarks thrown at you many times.'

Sybil groaned. 'I'm not sure I can stand being silently criticised every time I go about my work. It's not as if I made the job up for my own ends.' She sniffed. 'I'm just lucky it happens to be exactly what I want to do, war or not, but it feels as if it's both a blessing and a curse at the same time.'

A grey-collared dove cooed outside the window and Michelangelo stretched then closed his eyes again.

Auntie Myrtle was quiet for a few moments, then she said, 'Feelings are heightened during this war on our doorstep. Hurt cuts deeper and happiness runs at a fevered pitch. You must know what I mean.'

'Yes, I think I do.'

'May I have a look at the piece, please?' Auntie Myrtle stretched out her hand.

'Are you an artist?' Sybil asked when the sketchbook was open on the coffee table. 'You're studying it as if you are.'

Auntie Myrtle pushed her spectacles up on her nose. 'I so wanted to be,' she said, longing in her voice. 'So did my sister, Fenella. Blanche's mother. That wouldn't have been possible in our circumstances, though, but we made sure Blanche had the opportunities. And she's done rather well, don't you think?'

Sybil wondered if Auntie Myrtle's family had been in the same situation as the Land Girl with ruddy cheeks who'd enjoyed drawing. She hoped that young woman had enough energy to keep her eyes open in the evenings and sketch a cover picture for

The Land Girl magazine. 'Very well indeed,' she answered Auntie Myrtle. 'A bronze at the Olympics. You must be very proud.'

'I am but I don't know much about how art works. I like what I like. What speaks to me.' Her laugh was a low chuckle. 'That's not a term an art critic would use, is it?'

'No, but as taught to me by Dame Lily, I believe that's the main purpose of art,' Sybil said. Waiting for Auntie Myrtle's verdict, she twiddled with her wedding ring and felt nervous, as if she were back in school again hoping the composition would be deemed likeable.

'What are the men looking at?' Auntie Myrtle asked. 'No, let me guess. A bomb site in the same bloody awful condition as the one they're sitting in. Am I right?'

A smile spread across Sybil's face, and she nodded.

Auntie Myrtle smiled back, the lines around her rumpled mouth ironed out for a moment. 'You've achieved that. And you've captured something remarkable in their eyes. There's a chink in the smokescreen over them that lets us know they're trying their hardest to be stoic and resilient against the horrors crushing in on them. However did you do that?'

'I didn't know I had,' Sybil said softly. 'I drew what I saw and let the men speak through the art.'

Auntie Myrtle flicked through the rest of the book and Sybil walked to the window. She stared out at the trees, new leaves pushing through into the light, clouds sculling across a sky that would no doubt see an armada of enemy aircraft hurtle fire and bombs and heartbreak down on them again that night. A woman walked past, pushing an empty pram towards the shops, the toddler who should have occupied the seat probably evacuated to some far-off place of safety. When she caught Sybil's eye, she put her head down and hurried along. Sybil would draw her later and make the childless buggy prominent by clouding the street surrounding it.

If what Dame Lily, the WAAC and Auntie Myrtle were telling her was true, she was able to produce genuine, honest depictions of the country at war, and she would carry on despite barbed comments and pointed looks, lack of a familiar face close by and the uncertainty of not knowing if her finished pictures would be accepted. All she had to do – like the two men she'd drawn and the woman using her baby's forsaken buggy as a shopping trolley – was to be strong and get on with it.

A halo of yellow from a little lamp shone onto the table in the carriage and Sybil placed her sketchbook in the glow. As she turned the pages, twenty-seven sketches she'd created during her week in London stared back at her. There was the one of the mews she'd found hidden away behind Harrod's – one house intact with empty milk bottles standing proud on the step next to a demolished reflection of itself.

Next was the sketch of a long queue of people outside the doors of a doctor's surgery, each of them nursing an elbow or forehead or some other minor injury. In the corner of each page, she scribbled the details of where and when the drawing had been composed, although she couldn't imagine she would ever forget. Something about each scene had moved her deep inside and made her feel a rush of emotions that left her weak, and that applied to the cheerful as well as the grave. A wedding in Forest Gate; a kiss on the platform of Waterloo Station; three men gossiping outside a pub close to London Bridge; a group of women laughing as they sorted through a bag of rags; unevacuated children chasing each other down the middle of a road in Paddington. She'd tried to capture the determination and hope in each of them.

Then she began to plan how she could improve the sketch of the two men on the bomb site. She remembered the resigned slump of their shoulders and the way they refused to look at each other when they spoke – as if whatever they saw there might be reflected in their own eyes and would be too much to bear.

The scenery beyond the train flashed past and seemed to change in time with every rhythmic clack of the wheels. *That*, she thought, *is what my sketchbook will be like soon.* One glimmer of war life in Britain after another, each lasting as long as a glimpse from a moving train.

But she had to make her pictures amount to more than that. She framed the two subjects with her hands and decided this one would benefit from retaining the background – the rubble was integral to the story and the end product would be nothing without it.

Alone in the carriage, she spread out her supplies and set about sketching a few versions of the picture, then she would move on to another. Eventually, she would have to choose one to complete and present to the Committee, as she'd never be able to produce all of them in finished form until her commission came to an end and she had more time – but if she did that, she'd have no money to live on. That was a dilemma she would soon have to solve.

The train slowed to a stop outside a station and Sybil craned her neck to see where she was. With a jolt, the train jumped forward and the inspector announced Doncaster, just as a sign came into view.

Sybil watched a guard saunter along the grey platform. The station looked much like Luton, and the passengers milling around indistinguishable from those she'd seen there. The scene would be a good example of how things were the same as they'd ever been, yet impossibly different during this period of time.

Quickly, she snatched at a piece of charcoal and drew what she saw, paying particular attention to an older man shivering on a bench, his hand held out to a greedy loft of pigeons.

As the train pulled out, she thought she had enough on paper and would be able to fill in the rest later, then she turned back to her drawing of the two men. Deep in concentration when the compartment door opened, she was surprised by a whoosh of cold air, followed by a woman carrying a suitcase with one hand and manoeuvring a small dog on a lead with the other. 'Good morning,' Sybil said. 'Can I help you?'

'If you wouldn't mind holding Jasper for a minute, I'd be most grateful,' the woman said.

She took the lead but didn't know what else to do except stay glued to her seat.

'He's a good little fellow, he won't bite.' The woman swung her case into the luggage rack.

'I'm not worried about that,' Sybil said. 'But I've just realised this is the first time I've held a dog's lead. Isn't that odd?'

'I've barely had one out of my hands my entire life.' The woman looked down at Sybil's things, taking up every inch of the table, glanced at her ticket and said,' I believe this is my seat?'

'Oh yes, of course.' She handed the lead back so she could tidy up. 'I beg your pardon.'

With a few moans and groans, the woman settled herself down, took off her outdoor things and fussed over Jasper, who made himself comfy in her lap.

With less space to work on, Sybil thought that was that for now, until the older woman tapped the table and said, 'What are you up to, if you don't mind me asking?'

Steeling herself for criticism, Sybil flashed her badge and said she was a war artist on a temporary contract.

The woman's sparse eyebrows shot up and she gawped at Sybil. 'Well, good on you,' she said, caressing the dog's ears. 'Are they sending you to the Front?'

Sybil felt relieved to hear the approval in the woman's voice. She shook her head and said, 'No, women won't be sent overseas. We're commissioned to draw what's happening here.'

The woman sniffed and seemed to lose a bit of interest when she heard that. 'Same old story. Men get all the fun and all the praise.'

'Well, I wouldn't call moving along with an active battalion fun.'

The woman looked at Sybil as if she thought she should know better. 'Adventure, then. Excitement or a whiff of danger you have to use your wits to get out of. They're probably given training, so I don't suppose they're exposed to much jeopardy. But when they come back their pieces will be fawned over – much more so than your sketches of …' she glanced over at Sybil's artwork, 'bomb sites in London.'

Sybil closed her book and gazed out of the window again. She thought that was probably true but deserved, as the artists on the Front were bringing home pictures of situations that people hadn't seen and she was drawing scenes that most of them were forced to view every day of the week. She decided it was too wearying to carry on the conversation, so thought she'd pack her things and have a meal in the restaurant carriage.

'Oh, don't stop on my account,' the woman sounded horrified. 'I was about to add that on reflection there is plenty going on in this country that's dangerous. You only have to step out of your front door and you're exposed to all manner of peril. That's if your door hasn't been blown off its hinges.'

Sybil managed a smile. 'Yes, and we haven't been given any safety training other than how to put on a gas mask.'

The woman was quiet for a few moments, Jasper's spine twitching under her hands. 'You've been given a marvellous opportunity in such an inopportune time,' she said. 'And I can tell you're going to grab it with both hands, and your heart, and run with it. I worked in a munitions factory during the last war, and I loved it.' Her face brightened at the thought of it.

'I was on an assembly line next to my sister on one side and my cousin on the other. We had so much fun. Then when the war was over, I had to go home and face life without my fiancé but with a disfigured, wretchedly miserable father to care for. I'm afraid,' she said, blinking at the changing scenery, 'I've become rather bitter about it.'

Sybil gave her ring a few swivels and felt pity for the older woman, along with a strong bond of affinity. No, not quite that. It was more a sense of understanding, which softened her attitude.

'Will you draw me and Jasper?' The woman held the dog up

to her cheek and did her best to look appealing. 'I am living through the war, after all and doing my best to keep jolly and optimistic.' She laughed to show a gap in her bottom teeth and although Sybil knew she shouldn't waste charcoal and paper, she produced a quick sketch, signed it and handed it to her travelling companion who squirreled it away as if it were a sheet of gold leaf.

'Marvellous,' the woman said. 'Now I must get ready to alight at York. Are you getting off there or carrying on?'

York was on Sybil's list and under it a rather long catalogue of possible subject matter, so why not stop there and see what the place had to offer. 'Yes, I am,' Sybil said with a sudden surge of confidence. 'Can I help you by holding Jasper's lead again?

She found a room at the Minster Hotel which she barely glanced at before heading out, her art supplies in her new waterproof oilskin bag. The afternoon was chilly and, with no bombing raids to contend with, the air felt fresher than it had in London. Blue sky canopied above her and daffodils trembled around the trunks of trees. Sybil took a deep breath, lifted her face to the light and let the warmth seep in. Other than having Graeme home with all their troubles sorted out, she couldn't think of any way in which she would have changed her current situation – given the circumstances. The determination she'd felt half an hour ago remained, although now an insidious edge of disquiet had wormed itself in. *But that isn't a bad thing*, she told herself. She would use it to her advantage when facing the inevitable adventure, excitement and danger that was part and parcel of her commission.

The towering Minster was chilling as it blindly surveyed the town from blank, boarded windows. She walked towards it and although it looked close, she found herself wending through cobbled lanes and back streets without getting any nearer. She passed the usual bakeries, butchers, greengrocers and haberdashers with low doorways and black-framed, skewwhiff windows. Quaint was the first word that popped into her mind.

Women bustled from one shop to another, woollen headscarves tied under their chins; a ladder was propped against a building whilst a workman cleared guttering; a lad on a bicycle bumped along. She knew the cemetery had suffered when four bombs fell on the city five months ago and the waterworks had a near miss around the same time, but none of that was on show here. Surrounding her was the quintessential British idyll and if she'd been contracted to create artwork for chocolate boxes, she wouldn't have had to look any further. It was two hundred or so miles from London, but it seemed a world removed; then she spotted the signs: *Dig for Victory*! It was as if the people of York knew they'd been lucky so far and felt the acclamation was the least they could do.

For some reason, the posters brought on a surge of pride and represented how the entire country had bonded since September 1939. She leaned against the wall of a café, and as she sketched the lane with those subtle reminders of the war prominently on display, no one batted an eyelid.

When she turned, another sign caught her eye and made her laugh. *The girls are laying*, it read. *We have fresh eggs*! Despite trying to control herself, saliva pooled in her mouth. She felt like Ellen, whose appetite was insatiable.

A little bell over the door to the café heralded her arrival, but the hubbub probably rendered it mute to the people inside. One of the women behind the counter, wearing a white apron and a cap shaped like a tiara, smiled at her and asked if she'd like a table.

'For one, please,' Sybil said. She followed the waitress, who had a number of clumsy darns in her stockings, to a table tucked away right at the back. 'I love the sign in your window, and I do hope you have some eggs left.' She held up crossed fingers.

'They're my girls.' The waitress smiled. 'And they're great layers. One or two?'

Sybil was disbelieving. 'Two?' she asked. 'May I?'

'We have enough. Fried, poached or scrambled.'

'Fried, please. With toast, if possible.'

The woman nodded. 'Can't have eggs without bread. Tea to wash it down?'

'Yes, please,' Sybil said. 'How many hens do you have? If you don't mind me asking.'

'Twenty, give or take. Some of the eggs are sold to the café and the rest to RAF bases. We have a smallholding, me and my husband. On the outskirts of town. We've taken our other poster to heart and we dig for victory, along with most of York. But I told him, my Henry that is, we're keeping our girls no matter what and everyone is glad we did.' She swooped her eyes around the full café. 'As you can see.'

'You certainly are busy.' Another three people filled the doorway.

'I'll put in your order now, my love.'

For once, Sybil was glad to be sitting in dim light, away from the windows at the front of the shop. A china hen sat on an old sideboard, its talons tucked under its chipped white feathers. Quickly, before the waitress returned, she sketched the ornament, adding a pile of eggs around it and the waitress holding the sign that was in the window.

Then she rooted in her bag for her list and spread it out. York – right at the bottom of the document. Under the heading was the list of suggestions for compositions, and Sybil thought she'd start with the former Rowntree's office block in Haxby Road, where the gum section had been requisitioned as a fuse factory and the cream department was being used for the production of Ryvita. Next there was Hill's, who manufactured and repaired aeroplane blades for propellers, and RAF Clifton where the Women's Auxiliary Air Force, or WAAFs, repaired bombers. Any of those would be worth a visit.

The waitress placed a steaming cup of tea and a plate of fried eggs in front of her. The yolks were golden and wobbly, the whites solid and shiny and the aroma more enticing than she remembered. 'Would you like any HP or Lea and Perrins?' the waitress asked.

'No, thank you,' Sybil said. 'I want to savour them as they are. But can you give me directions to any of these places?' She pointed to her list.

The woman's face turned ashen and she took a step back. 'Why do you want to know?' she asked. 'Are you a spy?'

'No, I can assure you. Nothing of the sort.' She produced her permits. 'I'm a war artist, commissioned to draw women at work throughout the country. This is my official list of possible subjects.'

The waitress stared at her as if she were speaking in a different language but scanned the documents from over Sybil's shoulder.

The woman's face remained confused, but she said, 'Ask anyone in town and they'll point you in the direction of Rowntree's, and if you go straight out into the country from behind the Minster, you'll eventually get to RAF Clifton.' She looked down at Sybil's shoes with disdain. 'You'll have problems in that footwear, though. It's about twenty minutes down a very muddy path.'

For an uncomfortable moment, the waitress sized her up. 'I'm not sure I've done right, giving you so much information.'

Sybil fiddled with her ring.

'Would it help if I came back and showed you what I've sketched? That might put your mind at rest.'

The waitress nodded. 'Yes, please, my duck,' she said. 'Ask for Jenny. Jenny Chapman.'

Then she hurried towards the front of the shop where a couple were waiting to be seated and Sybil cut into an egg, the yolk oozing over the toast like spillage from a tube of sunshine yellow paint. Nothing had ever tasted as good.

By the following morning, the crisp cobalt sky had disappeared, and in its place hung a sludge-coloured awning of dripping rain. Sybil was glad of her oilskin bag and only wished she could cover herself in the same material.

Walking along the lanes hadn't been too onerous, but now that she'd found her way past the town boundaries towards Clifton, there was nothing but sticky mud and bits of broken masonry underfoot.

She trudged on and was so bedraggled by the time she arrived, she wondered if the sentry on the gate would be able to appraise her through the mud she was caked in. But he waved her through, the clunk of the gate behind her sounding like a warning not to challenge its authority. She felt small as she walked across the airfield, like a dormouse scurrying for cover away from the neighbourhood tom. Insignificant, too, or a tiny part of something much larger than she could fathom.

As she stepped inside the first open hangar she came across, women in regulation RAF overalls were crawling all over six Halifax bombers. The sight made Sybil stop and stare, a broad smile on her face.

'Stop where you are!' a voice boomed above the rattle and hum of machinery.

For a beat, Sybil was unsure who the voice was shouting at, then realised that all work had stopped, and everyone was looking at her. Her legs almost buckled and with trembling hands, she fumbled for her permits.

'Don't take another step. Put down your things and put up your hands where I can see them.'

'I'm a …'

'Don't say a word.'

It felt as if ball bearings were loose in the pit of her stomach and, afraid she might disgrace herself, she did as she was told. A woman in smart RAF battledress warily came towards her. 'Explain yourself. Name, please.'

'Sybil Paige.' She didn't know how she got the words out.

'Reason for trespassing?'

'I'm not,' Sybil stuttered. 'I'm a war artist. I have permits and I was allowed to enter at the gate.'

The officer maintained her distance but held out her hand. Sybil didn't want to move, so stretched across and passed the documents to her. She wished she could ask the woman on the train if she thought this was enough danger, excitement and adventure.

At last the officer sighed deeply and handed back the permits. 'The gate should have acted on protocol and warned me. I shall be having a word with them,' she said in a voice no less loud and stern. 'I expect you need a cup of tea after that.'

'Yes, please.' Sybil could feel that her face was clammy and this time it wasn't anything to do with the rain. 'And the lavatory, if I may.'

'Follow me.' The officer stepped out smartly. 'Enough gawking, ladies,' she bawled. 'Back to work.'

After a quick freshen-up and cup of tea, Sybil was given free rein to sketch the women repairing the aircraft. She soon discovered that they worked in pairs or small groups, never on their own. They used rivet guns and spanners, hammers and screwdrivers as if they had been born with them welded to their hands. When they had a moment to look at her, some of the girls posed with puckered lips and others put their shoulders to their chins in the hopes of looking provocative. But when they went back to their work, they were nothing other than serious and urgent.

Like the Land Girls, their biceps formed hillocks under their sleeves and when they moved about, they were strong and confident. She captured them in various poses, but her favourite was of a young girl hanging from crossed legs under the nose of a plane. Her mate, standing on a wheel, was handing her a wrench. 'I used to swing from the branch of a tree like that years ago,' Sybil called up to her.

'Me, too,' the WAAF said. 'I thought I'd outgrown it, but here I am again.'

When she'd accrued ten drawings, she packed up her things, said goodbye to the officer and headed back to the gate. She thanked the sentry profusely, hoping it would make up in some small way for the bollocking he was in line for.

She decided to leave for Darlington early the next morning, so she had a lot to cram into the rest of the day. She found her way to Rowntree's where she sketched women in hair nets working on every aspect of producing Ryvita. When she saw the slurry being mixed before it went into the oven, she thought she might heave, but when it came out brittle and crunchy and evenly cooked, she would have bitten into one without hesitation, given the chance.

Again, she was amazed at how the women kept their eyes on measuring, packing and checking for anomalies. In a finished piece of the assembly line, she would clearly depict the label on one packet, but blur the others along with the women's hands, which reached back and forth like the arms on robots. With permission to wander the area, she chanced upon the rest room where she sketched a composition of four young girls chatting animatedly as they sat next to an older woman in a white coverall, asleep with her head lolling on her chest. That would tell the subject's exhaustion with clarity.

The work at Hill's was on a different level. She had to don a face covering not unlike a gas mask, but it failed to filter the appalling fumes that smelled like concentrated nail varnish remover. The huge space was cold, with lofty ceilings and concrete floors. Apart from the occasional chat or giggle, the women in the other factories had not said a word, but here, the silence was distracting. It seemed as though not so much as a smile was allowed. The girls' faces, as they laminated the propeller blades with the unctuous varnish, were pale and haunted. She longed to ask if the effects of working with such noxious chemicals were known and what was being done to protect the women handling them. But the answer would probably have been that no one knew, the job just had to be done.

Outside again, Sybil gulped in fresh, cool air and felt grateful for the war work she'd been assigned and overwhelmingly sad, at the same time, for the women stuck with those sickening factory conditions. They were a stark example of having to take the bad for the collective good. But when she thought of them as individuals, her eyes stung with angry tears.

Before she headed to her hotel, Sybil popped into the café and saw Mrs Chapman tidying the counter.

'Hello,' Sybil said. 'I've come to show you my sketches as promised.'

'No need, my duck. My Henry explained that your work is vital and completely above board.' Her face crumpled. 'He said I was very rude to you. I'm so sorry.'

'Please don't worry,' Sybil said. 'No harm done. You're not the first and you won't be the last to question what I'm doing.' She opened her bag. 'I can't show you everything,' she said. 'For security reasons. But here are a couple, along with one of you.'

Sybil produced the sketch of Mrs Chapman with the eggs and china hen, and the waitress laughed out loud. 'You've made me look like a film star.' She smoothed her hair. 'But wait one minute,' she said. 'I have something for you.'

Sybil felt embarrassed, as she didn't expect to be given anything for doing her job. She hoped it wouldn't be an egg as she had no means of cooking it or, worse still, a chicken that would have to be politely declined. But Mrs Chapman beamed when she came back from the kitchen carrying a pair of ankle-high overboots.

'Oh,' Sybil said. 'They look very handy. But you must need them, surely?'

'I haven't used them for ages, and they'll do you nicely. Pop them over your shoes and you'll arrive at your destination clean and dry.'

Tears clouded Sybil's eyes. 'Thank you, Mrs Chapman,' she said, touching the waitress's hand.

'We have to help each other during this bloody war,' she said. But Sybil thought the woman's kindness and generosity were a trait that wasn't bound by any specific time or place.

That evening after she'd packed, Sybil spread out her sketches, scribbled references in the corners and chose which ones she thought spoke most eloquently for the subject. Her first port of call had gone well, and she felt good about the work she'd produced. Perhaps, she thought, she'd gained enough resilience to draw that portrait of herself receiving the telegram about Graeme. She pulled out the sketchbook she saved for that purpose and tentatively put charcoal to paper, but no sooner had she started than she was shaking and heaving and sobbing. She tore out the sheet of paper, ripped it to shreds, threw it across the room, then spent ages on her hands and knees picking up the pieces and tossing them in the bin. It was going to take much more than one good day to enable her to set her grief aside long enough to sketch herself in the throes of it.

9

April 1941

As she stepped off the train, Sybil remembered that she should have been in Darlington yesterday, instead of York, and that she'd forgotten to notify Miss Butterworth of the change of plan. Her heart thudded and an electric shock like tiny darts attacked her hands and legs. How could she have forgotten? She felt foolish and unprofessional and hoped the WAAC hadn't urgently been trying to get in touch with her.

She stashed her belongings in a B&B and made her way to the main post office. Much to her relief, no telegrams were waiting for her, but she sent one of her own to Miss Butterworth, thankful she wouldn't have to give her the news of her incompetency face to face. When it was gone, she promised herself she wouldn't be that remiss again.

Besides wanting to start her commission far from anyone she knew, she'd chosen Darlington for two reasons. The North Road Locomotive Works and RAF Middleton St George, which both employed women, but now she doubted her choice as she'd used the same two examples in York and wanted to vary her pieces as much as possible. It wouldn't fulfil her contract if she went back to the WAAC with nothing but sketches of women in engineering works and on RAF stations.

Passing a row of terrace houses, she noticed a middle-aged woman in a worn tabard tending rows of vegetables in her front garden. From across the road, she watched as the woman hoed a strip of rich earth, bent over to pick out a few weeds and stood with a groan as she rubbed her back. Her legs were bare and her sleeves were rolled up to her elbows. A dog sat on the porch, its head on its paws and its tail lazily thumping the ground.

Sybil took a couple of steps back, hid under cover of a tree and retrieved her equipment. *Perhaps this is the way to do it*, she thought. Stay in the shadows and sketch ordinary women in everyday situations whenever she happened upon them. That way she wouldn't alarm anyone into thinking she was up to no good.

Immersed in her work, she looked up every few minutes to see how the woman moved or what vegetables she was gathering or how the light hit the glass in the greenhouse. Then she started when she gazed across to see the woman staring at her, the line of her mouth set rigid.

Without a polite preamble, the woman lifted her chin and called out, 'Do you mind explaining yourself?'

Sybil crossed over, took a deep breath and did just that, but the hard set of the woman's face didn't change.

'Why don't you concentrate on London?' she asked. 'And leave us in peace.'

Sybil thought that a strange turn of phrase to use during a war, as any peace to be found could be shattered in an instant. It made for living on a knife edge. She spun her ring around her finger and said, 'I've been commissioned to draw pictures of women on the home front up and down the country. And there were various things I wanted to capture in Darlington. You could be immortalised on canvas.' She tried to sound buoyant.

'Hmm,' the woman snorted. 'For all the wrong reasons. But if you're really interested in seeing the busy darlings of Darlington, there's a Women's Institute meeting this evening at seven.'

'Oh,' Sybil said, thinking the conversation had taken a helpful turn. 'Where is it going to be held?'

'The Methodist Church Hall.' The woman rubbed her back and grimaced.

'Thank you,' Sybil said. 'I hope to see you there.'

The woman nodded and turned back to her gardening without moving her face an inch towards a smile. Who knew what she might be going through – a son missing in action like Graeme; a daughter involved in nursing the wounded; a husband invalided from the Great War – but if that were the case, Sybil didn't think she'd have spoken so freely about living in peace. Perhaps she'd had to give up a garden of prize roses for the vegetables, or maybe her sore back pulled her features down. Whatever the cause, Sybil was quite sure she'd captured the essence of the woman in her sour face, and that look of deep displeasure would speak to many people.

If she wanted a meal and a freshen-up before the WI meeting, she knew she'd have to choose between the RAF station and the Locomotive Works, and as North Road was one short stop away on the train, Sybil decided on the second option. The day was cool but pleasant, and as she hurried through rows of houses, she was reminded of London and Auntie Myrtle. A spasm of homesickness gripped her stomach and she tried to massage the pain away with the flat of her hand. She'd only been gone a couple of days, but she looked back at her time in Wandsworth with a sense of nostalgic longing. She must make time to write to her adopted aunt and to Blanche and Ellen, who had been told to send their letters to her via the WAAC where the competent Miss Butterworth was sure to forward them immediately – if she had advance warning of where Sybil would be.

No sooner had she hopped on the train than it was time to alight, which suited her fine. With no one to regularly talk to, she sometimes felt burdened by her own thoughts and it helped to keep occupied. She should be used to it, she thought sardonically, as she'd spent so much time on her own in that pokey bedsit.

After she'd passed through the foyer of an enormous red brick building, she was directed to double doors that a guard opened for her. As she turned to thank him, she was almost blown off her feet by the noise. For a moment she stood, her hands over her ears and a tight grimace on her face until a supervisor bustled her into an office with windows facing the factory. The grating sound of metal on metal could still be heard, although it was muffled to some extent by the glass walls. 'I've read about the WAAC and the Recording Britain Project,' the supervisor said. She wore a knotted scarf around her head, a loose, beige work coat and red lipstick that had worn off in patches. She didn't give the impression that working in engineering was her lifelong career. 'But I never thought for a minute that an artist would make it to our Shop here in Darlington.' She beamed with excitement.

'I've been tasked with a mission to capture images of women's war work from far and wide.' Sybil felt caught up in the supervisor's enthusiasm. 'And this is a thriving factory manned, if you like, by women. It's perfect.'

'Well, there's a lot going on. We have women – and a few men – overhauling and manufacturing locomotives, plus another couple of hundred making munitions. I only have authority over a small section, but if I can get cover, would it be alright if I tag along with you? I'm very interested in seeing what you do.'

'Of course.' Sybil thought she'd enjoy a chat with this energetic woman, if the roar permitted, and she could be insightful into the work that went on in the 'Shop', as she called it. 'I'd be pleased of the company.'

'If you don't mind putting these on.' The woman handed her a smock-like coat and a pair of ear plugs. 'I'll be back in a couple of minutes.'

The coat was too large and the ear plugs too small, until she shoved and spiralled the hard little nuggets into position. Two colossal engines were within touching distance, and they appeared to be much larger than those used for passenger trains. Perhaps they were special models for transporting tanks and other large pieces of equipment from one place to another. Women in face visors welded parts of the chassis, attached wipers to the windscreens as large as picture windows and slid beneath the machine to inspect any damage to the undercarriage. Any and all of what she observed would make excellent sketches, but as she was about to get out her supplies, the supervisor came back into the office. 'Can you hear me?' she mouthed.

Sybil waved her hand about to signal that she could, but not very well.

'Good.' The woman gave a thumbs-up, produced a notepad and pencil and indicated that they would have to write on it to communicate, so Sybil wouldn't get the chat she'd so been looking forward to.

The woman beckoned her to follow and they made their way down onto the tracks. Above them, the overwhelming proportions of the locomotives loomed eerily. Sybil shivered and thought about how easy it would be to slip and be dragged under the rasping wheels of a moving engine. On the notepad she scribbled: *Have many people lost their lives in accidents?* The question didn't alarm the supervisor in the slightest. *That is classified information,* she wrote back and shrugged her shoulders. *Please just stop and draw whenever you feel inspired.* So Sybil sketched the towering locomotives with the women working on them as minuscule, but not feeble, in comparison.

They threaded through engine upon engine, Sybil stopping when a particular scene caught her eye. It was unnerving to have the supervisor watch every mark she made on the paper until it became apparent that the woman was not going to offer suggestions or criticism. All she did was beam, nod her head in approval and jot *excellent* or *well done* on the notebook.

The supervisor beckoned towards a door leaving the factory floor, but Sybil stopped, mesmerised by a furnace, a ball of orange flame roaring and sizzling in its belly. Two men were feeding it, and on the opposite side a woman was shovelling ash from its bowels. The supervisor followed Sybil's line of sight and shook her head. She jotted on the notepad that they had to stand back. *Can you take me as close as possible?* Sybil wrote and they inched forward to a red line drawn on the floor. The heat was immense and sweat began to trickle down Sybil's spine. For a moment she felt the world melting around her. She thought she might faint and knew she'd have to be quick if she wanted to get her sketch.

She wished she could tell how old the female stoker was and if she was slight or sturdy and whether or not her makeup, if she wore any, was sliding off her face. But she was covered in protective clothing, so those things were difficult to discern – Sybil would have to use her imagination which was never as effective as viewing the real subject.

Perspiration had made the stub of charcoal run, like black ink, over her fingers and when she looked up to gain perspective, the woman had stepped back and removed her face shield. The sight made a fist close around Sybil's heart. The woman was fifty at the very least, with a thin, gaunt face and greying hair, and Sybil thought it should be against the law to allow a woman of that age and build to undertake such a strenuous job. Wide eyed, she shot a look at the supervisor who she thought would put a stop to the woman's hard labour, but instead, all she did was wait patiently for Sybil to finish her drawing.

She sketched the subject wiping her forehead with a cloth but left enough of her face exposed to tell her age. Then for a split second, the woman locked eyes with Sybil. Her gaze was determined and as steely as the metal that dominated the factory. Something ran between them. A message or a moment of understanding. It happened too quickly to analyse – that would have to wait until later. But there was the soft jolt of immediate acknowledgement from one woman to another, who, in the midst of an upside-down world in which women took on the strangest of jobs, recognised that theirs were more bizarre and curious than most. The second passed so quickly that Sybil wondered if she'd imagined it because she longed for it to be so, then the woman started work again and Sybil gripped her charcoal to draw her shovelling ashes with all of her considerable might.

As she and the supervisor passed through the door, the connection she'd felt with the stoker ebbed, and guilt engulfed her at leaving the poor woman slaving away at such treacherous work. The second factory was much quieter than the first and Sybil followed the supervisor's lead in taking out her ear plugs, although there remained a muted version of the clash and clatter. The first question she asked was whether or not that woman should be working in such a terrible environment.

'Which woman?' the supervisor asked in innocence.

'The older woman shovelling ash out of the furnace. Surely that must be a younger, fitter person's job.'

'That woman,' the supervisor said. 'Worked here during the Great War but had to give her job back to a man when it came to an end. She could not wait to sign up when the gates were opened to women again, so there's really no need to feel sorry for her.'

Sybil thought about that for a few minutes and decided that she did still pity the woman, but not for the backbreaking work she was doing. Her heart felt heavy for all the years that workhorse hadn't been allowed to take up a job she loved and seemed to be very good at. Perhaps she'd done something in the intervening years. Worked in a shop, or an office or on a farm. More than likely she'd been confined to the home, especially if she had a husband and children. Sybil imagined her walking energetically to and from the shops and stopping longingly at the factory gates, hoping there might be a sign that female help was wanted again. Disappointed, she would have turned for home and set upon a pile of potatoes that needed peeling or whacked the dust out of a rug. *What a waste*. More than sympathy, Sybil felt anger as she realised she and the stoker had so much in common. If it hadn't been for the war and the lack of men, they would both be at home preparing meals and scrubbing tide marks off shirt collars.

Sybil wiped her grubby hands on a rag she kept in her bag. It was ridiculous to ban half the population from working outside the home if that's what they wanted to do. It was almost as preposterous as the appointment of one lone woman to the ranks of men given permanent commissions by the WAAC.

'This is the rather new munitions department,' the supervisor said. 'Are you interested?'

Yes, she was, very.

On one assembly line, women were making brass shell cartridges, and on another, metal tracks for tanks. Again, they had their heads down and looks of deep concentration on their faces. Why was that so unexpected, she wondered. Because whenever she'd thought about women in manufacturing, she'd imagined laughter and ribbing and chat – as the woman on the train to York had described. But nothing about these women was frivolous.

She captured a young woman as she picked up and cleaned cartridges with an oily cloth. She drew two others inspecting a sheet of metal tracks and a man showing a group of women how to work a piece of apparatus – all with the smiling, breezy supervisor at her elbow.

At last, she closed her sketchbook and said, 'I think that's enough for now. Thank you very much for making me so welcome.'

The supervisor's face crumpled like a piece of broken machinery. 'Are you sure?' she asked. 'There's the outdoor Shop to see.'

'A peek, perhaps,' Sybil said. 'I can't fill my books with one type of work, much as I'd like to. I have to draw as many women working in different roles, paid and unpaid, as possible.'

'Oh, I see,' the supervisor said. 'In that case, my mum's going to a WI meeting tonight at …' She was cut off by Sybil's laugh. 'Isn't that what you meant?'

'I'm sorry,' Sybil said. 'That's exactly what I meant. It's just that I stopped to draw a woman in town, and she told me about it too.'

The supervisor smiled. 'Well, Darlington isn't London,' she said. 'There isn't much to do here so we make the most of whatever's going on.'

The outdoor Shop consisted of a series of short platforms covered by awnings under which damaged engines were towed in and repaired engines tested before being returned to service. Women in the same knotted scarves as the supervisor appeared to be involved in every aspect of the operation with the exception of driving – that was left to the men. 'It amazes me that women are okay to empty ash from a furnace, but they're not allowed to drive a train,' Sybil said.

The supervisor shrugged again. 'It doesn't make a lot of sense, does it? But I believe it's the same everywhere. Women can be porters and guards, but not train drivers. Same in the Services. Women can drive trucks and tanks off assembly lines, but no further than that.'

A gust of wind blew across the platform they were standing on and whipped the pages of Sybil's sketchbook as she drew a woman testing a locomotive's whistle. 'Perhaps the authorities think we'll get upset if our nail varnish chips,' she said.

'I hate it when mine flakes.' The supervisor looked down at her hands. 'That's why most of us don't wear any. It would be a waste of time and money. But I think it's more to do with how men feel about themselves,' she said.

'What do you mean?' Sybil stopped drawing and gave all her attention to the supervisor.

'Well …' She hesitated as if she wasn't used to voicing her opinions. 'I suppose, if there were absolutely no men about then it wouldn't matter, but our lads are reserved and not allowed to join up. So if women did everything they do, they might feel … worthless or … I'm not sure what the word is. Not much like men.'

'Emasculated?' Sybil offered.

'That sounds right. Women certainly have more opportunities now than they did before this bloody war started, but what a God-awful way to get them.'

Perhaps the supervisor was right – it wasn't about women not being able to do certain things, but that given the chance they would do them too well and men's pride would suffer. 'That's very interesting,' Sybil said. 'And well thought out.'

The supervisor smiled. 'I've enjoyed your visit very much.'

'So have I. It's been inspiring, in many ways. Thank you.'

'And for me,' the supervisor said. She opened the door of a broom cupboard and said, 'I don't want to drag you back through the noisy factory, so you can take off your things in here and leave by that gate.'

As Sybil was ejected onto the street outside the Shop, she felt disorientated, as if she'd been visiting a much different, louder, dirtier world with a life and beating heart of its own.

Before getting ready for the WI meeting, she sat in her room, looked through her sketchbook and thought she would want to extend her work on the women crawling like ants around the engine that towered over them and, of course, the female stoker. She conjured the woman's bold look of pure resolve and wondered if the same glint had been mirrored in her own eyes. She stood and studied herself in the mirror, and what gazed back at her was the same lack of confidence she'd always seen there. More than recognition, perhaps the female stoker was giving her a glimpse of the story she wanted to share with the world. And that Sybil, too, should nurture the same courage and conviction.

But she needed to stop and think of more practical issues. There were two pages left in her sketchbook, and although she had another and could wire Miss Butterworth for further supplies, she couldn't possibly reproduce all of her drawings into a format that would be acceptable to the WAAC. If she tried, she'd still be hard at it no matter if umpteen years went by before the war came to an end. That thought made her shudder.

She needed a plan. She could go back to London tomorrow, set up her paints and an easel in Auntie Myrtle's dining room and get to work on a painting. But that was eating into the time when she could be travelling and gathering evidence and ideas. It would be best if she carried on for as long as she could, then went home at the beginning of September and tried to have a least one painting ready to present to the WAAC at the end of her tenure. That way she could live off the fee, if her piece was accepted, whilst she worked on another and another after that. Her homesickness would probably get worse, or she could throw back her shoulders with stoicism and it would abate. As for Graeme, her despair for him and their relationship would follow her wherever she went, so there was no need to add that to the equation.

It was time to close the bloody blackouts, as Dame Lily called them, and block out the natural light she loved so much. But now that she'd started to think about Graeme, her arms refused to reach up and pull them tight.

Signing up was admirable and she should have been proud of him, but he hadn't needed to go when he did, and she couldn't shake the feeling that he couldn't wait to get away from her. Had she asked him for what he couldn't or wouldn't give her? Perhaps she was too ambitious and he'd felt threatened – emasculated. Their intimate life had been so wonderful that she could feel his hands caressing and grabbing and kneading at her now. He'd wanted her over and over again. They'd spent hours under the covers on lazy weekend mornings, dizzy with love. Or at least she had been. Although he'd married her, perhaps all he'd wanted was sex, and when the fervour plateaued, it was over for him.

No, she told herself. That couldn't have been the case – she refused to believe it. She dragged the blackouts into place and turned on the lamp. She was overreacting, allowing her imagination to run away with her. Her husband was an honourable man who was probably lying wounded in a hospital or prisoner of war camp longing for her. With a twist of guilt, she thought it was easier to imagine him in that situation than purposefully turning his back on her.

The windows of the Methodist Church Hall were boarded, so

it wasn't until Sybil was inside the second set of double doors that she was dazzled by the light and the décor. The space was done up like a debutante going to her first ball. Tables covered in embroidered cloths had been set out and on them were all manner of goods and produce that the WI members had either crafted or grown themselves.

The women were wearing their best, too. Shoes had been polished, hats were perched on waved hair and brooches twinkled on lapels. Sybil was glad she'd put on a fresh blouse and a bit of makeup and pinned her hair behind her ears. She looked around for the woman she'd drawn earlier, but there were so many women milling around that it was hard to pick her out. The volume of chatter made her wish she'd kept hold of her ear plugs.

There was so much activity she wanted to capture, but she thought it would be disrespectful to start before she had permission from the woman in charge. She looked about, not sure how she'd be able to tell who was who in the hierarchy, when she saw her gardener near the podium whispering, her hand covering her mouth, to another woman. Both of them had their eyes trained on her. When they broke ranks, her acquaintance went one way and the other woman made her way towards her, hand outstretched.

'Hello,' she said. She was wearing a knee-length, well-worn ocelot coat and green paste earrings. 'I'm Mrs Margaret Dibcote, President of the Darlington Branch of the WI, and you must be the lady artist my vice president was telling me about.'

'Pleased to meet you,' Sybil said. 'I'm Sybil Paige, and I've been commissioned by the War Artists' Advisory Committee to sketch women at work. This meeting is wonderful. I have permits to draw in public, but may I please have your okay to do so?'

The woman smiled. 'It would be our honour,' she said. 'I'll announce your presence with the notices.'

'No need,' Sybil said, alarm at the thought of being singled out making a blush rise to her cheeks. 'I can just get on with it and introduce myself to individuals when I need to.'

'No,' the president was adamant. 'You must be formally announced. Also, I would like to ask a favour of you.'

Something shrank inside Sybil. She couldn't imagine what she could do to help the WI except draw a portrait of the Committee or design a new poster for their market stall campaign – the current one on show was abysmal. She didn't want to commit herself, so didn't say a word, but her face must have shown her apprehension because Mrs Dibcote touched her sleeve and said, 'Nothing at all to worry about. One of our speakers has had to back out and it would be wonderful if you could step in. I'm sure you're used to speaking in public.'

Nothing could be further from the truth and Sybil was sent into a spin at the thought of it. 'No,' she managed to stutter. 'I've never had to do that and don't think I'm equipped to ... I stand behind my sketchbook or easel and I speak for others through my compositions. That's all.' The self-portrait of her receiving the telegram about Graeme flashed through her mind and she was struck by the thought that besides the heartbreak involved in recreating that moment, maybe she couldn't get it down on paper because she deplored being the centre of attention.

Mrs Dibcote brushed aside her plaintive rejection of the suggestion, if she'd heard it at all, and acted as if Sybil had agreed without hesitation. 'Speak for about ten minutes and then perhaps you could pass around some of your sketches. Our members would love to see them. Now, I think I'll put you on last. After Mrs Smith and her onion sets.'

'No,' Sybil said again. Her voice sounded as if she was being strangled. 'Not last. I couldn't bear to wait until ...'

'Then first.'

'No, please. And I can't show my pictures to anyone. They're classified information.'

Mrs Dibcote's face fell. 'But soon they'll be on display in a gallery somewhere, won't they?'

'They might be,' Sybil said weakly. 'But if and when they are, they will have been carefully selected by people who know about these things. I'm just following orders. I'm not a speaker. I hate being the focus of a gathering. No one would enjoy it because I'd be rubbish.' Her voice was growing more familiar to her ears. 'I'm just doing my bit and all I want to do is draw the WI women doing theirs.'

Mrs Dibcote smiled at her fondly, almost as if she were a niece or her best friend's daughter. 'Well,' she said. 'Apart from a wobble right at the beginning, that speech was certainly eloquent.'

Sybil smiled wanly. The bustle in the hall had quietened and Sybil realised that the women were taking their seats ready for the evening's entertainment.

'I'm not going to force you,' Mrs Dibcote said. 'But you might be called upon in the future to stand up and talk to all manner of people about your work. Especially when you become well known. This might be a good chance for you to practise. If you do happen to stumble over your words, which I have every faith you won't, you don't have to worry about bumping into people you know tomorrow or the next day.'

She imagined herself at the podium, all eyes on her and she cringed inwardly.

'I tell you what,' Mrs Dibcote said. 'When I introduce you to the ladies, if you want to stand up and say a few words, give me a nod. And forget about the ten minutes. Just come to the front, say hello, tell us your job role and sit back down.'

Sybil felt as if she were turning to liquid. If it wasn't for Auntie Myrtle, Dame Lily, Blanche and Ellen, she thought she could stay here in Darlington and live the rest of her life in the folds of Mrs Dibcote's threadbare coat.

Mrs Dibcote took to the podium as if she were born to it. Her voice was pitched low, she was engaging and she made eye contact with the audience. 'We will have a presence at the market again on Wednesday. If you're interested in selling pies or surplus produce, please see Mrs Thompson. Any goods we don't sell will be given to RAF Goosepool.'

That base wasn't on Sybil's list, yet it couldn't be far away. She would enquire about it later.

'This week's knitting party will take place at Mrs Edgar's house. If you attend, please bring a cake or biscuits to share. As for tonight,' Mrs Dibcote smiled broadly, 'it is my utmost pleasure to introduce a commissioned war artist who has come all the way from London to draw our meeting.'

Sybil felt herself redden when Mrs Dibcote gestured towards her. All heads turned her way and the blood vessels in her face throbbed right up to the roots of her strawberry blonde hair. Mrs Dibcote waited for a beat and Sybil glimpsed again the encouraging flash of determination in the female stoker's eyes. On a deep breath she thought she would, after all, give it try. The president had been so kind, and she was right – Sybil had nothing to lose. She nodded her head and Mrs Dibcote's eyebrows shot up in surprise. When she made it to the front of the hall on shaky legs, Mrs Dibcote touched her sleeve and stood aside.

She tried to re-enact the ways in which Dame Lily and Mrs Dibcote captivated their audiences, but apart from a couple of times when she felt in control, the few minutes were an ordeal. She thanked the women, told them about her commission and said she would be drawing them during and after the talks. That was enough for her first public speaking engagement.

But the women thought otherwise. One hand after another shot up and she felt compelled to stay rooted to the spot and answer their questions as best she could.

'Will all your sketches become paintings?

'I don't think I'd have time to paint all of them,' Sybil said. 'And some of the decisions will be made by the War Artist's Advisory Committee who commissioned me.'

'Have you always wanted to be an artist?'

'I think so.' She had often wondered if her drive was led by others saying she was talented rather than her own ambitions. Now she was being forced to answer her own queries and it felt like a positive move. 'Teachers said I could draw, and one in particular took me under her wing and gave me extra tuition. Under that one-to-one instruction I could see how I improved, and before I knew it, there was nothing I wanted more.'

'Do you have a theme?'

As Sybil shifted her weight from one foot to the other, she realised her legs were no longer trembling. 'My theme,' she said with confidence, 'is enabling my subjects to speak to the viewer about their circumstances, their emotions, their lives. I like to think that if we weren't living through a war, the essence of my work would be the same, but I don't want to categorically state that to be the case.'

'What advice would you give to an amateur artist?'

'Don't give up, if you can possibly help it.' She thought back to how close she was to quitting when she'd had that chance meeting with Dame Lily. 'Be determined and single-minded and try to find a mentor to guide you.'

'How do you decide upon one scene rather than another?'

'That's difficult to do when all the subjects around me are crying out to tell their stories. But I've learned to sketch quickly so I can get quite a few scenes on paper in a short period of time. I also commit a lot to memory and draw them later.'

'In your opinion, has the war changed art?'

'Most definitely,' Sybil said. 'There are things we aren't allowed to draw and many we never thought we'd have to. The art world has been deprived of many artists who have joined up or are undertaking other war work or worse. And of course, the vast majority of our pieces must depict the war. In fact, all of them do as that is the reality of our lives now.'

The questions came thick and fast, and she would have liked a bit more time to think about her answers, but she did her best. When no more hands were on display, Mrs Dibcote thanked her, and after a rousing round of applause, the president announced Mrs Smith with her onions. Walking back to her seat, Sybil realised that although she felt exhausted, she walked with a light step and that, towards the end, her voice had been strong and resonant. She felt pleased with herself and grateful to Mrs Dibcote for talking her round, but more than anything she was impressed by the women. The little she knew about the WI had led her to believe that the institute consisted of women fussing and clucking over crochet needles and jam. But they were a lively, intelligent group who obviously read widely and were interested in what was going on in the world. *Shame on me*, she thought, and a blush attacked her cheeks again.

She drew Mrs Smith holding up small bulbs and black seeds, instructing the women on how to grow and harvest onion sets of their own. She made the process sound riveting.

After the talks, Sybil tried to sketch whilst balancing a slice of pound cake and a cup of tea and answering yet more well-thought-out questions. When the women began to pack up, Sybil found Mrs Dibcote and gave her a hug. 'Thank you for encouraging me,' she said. 'I feel as though I've surmounted something I imagined to be nerve-wracking, but it turned out to be nothing other than silly and insignificant.'

'I'm so glad you decided to speak,' Mrs Dibcote said. 'You were very interesting, and if it helps to know, you didn't come over the least bit nervous.'

Walking on a cloud, Sybil strode out amongst the beams of tissue paper covered torches dancing like a sparkle of fireflies in the blackout.

It had taken her ages to get to sleep and then she tossed and turned, so when the blast came, her first reaction was that it had been a dream. She sat bolt upright, clutching the bedsheets close to her chest. Then there was another boom followed by a deafening whoosh, as if something were falling from the sky. Shuffling and murmured cries of alarm came from other rooms. Sybil peeked around the blackouts and in the distance, she could see a ball of fire, rolling and spinning across the ground.

She cracked open her door and heard the landlady call out that she'd put on the kettle. Guests shambled downstairs and Sybil dressed quickly, picked up her bag and joined them.

'It's come from the direction of Goosepool,' the landlady said.

'Where is that?' Sybil asked. 'I was only aware of RAF Middleton St George.'

'One and the same,' the landlady said, handing out cups of weak tea. 'Goosepool was the name of the farm it's built on.'

Sybil felt it her duty to find out if there was anything going on that she should record. But the relatively safe confines of the kitchen and the warm bed waiting for her return held her back. The thought of what was out there turned her to ice. Besides, it probably had nothing to do with women's work and her commission.

Then she wondered what Dame Lily would tell her to do. 'Draw it from afar,' she would say. Blanche's advice would be to tuck herself back up under the covers and Ellen would tell her to go – with a friend. But the female stoker, with her ruthless determination to fulfil her ambition, won the day.

'I'm going to have a look,' Sybil said, with as much confidence as she could muster.

'It's five miles away.' The landlady was shocked. 'Over fields and down dark lanes. I won't allow it.'

The landlady delivered her decree with such authority that Sybil put down her bag and thought that would have to be the end of it. Then an image of the woman stoker flashed through her mind again and Sybil found her resolve. 'I have to,' she said. 'It's part of my war work.'

A hush came over everyone in the kitchen.

'Besides, I'm sure I won't be the only one making my way there.'

'No, probably not,' said a woman with a layer of cold cream on her face. 'Mind you, I think everyone should stay away, war work or not.'

Sybil let that remark pass, put on her outdoor things and stepped into the night. She'd been right, there were a number of people, mainly men in an agitated state, heading east out of the town so she fell in behind them.

In the distance, sparks ripped through the fabric of the black silk sky and fell back into the blazing object on the ground. Silhouetted men appeared, running backwards and forwards and hauling ropes or hoses behind them. The air fizzed and crackled and noxious smoke scorched her nostrils and throat. She pulled up her scarf and tried to make herself insignificant amongst the men, but some of them looked at her as though her husband or father should be ashamed for allowing her out by herself on such a night. Jittery with apprehension, she was aware of the danger of the situation and wondered if she'd been too hasty. If she'd thought speaking in front of a WI meeting was harrowing, this was in a completely different league. Perhaps she should have played it safe and stayed in the B&B, drinking tea with the landlady. But there was a part of her that felt a buzz of excitement, which would have been too awful to admit to anyone. Not an elated feeling of heightened pleasure or anticipation, but more an idea that she was part of a mutual sense of urgency to do whatever she could – even if that amounted to nothing more than drawing what she observed.

There was a low-pitched babble around her. Men softly calling out and clapping each other on their backs. She picked out the word Goosepool a number of times, along with bomb; RAF; bloody Jerries; fire; fight; they'll get what's coming to them; they'll wish they'd never come near Darlington. Shovels and pokers and chair legs were brandished and at the ready over shoulders. Sybil trudged along next to them, glad of her overshoes but wishing one of the men would offer her a drop of whatever it was they passed around in their flasks.

As they got closer to Goosepool, those more able broke into a run, and she was left to trot behind them. The air was acrid, and sooty flakes danced around before settling on her hair and clothes. Heat hit her in waves and she put up her hand to shield her eyes.

At the gates, two uniformed guards allowed certain men to pass, based, it seemed, on the size of their biceps. They were given orders to report to Sergeant Jenkins or join the line passing water buckets or trample down sparks that threatened to spread the blaze. Sybil was jostled against a rough woollen coat that smelled of cooking fat and hair oil, then nudged to one side by an oversized boot. When at last she got to the gate, she flashed her permits and said, 'War artist. Commissioned by the WAAC.'

One of the guards looked at her with disbelief. 'Move to the side, Miss,' he said forcefully. She followed orders, thinking he would turn his attention back to her, but it soon became clear that, as far as he was concerned, there was nothing else to say. She presented herself again, 'I have permits to restricted areas.'

'That's of no consequence here,' the man sounded angry and frustrated. 'Can't you see we have enough to do without worrying about a girl and her sketchpad?'

Sybil felt as if she'd been punched by what amounted to an insult rather than a remark. She lifted her chin and was about to the argue her case when he said, 'You can walk around the perimeter and draw all you like from there. Then come back in the morning when we can hopefully accommodate you.' With that, he turned his back on her and dealt with the next man in line.

She knew there was no point in trying to get him to change his mind so she began to prowl the fence and got quite a few reasonable drawings of two German planes, fire leaping from them where they'd come to rest in the middle of a field, lines of men dousing them from any kind of vessel that could hold water.

The two fighter pilots would not have stood a chance, and staring at the skeletons of the planes through a chain link fence, Sybil wondered about their names and ages. If they were tall or short and if they wore moustaches. She thought about who would miss them – mothers, fathers, wives, lovers, children – and if those people would be tormented when they received the telegram of their loved one's demise, as she had been.

When first light crept across the sky, Sybil dragged herself back to the gate, presented her permits again and this time, she was allowed in. The men of Darlington passed her on their way home, their whiskers shadowy and smuts engrained in their hands and faces.

Sergeant Jenkins introduced himself and accompanied her to the site of the planes, smouldering in the blackened grass. He looked exhausted and didn't say much. Sybil was pleased he stood and watched her circle the wreckage without making an attempt to follow her around.

She sketched the carcasses from different angles, ensuring that a half-destroyed swastika was visible in a number of them. Then she turned to the Sergeant and captured him, dark circles under his eyes, at the moment he lifted his cap to wipe the sweat from his forehead.

The walk back to town was long and filled with sadness and a sense of terrible waste. Those two young men, Graeme, the thousands killed on both sides. Her legs and heart felt as if they were filled with concrete. As for herself, she thought she'd been daring considering the circumstances. But how she wished this bloody war wasn't the way to teach her how to overcome her fears. Life would be so much easier if all she had to do to learn bravery and fortitude was stand up and make a speech in front of a hall full of women.

IO

MONDAY 14TH MAY 1941

SENT FROM COVENTRY POST OFFICE COVENTRY
WARWICKSHIRE

PRIORITY J BUTTERWORTH NATIONAL GALLERY
LONDON

TWO SKETCHBOOKS CHARCOALS MIXED PENCILS STOP
MAIN POST OFFICE STOP LYME REGIS STOP DORSET
STOP S PAIGE STOP

Miss Ellen Hewitt, NA,

Nurses' Quarters,
St Mary's Hospital,
Paddington,
London, W.2

Thursday, 15th May 1941

Mrs S. Paige,
c/o Miss J. Butterworth,
Personal Assistant to Sir Leonard Thwaites, CH KOB FB,
War Artists' Advisory Committee,
Ministry of Information,
The National Gallery,
Trafalgar Square,
London, W.C.2

Dear Sybil,

I can't tell you how pleased I was to hear from you at last.
I kicked off my shoes when I returned to my living quarters,
sat with a cup of tea and devoured all your news. Well, some
of it, as I know you're not allowed to give details. But you've
been all over the place, you lucky so-and-so, and you've only
just started. I know you'll have some wonderful sketches to
share with us when next you come home – have you any idea
when that will be?

You were probably surprised and a bit confused when you
saw my address at the top of the page and yes, I did what
I've been threatening to do for such a long time and signed
up with the Civil Nursing Reserve as a nursing auxiliary.
I underwent two weeks' training which means I am fully
adept at first aid, home nursing and practical hospital work.
Gone are my hair ribbons, and in their place, I wear a
starched white cap over my short, waved hair. I love the job,

Sybil, even the mucky bits, and feel that I've done something worthwhile at the end of every day.

But I haven't forgotten art and my ambitions in that field. Every sight I see at St Mary's is a potential composition, and most days I spend an hour or two of my off-duty time sketching and drawing and refining – believe it or not. I must be getting old as I'm learning the advantages of taking my time, except when I work at a clip on the wards.

Blanche was in Wandsworth last weekend, and I was able to join her and Auntie Myrtle for Sunday tea. I grabbed hold of them and felt as if I'd never let go. Your ears must have burned because we shared your letters and said how much we missed you. Blanche showed us some of the work she's going to present to the RBP very soon and I must say, it's of the highest quality.

London has been much quieter for the past week or so without our nightly visitors. Although no one trusts that this is the end for us, and we are living on our nerves wondering when the attacks will resume. I have heard that Jerry has gone to play in *** ****** ****, but who can read the mind of that nasty crowd of bullies.

I must report for duty in ten minutes so will have to close here. I'll be checking the post daily as I can't wait to hear from you again.

Lots of love,

Ellen XXX

P.S. I share a room with two other auxiliaries. One talks non-stop and the other doesn't say a word. Neither of them likes a laugh or a drink. I often think back to the lovely time I shared with Blanche and, to all intents and purposes, with you.

P.P.S. Please find enclosed a copy of the April edition of *The Land Girl* with my drawing on the cover! I'm going to get it framed.

Mrs S. Paige,
c/o Miss J. Butterworth,
Personal Assistant to Sir Leonard Thwaites, CH KOB FB,
War Artists' Advisory Committee,
Ministry of Information,
The National Gallery,
Trafalgar Square,
London, W.C.2

Wednesday, 21st May 1941

Miss Ellen Hewitt, NA,
Nurses' Quarters,
St Mary's Hospital,
Paddington,
London, W.2

Dear Ellen,

Thank you very much for your letter which I've just read and am replying to whilst on the train from Birmingham to Dorset. I think I could be much more efficient in the way I map out my itinerary, but I tend to follow my heart rather than my head. The Midlands, as I'm sure you know, is very industrialised, and after I'd finished there, I thought I'd like to compose in an area that's more rural and rugged.

You're absolutely right - I was most surprised when I saw your address. Very many congratulations! It isn't difficult to imagine you doing well in your new role as you are very empathetic but also practical. Do you think you'll eventually become a fully trained nurse? I can see you in your uniform with your neat hair and sensible clothes, wounded servicemen daring not to question your authority. May I draw you in uniform when I return, or perhaps I could come to the hospital and sketch on site, or would that be stepping on your toes – something I wouldn't want to do?

I find that I'm becoming more used to being away from home, up to the point where I'm really quite enjoying some aspects. I meet so many interesting people – and some not so compelling. I work hard as there are few distractions in the way of going to the pub or the cinema and I feel more independent and confident with only myself to rely on. That's not to say I don't miss all of you terribly. But I think I'm going to make the most of my commission, as I'm quite sure I won't get another, and stay away from London until the beginning of August. When we meet up then, we'll have so much to talk about. I'm feeling waves of homesickness just thinking about it.

Very many congratulations on the beautiful cover. You must feel deservedly proud. I'm so pleased for you.

With love and hopes for many more quiet nights in London,

Sybil X

Miss Blanche Northcutt,
Marylebone School of Art,
Old Manor House,
Luton,
Beds

Friday, 16th May 1941

Mrs S. Paige,
c/o Miss J. Butterworth,
Personal Assistant to Sir Leonard Thwaites, CH KOB FB,
War Artists' Advisory Committee,
Ministry of Information,
The National Gallery,
Trafalgar Square,
London, W.C.2

Dear Sybil,

Who knows where this letter will find you, but may I suggest you make your way to St Ives at some stage? I spent many a happy holiday in that picturesque place with my mother and father and Auntie Myrtle. The summer days seemed to go on forever. We would build sandcastles, paddle and feast on pasties – I insist you try one whilst there.

I am on the way back to Luton from Cambridgeshire where I spent the weekend drawing cobbled streets behind the university and punts on the Cam. I walked the length of the river to Grantchester and thought about Rupert Brooke who was bereft with homesickness when he wrote *The Old Vicarage, Grantchester* in 1912. How many other boys, not known for their poetry or similar achievements, are right now in some distant country thinking of the places and people they love here at home, your Graeme amongst them. I'm sorry if I've stirred up feelings that you may have tried to quash, but the sentiment needs to be aired.

Coming back from Grantchester, I walked past a slew of at least fifty homes that had been partially burned, which rather tarnished the shine on the city and reminded me that nowhere is safe from the next packet. I asked at a nearby teashop and was told that a couple of weeks ago the houses took a shower of incendiaries, but the fires were put out in minutes. The woman who served me a cup of tea seemed proud of that. I thought of you and some of the horrific sights you must have seen and was overcome with relief at the commission I have been given. However, since then, I've been thinking of trying my hand at some of the grittier aspects of the war as they are becoming increasingly difficult to ignore.

What do you think of our Ellen's new war work? I must say she is transformed – like a filly that's been broken. She looks the part and is often much more sedate, although she can still be immensely silly. I never thought I'd say this, but I do miss her. It's odd, isn't it, that two such disparate people could become close friends in the unlikeliest of circumstances.

Of course, it goes without saying, although I will, that you are very much missed, too. There's a new tutor in your old room, one Miss Edith Hopkins, who is very timid and has little or no opinion on anything. and her artwork is as dull as her personality. Mr Merton must be getting desperate. She's been cornered by the dreaded Morgan Langley and hasn't the gumption or wherewithal to tell him to sling his hook. Who knows, perhaps we'll have a wedding to go to soon.

With love and best wishes,

Blanche XX

Miss Myrtle Ashcroft,
78, Broxash Road,
Wandsworth,
London, S.W.11

Saturday, 17th May 1941

Mrs S. Paige,
c/o Miss J. Butterworth,
Personal Assistant to Sir Leonard Thwaites, CH KOB FB,
War Artists' Advisory Committee,
Ministry of Information,
The National Gallery,
Trafalgar Square,
London, W.C.2

My dearest Sybil,

No sooner had you come to live with me than you were gone, but when I see your possessions about the place, I know you'll be back and that raises my spirits – as did your most welcome letter.

Your travels have indeed taken you far and wide. I've not been to any of the places you mentioned, but they sound so different from each other that I had to remind myself they're all part of the British Isles. Blanche said she was going to recommend you pay a visit to St Ives where we holidayed between the wars. It was idyllic. Her mum and dad were always so kind and generous about sharing their lives with me. I think Blanche and I have such a strong connection because I was so involved with her right from the beginning. There were times as a toddler when she didn't seem to know the difference between me and her mother.

If you look up when you wander along the beach, you might see a pastel pink building above you. That was the boarding house we stayed in year after year. It was run by a Mrs Abelard. She was lovely, but some of her cooking left a lot to be desired, especially the watery, mushy cabbage she was very fond of. But I read somewhere that the entire coast is lined with pillboxes and structures known as 'dragons' teeth', so you probably won't be able to walk along the shore at any point.

Here in London, we are amazed that the nightly air raids appear to have stopped and it feels like a miracle. Sleep overcomes me whilst I'm in my bed rather than holed up in the shelter. The other night I slept for six hours straight off; a phenomenon that hasn't occurred since September last. I don't want to give you the impression that we are raid free, we're still enduring numerous sirens and bombs every day, but nothing like the last eight months. Then why, I ask myself, does everyone still look so ghastly? Well, there's rationing, and queuing for it, rubble everywhere waiting to be cleared away, the fear of what's to come, the worry about how long it will go on, the ache of bereavement and disbelief at what we're living through. Enough of all this! I'm sounding quite the world-weary, elderly person who can't stop moaning about the good old days, something you girls have never allowed me to become.

The blossom is out on the trees along the road and the pink and white is beautiful. Michelangelo is in his favourite place on the windowsill and I will have a bit of rabbit fricassee with dumplings for my dinner. Blanche and Ellen are coming to see me next Saturday although Blanche can only stay for an hour or so because she will have to get to Leighton Buzzard for her commission.

I cannot wait to hear about your adventures and see all of the wonderful artwork you've produced. Have you any idea when that might be?

Take care of yourself.

With lots of love from your Auntie Myrtle XX

Dame Lily Brampton, DBE RA ROI RWS,
Seagulls' Watch,
Cley-next-the-Sea,
Norfolk

Saturday, 17th May 1941

Mrs S. Paige,
c/o Miss J. Butterworth,
Personal Assistant to Sir Leonard Thwaites, CH KOB FB,
War Artists' Advisory Committee,
Ministry of Information,
The National Gallery,
Trafalgar Square,
London, W.C.2

Dearest Sybil,

The sketches that you described in your letter sound marvellous and each of them would surely be deserving of an opportunity to be shown. I know I will be awestruck by the woman with her onion sets, the women mending parachutes in the Midlands and the girls hanging off aeroplane fuselages with spanners in their hands. But the composition I'm most intrigued by is the female stoker – what a gruelling job for a middle-aged woman. You describe the intense heat and the glint of defiance in her eyes admirably, and I feel sure you'll be able to translate that into the woman telling her story through your artwork. But how on earth will you decide which one or ones to work on first? If you would like my opinion about that, you only need to ask.

I've continued to sketch seascapes giving prominence to the anti-invasion defences. Last week I worked on one that featured the grey, roiling sea as viewed through a roll of barbed wire, wildflowers crushed beneath the twisted spikes. I'm sure you'll come across many such measures on your travels.

Three of my paintings are now in New York as part of an exhibition to persuade the US to lend ******** and ******** support and give up their ****** misconceived idea of *********. One is of a young Corporal in the WAAFs, another is a woman hurrying to join the queue outside a butcher's shop and the last is of a schoolgirl receiving treatment in hospital for an injury received as the result of a bombing raid. I feel sure that your work will soon be included in such displays world-wide.

I was pleased to hear that your two lovely friends, Ellen and Blanche, are getting on so spectacularly. Becoming a nursing auxiliary will do young Ellen the world of good and give her a new outlook on life. And what a wealth of material she will have on hand. Blanche, too, must be in for some further success, and I shall look out for her work.

Much to my utter dismay, both Aloysius and Dominic have joined up. Dom completely disregarded our pleas for him to qualify first and said that there would be an opportunity for him to finish his medical training in the RAF. Whilst that has been so, he's also training for his wings, and that seems to have become the priority. As for Al, he's followed Iggy into the Army as an officer. My emotions are all over the place and shift hourly from being ecstatically proud of my three sons to wishing they were all back home with me, safely tucked up in their beds.

That, of course, brings me to your terrible situation. I suppose if there had been any news of Graeme you would have told me about it in your letter. It must be heartbreaking for you, but that's the price we pay when we live and love.

With all good wishes,

Lily X

6819913 L/Cpl Paige, G.J.,
9th Battalion,
Middlesex Regiment.
c/o Army PO

Wednesday, 17th April 1940

Mrs S. Paige,
Flat 3,
47 Flowerpot Close,
Haringey,
London, N.15

Dear Sybil,

I hope you are well and keeping busy. Do you have any news for me about your artwork? You are so very talented that I know it's only a matter of time before you are singled out for great things.

There is a chap here who draws whenever he has a minute to spare and his work is excellent. He sketches landscapes but prefers portraits. I would like to have his patience and tenacity but cannot seem to concentrate for more than a couple of minutes.

It is so wonderful to receive your letters and to know that you are thinking about me – as I am of you. But your words seem to lack a certain amount of warmth and I feel that a barrier has gone up between us, all my doing, I know. My leaving so abruptly and without much discussion must have confused and upset you, and I am so sorry from the bottom of my heart if I hurt you, something I never set out to do.

The truth of the matter is that I was feeling unsettled for a while before I joined up, and I know you noticed the change in me. I want to assure you it had nothing at all to do with you, but everything to do with someone I knew before I met you. Her name was Heather, and I should have told you all about her before I became so deeply involved with you. In my defence, I thought that if I did so I stood a good chance of losing you because you might have thought I wasn't over her, and it's with a heavy heart that I've come to realise that is probably the case. That's not to say I didn't fall deeply in love with you too. Now I've had time away, I realise that was a selfish and cowardly thing to do and it left you in the rotten position of not being able to make a choice about me based on all the facts. So I think it only fair to tell you everything now.

Heather was my sweetheart for a few years and we planned to … damn this ****** war! The ****** Army only allows us one sheet of this inferior paper. I will have to continue on another and send it separately.

With love,

Graeme XXX

11

May 1941

When Sybil startled awake, it took her a few minutes to get her bearings. Her head thumped, her heartbeat was erratic, she tried to steady herself with deep breaths which she couldn't seem to take in beyond the top of her chest. Sweat glued her nightgown to her body, and her tongue was stuck fast to the roof of her mouth. The smell of Spam frying in lard assaulted her, and she heaved into the wash basin balanced on the bedside cabinet.

A series of mewls and feeble grunts escaped her as, exhausted, she laid her head back down on the pillow, but not before she caught sight of herself in the mirror. She was a pasty shade of yellow with dark, ghoulish hollows under her eyes. Where it hadn't adhered to her clammy face, her hair was sticking out in tufts. Whatever had she done to herself? Hot tears spilled down her cheeks.

Hardly daring to move, she gingerly reached for the basin again and stopped still when her hand rustled a sheet of thin paper. It was Graeme's letter, crumpled and torn and stained. She stared at it, closed her eyes and recited the words from memory, then let it fall to the floor.

She'd been in shock and probably was now. When she'd pulled Graeme's letter from the packet Miss Butterworth had forwarded, she couldn't believe what she was seeing. Her initial reaction had been that it was a sick joke or that someone was being deliberately cruel and heartless. But she didn't know anyone who would be that sadistic. She'd tentatively taken out the one sheet of paper and known immediately that it was written by Graeme, the handwriting was unmistakable. It was dated the 17th of April 1940 – not long before he was listed as missing in action. Where had it been for 13 months? Hiding at the bottom of a postbag or wedged behind a counter in an office somewhere? And why had the ever-efficient Miss Butterworth shoved it into the parcel with all the others and not cautioned her with a telegram? Then she'd remembered that she hadn't checked the post office on her last day in Birmingham, so maybe the warning letter was there in a pigeonhole – unread and waiting.

Unable to sit in the crowded carriage for fear she'd fall apart, she'd stumbled to the compartment between cars, pushed down the window, taken a deep breath and unfolded the letter with shaking hands.

Everything became a blur, and she'd threaded her arm around a metal pole to keep herself upright. A couple passed close by and the woman looked at her, concern creasing her face, but the man must have said something funny, and the woman, distracted, carried on.

She'd read the letter again and again after that, trying hard to fill in the words that Graeme had cut short. So, she'd been right. That thought overwhelmed her, and she'd let out a soft moan. There was something wrong between them, but was that something Heather herself or the fact that her husband had failed to tell her about Heather's existence? Had Heather died? Had she given Graeme the heave-ho, or had it been the other way around? Was he intent on trying to rekindle his lost love, or was he going to try to reconcile with her, his wife? She'd never know until she received the next letter he'd written. But that wasn't a given and would depend on whether it was buried with him under piles of rubble or had a bullet through it when he took the shot that floored him or if he was in a field hospital unable to remember who she was. Or perhaps he hadn't had the chance to write another at all. How brutal – how callous – she'd wanted to scream out to anyone who would listen.

But she'd wiped her eyes, read the letter again, went back to her seat and read it a further four times before she'd disembarked in Lyme Regis.

Somehow, she'd found a B&B and thrown herself onto the bed where she'd read the letter over and over. Then she'd made her way to the nearest pub, not giving a second thought to the stares as she sat at a table on her own and downed four – or was it five – double gins on an empty stomach, reading the letter again after each mouthful.

Now, she squinted at the ceiling through sore eyes, nausea overcoming her and specks of perspiration dotting her face. Footsteps hurried along the hallway and stopped at her door. 'Mrs Paige,' the landlady called. 'Are you awake? Your breakfast is ready for you in the dining room.'

'I'm not well, Mrs Mansell.' Her voice quivered. 'Please give it to someone else or have it yourself. I'm sorry. I should have alerted you.'

'Shall I call the doctor?' the landlady asked. 'There's so much going around.'

'No need,' Sybil said. 'I'll be better soon.'

For a few beats, there was silence from the other side of the door then Mrs Mansell moved away and Sybil tried to sleep, but the writing in the letter appeared on the inside of her lids every time she closed her eyes.

Much later in the day, Sybil stood and tested her legs. She managed to clean the basin, rinse her hands and face and pin her hair. Without wearing a scrap of makeup, she picked up her oilskin bag and made it downstairs and out of the house. The light stung her eyes and she dug into the sockets roughly with her knuckles.

She knew what she needed was a cup of tea and something plain to eat. There was a café not far away where she found a table and ordered, hardly looking at the waitress. Apart from the hangover, she felt numb. When she'd received the telegram about Graeme, she knew in her heart that men missing in action rarely made it home alive, so she'd suffered a semblance of bereavement whilst trying to remain hopeful. But this letter left her more firmly in no-man's-land about two things – whether Graeme would come home or not and where she stood as his wife. She drank her tea and nibbled at the unbuttered toast. Compelled to both read the letter again and head to a pub at opening time for another gin, she rationalised that neither would do her any good, so she resisted.

The following morning the letter was still there but her hangover wasn't, and for that, at least, she was grateful. She managed porridge and a sausage and debated whether or not she should go back to London, but she knew all she would do there was wallow, and she didn't want that. There were plenty in worse positions than her. She had war work to do and would stay and go about it to the best of her ability, and with that she made a shaky plan for the day.

Pillboxes and dragons' teeth weren't the only defences studded along the coast. There were minefields and gun emplacements, steel scaffolding and anti-tank walls, defended roadblocks and long, lonely stretches of barbed wire. That huge amount of security should have made her feel safe and protected, but instead she couldn't rid herself of the thought that there was only one reason for it – they could be invaded at any moment. She imagined the locals would be living under that same crippling cloud of consternation, but unlike her, they couldn't escape in a few days' time.

She walked for miles in pouring rain and blistering heat, with only screaming seagulls for company. On the top of a hillock, she was lucky enough to see a woman trailing ribbons of seaweed over the sides of a pillbox. Sybil introduced herself and asked if she could draw the woman at work, her voice thick with leftover tears.

'Makes no difference to me,' the woman said. 'Long as it doesn't get into enemy hands.'

Sybil assured the woman that wouldn't happen. She sat on the ground and tucked her skirt between her legs. Patches of sea campion were all around, and try as she might, she couldn't avoid squashing the fat leaves and tiny white flowers. 'Are you worried that the defences aren't camouflaged sufficiently?' she asked. 'Is that why you're covering them?'

The woman stood back with her hands on her hips and surveyed what she'd achieved so far. She was wearing grey corduroy trousers, black gumboots and a striped, knitted hat. 'This one is new,' she said. 'So it hasn't been weathered yet.'

Sybil thought it wouldn't take more than a strong gust of wind to blow the fronds of kelp from their precarious position or else they would rot and wither to the ground. But the woman turned back to her work and Sybil to hers.

Much to her surprise, the woman then said, 'Someone else sketched me last week. Whilst I was winkling in the rockpools.'

'I didn't think anyone was allowed down to the sea.'

'Not officially, but most of the locals know a way.'

'Oh,' Sybil said, hoping the woman would share her secret. When it wasn't forthcoming, she took a deep breath and asked.

'No. You're not from around here, so I can't. Sorry.'

Although she was half-expecting that reply, she felt disappointed and very much the outsider. 'Was it another war artist who drew you?' she asked. If it was, she would leave by the next train as Dorset would have already been covered.

The woman shook her head, long tendrils of grey hair that mirrored the seaweed escaping from her hat. 'No,' she said. 'Someone renting Old Ship Cottage. He's come from London, I think. Dorset acts like a magnet to artists, so that's not unusual. Well, not so usual since the war started and we have a plague of these ugly things eating into our landscape.' She pounded on the pillbox. 'I'm amazed you want to draw them at all.'

'It's my war work,' Sybil said wearily.

The woman reached into her bucket, took out another dripping chain of seaweed and gave it a good shake. She looked over at Sybil and smiled tightly. 'I know, my dear. I know.'

The sudden softness in her voice made Sybil want to cry.

'If you go to The Sloop tonight about seven, you'll see the Home Guard gathering for their pints. Not all of them, mind, some have to stay sober in case the Jerries make it past my seaweed.'

That made Sybil laugh.

The woman picked up her empty pail, surveyed her handiwork one last time and started down the hill to the shore. 'Don't follow me,' she said, turning. 'It's much too dangerous.'

'I won't,' Sybil said. If she had happened to be up to it, her overshoes certainly weren't. 'Thank you for your help.'

The woman seemed to drop from view in no time. Sybil raised her hand as she peered over the edge of the sheer cliff and the woman waved back.

That evening, she sat outside the pub and let a cold glass of cider slip down her throat. She didn't know if it was a good idea, but when the first sip hit her tongue, she wondered why she hadn't tried the hair of the dog yesterday.

The Home Guard marched to the forecourt where they were dismissed by a Warrant Officer. Each of them followed him into the pub and trickled out with a glass in hand. Sybil captured a number of scenes which might not be of use given the lack of women involved, but it was comforting to sit in the sunshine sketching them.

As she turned back the pages of her sketchbook to scrutinise her work, a shadow slid across the wooden table and she looked up to see a man hovering above her, easel and shooting stick in his hands. 'May I join you?' he asked.

Sybil was a bit startled. There were plenty of empty tables, or the stranger could have joined one of the men who was sitting on his own. She placed her left hand on the table and tinkered with her wedding ring, but a knife twisted deep into the bruised area beneath her ribs when she thought of Graeme. The man smiled down at her and with a sense of relief, she realised he had singled her out as a fellow artist. 'Of course,' she said.

He was in his forties, tall with thick, windswept dark hair. She wondered why he wasn't in the Services or involved in some sort of war work and found it difficult to look at him without narrowing her eyes in judgement. But when he made to sit down, it was obvious that he limped heavily on his left hip, and she felt a bit easier about being seen with him.

'Hector Ainsworth.' The man held out his hand. 'Are you the official war artist? Someone told me you were visiting.'

The man's handshake was as far removed from Morgan Langley's limp fish as was possible. 'And who was that someone?'

'One of the locals named Martha. She gets here, there and everywhere. Long greying hair. Wears men's clothes.'

'Yes, I thought so. I sketched her up there.' Sybil pointed towards the cliffs. 'She was hanging seaweed on a coastal defence.'

Hector threw back his head and laughed. 'That sounds about right for Martha.'

'Are you the artist renting Old Ship Cottage?'

'That's right,' Hector said. 'So, what's your commission?'

Sybil explained.

'I'm thinking of approaching the WAAC myself.' A glint of light passed over Hector's face, and he put up his hand to shield his eyes. In the shadow, she saw that one of his cheeks was thick with raised scars. He didn't rush to hide them from her, but she blushed, not wanting to be caught staring.

'Why are you hesitating?' she asked.

'That's a good question,' Hector said. 'Two reasons, really. Art is a recent hobby for me, and I'm not very confident or very good.'

Sybil took another sip of her drink. 'May I have a look?'

With a grin, Hector said, 'You show me yours and I'll show you mine.' And with that, she was no longer concerned with her circumstances or his – they no longer mattered. He was flirting with her, and that was enough to mask the rejection she was sure Graeme had been on the verge of delivering. Gin had numbed her through the previous night, perhaps this man and his attention would get her over the hours until dawn.

Sybil gave him her usual spiel of not being allowed to show her drawings to the public, but leafed through her sketchbook and came up with three that were innocuous. Hector leaned towards her and studied each of them for some time.

'Well,' he said. 'If this is the standard, that's another reason not to present my pieces to the WAAC. Or anyone, for that matter.'

This time her face burned with the flattery. 'Perhaps,' she said, 'you'll let me be the judge of that?'

He slid his book towards her. 'Let me get us another drink,' he said. 'That way I won't have to see your reaction first-hand.'

She thought about the awful effects of the alcohol she'd downed a couple of nights ago and the reason she'd got herself into such a state. Then she looked up at Hector, his handsome, damaged features waiting hopefully and decided that one more wouldn't hurt. 'Thank you,' she said. 'A Gin and It, if possible.'

He disappeared into the gloom of the pub and for a minute, Sybil sat quietly taking in the sunshine, the glimpse of the sea between the rooftops, the discordant ages of the Home Guard, the feel of the sketchbook under her fingers. And, perhaps because she had the promise of a distraction with Hector, she felt calmer than she had since receiving Graeme's letter.

She was reminded of the afternoon she'd sat in the pub with Dame Lily all those months ago. Then, she'd been the one who'd sought the cover of the bar after reluctantly handing over her pieces for scrutiny. She knew she was more confident now – or had been – until the setback that came with the letter from Graeme. Receiving it should have been the miracle she'd been waiting for, but the way it had finished – or not finished – made her wish it had never found its way to her.

Hector turned a few heads when he came back towards her, either because of the handsome side of his face, or the half that was flawed. Sybil opened his sketchbook to the first page and looked down at the bombed House of Commons. It wasn't very good. There wasn't enough definition between the shadows and some people in the background were larger than those in the foreground. Sybil didn't know what to say; she'd never had to review this level of amateurish work. And to make things worse, the person presenting them to her was full to the brim with enthusiasm.

'What do you think?' Hector asked.

Not sure she could find the right words, she played for time. 'I'll appraise a few more before I give my verdict.' The next sketch was of the razed Surrey Commercial Docks in Rotherhithe, a scene that many artists had turned their hand to, and it was of an equally low standard. All of those following were depictions of Lyme Regis. 'Oh, there's Martha,' Sybil said. 'Rock pooling. How did you get onto the beach? She wouldn't tell me the way.'

'Nor me, but I found a chink in the armour. I could show you tomorrow, if you'd like.'

Sybil looked up and Hector's entire face seemed to be twinkling.

Tomorrow. She thought that signalled there would be a tonight when she could forget about the rebuff from Graeme and regain a feeling of being wanted and needed. 'I'd like that.' She returned his smile, then realised she'd better think of something to say about his compositions.

She so wanted to model herself on Blanche and Ellen, who prided themselves on always telling the truth when it came to others' work, but this time that admirable trait wouldn't do. 'You must remember perspective,' she offered.

'Yes,' he said eagerly. 'I know I often get that wrong. I borrowed a book from the library that explained how to hone that skill, and I've been trying to improve.'

Sybil didn't think any book could help Hector. 'Sometimes it takes ages to get it right.'

'I'll bet you didn't have to practise,' he said without a trace of sullenness.

'Oh, I still do,' she said. 'We never stop learning. And one other comment. Shadows come in very many different shades, not just black or grey.'

She handed the book back to him and he opened it again, studying his drawings in light of her suggestions. Then he sighed and said, 'I don't think I'm ready for the WAAC yet.'

'Perhaps try to improve those skills first, then you'll be in a better position to impress them.'

The Home Guard wandered off in twos and threes and a chill passed through the courtyard. Hector ordered himself another pint, but Sybil was strong and refused. There was a current running between them, and she wanted to be alert to what she envisaged would be a cosy end to the evening. Much to her surprise, that didn't horrify her. Was she so shallow, she questioned herself? To allow one letter from her missing husband, that really did nothing but verify what she'd known all along, to throw her into the arms of a stranger? Of course she wasn't, and then in the next beat of her heart, she hoped she was – at least this once.

They talked about Churchill, how they both missed but were glad to get away from London, their favourite artists, which rationed foods they missed the most. Hector smoked two cigarettes, flicking the ash through the gaps in the table. Then Sybil said, 'How long do you spend refining your work?'

With a groan like Ellen's, he said he hated that aspect of being an artist.

'It's completely necessary,' Sybil said in a clipped voice. 'And you should take hours, days and months on the process.'

He sighed deeply and shook his head. 'I've had a go at reworking a particular piece, but without much enthusiasm, I'm afraid. Would you care to see it? It's on an easel in Old Ship Cottage. I could cook something for us.' He sounded as if the idea had just occurred to him. 'Sprats on toast, or some such delicacy.'

Propriety was the only thing stopping her from saying yes – or was it? She no longer knew and thought that for now she didn't want to care. A few moments passed whilst she gazed out towards the horizon and told herself she was considering what she should do from every angle, but in reality, she'd made up her mind. 'Thank you,' she said, as properly as she could. 'I'd like that.'

As they ambled up the cliffs on the other side of town, they talked about how difficult it was to get about in the blackout and how they both loathed pulling the heavy curtains across the windows when night fell. Hector told her a funny story about an over-enthusiastic warden who used to walk along his road in London and rap on doors ages before the dark overtook light. He didn't ask about her wedding ring, and she didn't mention his scars.

Old Ship Cottage stood alone behind a broken gate. Hector retrieved a key from under a plant pot, and as he unlocked the door, his elbow brushed the top of her breast and she caught her breath. He didn't apologise and that made the place he'd touched feel tender and alive.

She helped to pull the curtains across windows that looked out over the sea. The scene must have been glorious in the daylight. Hector turned on a low lamp, said, 'Ta-dah!' and stood back with his arms wide. Without thinking, Sybil almost fell into them, until she realised he was gesturing to an easel, a seascape leaning against the wooden support.

'Oh,' was all she could manage to say when she took in what amounted to nothing better than a child's attempt at a holiday souvenir.

'Shall I turn up the light?'

Sybil didn't think that would make much difference, but to play for time she said yes.

'I'll put on the toast,' Hector said, busying himself in the small kitchen. 'Whilst you take a good look.'

That didn't take long, but wondering what she could possibly say to encourage him did. She wished he'd get down to what must surely be the real reason he'd asked her to his cottage, then for half an hour or so they could both forget about art and the war, his injuries and her husband.

The pungent aromas of bread and fish mingled with the salty air that found its way in through the blackouts. Hector lit a fire and it sparked and spat in the hearth. At last Sybil asked, 'Is this your first attempt to refine the piece?'

'Second,' Hector said. 'As I told you, I hate that process.'

'Hector,' she said, closing her eyes for a beat. 'It's very difficult to capture the sea, especially when it's in turmoil. Have you studied other seascapes? Dame Lily Brampton, for example.'

'Who's she?' he asked.

Oh dear, Sybil thought. She would have to be very careful not to hurt his ego, he had enough scars to be going on with.

'She's a very well-known artist. I suggest you try to get inspiration from her and some others.'

'I thought that would be cheating,' Hector said. 'I want to be unique.'

'I believe individuality comes after you learn how to emulate what others have perfected. That way you have the basics under your belt.' She looked away so he wouldn't see the blush slither up her face when she thought about his belt and what was underneath it.

'Sprats up,' he said.

She sat in an overstuffed armchair, and he sat opposite on a saggy sofa. He asked about the painting again, and she reiterated that he should vary the colour of shadows and not think of them in monotone. They had a cup of tea, and Hector said they should meet the following morning at eight to breach the barricades along the beach. Sybil sat up straight. It seemed as if he were bringing the evening to an end. But she'd been sure he wanted her as much as she longed for him. She was desperate to be held by someone for a short time, a few hours of comfort that wouldn't lead to worries about commitment or rejection or bewildering letters that left her life hanging mid-sentence.

'Oh, can I see the book you borrowed from the library, please?' she asked.

Hector grabbed it from a shelf and spread it out on his knees. Sybil took the opportunity to sit next to him on the sofa and hoped that being close would give him the same jolt of excitement that ran through her. He didn't move towards her, but nor did he move away. He handed her the book and leaned back, giving her time to skim through the pages. When she turned to comment, hoping his mouth would find hers, he was almost asleep, the gnarled side of his face in the folds of a cushion.

Disappointment caused a gnawing hollow in her stomach and in desperation she wondered if she should chance kissing him gently. But at that point, he breathed in loudly on a growl, then his breathing settled into a steady rhythm.

Sybil jiggled her wedding ring about on her finger as she watched him twitch and fidget. It dawned on her that everything she'd forecast for the evening had been conjured up by her imagination. All Hector had wanted was a companion whom he could talk to about art. Her face burned with shame, and she ran cold with the knowledge that her thinking was skewed. Had she misinterpreted Graeme too? His letter said he loved her and hadn't wanted to lose her, so perhaps not. But he'd ignored her pleas to stay when he'd joined up, and then there was Heather.

She glanced again at Hector and relief washed over her that the beer and sea air had sent him into a deep sleep. Embarrassment would have eaten her alive if she'd tried to take the situation further. And she didn't think she could bear another stark rejection now.

What was I thinking? She stood and covered him lightly with a blanket.

Ashamed, Sybil gathered her things and slunk towards the door. When she looked back, she wondered what had attracted him to her. He was good-looking and he was an artist, of sorts, and that, she thought, was about it. Then she almost cried out when she realised that her hidden scars seemed to be causing her more pain and anguish than his that were on display for the entire world to see.

At the B&B she made up her mind that by the time he woke, she would be gone. She packed her bags and pushed away humiliating thoughts of what Blanche, Ellen, Auntie Myrtle, Dame Lily and the female stoker would think of her if they'd seen her tonight or the night before last. She recited the letter from Graeme in her head, let tears glide down her cheeks and waited for dawn.

Completely wrung out and so ashamed she wanted nothing more than to hide away from herself, she escaped to St Ives to try to patch over her wounds.

It was every bit as beautiful as Blanche and Auntie Myrtle claimed it would be. The coastline, marred only by the ubiquitous sea defences, was vast and wild, and behind that, the tiered town gazed down in a genteel manner. Sybil found the pale pink boarding house, but there was no sign of Mrs Abelard, and the man in uniform who answered her knock said the large property had been seconded as an officers' mess. Despite the rain coming off the sea, she sketched the building and later, when she'd coloured it in pastels, she would post it to Blanche.

Determined to stay away from the pub, she favoured teashops and small restaurants and spent her evenings looking through the compositions she'd accrued that day, inwardly chanting lines from Graeme's letter that went round and round in her mind like a broken record.

Along Wheal Whidden, she came face to face with four uniformed girls, their arms around each other's waists and laughing as if they'd never heard the word war. They all wore dungarees and had dark, wavy hair under their steel helmets. 'I beg your pardon,' Sybil said, stepping to the side.

The girls sparkled and gleamed in her direction. One of them said, 'Thankee,' and nodded her head. It was then Sybil could see they were sisters or cousins at the very least.

As they passed by, Sybil brandished her permits and asked the girls if she could draw them. That suggestion caused another round of giggles. They looked at each other for guidance, then all agreed at once. They were very young, attractive and innocent – the very antithesis of how Sybil felt about herself – and she thought they symbolised hope and freedom and the future. ''Ere?' one asked, the 'r' round and full in her mouth.

'Well...' Sybil looked at the backdrop of trees and thought there must be somewhere better to tell their story. 'May I ask you what your war work is?'

'We be part of the Firewatching Service, and it's our shift soon.'

'So you can't be late. Perhaps I can sketch you there?'

The girls agreed that it would be fine with them, but she'd have to ask the Chief Warden at the Air Raid Precaution Headquarters. They broke apart to walk two together and led the way.

'Are you sisters?' Sybil asked.

'We be that,' she was told. 'And there are two more at home.'

'My goodness.' Sybil was shocked. With that many girls in the house there would always be someone for company. 'Any brothers?'

'One,' the first sister said. 'And he be the youngest. Eight years old.'

'Poor little fellow,' Sybil said. 'He must be overwhelmed with so many sisters.'

The girls laughed. 'He's our little luvver. We's always making a fuss of him.'

The sisters didn't stop smiling. Their cheerfulness was so infectious that Sybil realised her face was beaming too. Of course, they were younger than her and probably hadn't yet been visited by the hurt of distant husbands and cruel letters. Watching them jostle and rib and move the hair out of each other's eyes, she hoped they'd never have to experience such awful things.

They had as many questions for her as she had for them.

'Why have you come all this way?'

'To capture the war work that women are doing all over the country. What made you choose firewatching?'

The two eldest girls looked at each other as if they'd never given that a thought. 'We's wanted to do our bit,' one sister said. 'The men was all going off or joining the Home Guard, so when the call went out for firewatchers we thought we's should sign up.'

'Little Jory, our baby brother, does train with the Home Guard,' a sister said from behind. 'Mamm's sewing a uniform for him.'

Sybil was astonished. 'At his young age?' she asked. 'Surely he wouldn't be expected to confront the enemy if they were to invade ... or any such terrible thing.'

In a tone of equal amazement, she was told that he helped with everything else, so why not that?

The girls were greeted by every passer-by they met as they wended their way through the narrow streets, the pavements slick with the residue of salty seawater. Sybil sketched quickly as they walked, the girls competing to view the likenesses of themselves over her shoulder.

They came to a corrugated ARP hut not far from the beach and went inside. 'Chief Warden Rosewarne,' one of the girls shouted. 'We've gots a visitor for you.'

An elderly man with pale blue eyes in a rugged face appeared from a small office. 'How many times,' he said, 'do I have to say don't shout. When you need to, no one will believe there's anything wrong because you've called wolf so many times.'

Sybil thought of how Blanche reprimanded Ellen for banging doors and bouncing on beds. But her exuberance had evaporated with time and responsibility and that, no doubt, would be the same for these lovely sisters. For now, their only reaction to the ticking-off was another slew of giggles, and Sybil thought Chief Warden Rosewarne was probably the butt of quite a few of their jokes.

The Chief Warden read through Sybil's documentation at least three times, handed the permits back to her with overblown ceremony, then took off his cap and smoothed down his sparse hair. The girls tittered and Sybil, caught in the moment, had to stifle a laugh. 'If you can all go about your duties normally and naturally, then I can do the same,' she said.

The Chief Warden saluted, turned back to his office and the girls were joined by three other women and two men. Sybil followed them around as they readied their equipment in the freezing cold tin cabin that smelled of smoked mackerel. She drew them as they checked their gas masks and slung them over their shoulders; ticked their names off a roster; donned overcoats and looked in the stores to see how many sandbags were available.

'Sybil.' One of the sisters touched her lightly on the shoulder. 'We's about to go out and check on all the sandbags in our section. Are you coming with us or is it too dark to draw?'

'I'd like to tag along,' she said. 'I'm used to sketching at night and it gives an eerie atmosphere to the compositions.'

With low torches they walked around the town, the girls prodding burlap sacks to gauge the effectiveness of the stitching and ascertain whether the sand was still viable or not. They told her that the last time they'd made the rounds, they'd moved a pile of bags and unearthed a nest of rats. They shivered, their faces contorted with horror. It was the first time since she'd met them that they'd stopped smiling.

Sybil's legs began to drag, and she had to smother a yawn. The last few days had depleted her, and she needed to find her energy again. When they returned to headquarters, Sybil thanked the girls and said how pleased she was to have met them.

They murmured the same in reply, then one girl elbowed another and said, 'You ask, Nessa. You said you would.'

Sybil expected a question about where her paintings could be viewed or what life was like in London, but Nessa asked if she'd go home with them and draw her brother and their evacuee.

'You have an evacuee as well?' Sybil asked. That made a total of eight youngsters in their household.

'That we do. A boy. Everyone gots at least one. We had two, but the little girl goed to relatives in Hampshire in the end.'

'Please,' another sister begged. 'Mamm would be so happy to send it to Dad away with the war.'

'Will they be up this time of night?' she asked.

'They stays up until we get home.'

There was no way Sybil could say no, and it would be good to see how these kind, generous people housed an evacuee in what was probably an overcrowded house to begin with. 'Of course I will,' she said.

Nessa commanded the two youngest sisters to run ahead and warn their mother to spruce up the boys. When they arrived at the terraced house, they walked straight off the street into a cramped living room that was smoky from the remains of an ashy fire. Two girls sat at the scrubbed table. They were exact copies of their four firewatching sisters, except their hair was tied in long plaits. Their mother, a high point of colour on each cheek, looked as though she had once been as lovely as her daughters. She busied herself with the kettle, an apron tied around her waist. And on the couch sat the two little kings.

Although the girls had explained what Sybil was doing, their Mamm wanted to hear it for herself and when she did, she said she would be delighted if she could have a drawing of the boys together. Their faces scoured and their hair plastered down, except where it sprang back up in cowlicks, the two lads sat with their arms around each other, shy, cheeky grins on their faces. Sybil drew two quick sketches, gave one to their Mamm and kept the other in her notebook. Then she told all of them to huddle together. After much demurring, she captured a rough likeness of the family which made their mother, and Sybil, shed a few tears.

They asked her to stay for a cup of tea and a fairing to dunk in it, but she politely declined. 'Comes back in the morning, then,' Nessa said. 'And we'll find other things for you to draw.'

'I'm sorry,' Sybil said. 'But I have to move on tomorrow.'

A consensus of disappointment went around the room. Then she was caught off guard when in turn, they threw their arms around her to say goodbye. Multiple good wishes and appeals for her to mind herself, followed her out the door and back to her boarding house. When she turned the key in her bedroom door and was met with cold air, silence, emptiness and the words in Graeme's letter for company, she almost turned on her heels to bang on their door again.

For most of the long train journey to Cardiff, Sybil sat slumped in her seat, the creased letter in her hand. She hadn't reviewed her compositions, taken notice of her fellow passengers or looked at her list to plan what she would draw when she arrived at her destination. Hungry and starved of rest, she felt as if she were on the edge of a personal catastrophe – a breakdown or worse. She'd made up her mind to never again find herself in the position she'd been in with Hector. As far as men were concerned, she'd be purer than pure. But she'd yet to find a way out of the downward spin Graeme's letter had sent her into. Every time she got to the last sentence, she tormented herself by filling it in with an ending of her own. *Heather was my sweetheart for a few years and we planned to …*

… marry and have children, but she sadly passed away.

… spend our lives together but you somehow hoodwinked me into marrying you, which I regret every minute of every day.

… open an art gallery together.

… marry, but she threw me over for another man. I'm afraid I married you on the rebound and on reflection, I want out.

… become engaged. Then I met you, and I had to tell her that her time as my special friend was over. You're everything to me, but I am ashamed that I haven't spoken to you about Heather and what she meant to me once upon a time. Also, I didn't handle leaving her well and should have given her more of an explanation. Therefore, I am asking you to give me permission to write to her and say I'm terribly sorry for treating her badly. Knowing you as I do, I feel sure you will agree to me having contact with her one last time.

That was it. Sybil sat up tall. She folded the letter neatly and put it in her oilskin bag. There would be no need to look at it again. Each time she came to the end of the recitation in her mind, she would add that last paragraph and convince herself that was exactly what Graeme had intended to write.

12

Dame Lily Brampton, DBE RA ROI RWS,
Seagulls' Watch,
Cley-next-the-Sea,
Norfolk

Thursday, 14th August 1941

Mrs S. Paige,
c/o Miss J. Butterworth,
Personal Assistant to Sir Leonard Thwaites, CH KOB FB,
War Artists' Advisory Committee,
Ministry of Information,
The National Gallery,
Trafalgar Square,
London, W.C.2

My dearest Sybil,

I am writing to apologise from the bottom of my heart.
I have been insensitive and unthinking, although in my
defence I had no idea what you were going through, but
now, regrettably, I have.

Dominic has been listed as missing in action. The telegram
was delivered yesterday by one of those little messenger
boys – angels of death I've heard them called – and now I

know why. It said the deed had been done somewhere in the Middle East, so my guess is ******. My mind won't let me believe it, but each time I pick up the telegram and read it again, I'm faced with the terrible truth.

I have been a wreck, we all have, and I have to keep stopping to wipe my eyes whilst writing the letters that must be sent. Geoffrey is in the same state. We comfort each other one minute, and the next we push each other away and want to be alone in our grief.

Now that my heart's been severed in two, I cannot believe the way I spoke to you about Graeme. I recall that I asked if you'd had time to adjust. Adjust? How could that ever be possible. And even if I could, I do not think I want to. That would seem as if I were abandoning my beautiful son. And of course, saying you're not the only one is no help whatsoever. In fact, it makes it worse, doesn't it? To think there are so many other mothers, wives, sisters going through this same hell is an abomination. Hitler started on Manchester today and that means there will be hundreds of mothers in my position by the end of the night, and it will most probably be the same the following day and the day after that.

I cringe now when I remember that I advised you to stay busy and remind yourself that when one door closes another one ... etc., etc. A door has closed for me, and I know that another will never open in its place.

How do you do it, Sybil dear? How have you managed to keep going? You always look so lovely, and you talk to everyone with great interest and sympathy. And to take a commission and travel the country when I'm sure, like me, all you want to do is curl up at home and wait for communication from the authorities that your loved one is alive.

I cannot indulge in discussions about the WAAC, RBP, your drawings or art in general at this time. I do hope you'll understand.

Again, please accept my apologies for being so ignorant and unfeeling.

With love from,

Lily X

P.S. Please excuse the tiny burn marks in the paper. I'm chain smoking as I write and have no care for where the ash settles.

MONDAY 18TH AUGUST 1941

SENT FROM MAIN POST OFFICE SHREWSBURY SHROPSHIRE

PRIORITY DAME LILY BRAMPTON

SEAGULLS' WATCH CLEY NORFOLK

ARRIVING NORWICH THORPE STOP WEDNESDAY 20 AUGUST STOP 443PM STOP SYBIL STOP

13

August 1941

True to its name, Dame Lily's house was guarded by seagulls that stood on the tall chimney, screeching and squawking to announce Sybil's arrival. A housekeeper, dressed in black and white to match the timber frame, opened the door and ushered her into a rather cold, lofty hallway. Artworks hung on the wall and as Sybil shrugged out of her coat, she thought she'd love to spend an hour or so viewing them, if she could find an appropriate time.

'Pleased to meet you, Mrs Paige,' the housekeeper said. 'My name is Ida, and I'll show you to your room. Follow me, if you please.' She picked up Sybil's bags and headed for the stairs, but there was Dame Lily, a yellow and gold scarf thrown around her shoulders.

'Sybil,' she whispered. 'My dear.'

Without giving a thought to decorum, Sybil ran to her mentor and held her tight. Beneath the hug, Dame Lily's arms twitched and her heartbeat was erratic. When they drew apart, Sybil saw the toll the recent news had taken. She'd always thought Dame Lily looked younger than her years. Of course, she used makeup artfully, but that only enhanced her features, alive with interest in everything around her. Now her few wrinkles had multiplied, and two tiny, deflated balloons bagged under her inflamed eyes. Her hair had been pinned in some sort of bun, but strays like wire wool poked out here and there. Rather than an immediate tug of sympathy, Sybil thought Dame Lily honest and down to earth. She knew it was good for morale to put on a brave face, get on with things and have a stiff upper lip, but here was a woman allowing the natural reaction of grief to send her to her knees – at least in the privacy of her home.

Behind her, Dame Lily's husband appeared looking every bit as dishevelled and ghostly. He was wearing baggy trousers and a maroon jumper pocked with holes. 'This is Sir Geoffrey,' Dame Lily announced, and Sybil shook his hand despite it being covered in paint. 'Ida,' she said, her voice cracking. 'Mrs Paige can be shown to her room later. For now, we'll take tea in the drawing room. Thank you.'

Sir Geoffrey excused himself by saying he would be in his garden studio, and Dame Lily gestured for Sybil to follow her into the drawing room where a fire was lit, despite it being the height of summer.

There were no pleasantries. Dame Lily sat for a moment, closed her eyes and massaged her temples. 'I'm afraid,' she said at last. 'That I've rather gone to pieces, and I feel ashamed about that. I always thought I was made of sterner stuff.'

'You mustn't apologise. You've received a terrible blow and you're in shock. None of us knows how we'll react in these unprecedented circumstances. You must give yourself time to …'

'Adapt? I can hardly believe I used those ridiculous words when I spoke to you about Graeme.' With unsteady hands, she pulled a cigarette from a silver case and held a lighter to it.

A clock chimed the hour, which seemed to send the seagulls into a shrieking panic. Sybil jumped, but Dame Lily didn't seem to notice. 'I'm lucky that I can be so self-indulgent,' she continued. 'Most people who get the same terrible news have to go straight back out to work or tend to children or sick family members. You,' she eyed Sybil as if seeing her in a new light, 'had to carry on in that bedsit you detested and try to make a living for yourself with no one to turn to. How I admire you.'

Sybil felt herself blush. 'Please don't be fooled,' she said. 'I fell apart whenever I was alone. And often still do.'

Dame Lily reached across and clasped Sybil's hands. She wept and Sybil shed a few tears. She'd debated whether to tell her mentor about the letter from Graeme, and if she did, how much of the contents to divulge. Now, the argument resurfaced in her mind. She could choose not to say anything to anyone, but that might cause difficulties in the future if she received another letter or if Graeme came home. She could reveal it in its entirety, with or without the ending she told herself had been penned by him, and allow everyone to know the agony she was in. Or, and this was what she favoured, say the letter had arrived but not discuss what was in it. No one would be rude enough to ask.

Ida knocked, solemnly left a tray of tea things on a low table and closed the door quietly behind her. 'Believe it or not,' Dame Lily said. 'This house used to be full of fun. Everyone laughing and messing about, shouting to each other from different rooms with jibes and jokes that were ours alone. Especially Dom who was … is …' She shook her head. 'The most gregarious of all of us. It was warm, too.' She looked at the fire and shivered. 'Now we move around like undertakers.'

'But there's always hope,' Sybil said, taking a sip of her tea.

'I think I might have said something similar to you,' Dame Lily scoffed.

'Perhaps,' she said. 'Quite a few people did. But …' She hesitated, then made up her mind and ploughed on. 'Last month I received a letter from Graeme.'

Dame Lily gasped, her ashen face suddenly colourless. 'So he's alive.'

'I have no way of knowing,' she said. 'The letter was dated the 17th of April 1940 which was not long before he was reported missing.'

'Oh, my dear.' Dame Lily's cup clattered as she set it on the saucer. 'Talk about being in shock. And you were somewhere out there all by yourself.' She waved her hand towards a vague distant place.

'That was better than being in the cold bedsit on my own. At least I had purpose.' She cringed when she thought back to her behaviour after she'd received the letter, when her only purpose was to down as many gins as possible and gain the attention of the first man who looked at her.

'But what ...' Dame Lily managed to stop herself from asking what Graeme had written.

'The letter was cut short,' she said.

'By censors?' Dame Lily asked. 'They're always taking a pair of scissors or black pencil to what I write.'

'No.' She shook her head. 'Graeme ran out of space, he said he was going to continue on a fresh sheet. So far, though, I've had nothing else.'

Dame Lily stared at her. She started to speak a number of times but couldn't seem to find the right words. 'What a cruel blow,' she somehow managed.

'Yes, that sums it up only too well.'

'Sybil, my dear.' Dame Lily leaned forward. 'You are planning to stay for a while, aren't you?'

'I don't think so, Dame Lily.'

'But I insist.'

'I'm well aware that I invited myself. Besides, you need time to heal as a family and I must make the most of my commission before I head back to London and get at least one piece ready to present to the WAAC.'

Dame Lily groaned. 'What if I said that I think of you as the daughter I never had?'

Sybil raised her eyebrows in surprise and fiddled with the ring on her finger. 'Thank you, Dame Lily,' she said. 'I've always felt very close to you, too.'

Dame Lily nodded. 'And if that's not enough, perhaps I can sway you by saying there are so many things for you to draw in Norfolk and Suffolk, as I'm sure you'll know from your list, so you wouldn't be reneging on your contract. And for that, you might as well stay here with us than in lodgings elsewhere in the county.'

The thought of being in a proper household, although in the midst of grief, was very appealing.

'To be completely selfish, I think it would do me the world of good to have you here for a little while. Besides, Iggy is coming home tomorrow on leave, and it would help him to have another young person in the house.'

Sybil looked at Dame Lily, who seemed to be willing her to say yes. 'Thank you very much, Dame Lily,' she said. 'If you're sure.'

'That's wonderful, my dear.'

'But if I outstay my welcome at any time, please feel free to boot me out.'

Dame Lily forced herself to laugh and said, 'That won't happen, I can assure you.'

With dinner at eight, Sybil had time to tidy herself and change her clothes. She stared in the full-length mirror in her room and hoped meals wouldn't be too formal as all she had were the few serviceable things she'd packed for her travels. She sat in a chair by the window, listening for the bell Ida would tinkle. Low tide had stranded a few boats on the banks of the river Glaven, and the sea, which Dame Lily loved to capture, was a straight blue line across the horizon.

She thought back to what day-to-day life had been like before the bloody war but realised she had become so accustomed to the horrible changes they had to live with, that she could hardly remember. Everything had been much easier before it all started, that was certain. If Graeme had wanted to leave her for Heather, he would have had to tell her face to face and although hurtful, it would have been over quickly, and she could have started to get back on her feet without the interruptions of telegrams and letters with bad news. This war work, too, wouldn't have existed. Much as she was grateful for the opportunity that allowed her to do her bit and make a name for herself, she was well aware that there was no joy to be found in the grotesque reason behind the commissions and the recognition.

She thought about how Dame Lily seemed to view her in a different, elevated light. As if her own terrible experience gave her the hindsight to counsel others in the same position. She took the self-portrait sketchbook from her bag and wondered if now was the time to get that image on paper. The pencil in her hand hovered over the page, and there she appeared, a cold cup of tea on the table next to her, a ladder in her stockings, her head flung back in anguish and the telegram hanging limply by her side. Charcoal tears coursed down her sketched face and were smudged by the warm, salty drops that fell from her eyes. She heaved once, then slashed through her work with heavy black swipes.

The bell sounded and she sat for a moment, wiping her face and calming her breath. She didn't want to bother her hosts with her own tears – this was their time to cry.

Over breakfast the following morning, Sybil asked Dame Lily if she'd like to go with her to Thetford Forest to sketch women working for the Forestry Commission.

'I couldn't possibly, my dear.' Dame Lily inhaled deeply on her fourth cigarette. 'I want to be here when Iggy arrives.'

'You could take the car,' Geoffrey said. 'And be back for five.'

'That won't do, Geoffrey. Thetford is absolutely miles away. On the other side of the bloody county – you know that. Besides, the car's needed to pick up Iggy from the station.'

'Ah,' Sir Geoffrey said.

Sybil was afraid she'd become a bother. 'Please don't worry,' she said. 'I can get myself there. I'm used to getting to the most awkward places.'

'Why not go into Norwich today?' Sir Geoffrey suggested. 'Then you can meet Iggy and come home with him in the motor.'

Dame Lily's eyes lit up. 'What a good idea. Sometimes, Geoffrey, I think I married a genius.' She kissed her husband on his forehead. 'Sybil?'

It seemed as if Dame Lily wanted to stay close, and her insightful company would bring a fresh perspective to the artwork. 'I'd be delighted,' she said.

On the drive to the city, they looked out at the same herds of cattle and endless swathes of sky she'd passed when she'd arrived yesterday. A lone church stood in the middle of a field, the mist around its foundations making it seem as if it were hovering on a cloud. 'I can see why there are so many airfields in this area,' she said. 'The ground is perfectly flat for take-off and landing.'

'Indeed. Much as I adore the big city, Londoners think the world begins and ends with them, but the Battle of Britain started right here in sleepy Norfolk with three spitfires that took off from Coltishall. Are you planning to visit there?'

The car slowed to a stop and the women craned their necks to see a line of cows lumbering across the road towards a large barn. 'I have so many filled sketchbooks,' Sybil said. 'And too many compositions drawn on airfields. I'd like to capture different scenes now.' She unfolded the WAAC list and traced down it with her finger. 'I think there's a dairy training post somewhere near here. Shall we try to find it?'

Curiosity brightened Dame Lily's face. 'Archie.' She touched the driver lightly on his shoulder. 'Can you please look for ... The Broads Farm? If it's not too much trouble.'

'I know the one, Dame Lily. Cook gets some of her supplies from there.'

Archie turned down a lane towards a farmhouse, but when they came across a man studying the wheels of a tractor, Sybil asked him to stop. She opened her window, unveiled her permits and asked if she could draw the activity in the training centre.

'Not up to me, Miss,' the man said. 'You need the gaffer. He's in the barn now with the ladies. Shall I take you up there?'

Sybil looked around, not sure why the man had used the term 'up' as there was nothing but completely level ground as far as the eye could see. 'Dame Lily?' Sybil bent to look in the car.

'It ain't exactly good ground for walking, especially in them shoes,' the man said.

'I have my overshoes,' Sybil said.

Archie opened the boot and took out a pair of dark green wellies.

'And we don't drive anywhere without a pair of these.' Dame Lily leaned against the car to change her footwear.

They followed the farmhand, who had been right about the mess underfoot. It was muddy and slimy with cow pats, and the two women steadied each other as they picked their way through. The sound of gentle lowing came from the barn along with the soft chatter of young women. Ammonia stained the entryway yellow, and inside were two long lines of cows, each in a different stage of being milked. 'Ladies.' A man in tweed came towards them. 'Whatever are you doing here? Have you lost your way?'

'They want to draw you,' the farmhand said.

The herdsman looked surprised, but Sybil produced her documents and said, 'I'd like to draw the women at their training.'

'Well, I never,' the herdsman read through the documents, scratched his head under his hat and pointed towards the interior of the barn with an open hand.

Sybil got out her equipment and was pleased to see Dame Lily produce her own sketchbook and lump of charcoal. As they walked to separate ends of the barn, Sybil could feel the eyes of the girls on her. She sketched one of them sitting on a squat three-legged stool, gingerly pulling at the udders under a black and white cow. 'You don't have to worry,' said another girl, standing over her. 'They won't tear. They're as leathery and solid as they feel.'

The trainee wiped her brow. 'I'll never get the hang of this.'

'Don't be silly,' her tutor said, hunkering down next to her. 'In my first week it took me an hour and a half to get enough for a cup of tea.'

Sybil giggled. 'I wouldn't know where to begin,' she said, but the trainee was downhearted.

'Nor did I,' the girl said. 'I didn't know a bull from a cow, did I, Phyllis?'

'Oh, I see,' Sybil said. She thought even she could have made it over that hurdle.

Then the three women burst out laughing and Sybil moved along. A slender girl, her thick hair tied up in a scarf, poured a churn of milk into a larger container and Sybil captured the white waterfall as it hit the sides, not a drop wasted on the floor. 'Where does it go after this?' Sybil asked.

'Shops, markets, airfields, schools,' the woman said, her cheeks blazing from the effort.

'Do you enjoy the work?' she asked.

The young woman put down the churn and leaned on her hip. 'Some of it. It was this or somewhere farther afield, but I wanted to stay close to home to help my granny who's none too well.'

'I'm sorry,' Sybil said.

The woman shrugged. 'Needs be.'

Sybil was amazed by the number of sayings people used to convince themselves that life was as good as it could be given the circumstances. *Things are as they should be; take the good with the bad; God gives with one hand and takes away with the other; every good thing comes to those who wait.* She looked down at the drawing again and christened it: *Needs Be.*

By the time she'd made the rounds, Sybil had sketches of udders being cleaned, girls sluicing equipment in a huge sink, a woman teaching another to log milk yield, manure being carted away and a truck loaded for deliveries. Dame Lily had drawn one sketch of a trainee lifting a cow's tail so another could get to the teats more easily.

When they'd settled back in the car and resumed their journey, Dame Lily smiled and said she thought Sybil's commission was a good one. 'Putting aside the loneliness, you must have learned so much. I did from just that one visit.'

'Being on my own has been a blessing, in some ways. I believe it's made me more eager to meet my subjects and try to get to know them, so I can do my very best to tell their stories with the respect they deserve.'

That wasn't a piece of sycophantic nonsense, but the essence of what Sybil was trying to achieve, and it made Dame Lily smile broadly with her mouth, if not her eyes which were glazed with grief.

'May I?' Dame Lily asked, reaching for Sybil's sketchbook. Sybil held on to the cardboard cover for a moment too long until Dame Lily snapped her fingers at her, and she let it go. They both laughed at that, and when Dame Lily looked through the drawings, she said, 'Well, I am extremely impressed, my dear. It won't be long before you're snapping your fingers at me. There are more, I believe?'

'Yes,' Sybil said. 'But the ones I've filled have been sent back to Auntie Myrtle's house.' She nestled the book back in her oilskin bag.

'What about this one?' Before Sybil could stop her, Dame Lily plucked at the dedicated self-portrait book, opened it and perused page after page of defaced attempts to draw herself in the utmost distress. Mortified, her face burning with indignation, Sybil turned to the window and stared unseeing at the pastoral scene blurring past.

Aware of a rustle next to her, she heard Dame Lily replacing the book in the bag, then she reached across and rubbed Sybil's arm. 'How very vulgar of me,' she said. 'One shouldn't take such liberties with anyone, let alone with someone whom one considers to be a daughter.'

Sybil spun the ring around her finger and kept her eyes on the fields flashing by. She felt exposed and violated and wanted to be angry but couldn't bring herself to have words with this admirable woman who'd taken her under her wing.

'All I seem to do lately is apologise to you for one faux pas or another,' Dame Lily said. 'Much like members of all close families.'

That softened the blow and Sybil turned to Dame Lily with a small smile.

'If it helps,' Dame Lily said softly. 'I admire your artwork and your bravery now more than ever.'

'Thank you, Dame Lily,' Sybil said.

Archie dropped them in Gentleman's Walk, and it was arranged that he pick them up from the same spot at half past four. 'A cup of coffee to fortify us for the next round of drawing?' Dame Lily asked as she threaded her arm through Sybil's, all thoughts of the personal sketchbook seemingly vanished.

'Lovely,' Sybil said. 'Let's hope there's real milk as I have a craving for it after the dairy farm.'

They had, of course, to put up with substitute milk and sugar to go with the chicory blend. They sipped at it whilst they looked through Sybil's list together. 'Any thoughts?' Dame Lily said. 'I'll be guided by you.'

'A nursery for two- to five-year-olds. I haven't drawn teachers yet. It's next door to a shoe factory. So I could get some sketches there, too. And,' she leaned across the table and lowered her voice, 'you never know, we might get some cast-off shoes. Seconds or thirds.'

'How exciting. Have you received any other gifts?'

'My overshoes were a gift from a part-time waitress, part-time poultry keeper in York. Once or twice, I've been given a free second cup of tea or day-old scone, and a man in Lyme Regis bought me a couple of drinks and cooked tea for me. That's all. Other than that, I've been completely independent.'

'That way of life can become a habit. On that basis, how do you feel about going back to London and living under Auntie Myrtle's roof? It might prove difficult to keep to someone else's rules and regulations.' Dame Lily pressed a serviette to her mouth.

Sybil thought for a moment. She looked around at the white cups stacked on the counter and a display cabinet of Caley's Marching Chocolate. 'I'm looking forward to seeing my friends and having all my belongings in one place for a while. Auntie Myrtle won't have any rules, I'm quite sure, except the ones that pertain to everyone's health and happiness.'

'So would you take up another commission if it were offered to you?' Dame Lily asked.

Sybil smiled. 'I don't want to get ahead of myself,' she said. 'And the chances are that won't happen. I was extremely lucky to get this one, but that will be that.'

'After looking at your sketchbook.' Dame Lily coloured slightly, probably at the thought of her earlier indiscretion. 'I'll take bets on that not being the case.'

The weather had changed when they stepped outside, and they found themselves in the middle of a squall. 'This far away from the sea?' Sybil battled with her umbrella then gave it up.

'As you saw on your drives to and from Cley, there's nothing in between the coast and here to stop wind and rain. Where is this nursery school?'

'St George's Street,' Sybil said. 'Is that far?'

'Everywhere is far in this weather, my dear.'

There were twenty-three children in residence at the nursery and they had five nurses and teachers minding them. It was dinner time, and in one room, highchairs were lined up and little ones were being fed a meal that varied according to their ages. A small table squatted on a rug and five children sat around it, tucking into what looked like oatmeal and vegetable goulash.

In a room next door, tiny beds were made up and waiting for naptime. Two toddlers were crying and when they were placated, three others found their voices. Snot dribbled out of noses, babies were carried to a changing room, little voices asked for the potty, a small boy wanted his mummy and through it all, the nursery nurses remained cheerful, calm and patient.

A small boy with curly hair ran up with a book in his hand and suddenly, a pang of what some people called feeling broody, hit her. She wondered if the little fellow made Dame Lily think about Dominic at the same age – that must have been so much more heartbreaking.

She and Graeme had agreed they wanted children – but not before they'd had a few years on their own. It was bewildering that any husband could have had that sort of conversation with his wife when all along he was thinking about another woman. It made Sybil examine every aspect of their relationship along with her perception of it. That train of thought led her to query her ability to judge people and situations – again. She shook her head and repeated the last paragraph of Graeme's letter that she'd conjured up. Well aware that couldn't be the long-term solution, it was the best she could do now in order to keep her head above water.

A nurse found two adult-sized chairs and Sybil sat, sketching a toddler being fed spoonfuls of gruel. He was a bonny lad with ruddy cheeks and Sybil wondered how he, and the other little ones, could thrive so well on rations. Then a little girl who'd been set on her feet stumbled and burst into tears and Sybil drew her being soothed.

When the dishes had been cleared away and the children cleaned up, those tots who were still awake gathered together on the rug. A teacher sat on a chair in front of them and opened a book called *Little Dog*. The children were immediately mesmerised. A few slurped on their thumbs and others smoothed blankets they held onto tightly. The cream-coloured walls made the room feel cool, yet warm at the same time, and for a little while, it seemed as though nowhere else existed in the entire world. Swaddled in safety, the comforting cloy of warm milk and the soft drone of the teacher's voice surrounded them, and Sybil's eyes began to droop. She closed them for a minute and the next thing she knew, the wailing rise and fall of an air raid siren yanked her back into the real world.

She looked at Dame Lily whose mouth was set in a line as she stuffed her art supplies into her bag. The nurses didn't drop their serene demeanour for a second. They herded the children together, picked up those who couldn't walk and marched out of the building and down into the depths of a shelter. 'I'm so sorry,' Sybil said, as she and Dame Lily followed them through the door. 'We've nowhere else to go.'

'Of course you must come along with us,' a nurse said. Then she smiled mischievously. 'You'll be able to capture the reality of trying to keep more than twenty children entertained in a confined space.'

The children seemed to have found a second wind and despite knowing the drill and sitting nicely along two forms, there was a good deal of chatter and poking and whining. Babies were placed on a large rug laid out on the floor and someone put on the kettle.

'Shall we continue with our story?' The teacher asked.

A few children said yes or nodded their heads. One little boy started to cry, as did two of the babies and they were each pacified in turn. A couple of potties were brought out from a storage box and Sybil thought the reek in the shelter would soon be worse than it had been in the cows' shed, and who knew how long it would be before this place could be mucked out.

Dame Lily budged up next to Sybil on the end of a form. 'Bloody war,' she said from the side of her mouth.

Sybil started to laugh, both at the way Dame Lily tried to keep her voice from reaching the little ones' ears and at two toddlers who had lunged for the same building block at the same time. 'I'm guessing this is a regular occurrence in Norfolk?'

'I'm afraid so, my dear. As I said earlier, London isn't the be all and end all.' She took a cigarette case from her bag and mimed putting one to her lips. 'Do you think they'll mind if I ...?'

'Most probably,' Sybil said. 'With the children in such an enclosed space.'

Dame Lily sighed and clasped her hands on her lap.

Sybil began to sketch a teacher trying to engage five children with an abacus. 'How about,' she whispered. 'We give the older ones an art lesson. Then the nurses can concentrate on the babies or have a well-deserved break.'

'What a good idea,' Dame Lily said. 'It will help pass the time.'

They sat the children in a circle and Sybil handed out paper and pencils. 'Who'd like to draw a duckling?'

'Me, me, me!' children shouted out in their high-pitched voices.

'This is how you start.' Sybil drew a line across the middle of her paper and waited whilst Dame Lily guided the little hands that didn't quite get the instruction.

'Now a curve under it so it looks like a boat.'

'Is that because it swims in the water like a ship?' a small boy asked.

'That's very clever of you,' Dame Lily said. 'Yes, I suppose that's why they need the same shape.'

Sybil showed them how to make a narrow upside-down U on top for a head, pencil in a ring around the neck, colour in the eyes, fashion a triangle for a beak, draw wings, two legs and paddles for feet. She asked the children to go around the circle, say their name and hold up their drawing for everyone to see. Some of them were better than others, most of them looked as though they'd been drawn with trembling hands, all of them were unmistakably ducks. Dame Lily led a round of applause for each of them and they gave the children free rein to colour them in with pastels.

'Goodness knows what Miss Butterworth's going to say when I tell her why I need more supplies so quickly,' Sybil worried.

'Oh, don't mind her. I've got plenty of pencils and pastels at home that you can have. Have you any string, Nurse?' she asked. 'And a couple of thumb tacks, please?'

Together they strung up the pictures on one wall of the shelter and both the children and staff looked delighted with them. A little girl wearing a tartan pinafore put her hand in Sybil's and said, 'Can we do a puppy now? They're my favourite.'

As they set about the task, two very young nurses joined them, laughing and comparing their drawings with the children's. Cups of tea were handed round, and the little ones had a splash of milk topped up with water and a plain biscuit. 'Oh, that's it,' someone said, and they all stopped to listen to the flat note of the all-clear. Quickly, Sybil sketched the children leaving two by two, their ducks fluttering in the breeze from the open door.

'You can come again,' the nurse in charge said. 'The children have never had such a lovely time during an air raid. Nor have we.'

'Thank you for having us,' Sybil said. 'The children are lovely.'

'Did you notice how poised they were?' Dame Lily said, her arm through Sybil's again.

'The nurses? Yes, I don't suppose we should expect anything less. It must be their training. But the children. The way they accepted the situation as if they know no better, which of course …'

'They don't. That's very sad,' Dame Lily said.

'Let's hope the whole thing is over before they really understand what's going on.'

They'd lost a few hours so had to cut short their visit to the shoe factory. But it was interesting to sketch the women working on lasts to make army boots and slippers for hospital patients. All of them had blisters and calluses on the tips of their fingers where they pushed thick needles in and out of the leather. They didn't look up or talk to Sybil and Dame Lily. They'd lost time, too, and probably had to make up their quota before they collected their children from the nursery and started on their chores at home.

Archie stood outside the car, scanning the hordes coming in from

Liverpool Street. Dame Lily, too, peered through the windscreen hoping to glimpse her son the minute he appeared. Never having met Ignatius, Sybil wouldn't have been able to pick him out from all the other uniform-clad men arriving or departing. Then an officer broke away from the crowds and stepped smartly towards the car, his hand out to shake Archie's.

Although quite tall, he was shorter than Sybil had imagined; there was a chip of amber in his eyes and his hair a darker shade of auburn than hers. Dame Lily was dark, but Sir Geoffrey had the kind of fluffy white hair that would have been that same reddish colour when he was younger. Ignatius opened the back door, leaned in and grabbed his mother in a tight embrace. All Sybil could see was how the sun had caught the nape of his neck, and the golden hairs sprouting on the backs of his hands.

He and Dame Lily murmured to each other for a few moments, then he looked up, his face flushed, and his mother introduced Sybil to him as an ex-student who had a WAAC commission and huge potential as an artist. That made her face redden to match his.

He hopped into the front passenger seat, half-turned and held Dame Lily's hand for the entire two-hour drive back to Seagulls' Watch. It was a beautiful sight and Sybil hoped that later, she'd be able to capture the love and deep distress on their faces when they looked at each other. A tinge of jealousy crept over her, knowing there wasn't a father who would look out for her or a brother or husband who would hold her hand in that way. Had Graeme ever looked at her like that? She was sure that if he had, she would have been able to recall it in vivid detail.

During dinner that night, the conversation was composed and civilised. They talked a lot about art and Ignatius said that tomorrow he would share his sketches of Army life with them but warned that they might find some of them distressing. 'Your father has been to war, Iggy,' Dame Lily scoffed. 'And Sybil and I have seen some terrible sights in this country. We're not ones to faint, are we, my dear?'

'No, Dame Lily. 'We can't be so self-indulgent, but thank you, Iggy, for being chivalrous and thinking about our sensitivities.'

Ignatius sat back in his chair and shook his head. 'I don't think I'm going to win here,' he said. 'Especially now there are two of you. Do you know, Sybil, that Mama always won every discussion, conversation or debate even though it was four against one? Didn't she, Papa?'

'Don't forget, son,' Sir Geoffrey lowered his voice to a raspy whisper, 'we let her.'

Dame Lily feigned hurt with a loud inhale and a hand on her chest. 'How dare you, Geoffrey,' she said. 'You know very well I have no need to cheat.'

They carried on in the same manner for the rest of the evening – serious discussions followed by a bit of sarcastic ribbing which they all seemed to enjoy. Before the men excused themselves to take port in a different room, they decided that the next day they would all take the train to Thetford Forest so Sybil could draw the women working there. She did her utmost to dissuade them, saying she was quite capable of finding her own way and that they must want to stay at home together. But they disagreed, so plans were made, Ida was asked to organise a picnic and Sybil went up to her room to study the sketches she'd drawn in the nursery.

That set a precedent for the next few days. Sybil chose what she wanted to draw and at least one of the family members – Ignatius more often than not – would accompany her, despite her protests.

When plans were laid the previous evening, Sybil was surprised to feel the small ripple of an electric shock each time it was decided that Iggy alone would keep her company the following day. And in the mornings, she found herself taking extra care of her hair and scant makeup before they left the house. Despite the fact that every single composition depicted war work, the days took on the air of jolly jaunts, and during one sandwich lunch, sitting on the stump of a tree in the middle of a field, Iggy took out a sketchbook and passed it to her. 'Here's my work we talked about,' he said shyly. 'From my last tour of duty.'

'Oh.' Sybil was confused. 'I thought you were going to show it to all of us at the same time.'

Iggy inched towards her. 'I changed my mind about that,' he said. 'I don't think it would be fair on Mama and Papa given the circumstances. And please don't feel you have to look either.'

Sybil was aware of his sandalwood scent and the V of tanned skin framed by his unbuttoned collar. 'That's very considerate of you,' she said.

He shrugged and blushed and looked down at the ground.

She opened to the first page and looked into the faces of three officers standing at ease, their arms around each other's shoulders. 'Your pals?' she asked.

He nodded. 'This one we call Halfpence and this one was Shorty.'

'Was?' Sybil asked gently.

'Yes.' Iggy's voice faltered and she put her hand over his for a moment. 'And what do they call you?'

'Sir,' he said, and they both threw back their heads with laughter.

The rest of the sketches were more macabre and sent a shiver of repulsion through Sybil, but she thought that if Iggy had to live through those scenes then she could force herself to view them. The final sketch was of Dom, handsome and heartbreakingly young in his uniform.

'We don't look much alike,' Iggy said, studying the drawing with her.

'I can tell you're brothers,' she said.

'I intend to compose a portrait for Mama and Papa,' he said. 'But it's going to be a slow, hard, painful process.'

She wondered if she should tell him about her self-portrait book – perhaps show him a page or two. It would unite them in sympathy. But the savagery of the war was enough to do that.

'I'm so sorry.' She handed the book back to him. 'I don't suppose those images will ever leave your mind.'

'No.' He shook his head. 'Nor will the ones of the godawful things you've seen.'

They exchanged a bittersweet smile and the spell shifted. 'Time to get on,' she said. They packed up their things and walked towards the next port of call.

Sybil decided she would go back to London when Ignatius's leave was up. Dame Lily did her best to persuade her to stay a bit longer, but Sybil was adamant she had a painting to prepare for the WAAC and her mentor eventually acquiesced. She didn't want anything to stand in the way of Sybil's success.

Dame Lily held Ignatius close on the morning of their departure. Then she turned her attention to Sybil. 'I shall be in London soon, my dear. It would be lovely to see you and your friends and perhaps view how your first final piece is coming along.'

'I'll look forward to it, Dame Lily. Thank you for making me so welcome.' It had been lovely being part of a family, but saying goodbye would have been much more difficult if she had to go back to the cold bedsit rather than the warmth and comfort of Auntie Myrtle's house.

'And as for you, young man.' Dame Lily had to stop to compose herself. 'I will hear from you very soon, I'm sure.'

Ignatius rested his head on his mother's shoulder and all Sybil heard him say was, 'Mama.'

He shook his father's hand and clapped him on the back, then they sped off.

At the station, Ignatius carried Sybil's bags and handed them into the train for her. 'You're very kind, like your parents,' she said. 'It makes me wonder how I managed on my travels without you.' She laughed but Ignatius coloured. 'Perhaps our paths will cross again sometime.'

'I certainly hope so. In the meantime,' he said, his words coming out in a rush. 'May I write to you?'

Sybil felt flustered and was aware of another blush to match his creeping up her face. 'I … I …' She couldn't think of any reason why not, although it hadn't occurred to her that their ramblings in the name of art would lead to anything more. She couldn't tell him about what had happened with Hector in Lyme Regis or her vow not to become involved in any way with another man until she was sure of Graeme's fate. But he was her friend's son – her friend, now. He knew she was married; she knew he would be thousands of miles away. So it seemed churlish not to agree. 'Of course,' she said. 'Please feel free to get my address from Dame Lily.'

'Thank you,' he said, smiling as if he'd been commended for an act of bravery. For a moment he looked at her as if he could see into the workings of her mind – or wanted to. She'd been right. Graeme had never looked at her like that. It wasn't that she'd thought he would never gaze beyond her or take his eyes off her. But now she knew that he had often looked right through her – as if she didn't exist.

14

August 1941

Artwork was spread out on every surface in Auntie Myrtle's house, with pieces pinned to the walls, the backs of chairs and cluttering the floor. 'This reminds me of Luton,' Sybil said. 'Do you still put students' work along the stairs for advice from the tutors, Blanche?'

'No,' Blanche said from another room. 'Mr Merton put paid to that practice a while ago when he discovered someone was writing comments that were less than helpful.'

'Ah,' Sybil said. 'And how is Morgan Langley?'

Ellen snorted with laughter, sheaves of drawings in her hands.

'I hardly see him.' Blanche joined them in the living room. 'And I'm not complaining. I'm away weekends with the RBP and during the week he spends most of his time with the doe-eyed Miss Edith Hopkins. She follows him around like he's the last man on earth.'

'Even if he was, you could count me out,' Ellen said. 'Now, however are we going to narrow these down?' She looked around the room, hands on her hips. The change in her was remarkable. From her hair, to the way she walked and talked, to her demeanour of quiet confidence. She was a young woman now rather than a girl, although she hadn't lost her mischievous sense of humour. 'How can we look through everything?'

'We can't possibly,' Auntie Myrtle said. 'Why don't we pick out ten from each artist that we particularly like, then keep passing them around and eliminating until we get down to the final few. From which the artist herself should have the final say.'

Sybil looked at Blanche and Ellen. 'That should work,' she said.

Everyone nodded. 'But I suppose if there's one the artist really likes to begin with,' Blanche said. 'She could overrule the other's votes.'

'The artist can do whatever she wants with her own work,' Ellen scoffed. 'Having said that, what would be the point in asking for everyone else's opinion?'

'What I'm hoping is that my judgement will be verified,' Sybil said. 'And if it isn't, I shall be asking where I've gone wrong.'

'That's all fair enough,' Auntie Myrtle said. 'Feel free to start. I'll pour the tea.'

The wireless was tuned to the Forces Programme and they sang along to 'Hey, Little Hen', during which Ellen held up a drawing of the china chicken in the café in York with the lovely waitress, Jenny, displaying her sign next to it: *The girls are laying. We have fresh eggs!* 'What a coincidence,' she said. 'What's this all about?'

Whilst they rifled through sketch after sketch, Sybil told them the story of the poultry keeper in the café who'd given her a pair of galoshes. 'They aren't very elegant,' she said. 'But they've saved me from getting soaked a number of times.'

Ellen looked more closely at the drawing, then placed it on a separate pile for further consideration. 'She looks so happy and proud of herself,' Ellen said. 'You've certainly captured that.'

'You must all have so many stories to tell,' Auntie Myrtle said. A gust of wind blew rain sideways into the window, causing Michelangelo to stir. 'Tell us about this one, Blanche.'

They all looked over at the sketch Auntie Myrtle was holding. On it, a man was pushing a roller over a football pitch as small boys clutching a ball watched from behind the white lines.

'That one was in Ampthill.' Blanche blinked as she peered at the composition. 'I was surprised the lads were still playing at the end of May and when I enquired, the groundsman said it was good for them to chase around and have fun whilst they could. So he maintained the pitch for them all year round.'

'That one is certainly worth another perusal.' Auntie Myrtle put it aside.

They worked until quite late, when Sybil said they should take a break and go out for a drink. Auntie Myrtle preferred her own sloe gin so sat with her feet up, taking in the details of every drawing she picked up.

By the following evening, each of the artists had chosen two compositions to refine. For Sybil it was the woman shovelling ashes from the furnace in Darlington, to be followed by two trainee dairymaids milking a cow. She was both pleased and apprehensive to work on her female stoker. She so wanted to do justice to the woman who'd seemed fuelled by grit and steadfastness to do the job she loved – a man's job – and do it well. Would she be able to capture the look of pluck and nerve in the woman's eye as they'd bonded through the undulating heat haze? Viewers had to see the moment as she had, or else she would start again and again until she got it right. Each in their own way, Dame Lily and Auntie Myrtle were her mentors, but the female stoker spoke to her, too – *If I can do this, so can you. But you have to be as dogged and as immovable as me.*

Blanche had chosen to polish the drawing of the groundsman and another of tethered punts bobbing lazily on the Cam. The only subjects Ellen had drawn were Land Girls and staff or patients at St Mary's and as a result, her final two were one of each.

Then Blanche returned to Luton and Ellen to St Mary's, but not before Sybil made an arrangement to visit her at the hospital the following weekend. As she and Auntie Myrtle stood at the door and waved goodbye, Sybil felt that despite the uncertainties of living through a war and of the letter from Graeme, she was lucky to have a home, lovely friends and the opportunity to establish her name in the art world. All she had to do was emulate the female stoker – work hard with persistence and dedication – and hold on to the good in her life with all her might.

She set up camp at the far end of the living room where there was adequate light from the windows. There she could feel the benefit of the fire, when it was lit, listen to the wireless and talk to Auntie Myrtle whilst the older woman sat in her chair.

First, she attempted to improve the composition with various methods of shading, honing it from the original sketch and her memory. True to the style she'd made her own, the men stoking the furnace and the background were seen as ghostly, vaporous shapes. She remembered how shocked she'd felt when the stoker had removed her protective face shield and revealed herself to be a middle-aged woman. That shock was what she wanted her viewers to feel along with the rigid determination that had been in her eyes. There couldn't be the slightest suggestion that the woman was pitiful – she had to be portrayed as strong and capable.

When she thought she'd done as much as possible at that stage, she placed a precious canvas on the easel with quivering fingers. The story of the piece would be told in her preferred shades of white, black and grey, the only colour coming from the oranges, reds, blues and yellows of the lit furnace.

Her chosen pallet beside her, she stood with her brush poised when Auntie Myrtle peered over her shoulder. 'Oh, it's that time, is it? Do you want to stop now for dinner, or shall I save yours?'

The cheese, potato and streaky bacon pie, one of Auntie Myrtle's specialities, smelled wonderful. There would be carrots or sprouts or cabbage to go with it and some sort of pudding for afters. So Sybil thought she'd better have her break now.

They sat together at a small kitchen table and Auntie Myrtle asked her how she thought she was getting on.

'Now is the dangerous time,' she said. 'I have a vision of the finished piece in my head so I could be tempted to rush it onto canvas. On the other hand, if I'm too meticulous, I could become overcautious.'

'If you make a mistake,' Auntie Myrtle said, 'or if you're not pleased with the way it's going, do you have to start again? I mean, canvases must be so expensive.'

Sybil savoured a forkful of pie and when it disappeared, she said, 'All supplies are terribly expensive, so until I'm happy I'll paint over each attempt as I did in art school. That way I can reuse the canvas.'

'Sensible girl.' Auntie Myrtle nodded her approval. 'Rice pudding? I've a bit of jam to dollop on top.'

After Auntie Myrtle washed and Sybil dried, she felt as if she could sit in an armchair and drop off to sleep. But Auntie Myrtle announced she was going out for rations and would be calling on Mrs Myers around the corner, so Sybil would have the house to herself.

Michelangelo wriggled out the door before Auntie Myrtle closed it behind her and a peaceful hush descended. She listened to the house settling, then picked up her brush and began. Her sketches were close at hand so she could refer to them and she evoked her memory of the visit to the Locomotive Works to remind herself of what she was trying to achieve. Most importantly, she told herself over and over again that it was her duty to make the composition speak for the subject – and for the times they lived in. She forgot about Graeme and his cryptic letter, Dame Lily, Dom, Auntie Myrtle, Miss Butterworth, Michelangelo and Ignatius. But she didn't forget about the war. That was prominent in her mind. Not only the obvious – fighting and bombing and fear – but those consequences, like children having to play in underground shelters, changes to train timetables, rations and lack of equipment, that crept like insidious snakes into every corner of their lives.

By the time Auntie Myrtle arrived home, four whitewashed canvases stood drying against a wall and a fifth, standing on the easel, had been satisfactorily christened.

'Did you have a productive afternoon?' Auntie Myrtle asked.

'Yes, very much so.' Sybil took Auntie Myrtle's shopping bag.

'I think I'm in a position to carry on with this attempt,' she said. 'Although that could change. Have a look any time you like. As long as you give me your honest opinion.'

Auntie Myrtle peeked at the canvas and laughed. 'There's not much to say yet, except I like that shade of grey.'

'I know the mistakes I shouldn't make,' Sybil said. 'And what I want to achieve is much clearer in my mind.'

'Good,' Auntie Myrtle said. 'But if you'd rather, we can make the spare bedroom into your studio. After all, you've been on your own for quite a time, and you might work better without me chattering and clinking teacups and turning the wireless on and off.'

Earlier, Sybil had wondered if that might be the case. Dame Lily had suggested the same thing. Perhaps she was becoming a solitary creature, in training for life as a spinster in a bedsit if she made it to the end of the war. Then she reminded herself that knowing she had Auntie Myrtle to come back to had given her the impetus to be independent when she was travelling. On reflection, she had a good balance and didn't want to change a thing.

All evening, she was up and down from her chair, swiping a dash of grey here, a dab of black there. Nothing drastic, just tiny smidgens when they sprung to mind. 'That's an interesting way to work,' Auntie Myrtle said seriously.

'That's not how I usually paint.' Sybil laughed. 'I have been known to stand in front of a canvas for hours trying to perfect a piece. But now I think I'm overexcited, starting on this first one for my commission.'

Before she settled down that night, Sybil drew a few more sketches to refer to the next day, then she tentatively turned to her self-portrait book. She studied each page, trying to see the ravaged drawings through Dame Lily's eyes. Anger, frustration, fear and helplessness shouted out to her, and Dame Lily must have thought her undisciplined and a victim of her emotions. Could the success of her burgeoning piece of work earlier today give her the confidence and control she needed to get that devastating moment down on paper? The look in the female stoker's eyes was telling her she could, and Ignatius, if he'd known about her painful dilemma, would have gently reminded her that he was in the same agonising position with his portrait of Dom.

She picked up her sketchbook and thought about where to place her pencil, then she put both back on the bedside table. She couldn't face it. Of course, she knew why the moment loomed large with importance for her, but why was she obsessed with turning it into a piece of art? It wasn't as if she would forget the scene – it was indelibly etched in her mind. And if she were able to finish it, wouldn't her suffering prove too personal and private to share with others? She didn't understand, but thought it had something to do with not fully accepting the truth – and the last letter from Graeme didn't help with that. But what she did comprehend was that until she'd completed that sketch she wouldn't start to heal.

All week she worked steadily and logically on the painting until, by Saturday, it was well underway and she hoped there would be no turning back.

That was a good point to leave it for the day and visit Ellen. Flitting around other parts of the country had made her forget how blitzed London had been, with Paddington no exception. Rubble was everywhere. Interior rooms stood empty and naked, wallpaper hanging in shreds from what was left. Sooty washing was pegged limply on lines. A scrappy Jack Russell sniffed around her ankles until a woman called him off. 'What's his name?' Sybil asked.

The woman shrugged. 'No idea. He ain't mine, but I might take him in. The kids would like him.'

Scrawny herself, the woman didn't look as if she had enough to feed her family, let alone a pet, but Sybil admired her generous heart.

Ellen was waiting for her in the foyer, dressed in her blue cotton uniform, a red embroidered *NA* sewn onto the front. A simple white apron was fixed to the dress with safety pins, and she had a little cap on her head with a partial veil floating at the back, so in a roundabout way, she was still able to wear flimsy material in her hair.

Despite her newfound decorum, Ellen threw her arms around Sybil and gave her a hug. 'I can't tell you how pleased I am to see you,' she said.

'I wasn't sure if you'd be in or out of uniform. You're not still on shift, are you?'

'I've just finished,' Ellen said. 'But I thought it would be easier to show you around if I stayed dressed up. Did you bring your permits?'

Sybil patted her oilskin bag. 'I never go anywhere without them.'

They turned down a long corridor with a low, arched ceiling that made it seem as if they were walking through a tunnel. The walls were a muddy green and looked slimy, as if they'd been painted with water from the overcooked greens whose smell pervaded the stale air around them. A few chairs were occupied by people in various states of discomfort – arms in slings, puffy ankles, patches over eyes.

'I'm not sure how to go about this,' Sybil said. 'Without being insensitive. I mean, I can't just burst onto a ward and start drawing, permit or no permit.'

'I think what we'll do is wander around and if you see something in particular you'd like to sketch, we can ask Matron and the patients involved.'

'Will you draw?' They turned a number of corners and walked up a flight of stairs. Sybil was sure she wouldn't be able to find her way out if it came to it.

'No, that wouldn't be allowed.' Ellen rolled her eyes. 'Even though I am off shift. I draw from memory. I'll show you later. This is Queen Elizabeth Ward. It's women's orthopaedics, and the matron is lovely. It's quite busy but not as rammed as it is after a hit.'

The ceiling was higher here and the windows had been opened so the ward was airy and light. The tiled floor gleamed and the white curtains around each bed were pulled back so the women could chat to each other. Matron greeted them and when they explained their mission, she said she was happy for her patients to be sketched, if agreed by the individuals. She didn't want any of them to become agitated or upset.

Sybil sketched a cheerful woman whose leg was in a sling. She told Sybil and Ellen that she'd tripped over a loose paving slab running to help her neighbour after a gas explosion. 'And your friend?' Sybil asked. 'Was she alright?'

'Not a hair harmed on her head,' the woman said. 'She's been in today looking much better than me, I can tell you. She brought me an orange she managed to get from somewhere. Would you like a segment?' She held out the most tired piece of fruit Sybil had ever seen.

'Oh my goodness.' Sybil turned to Ellen, hoping she would take charge and confiscate the shrivelled orange before it upset the patient's stomach, but all Ellen did was smile. 'I hope she didn't use too many rations on it.'

'Shouldn't think so. She probably got it from someone who …' She winked and smiled and dug her finger under the rubbery peel.

When they left the woman's bedside, Sybil said, 'Her holding out that orange as if it's a golden orb will make a good one.'

'People will talk themselves into believing anything if it keeps them going.'

Sybil nodded in agreement and wondered what Ellen would think if she knew about the fantasy ending to Graeme's letter that she'd made up and reiterated to herself many times every day.

At the end of the ward, Sybil ignored a bed with the curtain drawn around it, but Ellen crept in and motioned for Sybil to follow. In the inner sanctum, Ellen placed her hand tenderly over the patient's and whispered, 'How are you, Mrs Trentham?'

'Good afternoon, Nurse Hewitt.' The patient opened her eyes and looked at Ellen as if she were her favourite. 'I think I'm getting on alright. According to the doctors, at any rate.'

The woman's thin hair was slicked into a bun, and she was wearing a regulation nightdress. Peeking out from under the bed were a pair of slippers like those Sybil had watched being stitched in Norwich, and something about that was comforting, as if everything and everyone in the world could be joined together by a willingness to help others.

The woman tried to sit up, but Ellen gently held her down. 'You must rest and let this do its work.' She checked a bag of liquid on a pole and ran her hand down a tube to where it was inserted in the woman's arm. 'This is my friend Sybil. She's an artist,' Ellen explained.

'Oh, like you,' Mrs Trentham said.

'Much better than me. The government have asked her to make drawings of the things that women are doing during this wretched war. Can she please draw you? She'd like that very much.'

Mrs Trentham made an attempt to smooth down her hair with her free hand. 'I don't mind at all. Not if Winnie says that's what should be done. How I love that man. But,' she managed a smile, 'can you make my hair a bit more presentable? I'm terribly vain about it.'

Sybil felt tears in her eyes. 'Of course,' she said. 'I'm well-known for making my subjects look like film stars.' She captured the patient and her medical equipment from a number of angles, then she and Ellen softly said their goodbyes, even though the woman had fallen back into a twitching sleep.

'I'm glad you got that,' Ellen said. 'I think it's important as that infection-fighting medicine is going to save so many lives, now and in the years to come.'

'Will Mrs Trentham live?' Sybil asked, scared of the answer.

'Most probably. She'll be weak for quite a while, but she'll stay with us.'

'Can you let me know, please?' Sybil fidgeted with the ring on her finger.

Ellen patted Sybil on the arm but didn't commit herself and Sybil wondered how Ellen, who had seemed so young and flighty at the Marylebone, could take these kinds of sights day in and day out. She didn't think she'd be able to do it – it would break her – but thank goodness for those who could.

Sybil said that rather than sketch any more patients, she would like to capture nurses at work. Women doctors, too, if there were any. There were two. One on the maternity unit who allowed Sybil to draw her as she frantically scrubbed her hands almost raw in readiness for an emergency operation, and another who was peering into tiny ears and noses on the children's ward. Along with a few charcoals of nursing auxiliaries changing beds, a nurse wheeling a patient along a corridor and another applying pressure to an open wound, those would more than suffice.

Then Ellen said she wanted to show Sybil where she did her own drawing. She expected to be taken to Ellen's shared room in the nurses' quarters, but instead they walked down a number of stairs until they were deep in the serpentine guts of the hospital.

'Ellen.' Sybil felt a sense of foreboding. 'Are you sure …?'

Ellen smiled. 'I know my way around,' she retorted.

Sybil followed meekly behind until they came to what looked like a huge understairs cupboard, where everything that wasn't used but might desperately be needed someday was stored. Broken leg and hip bones from discarded medical skeletons; rubber tubing off stethoscopes; white coats that were no longer white; three-legged trollies; broken lamps; lopsided chairs. And pushed up into a corner was an easel and a rickety table with art supplies spread out on it. 'Ellen.' Sybil was in awe. 'You enterprising girl.'

Ellen beamed. 'There's less room in my quarters than when I shared with Blanche,' she said. 'And I was frustrated to think the only time I would be able to draw was when I visited Auntie Myrtle. Then I found this place on one of my skulks.'

'I see.' Sybil laughed out loud. 'You skulk around, do you?'

'Not all of us have permits,' Ellen said. 'Besides, artists and writers are allowed to skulk and sneak. That's how we get inspiration.'

A shaft of light filtered through the gap between buildings and found its way past the bars on the basement window. Even here there were blackouts waiting to be closed, but there was an old desk lamp on the table which Ellen turned on.

She pulled out two chairs and said Sybil was welcome to look at her sketches. Like every other aspect of her life, Ellen's artwork had matured. Gone from her pieces was the sense that the drawing had been rushed and in its place was a depth of understanding that pulled the viewer into the subject's world.

She'd captured the nurses as competent and business-like, all of their faces devoid of emotion. Not that the compositions were lacking in empathy, quite the opposite. There was intense feeling in the way a nurse took a patient's pulse or returned a teddy bear to a child's arms or handed a cup of tea to a waiting relative. 'Ellen,' she said. 'They're marvellous. You could hand over the entire contents of these books to the WAAC and I'm sure they would take them as a complete study.'

'I'm not so sure about that. And first things first, I have two that were chosen for me by you and Blanche. You must remember.'

'Of course. And they're excellent, too. But why didn't we see these?'

Ellen shrugged. 'There were too many for me to carry so I just grabbed a selection.'

'I wonder if all female artists have the myriad of drawings we've accrued. If so, can you imagine the size of the space it would take to show all of them?'

'That would be a huge exhibition,' Ellen said. 'Perhaps part of a celebration for the end of the war.'

Sybil liked the sound of those events – but who knew when either of them would happen. And although she'd been told that her artwork was important for the future as well as the present, she did wonder if by the time the war was done and dusted, they would all be so sick of it they'd never want to see or hear a reference to it again.

She turned a page and there was the poorly woman hooked up to the lifesaving drip. The patient was leaning against a pile of pillows, looking past a nurse who was checking the bag of liquid as Ellen had done earlier.

'Why were you so keen for me to draw this patient?' She turned the open book towards Ellen. 'When yours is so much better than mine.'

'The world has a better chance of seeing it if it comes from you,' Ellen said.

'Oh, Ellen.' Sybil grasped Ellen's hand. 'Nothing of mine has been accepted yet. And might never be. So we're in the same position. More or less.'

'No, we're not.' Ellen was matter of fact. 'You're about to take off. Just wait and see.' She closed her sketchbooks and tidied the table. 'Now, come and have a look at my quarters. Then it's Lyons and the pub for us.'

Life settled into a routine. It was tempting to roam around London and draw everything she saw whilst she still had her permits, but she held herself back. It was more important at this stage to have something to present to the WAAC, so she was strict with her schedule. She got up early and spent the best part of the day working on the woman and the furnace, then she would take a walk and spend a little time sitting with Auntie Myrtle in the evening.

When the canvas was finished, she tried to look at it objectively but as she felt so close to the subject, that was difficult. She strived to rework every tiny flaw that jumped out at her and in her estimation, there were quite a few, except for the look in the woman's eyes. She thought she'd captured that as she'd experienced it, so left well alone,

Then she couldn't spin it out any longer and showed it to Blanche and Ellen during one of their weekend visits. Both gasped when they saw it. They said it was breathtaking and so realistic they could feel the heat from the flames and the same tiny dots of perspiration blossoming above their own mouths as appeared on the subject's top lip. They agreed that, despite the woman's age and exhaustion, they could sense the pride and usefulness she felt in doing her job.

'And the look in her eyes.' Blanche stood back and held her chin in her palm. 'She's gazing straight at me and daring me to …'

'Question her capabilities? Be as resilient and tenacious as her?' Ellen added.

'Certainly both of those,' Sybil said. 'So, what should I do now?'

'Whatever do you mean?' Ellen asked.

'Is there anything else I should refine?'

'For goodness' sake, you must be mad,' Blanche said. 'Show it to the WAAC, silly girl.'

'That's what I told her,' Auntie Myrtle added. 'Make an appointment through Miss …'

'Butterworth.'

'… that's it. They'll bite your hand off to have it.'

Now she was where she'd longed to be, she didn't know if she was quite ready to let her painting go. She felt as if she knew the female stoker intimately and that she was too invested in her and the moment she'd captured on canvas to let the image go into the world. What if she hadn't got it quite right and the public failed to see what she had seen? Did the painting do justice to the subject and her work during two world wars? Could she have put more effort into capturing the soul of the woman? There was only one way to find out.

On the day of the presentation, Auntie Myrtle helped her wrap the painting in a couple of old blankets and Sybil took the Tube to the National. Miss Butterworth greeted her warmly and said she hoped the letter from Graeme had been good news.

'It was a dreadful shock,' Sybil said. 'And had been written before he was listed as missing in action.'

'Didn't you get the telegram I sent about the letter?' Miss Butterworth looked as if she were racking her brain to remember if she'd failed to follow her own procedures, which of course she'd never do.

'It was my own fault,' Sybil said. 'I forgot to check the post office before I left Birmingham, so I suppose it's still sitting there.'

'Oh, Sybil.' Miss Butterworth closed her eyes for a moment as if that might keep her from feeling Sybil's pain. 'I'm so sorry. Well, let's get you to the Committee on time, shall we? She showed her into a huge, echoing room where eight men and two women sat around a horseshoe-shaped table. 'Mrs Sybil Paige. Eleven-thirty,' she announced and shut the doors behind her.

It sounded as if it was a day of viewings and Sybil didn't know if that was a good or bad thing. She hoped it was early enough for the ten members not to be fed-up or that they hadn't already found a masterpiece as nothing that came after would live up to it.

'Mrs Paige,' Sir Leonard addressed his colleagues. 'Was given a six-month commission to compose pieces that depict the war work women are undertaking throughout the length and breadth of the country. It's a pleasure to meet you again, Mrs Paige. I trust your commission went well. Miss Butterworth has informed me that you travelled far and wide.'

'Thank you, Sir Leonard. I tried to make the most of the opportunity.'

'Let's have a look at your offering,' Sir Leonard said. He beckoned to two men in overalls who took the painting from Sybil, unwrapped it and placed it on an easel at the front of the room. 'Please take a seat, Mrs Paige, whilst we consider the piece.'

Sybil was pleased to sit. She crossed her legs in the hope they would stop shaking and twirled her ring around her finger.

The committee filed past the painting. They each stared at it from multiple angles and scribbled in their notebooks. Some returned for a second look, others stood well back and perused the composition from a distance. At last they took their seats again, and Sir Leonard asked if anyone wanted to start the questioning.

That made Sybil sit up with a jolt. She hadn't been expecting questions. Surely they would view the piece, talk amongst themselves, then decide if it was a yes or a no. Besides, if they had to query her, that meant she hadn't succeeded in allowing the subject to speak for herself.

She took a deep breath and girded herself for the barrage. 'Where is the subject, please?'

'The North Road Locomotive Works in Darlington.'

'Was that location on your list or did you hunt it out yourself?'

'It was on my list.'

'What attracted you to that factory and to that particular subject?'

'I visited Darlington early in my travels and thought the Locomotive Works would provide plenty of material as far as women's roles are concerned.'

'And were you correct?'

'Yes, I managed to capture a number of valuable scenes. As regards the stoker, I saw her from the corner of my eye as I was passing from one section of the factory to another. She, and her work, immediately fascinated me. It was a piece of luck that she took off her protective shield and I realised she was a middle-aged woman.'

'How did you feel at that moment?'

'Disbelieving. And disgruntled on her behalf. I thought it cruel to engage a woman of that age and stature in such onerous work. But it was explained to me that the woman had thoroughly enjoyed the hard physical labour she'd undertaken at the same plant during the Great War, and it was then I could see things from a different perspective.'

She faltered – they might not be open to hearing more. But they were watching her and waiting for what she would say next. She took a deep breath. 'I didn't think she was aware of me or what I was doing, then she looked straight at me for a heartbeat, and I knew she wanted me to capture her iron will and pass that on as a tribute to all of the work that women undertake. Since then …' She lowered her eyes to her lap. 'I've felt close to her somehow. As if we're linked or connected. I hope I managed to partially get that into the painting.'

There was silence for a few moments. A woman in a navy-blue suit blinked rapidly.

'In my humble opinion,' Sir Leonard said. 'You have portrayed all of those emotions most admirably.'

There was a murmur of consent from the committee members which made Sybil colour.

Sir Leonard carried on. 'Mrs Paige, would you be good enough to sit outside for a few minutes whilst we confer?'

'Of course.' Sybil felt her petticoat sticking to her legs as Sir Leonard showed her through the huge doors again. She had no idea of the process these presentations took, although she had imagined she would simply leave her piece and be informed of the outcome by post. But it seemed that, for her at least, the decision would be announced to her face today. The workings of her stomach boiled and bubbled first with excitement, then with apprehension and finally dropped with disappointment as she convinced herself that the conclusion for her and the piece would be negative.

The door creaked open, and one of the lady committee

members gave her a small smile and beckoned her back into the room. *She was probably chosen to lead me to slaughter instead of one of the men in order to soften the blow*, Sybil thought. All eyes were on her as she sat again. Sir Leonard coughed and said, 'As a committee we are agreed that this piece, *Woman Stoker*, is quite remarkable.'

Tiny lights flashed in front of Sybil's eyes, and for one terrible moment, she thought she might faint. But she gathered herself together and managed to say thank you with a faltering voice.

'What are you working on now, Mrs Paige?'

'*Trainee Dairymaids Milking a Cow.*'

A number of heads nodded sagely.

'How many sketches did you make during your commission?'

'Oh,' Sybil said. 'I haven't counted them. But if I said eight sketchbooks completely full, that might give you some idea.'

The committee members turned as one to look at Sir Leonard. The great man sat back, crossed his legs and tapped his pen on his chin. 'Mrs Paige, this goes against procedure, as under normal circumstances we inform artists of our decision at a later date, but I would like you to know now that the WAAC is going to purchase your painting. Terms and conditions to follow in a letter.'

Sybil gasped and nearly lost her balance. That was twice she'd almost disgraced herself.

'And if your next painting comes anywhere near the standard of this,' he gestured to the easel. 'We will purchase that, too. However, with your permission we would like to peruse your sketchbooks with a view to commissioning from those.'

Portrayed emotions most admirably; quite remarkable; the WAAC is going to purchase your painting; if the next painting is of the same standard; peruse sketchbooks for further commissions. Those select phrases whirled around Sybil's mind until she heard Sir Leonard addressing her again. 'Therefore, you will be hearing from us promptly and in the meantime, if you could please make an appointment to drop off your sketchbooks with Miss Butterworth, I would be most grateful.'

Dazed, Sybil stood and said, 'Certainly, Sir Leonard. Thank you.'

Sir Leonard looked her in the eye. 'It is we who should be thanking you. You have made wonderful use of your commission, and we are most impressed with your finished composition. Very well done indeed.'

Sybil didn't know if it was the done thing, but she went around the table, thanked each of the committee members and shook their hands. They all smiled and offered their congratulations. Out of the vast room, she headed to the ladies' restroom on wobbling legs. In the mirror, her cheeks were aflame against her pink face.

She should have felt mortified that the committee had seen her in such a state, but she wasn't. She was honoured and excited and overawed and was glad they'd witnessed her reaction to their critique of her work.

She splashed water on her face, reapplied powder to hide her freckles and thought it a pity that Dame Lily wasn't in town so they could meet at The Marquis in Chandos Place to celebrate.

But there was Miss Butterworth to see, Auntie Myrtle waiting at home with a cup of tea and a painting she'd been commissioned to get on with. That was more than enough of a celebration for now.

15

War Artists' Advisory Committee,
Ministry of Information,
The National Gallery,
Trafalgar Square,
London, W.C.2

Friday, 4th September 1942

Mrs S. Paige,
c/o Miss Myrtle Ashcroft,
78, Broxash Road,
Wandsworth,
London, S.W.11

Dear Mrs Paige,

Please find enclosed a postal order for the sum of thirty guineas for your paintings entitled:

The Remains of a German Plane
Onion Sets at a Women's Institute Meeting
A Nursery School Art Lesson
Women in a Factory Restroom
An Empty Pram
Woman with a Rescue Dog

All of the above are exceptional, and on that basis, the Committee is pleased to commission a further two. The first to be a study of the woman camouflaging a coastal defence with seaweed, and the second a painting of the women queuing for rations in London. Please contact the undersigned, Miss J. Butterworth, with regard to contracts, etc.

At this period of time, the Committee would like to offer you a further commission that will, if accepted, widen your portfolio somewhat. You are being asked to visit each city that was bombed as a part of the Baedeker raids and capture the efforts being made to clear and rebuild them after the assaults. These should encompass the work being undertaken by both men and women. The members of the committee feel that you are eminently equipped to fulfil this commission and it is our sincere hope that you will agree to this important piece of war work. Again, please inform Miss Butterworth of your decision and she will draw up contracts accordingly.

Yours sincerely,

J. Butterworth (Miss),
Personal Assistant to Sir Leonard Thwaites, CH KOB FB

Mrs S. Paige,
c/o Miss Myrtle Ashcroft,
78, Broxash Road,
Wandsworth,
London, S.W.11

Monday, 7th September 1942

Miss J. Butterworth,
Personal Assistant to Sir Leonard Thwaites, CH KOB FB,
War Artists' Advisory Committee,
Ministry of Information,
The National Gallery,
Trafalgar Square,
London, W.C.2

Dear Miss Butterworth – Jane,

I would like to thank Sir Leonard for monies received for the six most recent compositions of mine acquired by the Committee. In addition, please inform the WAAC that I accept their commission to provide a further two paintings as outlined by them.

With reference to sketching compositions relating to the Baedeker raids, I am very grateful for the opportunity and look forward to an appointment with you to read and sign contracts.

Yours sincerely,

Sybil Paige

> War Artists' Advisory Committee,
> Ministry of Information,
> The National Gallery,
> Trafalgar Square,
> London, W.C.2

> Thursday, 10th September 1942

Mrs S. Paige,
c/o Miss Myrtle Ashcroft,
78, Broxash Road,
Wandsworth,
London, S.W.11

Dear Mrs Paige – Sybil,

You are singlehandedly keeping me very busy. Please come to my office on Tuesday, 15th of September 1942 at 2 p.m. to sign contracts for your six-month commission to draw the aftereffects of the Baedeker raids. I'll make sure the kettle is on for a nice cup of tea and a chat.

Yours,

Jane

TUESDAY 15TH SEPTEMBER 1942

SENT FROM POST OFFICE HIGH STREET WANDSWORTH LONDON

PRIORITY BLANCHE NORTHCUTT

OLD MANOR HOUSE LUTON BEDS

AUNTIE M FALLEN STOP LEG BANDAGED STOP DISTRICT NURSE CALLING STOP NO NEED TO CHANGE PLANS STOP SYBIL STOP

Miss Blanche Northcutt,
Marylebone School of Art,
Old Manor House,
Luton,
Beds

Wednesday, 16th September 1942

Mrs S. Paige,
c/o Miss Myrtle Ashcroft,
78, Broxash Road,
Wandsworth,
London, S.W.11

Dearest Sybil,

Thank you very much for your telegram and the late-night telephone call to reassure me that Auntie Myrtle is indeed doing well. As you know, I was frantic with worry and on the verge of hopping on the next train home.

Since the beginning of this ****** war it has been my nightmare that something dreadful would happen to Auntie Myrtle when I wasn't with her. Every time I round that corner from the Underground, I have to hold my breath until I see the house still standing, Auntie Myrtle safe inside it. I am so glad that we made the decision for you to live with her.

I was in such a state last night that I'm not sure I understood the sequence of events. Did it happen like this? You had a two o'clock appointment to sign contracts at the WAAC after which you met Dame Lily for a drink. When you arrived home at 6 p.m., you found poor Auntie Myrtle in a heap at the bottom of the stairs. Thank goodness she didn't bump her head. What a terrible shock for both of you. You did absolutely the right thing by calling for the doctor, and it's good that the district nurse will be changing the dressing on her shin every day.

This has left me with a terrible dilemma and one that I couldn't possibly talk about in earshot of Auntie Myrtle. She would have none of it. You will soon be off again for the WAAC – very many congratulations on that score – and I, too, have been offered another commission by the RBP. This time the Committee would like me to sketch phone and pillar boxes, architectural nuances such as thatched cottages and pub signs in and around the Bedfordshire area. However, I am considering leaving my post here at the Marylebone and coming home to be with Auntie Myrtle. I don't think I could swan around the countryside with a bag full of art supplies knowing my lovely old aunt is alone for days at a time.

Although Auntie Myrtle is not your responsibility, I would appreciate a few minutes alone with you on Saturday or Sunday to discuss the future. I hope you don't mind. We could go for a walk or to the pub for privacy.

Have you heard from Ellen? I was bitterly disappointed on her behalf when her drawings were turned down yet again. I don't pretend to understand it. Her talent is exceptional, and the sketches tell the story of hospital life vividly. The only reason I can think of for the repeated rejections is that there is a plethora of the same material and the WAAC can be picky. When I see her this weekend I might advise her to present them with a painting next time instead of a sketch. That way they will be able to view her work in more detail.

Do please telephone if there are any developments I should know about. To inject a little levity into the situation, your phone call last night woke up most of the house, including Edith Hopkins, who appeared from Morgan Langley's bedroom with a head full of pincurls. What a scandal! Members of staff have talked of nothing since. Some have even nicknamed the poor girl 'Lucky' and they whisper the name with inverted commas.

Yours,

Blanche XX

P.S. Have you heard any more about when our paintings will be shipped to America for the exhibitions in New York and beyond? B. XX

Mrs S. Paige,
c/o Miss Myrtle Ashcroft,
78, Broxash Road,
Wandsworth,
London, S.W.11

Monday, 21ˢᵗ September 1942

Miss Blanche Northcutt,
Marylebone School of Art,
Old Manor House,
Luton,
Beds

Dear Blanche,

What a lovely weekend with all of us together again.

I'm so pleased we put to rights your silly idea that Auntie Myrtle isn't my responsibility. I know, as does Ellen, that's she's not my aunt by birth, but you and she have offered me a home and a family which I'm most grateful for and therefore, her well-being and safety has everything to do with me. And that's exactly how I want things to be.

So, we have two avenues to explore. You can ask the RBP to revise your contract so that you cover the same aspects but in the London area rather than Bedfordshire, or I can tear up my commission and concentrate on painting from the sketches I've already accrued. Either way, those outcomes would enable one or other of us to be with Auntie Myrtle for the most part of every day. I agree with you that, in this instance, it would be better for you to approach the RBP first with your proposal and once we have a reply, we can take things from there.

I'm so glad Ellen liked your suggestion to show a painting rather than drawings to the WAAC. How some things change! A few years ago, she wouldn't take any advice from either of us. Her time, though, might be much more constrained now that she's working towards becoming a fully trained nurse, but she certainly seems determined.

Must go, there's a knock at the door. It's probably the district nurse.

With love,

Sybil XX

Dame Lily Brampton, DBE RA ROI RWS,
Seagulls' Watch,
Cley-next-the-Sea,
Norfolk

Wednesday, 23rd September 1942

Mrs S. Paige,
c/o Miss Myrtle Ashcroft,
78, Broxash Road,
Wandsworth,
London, S.W.11

My dear,
I simply cannot keep up with you. Have you read the reviews of the latest WAAC exhibition? From *The Times* to

the *Daily Sketch* to *The Spectator*, it's all Sybil Paige this and Sybil Paige that. Needless to say, I am delighted for you and always held the strongest belief that you would get to this point.

Congratulations are in order, too, on your latest commission. I have no doubt you will fulfil it commendably. Unhappily, we know that Norwich is on your list of places visited by the ****** Jerries in the Baedeker raids, so I insist you come and stay with us whilst in the Fine City.

I wait for the post every day, hoping there will be something from Dom to indicate that he is alive somewhere in the world. I know you would tell me if you had, but I can't help asking if you've heard again from Graeme? If you received something from him written after his official missing-in-action date, it would give me tremendous hope.

I'm not sure if you've been informed, but the ship with a curated selection of our paintings in its hold is sailing tomorrow for New York. It's very exciting, but such a pity that we can't accompany them.

I'm in London next week. How about a farewell drink at The Marquis on Wednesday 30th September at 6 p.m.? As always, your friends are welcome to join us.

With love,

Lily X

7709567 Capt. Fortescue, I.G.,
2nd Battalion,
Royal Norfolk Regiment,
c/o APO England

Friday, 25th September 1942

Mrs S. Paige,
c/o Miss Myrtle Ashcroft,
78, Broxash Road,
Wandsworth,
London, S.W.11

Dear Sybil,

Thank you for your newsy letter. You're doing remarkably well with your art career, and I wish you continued success.

You asked if I've had opportunities to draw during my current posting. There are always chances and moments to be seized, but other than sketching Dom, I haven't put pencil or charcoal to paper since I was last on leave. I know Mama told you I want to follow in her and Papa's footsteps, and that was true during one period of my life, but since I've been away with the Army I think I've changed my mind. Believe it or not, I now use any free moments to sit in silence and think, and my thoughts seem to lead me in one of two directions. I either turn completely inward and concentrate on me and my innermost feelings, or I contemplate the wider world and the universe from a philosophical point of view. There doesn't seem to be anything in between.

But one thing connects the inner and the outer for me and that is medicine. Initially, I was rather perturbed to think I was drawn to that profession as an homage to Dom, and whilst that might be partially true, it is the one job in which I can see myself helping others and making a difference. What is your opinion?

I hope you don't mind me writing to you about such things, but at this stage I don't think it would be wise to talk to my mother or father. They are much too burdened with worry and grief, and I don't want to add to their disquiet.

What I'm gazing at now is the full moon. When it's visible on a clear night like tonight, it looks as though it's suspended just above our heads. It's starkly white and makes me think of doves and peace, and I wish you could see it, paint it and share it with the world.

Yours,

Iggy

Mrs S. Paige,
c/o Miss Myrtle Ashcroft,
78, Broxash Road,
Wandsworth,
London, S.W.11

Saturday, 3rd October 1942

7709567 Capt. Fortescue, I.G.,
2nd Battalion,
Royal Norfolk Regiment,
c/o APO England

Dear Ignatius,

It was lovely to receive your letter yesterday. I can picture you in a rare quiet moment, gazing up at the moon and thinking about your future. How I would love to see the view from your where you are. Perhaps you could sketch it for me and enclose it in your next letter?

Things have been hectic here. In a nutshell, I have been offered another WAAC commission that involves travelling so I shall soon be packing up and boarding another train. I must admit that, whilst I was glad to put down roots at home for a few months, I have missed wending my way around the country. One never knows whom one might meet, and I met many wonderful characters who have left a lasting impression on me. During the days I'm too busy to think deeply, which is a relief, but at night when I'm alone in my B&B, my thoughts, like yours, become overbearingly insular. When I try to turn them towards the wider world, I'm stopped in my tracks by the thought that, because of this ****** war, none of us knows what the future holds.

I don't think you should be at all uneasy that your idea about becoming a doctor might have grown out of your grief for Dominic. If that is the case, I think he would be immensely honoured. It was very kind of you to ask my opinion, although I can't possibly have much say in the matter. But for what it's worth, if it's what you feel passionate about, then I think it's a marvellous ambition. Whilst I understand your apprehension about broaching the subject with your parents, I don't think you have anything to worry about. I think they will be immensely proud of you whatever you do. You can rest assured that I won't betray your confidence by sharing the contents of your letter with Dame Lily.

Yours,

Sybil

P.S. When you next write, please use my previous address – c/o Miss J. Butterworth. S.

16

November 1942

The Baedeker raids had finished in May, but the same bombing campaign continued under different names. Canterbury took it twice in June with forty-five people dead and a similar number injured. Houses, shops, the Corn Exchange, the bus depot, churches, schools and the City Market were destroyed. Then the Luftwaffe paid them another call a couple of days before Sybil arrived and targeted anything left standing.

Ready with her permits, she started to draw the minute she alighted from the train. Men stood and stared at mountains of rubble that would have to be picked through and moved and rebuilt. As she sketched, one man who was dressed as if for work in a hat, three-piece suit and tie turned with a lost look in his eyes that stabbed her through the heart. There was at least an inch of dust on his shoulders and shoes. He turned back to the bomb site, his arms hanging helplessly at his sides, then made his way towards her.

Sybil snapped her sketchbook closed, held out her hand and introduced herself. The man nodded and seemed to take in the information, but he remained dazed. 'Did this happen last Saturday?' she asked in a soft tone of voice.

The man moved his head up and down slowly, as if he wasn't sure. 'Yes,' he said. 'I think so. What's today?'

'Monday,' she said. 'Do you need some help? I think you might be in shock.'

'It seems unlikely that anyone could help me. My shop's under there.' He pointed with his chin to somewhere in the middle of the mess. 'And my wife and kiddies were in the flat that used to be above it.'

'I am so very sorry,' Sybil said, touching his sleeve.

He closed his eyes for a moment. 'I'd had cross words with Mildred, about me going to the pub. She'd wanted me to stay home for once and how I wish I had.'

'Please accept my—'

'Excuse me,' the man interrupted her as if there was absolutely nothing she could say to comfort him. 'I have to get on with my digging.' Then he stabbed violently at her sketchbook with his finger. 'Get it all down,' he snarled. 'Every single disgusting, pathetic detail. And shove it in their faces.'

When he turned his back, Sybil picked up her pencil with shaking fingers. She quickly finished her sketch and drew another of the man's face in close-up, spittle flecking his lips, rage contorting his face, bitterness in his eyes.

Finding somewhere to stay was difficult, but at last she found a room in a pub on the outskirts of town where the bomb damage wasn't as bad. She should have hurried back out to take advantage of the light, but she sat on the lumpy bed and gazed out of the window. Rows of vegetables had been planted in the pub garden, and beyond that, smoke spiralled towards the sky in sad, grey swirls. In a sickening lurch, her stomach flipped at the thought that the German planes could return that night. But she reminded herself that Jerry could hit anywhere at any time. Tonight would be no different from every other in that respect.

She curled up on the bed, pillows behind her, and thought about the man she'd sketched earlier. How he must loathe himself for having argued with his wife about something as trivial as going to the pub. So many people were in the same position of telling themselves that their last minutes with their loved ones would have been different – if only they'd known that was going to be the last time they'd see them.

She harboured regrets for the way she'd handled herself with Hector, although no one would ever know about that except her, and she hoped she wouldn't lament the day she'd made the decision to take the commission instead of looking after Auntie Myrtle. Most of all, she felt remorse for her time with Graeme. For the fact that she hadn't asked him to tell her the truth about why he was so anxious to leave; that now he was lost to her forever whether he returned alive or not. And the continuing regret of being unable to capture herself in the terrible throes of her own story.

She thought about the bereaved man again, and whilst she'd been alarmed at his sudden aggression, she'd handled the situation much more confidently than she would have done a year or so ago. With that in mind, she spread out her art supplies and took up the self-portrait sketchbook. Calmly this time, she turned over the pages and studied each picture she'd tried to destroy. She'd obliterated her face in every one, but the telegram was there, hanging from her hand. Perhaps if she left her face vacant and lifeless and completed the rest of the scene first, she might be able to make some semblance of a whole and keep going with it to completion.

Determined to remain business-like, she drafted a blank oval and worked her way down to her dress and legs, the chair, her arms and the telegram. Then it hit her that the portrait was of her – not a subject she'd met on the street or in a factory who, no matter how much sympathy she felt for them, she could walk away from and leave behind. She had to carry this woman around with her forever and the burden was heavy. Still composed, she drew thick lines across the page and closed the book. Tears started then, and after she'd roughly brushed them away, she picked up her things and headed back to the centre of town.

That afternoon she drew a group of women handing out clothes, cups of tea and plates of stew to people who'd been bombed out. She found the cathedral and sketched it as it stood like an oasis amidst fragments of wood and the ruins of concrete. Cathedrals were the main targets of Baedeker raids, but the Jerries had missed this one. Something about that gave her hope – they must be getting tired or scared to leave such an easy target standing.

Despite being completely boarded up, a café advertised that it was open for business, and she wandered around looking for an entrance. 'Over there, love.' A man cleaning a window pointed to an alley that ran around the back.

'Oh yes, I can see it now,' Sybil said. 'Thank you.'

The workman nodded and resumed his task, whistling thinly through his teeth.

'May I draw you?' Sybil shouted. 'It's my war work.'

'Of course, my duck. But I'm no oil painting, and my job isn't worth writing home about.'

Sybil laughed. 'Neither of those things matter,' she said. 'I'll just sketch whilst you carry on.'

Every time the man banged a nail into a plank of wood, the note of his whistle sounded driven by the force. This time Sybil recognised the tune as 'Jingle Jangle Jingle' and it made her smile.

'You don't see many of those around here at the minute,' the man called down to her.

'What, sketchbooks?'

'No, smiles.'

'And you don't hear many people whistling such a jolly tune.'

'I have a lot of bad habits and two good ones,' he said. 'And they're keeping busy and keeping cheerful.' He rinsed his cloth in a bucket and looked at her. 'But whistling seems a bit irreverent now, so I keep stopping myself.'

'I think it's lovely, and I'm sure most people would say the same.'

'Things can't stand still,' the workman said. 'They have to move on or, if that's not possible, at least tick over.'

Sybil thought about the man who'd lost everything and wondered what he would say to that. He might find it a comfort to see some parts of the life he'd known carry on regardless, or it might make him senseless with frustration. But she knew in her heart that all he really wanted was to go back in time so he could have been annihilated with his wife and children.

The café was serving a reduced menu, but the powdered egg omelette and toast were good. When she was down to the last crust, she noticed that it was speckled with mould, but she was hungry, so she ate it regardless.

At the end of five days, she felt she'd captured every nuance of life in Canterbury after their share of the Baedeker raids and made her way to Bath.

On the train, she looked through her full sketchbook and wondered how she could possibly find anything different to sketch in each of the cities that had been bombarded in the same way.

Despite trying hard not to become cynical or world-weary, she felt as if that way of thinking was creeping up on her. Rubble and broken glass, craters in the ground, small homes and mighty edifices broken as if they were matchsticks. Shocked, grieving people. If Dame Lily could read her thoughts from afar, she would be appalled. *'Are you forgetting, my dear? We don't want to see the same old story over and over again. We want to see the personal stories of the people involved. That is your job.'* So, capturing the look on the face of someone in shock or viewing scenes through the eyes of those affected – that was where the differences came in.

She'd never been to Bath, but knew it was a lovely old Georgian town with ancient Roman baths still in working order. If anything, on first sight it looked as though the city had taken it worse than Canterbury, if that were possible. But she immediately quashed her cynicism *Statistically speaking that might be true*, she thought. *But in reality, a single bomb is one too many.*

She looked in awe at the abbey, again relatively unscathed. A bomb had fallen close by and as a result, the Great East Window had been badly damaged. As she sketched the scene, two women picked through the rubble close by and put little things they found into a shopping bag. 'Hello,' Sybil called out to them.

They looked up and nodded, then turned back to their search.

She made her way over the bomb site towards them. 'What a pity that magnificent window wasn't boarded up.'

One of the women, a thin scarf tied under her chin, stood and looked at her. 'You're not from around here, are you? Else you'd know the answer to that.'

'No, I'm a war artist from London on official business.'

The other woman stopped rummaging and joined her friend in staring at Sybil. 'Oh, I say. Well, I suppose someone's got to do it.'

'There are quite a few of us,' Sybil defended her colleagues.

'First one I've seen. You too, Gertie. So I reckon.'

'That's right, Maggie,' Gertie said.

'It's good to meet you.' Sybil held out her hand.

'No', Gertie said. 'We're much too grubby to shake.'

'If you don't mind me asking, why weren't the windows boarded?'

'Well,' Maggie started. 'Some call it foolhardy. Others, complacency.'

Sybil was not expecting that response. 'Really?' she said.

'The only hits we'd taken before these,' Gertie continued, 'were from the wicked Jerries losing their bearings on their way to Bristol.'

Sybil knew that city had taken it many times over.

'Besides, we never thought we had anything much they wanted.'

'All we've got – or had,' Maggie said, 'is old buildings and such like.' Tears made her eyes cloudy. 'Turns out that's exactly what they came for.'

'But they didn't get all of them, as you can see.' Gertie pointed to the abbey. 'And some of the Crescent is still standing.'

'Along with parts of Queen Square and the Francis Hotel,' Maggie said. 'But they burned out the Assembly Rooms. My cousin's husband has just come back from London, and he overheard someone on the Tube say that it's about time other cities took it so they would know we were in the middle of a war. Don't you think that's a wicked thing to say?'

The intensity of cynicism in that remark reassured Sybil that she was not jaded just yet. 'Yes, I do,' Sybil said. 'It's awful. We're all in this together. If it's not too painful, can you tell me a little bit more about the raids? You know, your feelings and so forth.'

The two women looked at each other. 'Probably much the same as yours when bombs have fallen near you.'

Sybil knew only too well the visceral sparks that ran up and down her arms, legs and spine whenever she heard a blast. The way her stomach seemed to drop and then rise in a nauseous wave. Then the command – move – from brain to legs and the frantic search for the nearest shelter. They each might have a different means of coping on the outside, but inwardly their bodies reacted in the same way.

'We're neighbours.' Maggie and Gertie nodded towards each other. 'Both our homes went sky high and when they came down that was them done for.'

'You were displaced then,' Sybil said. 'Have you somewhere to go now?'

'We're together in a room not far from here.' Maggie pointed to the left. 'It's not so bad.'

'Not as horrible as when we slept outside for a few nights.'

'Oh.' Sybil was taken aback. 'I didn't realise that happened.'

'In the countryside,' Gertie said. 'Thousands did the same. If the city was being bombed, we thought we'd be safe there.'

'Would you like to draw our camp?' Maggie sounded excited. 'It's still there, as far as I know and it's not all that far.'

Sybil's eyes widened. 'If you don't mind,' she said. 'That would be most helpful.'

They slogged along through country lanes and thickets. Every time they came to a wooded area, the evidence of people having eaten and slept under trees and next to hedges appeared. Sybil nearly lost her footing a couple of times as she jotted down as many details as possible. It must have been terrible lying on the cold, hard ground hearing the Luftwaffe overhead and wondering what the place you called home would look like when you crept back to it the following morning. The landscape would have looked very different last Spring, too. Daffodils and crocuses nodding their colourful heads. But she doubted the people of Bath would have been bothered if they'd squashed any number of flowers as they laid down their exhausted heads.

'Here we are,' Maggie said. She sounded proud and disbelieving at the same time. A sheet was attached to a large tree trunk with thumb tacks. 'It's just the same.'

The women lifted the sides of the sheet, peered into what had been their den and started to giggle. 'Oh my goodness,' Gertie said. 'That old cushion is alive with crawling things.'

'It was probably like that whilst we were here, but we were too preoccupied to notice.'

The thought made Gertie shiver.

Sybil sat on a log and drew Maggie and Gertie as they inspected their camp. They dragged their feet across the earth to level it and shook the covering before pulling it back over the space. Then they sat inside, hugging their knees to their chins, both lost in their own thoughts.

'Would you sleep out here again?' Sybil asked.

'If the warning sounds,' Maggie said. 'Then we'll have to.'

As they walked back, Gertie and Maggie discussed what they were going to have for tea and decided on crumpets they would toast over the fire, if they could get the flour. 'We have to walk past our old road to get to the shops,' Maggie said. 'Shall we show you where we used to live?'

Sybil thought she could dedicate an entire sketchbook to these two women. 'You're very kind,' she said. 'I'd like that, if it's not an inconvenience.'

'We're having a lovely time, aren't we, Maggie?' Gertie said.

Gertie nodded. 'It's a welcome change.'

They turned down a damaged street, clogged with debris and passed pile after pile of what used to be houses and shops. 'Here we are,' Gertie said. She stopped at a mountain of bricks and mortar no different from the others, except this one had a small, ragged Union Jack hanging from the remains of a window frame. As they watched, a breeze stirred, and it fluttered from side to side. Sybil couldn't remember the last time she'd seen such a heartwarming sight. Tears flooded her eyes. 'Did you put this up?'

Maggie and Gertie nodded.

What better symbol to display the hearts of these two friends, Sybil thought. And of Bath and the whole country. She sketched a drawing of Gertie and Maggie on either side of the flag and another of the standard alone, holding on with all its might amidst the ruins around it.

Sybil shuddered when the train terminated in Exeter. She picked up her belongings and thought about being so close in proximity to Hector – if he happened to stray over the county line from St Ives. That was much too close for her liking. Absurd as it seemed, she was petrified of bumping into him. If she did, she would have to make some lame excuse and get away as quickly as possible. Because of that, and Exeter having gotten off lightly in comparison, Sybil decided to cut her visit short. She would stay one night and wouldn't allow herself to get waylaid by friendly eyewitnesses, eager to share their experiences of the dreadful nights they'd lived through.

How wrong she'd been in her assumption that Exeter hadn't taken it badly. She sketched the centre of the city, which had suffered the brunt of the attacks, and walked along what used to be Sidwell Street. At the bottom end, she came across a church with nothing left standing except the tower. It looked both magnificent and desolate at the same time. Onlookers stood around whilst workmen crawled all over the site, measuring, moving rubble, consulting blueprints. 'Stand back, Miss,' one of them addressed her. He had a rope in his hands to cordon off the area.

'I have permission,' she said.

'Permission to be this close to something so hazardous? I don't think so.'

She flashed her documents, and he scratched his head.

'And you want to make a picture of us tearing down the tower, do you?'

'If that's what's about to happen,' she said. 'It would be perfect for my commission.'

'I'll have to refer this to the man in charge. But please, for now, don't step past the rope.'

If the foreman banned her from the site despite the permits, Sybil supposed she could get a reasonable view from where she was, but she hoped he would give her the thumbs-up. 'If it were left to me, you'd stay where you are,' the returning workman said. He lifted the cordon, and she scuttled underneath. 'But the gaffer says you're in.'

'Thank you for your help,' Sybil said. As she walked around the site, narrowed eyes followed her suspiciously, but no one challenged her. She captured the one intact bell as it was lifted and placed in a straw-filled box, ropes being attached to the tower to raze it to the ground.

Since her first commission, most of her artwork had been centred on women, and drawing men again was very different but not unpleasant. Although all the women she'd met were steely, the lines she used to draw them were soft and flowing. For men, the outlines were harsher and more severe. It was only when she got closer, as she had to the bereaved man in Canterbury, that she saw the same chink of vulnerability in their eyes.

Then everyone was asked to move well back. A hush fell on the site, bulldozers hit the tower at the same time as the ropes were pulled and the Gothic-style masterpiece, which had stood for over a hundred years, crumpled to the ground. She thought the workmen might cheer because they'd done their job without any casualties. Instead, both they and the crowd gasped and grumbled with regret for another fallen landmark. 'Will another church be built?' she asked a man next to her.

'Not today,' he said.

She laughed at that. 'Perhaps in the future.'

'Hard to say. We've houses to rebuild first and we can barely keep up with that. Have you been to Hoopern Fields? There's a bomb crater there which I don't think can ever be filled in.'

Following the vague directions she'd been given, she found her way to Hoopern where she stood with a number of other people and gawped at the almighty hole in the ground. Unlike the church, the site wasn't roped off and Sybil walked right to the edge and looked down into the depths. Then she felt spooked and took a step back. If that bomb had fallen in a built-up area, the entire city and its population would have caved in with it. Then it dawned on her that the same amount of devastation had been hewn deep into the city, and many others, but the ruins had toppled into the pits and disguised them. She imagined the entire earth dented and hollowed and for a moment she felt giddy. Quickly, she drafted what she could see, the crater mysterious and foreboding with the skyline of the battered city in the background.

What had been the elegant Bedford Circus was gone as was the City Library. She walked around the remains of the Vicar's Choral Hall and startled a young couple cuddled together in a corner of what was left of the masonry. They forced themselves apart and looked at her with wide eyes, afraid of her reaction. But all she did was turn her back and walk away, hoping they would enjoy whatever they got up to. Later, she'd sketch the scene in her sketchbook.

As she walked back to her lodgings, she wondered whether or not she would feel the same passion for Graeme, if he came back, as that couple very obviously felt for each other. Perhaps she would if he lived and if he told her why he'd wanted to leave in such a hurry and if he finished the explanation he'd started in his letter. All those ifs and a few more besides made her think that no, the fervour she'd felt for and with Graeme had gone. That didn't mean she wouldn't live with him should he return – she might have to – or marry someone else if he didn't, but she couldn't imagine ever again reaching the same level of devotion and excitement she'd felt with her husband for such a short period of time. Or maybe she wouldn't allow herself to do so. She would have to think carefully about letting herself get deeply involved with anyone in the future. The pros and cons would have to be weighed up. She would have the difficult job of vetting them and wondering if their feelings for her were legitimate, or if she were being used, however unconsciously, to plaster over holes in the other person's life. And she'd have to delve into her own motives, too. Perhaps she could be a free spirit, like so many artists were. Loving and leaving and moving on to the next whilst holding onto art as their primary love affair. Maybe that was what she had envisaged for her night with Hector, and she could feel her face reddening as she thought about how that had turned out.

She was pleased to leave Exeter and board the train to York the following morning. It almost felt as if she were returning to somewhere that had once been home. She knew there would be huge changes and that they would tear her apart, but she hoped what made the city distinct and recognisable stood undamaged.

She wanted to know if the girls were still laying and she would pop into the café, wearing her overshoes to show Jenny Chapman how useful they were. There might be an egg up for grabs, too, and her mouth watered when she thought she would have hers fried again.

Rain had hammered her window during the night, and she'd

thought for too long about Maggie and Gertie and the thousands of others who'd braved the elements during the frightening bombing raids, so it didn't take much for her eyes to close. Weak winter sun warmed the carriage, and she listened to fragments of conversation about knitting and babies and recipes as she slipped into sleep. When images of bomb sites and church towers and lovers in a clinch filled her head, she thought her fellow passengers' lives seemed simple in comparison to hers, and hers was not bad compared to others.

The railway network seemed to have been the Luftwaffe target in York. But despite that, the station was running remarkably well around the clean-up operation. Women in overalls with knotted scarves on their heads swept never-ending piles of dust from the platforms, and passengers were advised to make their way to the tearoom which had been turned into a temporary ticket office. Sybil found a quiet corner and sketched what she saw around her. From her previous visit, she remembered a lovely glass roof. She'd thought the light filtering through it was sublime. Now it had been replaced by wooden boards which left the station dark and ominous, but safe.

She felt lucky to find a room in the Minster Hotel where she again dropped her bags and headed out. Her hope that the city might be more or less unchanged didn't come to fruition. It was in the same sorry state as the others targeted by the raids. Strangely, the cathedral stood like the others, but perhaps here it was because the Jerries had been after industry instead of culture.

There weren't many *Dig for Victory*! signs left, but gardens and allotments not covered in rubble were still abundant with vegetables. Teetering on the cobbles, she found the café and was cheered by the tinkle of the bell over the door. It was busy, but not packed as it had been last time, and right away, she saw Jenny, her back to the counter. 'Won't keep you a moment,' Jenny said, a loaf of bread in her hand.

When she turned, she said,' I hope you haven't come for eggs. I'm afraid there won't be any more.' For a beat, a puzzled look crossed her face, then Sybil pointed to her overshoes and Jenny's eyes widened. 'Sybil,' she said. 'That is right, isn't it? How lovely to see you.'

Jenny came out from behind the counter and the two women hugged. 'I've thought of you so many times,' she said.

'I have you, too. You were the first person I thought of when I heard about your terrible raids,' Sybil said. 'I was almost afraid to seek you out for fear of what I might or might not find.'

Jenny lowered her voice to a whisper. 'Come out the back. I have something to show you.'

The kitchen was small and cluttered. The oven door stood open which made the space feel cosy and the smell of toast and buns was distracting. Jenny moved a few things around and there, half hidden, was a bowl of fresh eggs.

'I thought you said you didn't have …'

'Shh,' Jenny said. 'We keep them for special customers. Fried?'

Sybil couldn't believe her luck and although every bit of her longed for one, she did her best to be noble. 'So the girls are still laying,' she said. 'But save them for children or the infirm.'

Jenny shook her head. 'I'm only allowed to keep the eggs that me and Henry will eat. Do you know where the rest go now? To Rowntree's where they're manufacturing tins of powdered egg. So you might as well get the benefit of what would be considered contraband.'

Sybil wasn't sure if that was quite the case, but understood the argument so watched as Jenny dropped a couple into spitting fat and toasted two slices of bread.

Another waitress who bustled in and out must have been in on the secret because she didn't turn a hair. 'Mr Williamson is in,' she said. 'And he'll have his usual scrambled, please. I'll sit him at the back.'

Jenny set another pan on the stove. 'The people we give the fresh eggs to are specially chosen,' she said. 'They might be sick or missing someone or lonely.' She turned to Sybil and winked. 'So we're still doing our bit.'

'But I'm none of those,' Sybil said, knowing she hadn't spoken with Jenny about her circumstances.

Jenny looked at Sybil for a moment too long, then softly said she thought Sybil was at least one of those. That helped Sybil feel easier about tucking in when the plate was put in front of her, but she also wondered what it was about her demeanour that gave her away. She wasn't ill. Hungry and tired like everyone else, but she was well and grateful to be so. Was she missing Graeme? Not from her life as it was now. She was grieving for him or for the promise of what they might have had were it not for the war and the ghostly shadow of Heather. There were others she did miss, though, with desperation. Auntie Myrtle; Blanche; Ellen; Dame Lily. And snippets of concern would come into her head day and night about the female stoker, the firewatching sisters, the angry man. As they'd done about Jenny. Maybe the fact that she was here, seeking out the company of a woman she'd had such a short interaction with eighteen months ago was what made Jenny think she was lonely. For a beat she recognised the loneliness in herself and a forkful of egg and toast stuck to the lump in her throat. She swallowed a mouthful of tea to dislodge it and with it disappeared the moment of self-pity.

'Are you still on the same commission?' Jenny asked. She looked very pleased with herself as she watched Sybil eat.

'No,' Sybil said. 'Some of my paintings were accepted, and I was given a new contract to log the aftermath of the Baedeker raids.'

Jenny shook her head as she wiped the draining board. 'Well, I can tell you all about how those went, here in York at any rate.'

'Yes, please,' Sybil said. 'So far I've seen the devastation in Canterbury, Exeter and Bath and I suppose dear old York has been left in the same situation.'

'We certainly took our fair share here. We were expecting it, because the news said the Jerries were after old buildings and such like. But what with the industry around here we took a double whammy. Still, it caught us unawares. By the time the sirens started, they were on top of us, so we didn't get much of a warning at all.'

'It must have been very frightening for you.' Sybil put her hand on Jenny's.

'Oh, you should have heard the dogs and hens. Barking and squawking and running around in circles. Me and Henry ran outside in our dressing gowns and the sky was lit up like the inside of a theatre and what a horrible show it was.' The bell tinkled and Jenny hopped off her chair. 'One minute,' she said.

Sybil sighed long and deep and felt as if she hadn't been so full for months. She washed her plate and cutlery in the sink along with anything else that had been lying around.

'You needn't have done that,' Jenny said when she returned with an order in her hand. 'But thanks very much. No eggs for this one,' she said. 'She's as fit and healthy as they come. I'll make you another cup of tea in a minute.'

'Do you want to carry on with your story or is it too painful?'

Jenny looked surprised. 'No, I don't mind telling you. Everyone talks about it over and over again.'

Sybil sat and watched Jenny fry two slices of Spam.

'The planes were so low,' Jenny continued. 'That we could see the pilots. I know lots of people say that, but it really was true. I'd like to say they were all ugly buggers, but most of them looked young and handsome. Each of them someone's husband or son.' She looked into the distance as if she were seeing those faces again. 'So sad. Then they dive-bombed the city and strafed it with machine gun fire. It came thick and fast, and no one could have run from it.'

They were quiet for a few moments. Jenny put the Spam sandwich on a plate and handed it through to the other waitress. 'It didn't go on for long,' she said. 'But by God, when it was over. The railways were a mess. One of Rowntree's warehouses took a direct hit. Coney Street, the lovely old Guildhall, Burton Stone housing estate, all gone. Twenty rest centres had to be opened and three of them closed soon after because they were unsafe. But do you know.' Her face lit up. 'The station was open again the next day. We're all proud of that,' she said.

'You should be. That's remarkable.'

'Is that the kind of thing you can get down in a picture?'

'I'd certainly like to try,' Sybil said.

'I'm not telling you how to do your job or anything, but you should pay a visit to the powdered egg factory. I know it's nothing to do with the raids, but it's really something to think the whole world is eating that rather than the real thing.'

'Except for me.' Sybil patted her stomach.

'And one or two others.' Jenny winked again.

'Any other tips for me?'

'The Guildhall, definitely. And Betty's.'

'Isn't that your rival?'

'Not really. This is a café and that's a teashop. Canadian airmen from RAF Linton-on-Ouse go into the basement Oak Room and etch their names into the mirror with a special pen.'

Sybil liked the sound of that, although it didn't quite meet her commission. But it was another slice of history that someone should document, and that person might as well be her.

The assembly lines at Rowntree's were much as they had been when the women were producing packets of Ryvita. They wore the same hair nets and had the same looks of deep concentration on their faces. Despite that, Sybil sketched several charcoals of the eggs being spray dried whilst she listened to a monologue of the entire process from a supervisor. 'The powder contains the whole egg. One tin is equivalent to twelve fresh eggs and keeps for five to ten years in a cool place. War or no war, who wouldn't choose powdered?'

Sybil smiled politely. *Me for one*, she thought, the fresh ones she'd eaten emitting a warm glow in her stomach.

She drew images of the Guildhall and a woman in a rest centre tending to a toddler who'd tripped over a pile of timber and gouged her knee. The wound looked sore and inflamed, and

Sybil hoped he'd be able to get some of the new medicine to fight infection if he needed it.

It was early evening by the time she got to Betty's. When she climbed down the stairs to the Oak Room, she could not believe her eyes. The cake counter had been replaced by a bar and every table was crammed with Canadian Air-Force men languishing as if they'd strolled in from their homes in Calgary or Montreal or Toronto. Amongst them were local women drinking, eating, jigging about to band music and having the time of their lives. Sybil stood and gawped and was gawped at in return. 'Are you meeting someone, love?' a waitress asked.

Sybil shook her head and produced her permits. 'I was going to ask for a quiet spot to sit in and observe, but I don't think that will be possible here.'

'No.' The waitress laughed. 'You won't find quiet in the Dive.'

Sybil looked around at the name on the door. 'Am I not in the Oak Room?'

'Officially, but the guys – as they call themselves – have renamed it. I could find you a chair and put you in that corner over there?' The waitress pointed to a dark, shadowy alcove.

'That would have been perfect, but it's a bit too dark,' Sybil said. 'How about just there, against the back wall.'

'I'll fetch the chair and a menu.'

As she manoeuvred through the crowds with her oilskin bag and overshoes, she felt her face colour. Every set of eyes was on her – not in a hard, lewd way but with appreciation. Yet it was unnerving, and more than once she imagined herself dropping her belongings or coming a cropper and taking a spin across the tiled floor. When she at last made it to her place, she was relieved to take off the scarf prickling her neck and try to blend into the wall.

Gradually the novelty of a new girl in the bar wore off, and she was able to take a good look around. Most of the Canadians were much taller and broader than their British counterparts. They had clean, fresh faces, neat hair and nails and a way of sitting that made them look as if they couldn't care less about the manly appearance they exuded. Sybil ordered a cup of tea and a plate of chips and retrieved her sketchbook and pencils from her bag. That caused another onslaught of stares, but she kept her head down and got on with it.

'Hey,' a soft voice said. 'I'm Larry. Corporal Larry McEnnis.'

Sybil looked up to see a young man with bright blue eyes and vivid white teeth smiling at her. 'My buddies and me,' he gestured to a table with five uniformed men sitting around it, 'were wondering what you're up to. Mind if I join you?'

She'd heard about North American servicemen and wouldn't have been surprised if they'd drawn lots to chat her up. She reminded herself that she had important war work to do and that she'd vowed never to get involved in another ill-judged encounter. But having thought all that, she said, 'Yes, of course.' Then tinkered with the ring on her finger so he would see it before she turned back to her sketch.

Larry pulled up a chair, crossed his legs and studied her sketchbook. 'Drawing,' he said with a drawl. 'That's a nice hobby.'

Sybil hoped to send him packing with a withering look. 'I'm a commissioned war artist and I'm on duty,' she said.

He looked as though someone had got hold of his trousers and pulled them up with all their might. When he fidgeted on his seat, she felt sorry for answering him so harshly. 'Is it one of your hobbies?' She tried to redeem herself with the question.

Larry shook his head. 'I'm not that clever or talented,' he said. 'But my sister back in Winnipeg is very arty. What did you say your name is? She might have heard of you.'

'My name's Sybil Paige and I doubt that very much,' she said. 'What does your sister like to draw?'

'Trees, flowers, birds. She drew a picture of our mom for me before I came away and it's a really good likeness.' He pulled a folded piece of paper from his pocket and put it down in front of her. The middle-aged woman in the pencilled portrait wore her hair in a twist and an apron was tied over her dress. 'It's lovely,' Sybil said. 'I'm sure you treasure it.'

'I do,' Larry said. He smiled at the drawing before putting it away.

'Would you like me to draw one of you to send back to your mom?'

For one awful minute tears glazed Larry's eyes and Sybil didn't know what she would do if he started to cry. Then he quickly gathered himself together and nodded. 'Yes, please. I'd appreciate that.'

When she handed it to him, he considered it for a few moments. 'Mom would send you a very big thank you if she could,' he said when he'd nestled the sketch in his pocket. 'Let me buy you a drink.' His demeanour brightened.

Sybil thought about the terrible hangover that had made her feel as if she wanted to die, but knew she'd be kinder to herself this time and stop at one or two. What harm would that do?

'Gin and It, please.'

'You got it,' he said. 'Then I'll show you our mirror.'

The drink was good, and she let one of Larry's friends buy her another. They showed off the mirror with great pride, and whilst she sketched, one of them carved his name in amongst the others. 'I sure hope this whole thing lasts,' Larry said, tapping it with his finger.

'Me, too,' another man said. 'Then there'll always be evidence that Herbie wuz here.'

Another raucous round was called for, but Sybil politely declined, and no one tried to persuade her. When she was leaving, Larry tipped his head and said he'd been very glad to meet her, then he smiled and touched his pocket where the portrait was safely snuggled.

17

MONDAY 30TH NOVEMBER 1942

SENT FROM CHARING CROSS POST OFFICE LONDON

PRIORITY DAME LILY BRAMPTON AND MRS S PAIGE

SEAGULLS' WATCH CLEY NORFOLK

MANDATORY MEETING FRIDAY 4TH DECEMBER 1942
STOP NINE AM STOP NATIONAL PORTRAIT GALLERY
STOP NO LOSS OF WAAC LIFE OR LIMB STOP

18

December 1942

Sybil hadn't known whether to be alarmed or merely curious about the telegram that had arrived a few days earlier. She felt both along with anxiety and bewilderment. Norwich was the last stop of official Baedeker-raided cities on her list, and once again, she had been staying with Dame Lily at Seagulls' Watch. Together they'd read the wording for the umpteenth time.

'What could have happened to call us back to London so suddenly?' she'd asked.

'Lack of funding,' Dame Lily had said. 'I expect the government has pulled the plug as the money's needed for more immediate things like weapons and food.'

There wasn't anything else it could possibly be, so Sybil settled on that reasoning and it soothed her, as did the final paragraph of Graeme's letter that didn't exist anywhere but in her mind.

After travelling together to Liverpool Street, Sybil and Dame Lily made an arrangement to meet at the National the following morning. Then Dame Lily headed to Chelsea and Sybil to Wandsworth where she was most surprised to see Blanche waiting for her – a telegram of her own in her hands. 'Dame Lily thinks it must be something do with money, or lack of it,' Sybil said.

Blanche, clearly agitated, said, 'That would make sense, but the Recording Britain Project is funded by the Pilgrim Trust, so why have I been called in, too?'

Sybil had no answer to that, but it certainly added to the mystery.

'I don't care what the reason is,' Auntie Myrtle said, her swollen, bandaged leg resting on the leather pouffe. 'I'm just glad to have you girls home. I'm steaming a meat and suet pudding for dinner to celebrate.'

'That will make a lovely change from vegetable and oatmeal goulash,' Blanche said.

'But are you well enough?' Sybil raised her eyebrows. 'We can sort out the dinner.'

'The nurse has given permission for me to potter in the house, hasn't she, Blanche?'

Blanche nodded. 'Yes, but sometimes you and I have a different view of what pottering means, Auntie Myrtle. We'll give you fifteen minutes, then we're taking over.'

Sybil enthused about Blanche's sketchbooks full of drawings of pub signs, post boxes and telephone kiosks, black cabs and red double-decker buses.

Auntie Myrtle and Blanche thought Sybil's sketches were up to her usual high standard and gave special praise to the ones of Maggie and Gertie's camp, their Union Jack and the courting couple in Exeter.

'We haven't amassed so many this time,' Blanche said. 'So they won't take up as much space when we come to choose what to work on first. Shall we do that now?'

Sybil was tempted but decided it wouldn't be worth it. 'I think we should leave it until after the meeting tomorrow.'

'I suppose that's advisable,' Blanche said and instead, they spent the evening huddled together in the living room playing cards with Auntie Myrtle. When they went up to bed, Sybil tossed and turned through a fitful night.

A number of artists made their way into the hall with Dame Lily, Sybil and Blanche, but not nearly as many as were on the WAAC's books. Jane Butterworth stood by the door and greeted each of them with a solemn look on her face. There was a bit of fidgeting and coughing, then Sir Leonard walked towards the podium with a few sheets of typed paper in his hands. Sybil fancied he was thinner and more pale than she remembered. His hair, too, seemed to have a thicker dusting of grey, but that might have been the lighting. Perhaps he was ill, Sybil thought, and standing down. But if that were the case, why had only a select few been invited to the announcement?

When he looked at his audience, the shuffling stopped and after a few beats, he said, 'Ladies and gentlemen, fellow artists. Thank you for answering the call and meeting with me today. I have some news for you that I wanted to impart in person.

'It is with great sadness that I must tell you that the ship taking your – our – beloved paintings to the United States of America and beyond has been sunk by an enemy torpedo.'

Stifled gasps filled the hall. A spasm of grief stabbed and twisted between Sybil's ribs, and she touched the sore spot with her fingertips. As if she were flailing in the dark, Blanche found Sybil's hand without turning to look at her and Sybil held on tight. Dame Lily wound her turquoise scarf around her neck, and her nostrils flared in defiance.

'Not wanting to alarm you unduly, I was very specific when I related in my telegrams that there has been no loss of WAAC life or limb. However, all crew on board the ship went down and I'm sure you will want to join me in offering heartfelt sympathy to all the bereaved.'

All those families who've lost someone to the sea. Sybil felt distraught for them. They would be denied the most basic of human rights – the grave of a loved one to visit.

Blanche dropped Sybil's hand and sat rigid, eyes on her lap. Sir Leonard looked into the distance, and when he'd given everyone time to pay their silent respects to the lost crew, he said, 'As for the paintings, there will, of course, be no search for them, so we must get used to the idea that they've gone forever.

Their loss is a personal sacrifice that we must all bear, myself included.'

Thank goodness, Sybil thought, *that the WAAC had forbidden any artists' entire portfolio from being sent.* A wave of nausea that she might have lost the *Woman Stoker* left her trembling and clammy. She couldn't bear the thought of that example of stoicism and independence lying at the bottom of a cold, dark, unforgiving ocean where no one would get the benefit of seeing the challenging speck in the subject's eyes, or the sweat pouring down the runnels of her face, or the chance to understand her story.

But the cheerful dairymaids, giggling as they tugged on udders were gone. And the nursery school art lesson; the woman about to surprise her children with a ragged dog. Ordinary, everyday women whose extraordinary stories were now nothing more than flotsam and jetsam. Hot tears stung the backs of Sybil's eyes.

'What I propose to happen now,' Sir Leonard continued, 'is that those amongst you who can face it, should consider producing works identical to those lost.'

There were a few involuntary grunts and groans at that suggestion and Sybil could understand why – that task seemed impossible.

Sir Leonard put up his hand as if he were silencing an orchestra. 'I am aware that the originals can never be reproduced perfectly, but nevertheless, some of you might want to create a piece that is a good likeness. And you never know.' He allowed himself a small smile. 'Your second attempts might be an improvement on the first. If that were possible.'

A few titters rippled the hall.

'It is perfectly understandable, though, that some of you might not be able to see your way to achieving that suggestion. If that is the case, you must continue, for the sake of art now and in the future, with your commissions, and bring your finished compositions to the Committee as soon as possible.

This news is confidential until the information is released to the public on Monday the 7th. I must remind you of the secrecy documents you signed when you were offered contracts and ask that you not tell anyone about this incident until that date.

Thank you for your time today. Miss Butterworth will direct you to the refreshments.'

Sir Leonard left the platform, and that was it. Sybil didn't know what she expected after such an announcement, but it was something more than that. Their paintings would be attracting barnacles and sinking into sand and that was all that was going to be said about them. They were expected to sip tea and nibble on almost inedible slices of parsnip cake, go home, remain stolid and churn out another painting.

There was no question that one life or one useful ship was worth much more than a pallet full of paintings, but that didn't mean they were worthless. And it didn't mean they shouldn't be grieved for, especially by the artists who had so lovingly and painstakingly nurtured them to life.

'Sybil,' Dame Lily was saying. 'My dear, are you quite alright? You look a bit pale.'

'It feels as if the Jerries have drowned all those people whose stories I tried desperately to tell. I can't separate the paintings from the subjects.' Sybil closed her eyes and felt the room sway around her.

'I know, my dear, I know.' There was the threat of tears in Dame Lily's voice. 'I must go and meet with Sir Leonard. You and Blanche make your way to the refreshment area, and I'll see both of you there soon.'

Blanche seemed as dazed as Sybil, and looking around, the shock was mirrored on everyone else's face, too. They each took tea and a bit of cake to a table and sat looking at the food and each other for a few moments without eating or speaking. Despite Sybil's best efforts, resentment ate into her. She only had to look around to see it wasn't only her – there were so many in the same situation, or worse – but that didn't make her feel any better.

'For goodness' sake, what a blow,' Blanche said at last. She pushed her spectacles up on her nose. 'Bloody war.'

'I suppose we'd better try to put something in our stomachs,' Sybil said. But the tea was as weak as dishwater, and the cake stuck in her throat.

'What are you going to do?' Blanche asked at the exact moment the woman behind them asked the same question to her companion. 'Try to replicate your lost paintings or carry on with your new ideas?'

'I'm not sure.' Sybil took a deep breath. 'If it had been the *Woman Stoker* I would probably have had another go, although I doubt I could have faithfully replicated it.'

Blanche was thoughtful for a beat. 'They must haunt you in a way that ducks and telephone kiosks never could.'

'Not unless those representations of quintessential England are here one day and poof,' she clicked her fingers, 'gone the next. I think for now, I'll get on with what I intended to paint next, then see how I feel about reproducing some of the ones lost, although it seems to me it might be best to let them lie in peace as one would anything that's passed away. What about you?'

Blanche toyed with her cake. 'Like you, I shall carry on with new subjects before I look back.' Her smile was weak. 'At least we still have our sketchbooks to work from.'

'The bright side.' Sybil toasted Blanche with her cup. 'I'll drink to that.'

Dame Lily refused the refreshments saying she'd had coffee with Sir Leonard. 'There really is nothing to be done about the paintings, I'm afraid,' she reiterated.

'Except get on with it.' Sybil tried to persuade herself as much as anyone else.

'Shall we go to the pub and raise a glass to taking it on the chin?'

As they gathered their things, Jane Butterworth strode towards them. 'I can't tell you how sorry I am.' She looked at each of them in turn. 'I know it's no consolation, but I feel as if I've lived through the life cycle of every one of your beautiful paintings with you. However, this topsy-turvy life goes on. Will you be on the move again for your current commission, Sybil?'

'Actually, I've visited the five raided cities and am going to start painting tomorrow.'

'Well done,' Jane said.

'We're off to The Marquis. Care to join us?' Dame Lily asked.

'I'll try to pop in during my dinner break,' Jane said.

They'd had a few before Jane turned up and then they had a couple more. Banter flew backwards and forwards about what state their paintings were in now. 'I was never very fond of how they'd framed my ducks on the pond,' Blanche said. 'So good riddance to that one at any rate.'

'The only viewers those paintings will ever have are fish and strange deep-water creatures. I wonder what they'll think?'

'We'll never know as they can't write reviews or critiques, which might be a good thing.'

'I expect the canvases will make excellent burrows for crabs and suchlike.'

'Years from now one or two might get trawled up and salvaged.'

'One look at them and the fishermen will haul them back over the side. After all, you can't eat them with chips.'

'Are you coming back to Norfolk with me?' Dame Lily asked Sybil. 'The light's marvellous for painting.'

'Yes, it really is,' Sybil said. 'But I'll stay, thank you. That will give me a chance to sit with Auntie Mrytle and let Blanche go off for longer periods of time if she'd like to.'

Dame Lily looked disappointed but was as gracious as ever. They had one final drink then went their separate ways to start afresh – yet again.

When the news broke, Blanche and Sybil were able to talk to

Auntie Myrtle freely about the fate of their paintings. 'I see first-hand how much you put into those compositions,' she said. 'Your hearts, your souls, your energy. It really is too bad.'

Sybil said she was trying to resign herself to the misfortune and thought Blanche was, too. 'It was a shock when we first heard the news, but it has to be thought about in proportion. Don't you think, Blanche?'

'It's the only way to look at things, for goodness' sake.' Blanche blinked behind her spectacles. 'If you don't want to go doolally.'

'Something good will come of it.' Auntie Myrtle sounded sure of herself. 'Wait and see.'

Sybil twisted the ring on her finger, thought of her paintings at the bottom of a tumultuous sea, of Graeme and of Dom, and although she didn't want to disagree with Auntie Myrtle aloud, she didn't believe that was true.

They were quiet for a few moments, listening to the low mumble of the radio and watching Michelangelo lick his paws on the windowsill.

'It's quite alright,' Auntie Myrtle said. 'To feel sorry for ourselves when something awful happens. It's part of the human condition.'

Sybil knew that but thought Auntie Myrtle had probably never experienced a moment of selfishness in her entire life. 'Then you're probably not human,' she said.

Auntie Myrtle scoffed. 'You don't know the half of it. But I try not to get caught up in ruminating. I've just come to expect and accept that I'm going to experience ups and downs and leave it at that.'

Blanche squeezed Sybil's shoulder and gathered together the teacups.

The following morning, Sybil decided that she would try to paint two pictures in quick succession. The first of the ragged Union Jack and the second of the tower of St Sidwell's Church harnessed and waiting to be pulled down. After drafting two separate versions, she made the decision to include Maggie and Gertie in the composition with the flag but keep them in soft focus so the poignancy of the tattered and threadbare standard would take centre stage.

She set up her easel and paints and after a few faltering attempts, began in earnest. Blanche ventured further afield most days, the district nurse called and Sybil took Auntie Myrtle for a daily walk. Rations were bought, Auntie Myrtle cooked a meal, Sybil washed up and the painting developed. 'That's one of the only times I've seen you use colour,' Auntie Myrtle said when the red, white and blue appeared on the flag. 'Except for a flash of fire or red brick here and there.'

Sybil stood back and studied the canvas. 'I know. We're working in and with shadows now, I'm afraid. I've tried to make the flag tattered and dusty, so do you think the colours are too vivid?

'Not at all. They contrast beautifully with the muck and rubble and destruction. As usual, you've hit the nail on the ...' An assured knock on the door stopped Auntie Myrtle mid-sentence. 'Were you expecting someone?'

'No.' Sybil laughed. No one visited them except the district nurse, Mrs Myers and a few other neighbours and Ellen, who had a key of her own. 'I'll go.'

'No, I will. You carry on at your easel whilst it's going so well.'

Sybil picked up her brush again and listened to Auntie Myrtle and the deep rumblings of a man's voice from the open door. *That's strange*, she thought. Men don't usually call on two women alone in a house. *Must be the rag and bone man or the milkman come for his money*. Then the door closed and Auntie Myrtle said, 'Sybil,' in a voice that sounded as if she were being strangled.

Sybil turned and Auntie Myrtle was drained of all colour. She caught her under the elbow and guided her to a chair. 'Whatever is it?' she asked.

'It's ... it's ... Graeme. He's at the door.'

'Graeme?' Sybil echoed. 'Are you sure? That can't possibly be.'

'Go,' Auntie Myrtle said. 'Go to him.'

Shaking from head to foot, Sybil caught sight of herself in the hall mirror and the face that looked back at her was at least as apparitional as Auntie Myrtle's. What would she say? What would she do? What did he expect to happen between them now? She wasn't at all prepared for what she might find, but there was nothing else for it. She took a deep breath and pulled open the door.

There in front of her, looking concerned, stood Ignatius. 'I'm so sorry,' he said. 'I didn't mean to frighten your aunt. Is she quite alright?'

Relief flooded her and she almost launched herself at him. 'Ignatius,' she said. She shook her head to clear it and tried to steady her nerves. 'It was a case of mistaken identity, that's all. I must check on her. Come in.'

'Do you need the smelling salts, Auntie Myrtle? It's not Graeme, it's Ignatius. One of Dame Lily's sons.'

Her face waxen and sweaty, Auntie Myrtle peered at Ignatius as he stood twirling his cap in his hands.

'I beg your forgiveness,' Ignatius said. 'I didn't mean to startle you.'

'How silly of me,' Auntie Myrtle said. 'If I'd given you time to tell me your name, I would have known you weren't Graeme. I just presumed … when you asked for Sybil … shall we have a cup of tea?'

Sybil draped a blanket over Auntie Myrtle's knees and pointed Ignatius towards a chair. In the kitchen she held on to the worktop and commanded her quaking arms and legs to keep still. The voices from the sitting room were quiet and polite, and she wondered what Dame Lily's son was doing here, how long it would take Auntie Myrtle to recover from the shock, when she would be able to get back to her painting and, most alarmingly, why she had felt dread instead of joy when she thought Graeme had returned.

With a cup of tea and a biscuit inside her, the colour rose in Auntie Myrtle's cheeks, and she was able to laugh about her mistake. 'I don't know what came over me,' she said. 'You look nothing like Sybil's description of her husband.'

At the mention of Sybil's husband, Ignatius looked uncomfortable and quickly changed the subject. 'Mama told me about your paintings and I'm so sorry,' he said. 'It's such a pity for all involved.'

'Something else to blame Hitler for,' Sybil said. 'I'm keeping myself busy, though. He can't stop us from picking up where we left off.'

'Quite. May I see?' Ignatius pointed to the easel.

'I'm afraid not. The piece is hush-hush for now.'

Auntie Myrtle asked him about his posting but that was top-secret, too. They talked about Ignatius being on military business in London, how long it had taken him to find them because of a burst gas main, art in general, the weather. One more cup of tea, then there was an awkward silence.

Sybil was none the wiser about why Ignatius had paid her a visit when he stood, shook Auntie Myrtle's hand, apologised yet again and said goodbye. Sybil walked him to the door where he turned abruptly and asked if she'd like to walk out with him for a cup of tea – his treat. Swimming in tea already, Sybil wondered what he could possibly want with another cup and there was also Auntie Myrtle to consider.

'I'm afraid I can't,' she said.

'Can't or ...'

'I must get on with my painting and I really will have to stay with my aunt until Blanche gets home this evening.'

'A drink then,' Ignatius pounced. 'This is my only day of leave whilst I'm in London and it would be lovely to have company.'

When he turned a certain way he reminded her of Dame Lily, then in another light he looked like Sir Geoffrey. His hair was shorter and neater than it had been during the time they'd spent together in windswept Norfolk, and he seemed a bit broader in his immaculate uniform. They'd enjoyed each other's company at Seagulls' Watch, and she thought they probably would again, if the situation was less gauche. But she couldn't think of any reason to turn him down so said, 'Thank you. I'd like that.'

His shoulders went back, and he looked pleased. 'Are you alright to get to Covent Garden tube at about seven-thirty?' he asked.

'Yes,' she said. 'That won't be a problem.'

'Then I'll meet you just inside.' He grinned and Sybil watched him walk away at a jaunty pace.

'What a lovely young man,' Auntie Myrtle said. 'So like Dame Lily to look at.'

It had been a strange day, and a visit to the pub would be very welcome. Although as she sorted out the tea things, something was bothering her and it wasn't Ignatius. Him turning up unannounced could so easily have been misconstrued, but it was obvious from the affable letters they'd exchanged that there was nothing more between them than friendship. He'd come looking for her in London as a good way to pass a bit of leave time, that's all. The problem was Graeme and the way she'd reacted when faced with the sudden thought that he'd returned. She'd imagined it so many times. The knock on the door, his injuries and disfigurements, her falling to the ground at his feet and clinging to him as he picked her up as easily as if she were a piece of parachute silk and laid her lovingly on the sofa. The look on his face as he bent over her would be one of relief at how ecstatic she was to have him home.

But that wasn't how she'd felt when the moment might have been coming true. She'd been anxious and worried and resentful about how the whole chaos of his return would eat into her painting time. In those few minutes before she opened the door, it flashed through her mind that she might have to give up the WAAC commission; find somewhere for the two of them to live; apply for his rations; take him to and from the doctor; wash his clothes; cook his meals. In short, she thought guiltily, he would be a dreadful inconvenience, and seeing Ignatius, who wanted nothing more from her than a quiet drink, had been a huge relief.

She tried to be logical. Servicemen missing in action didn't show up with no warning, did they? If Graeme was found alive, surely she would get some kind of communication from the authorities. A telegram to say he was in a hospital overseas and she could see him when he was well enough to be sent home. Or a letter from a nurse setting out his hopes that she would still want him despite the extent of his injuries. That way she could get used to the idea that he was coming back, and she'd have time to make some kind of contingency for them to muddle through. Because that is how it would have to happen. They'd have to make a go of it whether they had it out about the contents of his last letter or not. How, she wondered, would she cope with all of that? She'd get used to it, she supposed. And in some ways, it might be preferable to slinking back to another dreary bedsit when Auntie Myrtle could no longer have her, which was bound to happen in time.

When Blanche came home, Auntie Myrtle told her about the earlier mix-up, and they all had a good laugh about it. Blanche showed them the sketches she'd created that day and another that she'd been working on for a few weeks. It was of an archetypal red telephone box drawn on a dark, rainy night. Inside, behind the mosaic of square windows was a fragmented Sybil, the receiver tight against her face. 'I hope you're not offended that I used you as a subject without your permission. It's how I imagine you looked on the night you called to tell me about Auntie Myrtle's fall.'

Sybil and Auntie Myrtle stared at the sketch. 'I don't mind at all,' Sybil said slowly. She shivered and felt unnerved. 'The way you've captured my dismay is uncanny.' Now that drink would be more appreciated than ever.

When Ignatius turned and saw her, the first thing he said was how lovely she looked. That filled her with shame as it hadn't occurred to her to take much time with her appearance, after all it was nothing more than a friendly drink.

As for him, he'd shaved and brushed his uniform, slicked back his thick auburn hair with something that made it shine and smelled strongly of his spicy sandalwood scent.

As they strolled towards the Lamb and Flag, Ignatius thanked her again for meeting him. 'It's my pleasure,' she said. 'I feel I know you quite well from your letters, but it's nice to chat face to face.'

The place was crowded with servicemen. They were lucky to find two bar stools and when Ignatius ordered for them, he said they could go somewhere else if it was too noisy to talk. But Sybil liked the raucous crush, the music and the Gin and It as it slipped down her throat. Laughter exploded from a table on the other side of the pub, and she caught the whiff of mothballs from the pin-striped suit of a man who leaned across her to reach the bar.

Although Dame Lily had vaguely explained, Ignatius hadn't quite understood that Auntie Myrtle wasn't a blood relative. Sybil talked him through the convoluted story, and when she mentioned how she'd lived in the bedsit and the displaced Marylebone, he said he could see why her present home was more desirable.

She asked if he'd spoken to his parents about wanting to be a doctor, and he said he was waiting until he was absolutely sure before he broached the subject. 'They might think that another five years of study after this bloody war ends, whenever that might be, is too much to go through. And then, of course, they had great hopes for my career in art.'

'Well, all I can only repeat that I'm sure they'll be proud of you whatever you decide to do.' Then without thinking she opened her mouth and out came, 'Do you want me to talk to Dame Lily for you?' She could have cut off her tongue. It was none of her business and getting involved could mean she'd alienate mother from son or either of them from her, and she didn't want that. But she'd said it now and couldn't take it back.

Ignatius smiled, and much to her surprise, he reached out and lightly put his fingers on hers. The gesture made her blush, and he followed suit. He pulled his hand away, coughed awkwardly and looked as though he were concentrating very hard on her question.

But the gesture had made her feel jittery. There hadn't been any indication that they were on a date, not unless she'd read the signals incorrectly, which she now knew had been the case with Hector and her own husband. She didn't want him to touch her again – it would complicate things. To remind him of her situation, she twisted her ring first one way and then the other.

He watched her intently then said, 'Hmm. Yes and no. I certainly wouldn't want anyone else to do my dirty work for me. But if it should ever come up ...'

'That you're thinking of going into medicine. Might it?'

'No, that I'm not so keen on art as a career.'

'Oh, I see,' Sybil said. 'Should it, I'll let you know your mother's opinion.'

'Great,' he said with a smile. 'Another?'

'Please.' She watched him from the corner of her eye whilst he ordered, and thought he was an odd combination of seriousness and laissez-faire, vulnerability and composure, deep thoughts and superficial laughter, the simplicity of Norfolk and the clamour of London.

He brought the subject around to Dominic and asked how she thought his parents were doing. That seemed to lead naturally to Graeme. 'You must wait for his knock on the door every single day,' he said. 'As Mama hopes for Dom's return.'

She shook her head. 'I don't think it will happen like that. If it happens at all.'

He nodded. 'Does it upset you to talk about it?'

'I'd rather not,' she said.

'Same here. So, do you like dancing?'

The quick switch in the conversation made her laugh out loud. 'I love dancing. Or watching other people dance, anyway. I'm a baby elephant.'

'But you look so elegant,' he said in a mock disappointed tone.

She laughed again. 'How about you?'

'These,' he pointed at his feet, 'are both left. But everyone has a go, so do you fancy bumbling around the dance floor with me?'

Suddenly, it seemed as though nothing would be as much fun. Ignatius led them down alleyways and dark streets to the Mecca Dance Hall. It was quiet and dreary from the outside, but once in, it felt as if the whole building was jumping in time with the crowds who danced the foxtrot, the waltz and the jitterbug. The masses seethed and blurred into one as they moved from one jammed end of the floor to another. Ignatius bought them a drink, put the glasses amongst a glut of others on a table and said, 'I don't know if they'll be there when we get back, but ...' He shrugged. 'Let's throw ourselves into the mix.'

The band was playing a quickstep and they tagged onto the end of a line of couples turning the floor at the corner. They laughed and tried to make themselves small as they missed their footing, started off again and tried to keep pace with the throng. 'Has dancing always been so popular,' Ignatius said. 'Or is it just because of the bloody war? Oops, sorry. Was that your foot?'

'No,' Sybil giggled. 'Must have been someone else's. I think people like it now more than ever,' she said. 'We seem to crave entertainment and being with others.'

'And look, there are rather more women dancing with women than with men.' He shook his head. 'There's just not enough of us to go around.'

'So thank goodness for you and the Americans.'

No matter how many times they went around the floor, they couldn't maintain the dance pattern. When their arms were in the right position, their legs were muddled, and when everything fit, their timing was off. The lights came on and a break was announced. As predicted their drinks had disappeared and despite Sybil's protests, Ignatius insisted on buying them another round.

She followed the crowds of women to the ladies' room and stood stock still with surprise when she came face to face with her reflection in the mirror for the second time that day. Her pale freckles were hidden under a flush that made her glow, and the curls around her hairline were damp with perspiration. Her eyes were bright and most importantly, she'd been completely unaware that she was smiling broadly. *A couple of gins and a twirl on the dance floor*, she thought. Was that all it took to raise the colour in her cheeks and make her look happy and hopeful? In that respect, she was no different from everyone else. She glanced at the other women chatting, rearranging their hair, applying lipstick and wondered what kind of worries they'd put to one side for a few hours of heady respite. They'd face tomorrow when it rolled around.

Back in the hall, she picked out Ignatius talking and laughing with a group of women who had surrounded him. She stood to one side and watched as he spoke to one, then turned his head and concentrated on another. He held a drink in each hand, and every once in a while he looked around in search of her. He'd been right about there being more women than men, and with the lights up, the ladies were making their way around those that seemed available in hopes of a dance or a drink or something more. A startling twinge of jealousy grabbed her stomach and squeezed hard. He was her friend, they'd come out for a bit of fun on that basis, she was married – confusing as that relationship was – and she should be pleased, if anything, that he might find a girl of his own here tonight.

Suddenly, she felt awkward and out of place and as bothered as she'd been by the shock earlier when she'd thought Graeme had returned. The two things seemed to be intertwined in a jumbled way, and she didn't think she should be experiencing the feelings they brought with them.

She wanted to be at home with Auntie Myrtle and Blanche, the smell of paint and a sultana loaf cake spiralling through the house. In her room, she would look through her sketchbooks and decide what to paint next.

For one ugly moment she thought she might turn and flee, but that would mean Ignatius would be frantic with worry and he didn't deserve that. He'd either send a telegram or knock on the door again to make sure she was alright, and she couldn't face either. As the lights went down, the women around Ignatius moved away and she made out his shadowy figure standing alone. She braced herself and walked towards him where she put her fingers to her temples and feigned a headache. 'Oh no,' he said. 'Is it the noise or the gin?'

'Probably a bit of both.' She did her best to sound aloof. 'But I'm going to head home now. Thank you for a lovely evening.'

'Wait for me. I'll make sure you get back okay.'

'No need.' There was an edge of ice in her voice which made her wince. 'Stay and enjoy yourself.'

'I won't be able to without …'

But she turned abruptly and left him clutching a drink in each hand, couples swarming around the dance floor next to him.

The house was dark and quiet when she arrived home, and she tiptoed in as if she were a schoolgirl who'd been out too late. As she sat on the edge of her bed, she recited the last paragraph of Graeme's letter that she'd made up and tried, once again, to sketch herself with the telegram in her hand. She thought she might be getting somewhere with it, then she was overcome with turmoil when the day's events flashed through her mind. She slashed through what she'd accomplished, tore the page from the book, crumpled the paper and left it on the floor. Tomorrow morning it would go on the fire. And from then on, she would do nothing else with her time except produce one painting after another.

19

7709567 Capt. Fortescue, I.G.,
2nd Battalion,
Royal Norfolk Regiment,
c/o APO England

Friday, 18th December 1942

Mrs S. Paige,
c/o Miss Myrtle Ashcroft,
78, Broxash Road,
Wandsworth,
London, S.W.11

Dear Sybil,

I've been beside myself with worry about you and your headache. You left the dance hall so abruptly and insisted you make your own way home, that I'm afraid I was stunned into inertia. When I pulled myself together, I ran out looking for you, but you were nowhere to be seen. I went back to the Mecca and downed both our drinks in quick succession before returning to barracks. Today, I asked for an hour's leave to race across London and check on you, but my application was turned down. Please let me know by return post that you are alright.

I do hope your incapacity wasn't any fault of mine. Did I say something inappropriate? I thought we'd been getting on well and having a fun evening, so the turn of events led to me ruminating on what we'd discussed prior to you being indisposed, and I can't come up with anything we spoke about that might have caused you to be poorly. But I can be a thoughtless oaf sometimes, so do let me know.

When I finish in London, I will have forty-eight hours leave to visit my parents before my next posting. Wish me luck, as I will be tackling the subject of medicine as my chosen career. Are you planning on spending time at Seagulls' Watch soon? If so, perhaps we could coordinate our visits.

I look forward to hearing from you soon.

With best wishes,

Iggy

Mrs S. Paige,
c/o Miss Myrtle Ashcroft,
78, Broxash Road,
Wandsworth,
London, S.W.11

Monday, 21st December 1942

7709567 Capt. Fortescue, I.G.,
2nd Battalion,
Royal Norfolk Regiment,
c/o APO England

Dear Ignatius,

Thank you for your letter and I must apologise for giving you so much worry.

As soon as I got out of the dance hall and into the fresh air, I began to feel much better. I was lucky enough to hop straight onto a tube, so that is probably why you couldn't find me.

I hope your time in London was useful and that your next posting is reasonable. I'm afraid I don't have any plans to visit Norfolk in the near future, but I wish you the best of luck with talking to your parents.

Sybil

Dame Lily Brampton, DBE RA ROI RWS,
Seagulls' Watch,
Cley-next-the-Sea,
Norfolk

Tuesday, 22nd December 1942

Mrs S. Paige,
c/o Miss Myrtle Ashcroft,
78, Broxash Road,
Wandsworth,
London, S.W.11

My dearest Sybil,

I hope you are well and managing to get on with your painting after the disaster at sea.

We had Iggy here for a few days before he was sent off to God knows where. How I longed to beg him to stay, but that wouldn't do, would it? He mentioned having seen you whilst he was in London, and I wonder what you made of him. He was a bit off with us – not rude or surly, he's never that. Distracted and distant would be a better description. Did he come across like that with you? There's so much pressure on everyone during this ****** war. It must play on young men's minds when they're about to be posted as it plays on ours left behind. But none of us speaks about it much. We put on a brave face for each other as I suppose there's nothing else we can do.

He seemed a bit easier after he told us he'd made the decision to study medicine when the ****** war is over. For some reason, he had it in his mind that we'd disapprove on the grounds that up until now he'd wanted to pursue an art career. Silly boy! We're proud of him no matter what he does in life. Alive and as healthy as possible – that is our dearest hope for all three of our sons.

I am working furiously on a piece for the WAAC, and I presume you're doing the same. Let's try to present on the same day so we can meet up afterwards.

Yours,

Lily X

Miss E. Hewitt, NA,
Nurses' Quarters,
St Mary's Hospital,
Paddington,
London, W.2

Wednesday, 23rd December 1942

Miss B. Northcutt,
and Mrs S. Paige,
c/o Miss Myrtle Ashcroft,
78, Broxash Road,
Wandsworth,
London, S.W.11

Dear Blanche and Sybil,

I can't believe I've been lucky enough to get leave on Christmas Day! I've got the entire morning and afternoon off but will have to report back for duty at 9 p.m., so we should have plenty of time to celebrate together.

Would it alright if I bring a friend with me? He's a very kind, funny American serviceman named Chuck (Yankee for Charles) Walker. He hails from El Paso in Texas, and I'm sure you'll like him. I met him on a night out with some other nurses and he's at a loose end over Christmas.

I have two important and exciting things to tell you. The first is that I applied to continue my training overseas and I've been accepted! I'll give you all the details when I see you. I was egged on by another nurse, although I never thought I'd be chosen. I'm looking forward to it with some trepidation, which I suppose is only to be expected.

My second piece of news is that the WAAC has accepted one of my paintings – something I thought would never happen. It's the one of my female patient hooked up to a line of special medicine. Do you remember, Sybil? What a boost this has given me! I was also told they would consider more from me so I must get busy.

I'm looking forward to spending Christmas with both of you.

All my love,

Ellen XXX

P.S. I'll bring the Christmas pud and make a bit of custard.

20

July 1943

Jane Butterworth smiled but looked weary when Sybil walked into her office. Immaculate, her red nails and lips shone in their usual manner, but there was a tinge of blue under her eyes and her complexion was sallow. She'd become a friend of sorts, greeting Sybil fondly and meeting her occasionally for a drink. She listened and sympathised and asked all the right questions but didn't give much of herself away other than that she lived with her mother, for her lapdog, and had a very long-term beau named Cyril who was away with the Services.

'Morning, Jane.' Sybil dragged her wrapped canvas into the cramped space.

'Hello, Sybil. Punctual as always. Lovely to see you. I know you have an appointment with Sir Leonard, but I wasn't aware that he'd asked you to bring in your latest effort?'

Sybil smiled. Jane knew the minutiae of Sir Leonard's diary and sounded aggrieved when she thought he'd failed to tell her the smallest detail. 'He didn't. I couldn't imagine what else he wanted to see me about, so I brought it along. It won't do any harm, will it?'

Jane raised an eyebrow and looked as if she wasn't sure about that. 'Have we time for a cuppa?' She turned to look at the clock and decided against it. 'It'll have to wait,' she said. 'Let me show you in.'

Sir Leonard rushed to help and set her canvas against a

bookcase. 'I haven't an easel set up as that's not the reason for our meeting. But as you've brought it along, we can unwrap it later and I'll have a look.'

He was remarkably well-turned out with a spotted silk tie and a matching handkerchief in his breast pocket. There was a large folder on his lap and another on the little table between two chairs. She sat in the one she was guided towards and waited.

'Coffee?' Sir Leonard asked. 'Or chicory blend as it is now?'

'Thank you,' she said.

He put his head out of the door, gave his order to Jane and sat down again. The artwork on the walls must have been commissioned by the WAAC as the scenes they depicted were barrage balloons over London, an abstract of civilians filing down into the Underground and a portrait of Churchill. Looking around rather furtively he put down the folder, went to his desk and lit a cigarette. 'Do you?' he asked.

'No, thank you.' She shook her head.

There was one sharp rap at the door and Jane came in carrying a tray. 'On the table, Sir Leonard?'

'My desk, please, Miss Butterworth.'

The only sound in the room was the ticking of a clock and the click of Jane's heels as she walked across the parquet floor. 'Anything else, Sir Leonard?' she asked.

'That will be all, Miss Butterworth. Thank you.'

When she closed the door behind her, Sir Leonard checked it himself then poured them both a cup of coffee.

By that time, Sybil felt so fidgety, she didn't know how she remained composed on her chair.

'... Have you heard about the paintings from this gallery being hidden somewhere?'

Sybil's eyes widened. 'Yes,' she said. 'That seems to be a commonly held belief. Although no one knows where. And those who do aren't saying.'

'Good,' he said. 'So they shouldn't.' He sat down again and

looked at her intently. 'How I wish now that I'd stored your WAAC paintings with them instead of sending them off on that doomed ship.' He threw his arms in the air and let them drop to his lap. 'This war is a catastrophe.'

Sybil certainly agreed with that but could not fathom what it had to do with her. She thought she might ask so placed her saucer on the table, then Sir Leonard carried on.

'Your paintings, though, were not meant to be hidden away. They were supposed to show the entire world what was happening here in Britain and broker support for the Allies. But our collection of masterpieces had to stay here in Britain. Churchill said,' he gestured towards the stately portrait on the wall, 'that we were to hide them in caves and cellars, "but not one picture shall leave this island". And now we want to capture how we've gone about keeping them safe.' He stopped, and Sybil followed his gaze as he looked around the room again. 'You do remember the secrecy document you signed, Mrs Paige?'

'Yes, Sir Leonard, I do.' She felt for her wedding ring and twisted it a few times. 'And I can assure you I haven't broken it.'

'Very well,' he said. 'There will be another to sign today and others in the future if you decide to take on the next commission the Committee is going to offer you.'

'Another commission?' Sybil was delighted. 'Thank you very much. I'm most grateful.'

'The National Gallery art treasures have found a sanctuary in,' Sir Leonard lowered his voice, 'the Manod slate mines near the town of Blaenau Ffestiniog.'

Sybil had never heard of that, but she took a stab at where it was located. 'In Wales?' she ventured.

Sir Leonard nodded. 'North Wales. They're safe and sound hundreds of metres underground in a labyrinth of tunnels. Brick bunkers have been built, each with their own air conditioning, and Professor Justin Hazelmere, who's resident on the site, is making remarkable inroads into how to preserve old masterpieces from the hazards of humidity.'

Sybil thought about Auntie Myrtle and how she tried to look for the positive in every situation. 'Something good has come out of the war then,' she said.

'That appears to be so. In this instance. I'm sure you'll agree that it's a fascinating place when you see it. If you accept your next commission.'

Sybil leaned forward and listened intently.

'The Committee has been debating for some time about sending an artist to sketch the subterranean space.'

'My goodness, what a task,' Sybil said. 'But how can anyone except Constable or Monet paint Constable or Monet?'

'No, Mrs Paige. The WAAC doesn't want drawings of the masterpieces. We want a renowned artist to sketch the way in which the paintings are being stored and protected. The tunnels. The brick shelters. The equipment used to provide variations in humidity and temperature. In other words, the whole outfit.'

Sybil felt as if she'd had the breath kicked out of her. Could this be her next commission? It hardly seemed possible that she was being referred to as a renowned artist and that she would be entrusted with such a crucial and extensive portfolio of work.

'We have been considering a number of very worthy artists for this role, but agreed unanimously that you would fulfil the commission most admirably.

Suddenly, her tongue refused to form words, her legs felt wobbly and her palms were sweating. 'I'm ... I'm ... very flattered,' she managed at last. 'But ...'

'Of course, you have questions,' Sir Leonard said. 'I had no doubt you would. Fire away, I'm sure I can answer most of them here and now.'

'How long will the commission last?'

'Six months.'

'With opportunities to visit home during that time?'

'I'm afraid not. You will have to be in situ for the duration.'

'Will I be able to send and receive post?'

'Via Miss Butterworth. No one must know where you are.'

'Where will I stay?'

'In Professor Hazelmere's cottage not far from the site. He will be returning to London for research during that time.'

'Is part of the commission to compose paintings from the sketches?'

'Not at this time,' he said. 'What we require is an extensive series of detailed drawings.'

The room was filled with silence. Sybil couldn't think of any further questions, and it appeared that Sir Leonard had run out of anything else to add. 'Would you like a few days to think about it?' he asked.

In a small voice Sybil said, 'Would that seem terribly ungrateful?'

'Absolutely not.' Sir Leonard smiled at her kindly. 'It's a very different kind of commission and therefore a huge decision. However, I am going to remain hopeful that you'll accept, so I shall ask Miss Butterworth to draw up the contracts. Do you think it would be reasonable to ask that you contact her with a decision by Monday next? That's the 19ᵗʰ.'

'More than reasonable, Sir Leonard. And please pass on my thanks to the Committee for considering me for this opportunity.'

'I will, Mrs Paige. Thank you for your time. And please, you must not, under any circumstances, discuss this with anyone.'

'I understand, Sir Leonard.'

'Now.' He rubbed his hands together. 'Shall we have a look at your painting?' He started to untie the string around the covers.

'Do you know,' she said. 'I'd completely forgotten about that.'

He stood back and cupped his chin in his hand, a look of deep concentration on his face. Then he kneeled in front of the canvas so he could scrutinise it at eye level. The lost man, as she'd come to think of the poor soul in Canterbury whose business and family were eradicated in one fell swoop, stared back at the director of the WAAC with venom in his eyes. The subject was in close-up, and one could only imagine the invective stream being hurled from his twisted mouth. Every sinew in his neck was taut as he pointed behind him to the immense pile of rubble he had called home. And over his eyes was a film of dusty tears.

Sir Leonard crossed his arms, gave her a bittersweet smile and nodded. 'May I have your permission to keep this and show it to the committee?' he asked.

'Thank you,' Sybil said. 'I'd be honoured.'

They shook hands and he saw her to the door. She knew Jane would have the kettle on, but she slipped past her office. Unable to ask anyone for advice about her next possible commission, all she wanted to do was think through the pros and cons and come to a decision.

Outside, warm summer rain stirred up an acrid smell of soil and soot. Sybil turned up her collar and breathed in deeply. She didn't want to go home because Blanche and Auntie Myrtle would ask her about the meeting, and she needed time to think about how she would get around their questions. What she would have liked was a couple of Gin and Its, but she hadn't been into a pub on her own since that fateful night in Lyme Regis and didn't want to start again now. That left a café, so she ducked into Lyons on Piccadilly and found a quiet table next to a window.

A cup of tea and a scone with a dab of margarine and jam were placed in front of her and she looked down at them as if she didn't know where they'd come from. There were so many things to think about, not least that Sir Leonard had said she was renowned. That must mean she was acclaimed, eminent – but how had that happened? She felt the same and apart from being a bit older, she looked the same. Did that mean she was established in the art world, like Dame Lily, and would never have to worry about her career again? The two seemed to be no more than tenuously connected. Dame Lily's reputation was built on works of art stretching back to well before the war started. But her own career might turn out to be no longer or shorter than the war itself, and if that were the case, she should be grasping every opportunity to cement her fleeting distinction now whilst she had the chance.

She stirred her tea into a raging whirlpool and took a bite of the crumbling scone. Outside, black umbrellas rushed past, the people beneath them hidden from view.

She recalled the evening in Luton when she was worried that, if she left the Marylebone, she'd be rootless. That had been solved by Auntie Myrtle and Blanche offering her a permanent home. She'd come to love her situation and to appreciate that when she was away on commission, she could return home for rest and respite at a moment's notice, whether she chose to or not. But six months alone in a cottage in North Wales seemed as if it would be completely isolating. It felt as if she were being handed a prison sentence along with the marvellous opportunity.

During her first stint away, she'd become accustomed to being on her own in B&Bs and lodging houses. And there were some evenings when she'd welcomed the solitude to look through her sketchbooks and ruminate on what she'd seen that day and where she would go next. But she could have stepped out to a café or followed a lead that gave her the chance to talk to others about their experiences. She couldn't imagine there being any such distractions in the midst of remote slate mines. She would be occupied, but she envisaged long stretches of time to recite the last, fanciful paragraph of Graeme's letter over and over; to worry about how she would cope if her husband came home, or if he didn't; to think about her fate if and when something happened to Auntie Myrtle. In other words, she would be faced with her own fears, and she didn't relish that.

What would the female stoker say about this situation, if Sybil could speak to her about it? If she knew about the commission on offer, she would no doubt ask Sybil to articulate what exactly she wanted out of life. A career as an artist; the courage to be independent; finish the self-portrait; overcome her anxieties. She remembered how the older woman had stared at her for a second and knew she'd been telling Sybil that she must find that same sheer conviction within herself.

She paid her bill, then walked for miles around London. Everything was as grey as she thought it must be in Wales. Destruction was everywhere – broken buildings; putrid potholes, worse-for-wear woollen coats; red, sore eyes; limps; children in clothes three sizes too small. And yet – there was a frisson of resolve. There was purpose and, most surprisingly, order. They all had a task, they all knew what it was, and they went about it with dignity and determination.

Gazing out from Westminster Bridge, Sybil thought about the part she played as a war artist. She'd longed for the job and now it was well and truly hers. So, was she going to turn her back on this next commission on the basis that she hated living alone and would, without doubt, be lonely and a victim of her own thoughts? With the memory of the female stoker firmly planted in her mind, she turned on her heels and headed back to the National Gallery. If she hurried, she could catch Jane before she left for the day.

Euston to Chester, Chester to Llandudno Junction, Llandudno Junction to Blaenau Ffestiniog. It had been a long journey. Sybil stood outside the station and scanned the road for the car Sir Leonard said would collect her, although she would believe that when she saw it. Her experience when she arrived in Luton had taught her a lesson as far as that was concerned. Leaning against the wall were her oilskin bag, full of new supplies, and one small case as she didn't think she'd need much except warm clothes and her overshoes. It had been raining on and off all day, although the rain here came down in sheets rather than individual drops. Smoke spiralled out of chimneys, and the stone cottages and shops were so thoroughly soaked they were almost black.

Sybil leaned on one hip and stifled a yawn. Then, from over a bridge chugged a car. Perhaps she was going to get her ride in a motor, after all. She watched its progress until it stopped next to her where, much to her surprise, Sir Leonard hopped out and greeted her. He wore an open-necked shirt and a woolly waistcoat and seemed much less formal than he did when she met with him in London.

'Mrs Paige.' He offered his hand. 'Please forgive me for being late. Farmyard animals take priority here. Allow me.'

He stowed her bags and opened the passenger door for her. She wished now she'd worn something nicer or had reapplied her scant makeup, but it was too late to worry about that. 'I didn't expect to see you, Sir Leonard,' she said.

'I come to the mine about once a month.' He raised his voice above the noise of the engine. 'I feel assured when I see for myself that everything is ticking over. And I thought this would be a good opportunity to give you a personal tour of the tunnels and introduce you to the men who work for us.'

'I wasn't aware that anyone other than Professor Hazelmere was at the mine,' she said.

'I'm sorry if I didn't make that clear, but a number of workers man the site around the clock on a shift basis. Mrs Edwards, a local woman, walks over from the village every day to cook and clean.'

That information made Sybil feel a little less anxious. At least there would be people nearby should she need them. The hills were soft and undulating and studded with sheep. Stone walls marked one field from another, and in the distance, slate quarries scarred the idyllic landscape.

'Does it rain all the time?' she asked.

Sir Leonard laughed out loud. 'I'd love to say no, but you'd soon find me out. It pours a good deal, but on the few days the sun shines, the light is extraordinary. You will feel like a different person.'

The car followed a track around a hill, then dropped down towards what looked like a thriving hamlet.

'Here we are,' Sir Leonard said. 'Professor Hazelmere is leaving with me tomorrow evening, so tonight, he and I will stay in the studio where conservation work is carried out.' He pointed to the small building next to where they'd parked. 'But first of all, I'm going to make you a cup of tea and carry out a few introductions. Then I'll take you to your cottage and the three of us can meet here for dinner later. Tomorrow, I'll give you the big tour. How does that sound?'

'Thank you, Sir Leonard,' she said. 'That's all very well for me.'

The professor was a slight man who had also forsaken his tie and folded his shirt sleeves to his elbows. She met the men on duty, who were lined up at the gates of the cave, and Mrs Edwards said it was lovely to have another woman about the place.

'Did you choose this cave because of its unusually huge entrance?' she asked.

Sir Leonard shook his head. 'We had to do a lot of engineering work before the cave was fit for purpose, including enlarging the entranceway with explosives and developing an existing railway to move the paintings around, which you'll see tomorrow.'

'My goodness. I never imagined such a mammoth operation. It's fascinating. No wonder you need me here for six months.'

Her cottage was a muddy five-minute walk away, but once inside, it was clean and cosy. Alone, she flopped exhausted on the bed, shut her eyes and let a sense of relief that the mines were not as isolated as she'd feared wash over her.

She wore the most acceptable dress she'd brought with her, applied a thin coating of makeup and put her hair up in two clips. A dirt path had been beaten from the cottage to the cave and it wasn't unpleasant to walk across. From under an umbrella, Sybil gazed at shifting clouds, rolling hills and clumps of yellow, round-headed tansy. But the thought of walking back and forth during the colder months made her shiver.

The aromas of leek tart and pear pudding filled the studio, and it was then Sybil realised how hungry she was. There was wine and beer on a small table that was simply set. When they sat down and clinked glasses, Sybil asked how the space was used for conservation work.

Sir Leonard looked at Professor Hazelmere, who thought for a few moments before he replied. 'Usually, I have up to six paintings in varying states of preservation in here and I log the outcomes of different temperatures and air conditioning on each. There aren't any such controls in the National, so it's helpful to have the time and place to carry out experiments.'

Sybil nodded and thought about how much that would benefit the art world.

With the meal well underway, Sir Leonard said he would like her help with something else. She thought that by this time in her war artist career, nothing should surprise her, yet here she was – baffled again. 'The decision has been made to take one painting a month out of storage and display it at the National.'

She widened her eyes. 'It's not my place to query those kinds of decisions,' she said. 'But is that wise after you and many others took such pains to keep them safe? And what would Churchill say?'

'He's all for it,' Professor Hazelmere said. 'He thinks it would be a fantastic way to boost spirits.'

'Oh, I see,' she said. 'In that case, it must be a sound idea. What are you going to start with?'

'We can't decide,' said Sir Leonard. 'Something deeply emotional. But it needs to be chosen very carefully.'

Sybil agreed as she pierced a piece of leek with her fork.

'We've narrowed it down, but we hope you might help us make the final decision tomorrow.'

Sybil didn't feel she had enough authority to do anything of the sort but didn't want to come across as falsely demure, so she said she would do her best but would ultimately be guided by them.

The pleasant evening ended with a glass of port and a small portion of Caerphilly cheese. The two men walked her home in the rain-washed moonlight, reminded her to always have her torch with her and left her at the door. As they made their way back down the path, she heard their voices deep in conversation, but she couldn't make out what they were saying.

It was much quieter and more remote than it had been in any of the other places she'd stayed on commission, and she thought the eerie silence would keep her awake all night. But the opposite was true. Before she had time to dwell on Graeme or the war, motorcars or masterpieces in caves, she was deep in sleep.

The following morning, it felt as if her stomach stayed at ground level whilst a lift dropped the three of them down into the bedrock of the mine. There, nothing was how she imagined it would be. The air was cool and brushed against her face and hands gently. Through every twist and turn and cavernous space, the area was bustling with people. Several men in lab coats carried telephone receivers they could plug into sockets to report back to others on the condition of certain pieces. Small skips were mounted on train tracks, and they chuntered past carrying artwork from one location to another.

Sybil could do nothing but stand and stare. 'I had no idea,' she said at last.

'Amazing, isn't it?' Sir Leonard smiled as if he were showing off his first born.

'There are no words. I must congratulate you, Sir Leonard. Both of you.' She included Professor Hazelmere. 'You've created a thriving purpose-built city – or world.'

'Let's start here.' Sir Leonard led them through a tunnel in which pallets, designed to hold paintings upright, were stacked along the walls.

Sybil tried to catch a glimpse of them, but they were covered with tarpaulin.

'You'll find tunnel after tunnel of these pallets. And each of them needs to be sketched.' Sir Leonard crouched down. 'Only draw them uncovered if you find them that way. Please don't uncover them yourself. And remember that the mechanical intricacies need to be catalogued. The wheels for transportation and such like.'

Sybil imagined herself sitting on the ground sketching the minutiae of everything she came across to her heart's content. She would ask Mrs Edwards to find her a pair of slacks to wear – no one would care about protocol or propriety here.

The tunnel opened out into a huge, high-ceilinged cave which took Sybil's breath away. Two brick bunkers, each bigger than the bedsit she'd once lived in, stood in the space. 'These,' Professor Hazelmere said, 'Are the bungalows we were telling you about. There are four more in another cave. The humidity and temperature are scrupulously monitored and adjusted on a daily basis. When you enter and leave, you must close the door firmly, and if you touch anything, you must wear gloves. There's a stash of them in the studio. In this one.' He ushered them in and made sure the handle clicked behind them. 'There are some of the National's library of books and a—'

'Botticelli.' She breathed out the word on an exhale.

Whilst the two men checked the state of the bookcases, Sybil's eyes were glued to the masterpiece. She couldn't believe she would have access to such treasures for six months. How could she ever have thought she'd be lonely with these pieces of art for company?

They viewed the other bunkers, each as fascinating as the first; watched workmen lifting and checking the pieces under tarpaulin; walked through an endless network of tunnels, and when the tour came to an end, she had a clear understanding of her commission. 'Extraordinary,' she said. 'Thank you, Sir Leonard, for giving me this role. I can assure you I will take it seriously.'

Sir Leonard rubbed his hands together. 'I have no doubt,' he said. 'Now, should "Picture of the Month" be Titian's *Noli me Tangere* or Velázquez's *The Rokeby Venus*? Let's talk about it over lunch.'

Mrs Edwards did them proud again, and Sybil congratulated her on being so resourceful with rations. When she asked about the slacks, the older woman said it wouldn't be a problem and she would find two comfortable pairs for her. After some debate, they decided on the Velázquez, and Sir Leonard asked if she'd like to watch it being loaded into an elephant case.

Sybil laughed. 'I certainly hope the elephant's not still in it as the poor painting will be kicked and worse.'

'No, that's just what we call them. They're huge cages used to transport our larger and more fragile pieces.'

She watched in awe as the painting was removed from the wall of a bunker, a typewritten label of details pinned in its place. All the men involved wore white gloves and handled the masterpiece with the respect it was due. Two of them sat with it on a little train to keep it steady, then they loaded it into the elephant case, secured it and covered the whole contraption with a waterproof camouflaged cover.

'You must write or telegram if you have any concerns or queries,' Sir Leonard said as he shook her hand goodbye. 'If not, I shall see you in about a month's time during which I hope all goes well.'

Professor Hazelmere hopped into the seat beside Sir Leonard and Sybil watched as the car, elephant cage attached, made its way out of the valley and disappeared from view. She looked around and, despite the milling workmen, a wave of intense melancholy came over her. But she fought it when she remembered how excited her task had made her feel earlier.

It was too late in the afternoon to start, so she wandered back up to her cottage and decided to use the couple of hours until dinner to organise her equipment and write to her friends that she'd arrived safe and well at her secret destination.

The next morning, Sybil wondered why one had to be considered Bohemian to wear a pair of trousers in civilian life. They were so marvellously comfortable and practical that, given the chance, women would choose them instead of skirts every time. She picked up her oilskin bag and headed out through the ceaseless rain. At least she would be dry in her subterranean world.

She decided to work logically and follow each tunnel to its endpoint, that way she hoped not to miss a thing. The men greeted her with a hello or friendly nod. The foreman introduced himself and said she must ask him if she needed anything, and if not, she would be left alone to get on with her task. 'Do you have a watch?' he asked.

'I left it at the cottage. Is that a problem?'

'It might be a good idea to wear it as it's difficult to tell the time underground. I'll give you a shout today at lunchtime and again at the end of the day. You wouldn't want to go without your meals, would you?'

She set about her work, and when the foreman called her for lunch, she thought there must have been some mistake with timings. Then the afternoon passed at least as quickly. She was as content as she'd imagined she would be, tucked up between pallets. She sketched close-ups of the tiniest pieces of apparatus, larger scenes encompassing whole walls and everything in between. By the end of the day, she had a profusion of drawings but had barely made any headway through the mine.

Tired after her full day, she thought she might have a lie down before dinner, but it struck her that she would soon turn into a pale, weak, wraithlike creature if she didn't have a walk outside. Once on the hills, she was revived, and newfound energy flooded her. It was raining, of course, but she took in deep breaths of fresh air and enjoyed the grey and yellow she could see. She turned and looked down at the mouth of the mine. Although there were a fair few men coming and going, no one would guess that it held anything other than slate. When she thought about what was down there and what she'd been privileged to see, her stomach flipped. The fortress guarded history and culture, intellect and philosophy. The development of humanity. And she was a minute part of that, which was enough to make her happy and proud.

Mrs Edwards stopped her at the cottage door. 'I saw you on the hill,' she said. 'There are some lovely walks here.'

'Yes,' Sybil said. 'I thought I might fade away if I didn't get outside for six months. But I think I'll take my walk early each morning. That seems sensible.'

'Especially once the nights draw in,' Mrs Edwards agreed. Your overshoes and coat aren't nearly adequate enough. Professor Hazelmere's walking boots and waterproofs are in the studio. I'll dig them out for you. They'll be too big, but ...' she shrugged, 'It's not London, is it.'

'It certainly isn't.' Sybil laughed. 'And most Londoners wouldn't believe the work that goes on here.'

After dinner, Sybil returned to the cottage, turned off all the lights and sat in an open window looking at the stars. It seemed as if the velvet curtain of sky had been pinpricked a thousand times over. The only noises were the sounds of whatever creatures lived in the wilds of Wales and the occasional clang of the gate to the mine being opened or closed. The feelings of loneliness or isolation she experienced weren't as crippling as she thought they would be. They soon washed over her, and she thought she could cope with them for six months. But nor did she want to live alone forever – she recognised that. With that out of the way, the next obstacle to face was Graeme and the self-portrait, but there was plenty of time for that. Tonight, she would enjoy the stars that were close enough to reach out and touch.

Sir Leonard had been and gone four times. During each visit he checked every aspect of the makeshift gallery, and together they chose a new masterpiece for 'Picture of the Month'. They'd been a huge success, apparently, with upwards of 30,000 people queuing to view them, and it was reported that they had lifted the hearts and spirits of the nation. He complimented her on her sketches, took her finished works with him and left fresh supplies. On one such occasion, she'd been feeling particularly homesick and almost blurted out that she wanted to go back to London with him. But she bit her tongue and imagined the female stoker's eyes daring her to give up. She couldn't let her down. She drew on that woman's determination and the strength and sense of contentment with her own company that she'd found during the time she'd managed on her own.

Every time a bundle of letters came for her, she shook the packet in the hopes that one from her husband was stuck at the bottom. But that never happened, and she slowly began to get used to the idea that it never would.

One evening, she got out the letter from Graeme. Although she knew it by heart, she read it over again. This time, she examined it for a meaning that she might have missed. A word or line that would tell her, one way or another, what his intentions had been. But there was nothing there that she hadn't already determined.

When she finished reading, she folded the letter and began to automatically recite the bogus paragraph she couldn't get out of her mind. It had helped her initially, but now it drove her mad and she hated it. It seemed to be stuck fast somewhere deep in her brain where she couldn't get at it and prise it free. Halfway through, she closed her eyes and forced herself to stop mid-sentence. Her breathing was shallow and her heartbeat was fast. The sketchbook lay open on the table next to her and flames crackled in the fireplace. With great will, she did not allow herself to chant the rest, and the world didn't come to an end. That felt like a good beginning.

Then she got out her self-portrait sketchbook and opened it to the next blank page. Carefully, she took up a pencil and began to sketch. She didn't draw much – a sliver of wall and her crumpled forehead. Then, instead of drawing her eyes closed tight against the terrible news she clasped in her hand, she left them open and the same fragment of defiance she'd seen in the female stoker's eyes filtered through. It must have been there the whole time, although she hadn't been aware of it. The older woman had, and that must have been the frisson that had passed between them.

She stared at the sketch in disbelief. This time, the effort didn't end up crumpled on the floor. She was pleased with how calm and contained she felt and thought that now she could start to tackle it – inch by inch.

21

58223814, Staff Nurse, Hewitt, E.H.,
QAIMNS,
c/o British Military Hospital 133

Monday, 3rd January 1944

Mrs S. Paige,
c/o Miss J. Butterworth,
Personal Assistant to Sir Leonard Thwaites, CH KOB FB,
War Artists' Advisory Committee,
Ministry of Information,
The National Gallery,
Trafalgar Square,
London, W.C.2

Dear Sybil,

Happy New Year from *******. I've always longed to visit ***** and view the artwork first-hand and here I am, but for an altogether different, less genteel, reason.

I am so glad I was given this posting. Living somewhat like a soldier has given me a whole new perspective on what the poor buggers we treat have to go through. It's humbling to say the least. Believe it or not, these lads hop out of bed the minute they think they feel better. And what do they do?

They lend a hand with odd jobs so we can see to others feeling worse than themselves. When they ask one of us to write home for them, they insist we make light of their injuries so their mothers, sisters and wives won't worry. They are truly remarkable.

You kindly asked about my American friend, Chuck Walker. He, too, has been posted, and I hear from him occasionally when letters get through. He was a great 'guy', wasn't he? But I realised after a while that, although I missed him and wished him well, I didn't miss him enough. That made me feel a bit sad as I thought at one time things might go further between us, but we didn't have a lot in common, so our relationship was destined to come to a full stop. Never mind, there's plenty more lads out there and not enough time to meet them, but that will hopefully change at the end of this ****** war.

I know you can't tell me any details about your commission, but it sounds as if it's going well. Six months! By now you must have amassed thousands of sketches of whatever it is you're drawing.

You'll be back in London soon, and writing that has made a lump form in my throat. I sometimes feel intense flashes of homesickness when I swear I can smell fish and chips and see lines of people queuing up outside shops for their rations. I have written to Blanche and Auntie Myrtle, but please give them a hug from me and have one for yourself, too.

Oh, I almost forgot! Please find enclosed two drawings that I would appreciate you giving to Sir Leonard when you see him. It pains me to say that the young man whose hand is being held by a nurse passed away soon after I sketched him. Ian, the one having his arm set in a splint, is doing well. He is from Hertfordshire and wants to write to me when he's sent home.

With love,

Ellen XXX
(Encs)

Dame Lily Brampton, DBE RA ROI RWS,
Seagulls' Watch,
Cley-next-the-Sea,
Norfolk

Saturday, 8th January 1944

Mrs S. Paige,
c/o Miss J. Butterworth,
Personal Assistant to Sir Leonard Thwaites, CH KOB FB,
War Artists' Advisory Committee,
Ministry of Information,
The National Gallery,
Trafalgar Square,
London, W.C.2

My dearest Sybil,

I do hope you managed to have a reasonable Christmas wherever you may be. This year, it was just Sir Geoffrey and me with my sister and her husband. Neither Iggy nor Al could get leave and Dom – well, you know about Dom. We spent a lot of time talking about him and laughing at his antics when he was growing up. At times it felt almost like a wake, but I pulled it back by repeating the phrase, 'when (rather than if) he comes home' and everyone followed suit.

It's not long now until you return triumphant to London. Will you be able to put us all out of our misery and tell us where you've been and what you've been up to, or will the commission remain top secret? Whatever the situation, I am so looking forward to welcoming you back.

Do you remember me telling you about 'Picture of the Month' at the National? My dear, what a success it has been. Luckily, I have been able to view them without joining the monstrous queues, and I must say, Sir Leonard has done a splendid job of choosing which masterpieces to put on display. Last month's was a Titian that was awe-inspiring.

Iggy is celebrating his thirtieth birthday next week and we asked him to apply for leave so we could throw a low-key party for him. Sir Geoffrey and I think that everything good that happens must be acknowledged. However, he was refused, but please raise a glass to him on the 18th of February and we will be doing the same here.

Yours,

Lily X

Mrs S. Paige,
c/o Miss J. Butterworth,
Personal Assistant to Sir Leonard Thwaites, CH KOB FB,
War Artists' Advisory Committee,
Ministry of Information,
The National Gallery,
Trafalgar Square,
London, W.C.2

Wednesday, 12th January 1944

Dame Lily Brampton, DBE RA ROI RWS,
Seagulls' Watch,
Cley-next-the-Sea,
Norfolk

Dear Dame Lily,

Thank you very much for your letter which arrived today.

It hardly seems possible that the six months' commission is coming to an end, but here I am thinking about packing up my belongings. Strangely, it has both flown by and seemed interminably drawn out at the same time. But it has been very worthwhile, and I hope Sir Leonard and the Committee think I have fulfilled the contract well. I'm afraid I'm going to disappoint you and my other friends by saying that when I arrive home, I cannot reveal what I have been doing. The secrecy document I signed is going to remain applicable until Sir Leonard decrees otherwise.

I think you and Sir Geoffrey were very brave to think about hosting a birthday party for Ignatius given your terrible uncertainty about Dominic. I'm so sorry your plans were thwarted by the ****** war, but I will certainly toast Ignatius on the day.

With all good wishes,

Sybil X

Miss Myrtle Ashcroft,
78, Broxash Road,
Wandsworth,
London, S.W.11

Friday, 14th January 1944

Mrs S. Paige,
c/o Miss J. Butterworth,
Personal Assistant to Sir Leonard Thwaites, CH KOB FB,
War Artists' Advisory Committee,
Ministry of Information,
The National Gallery,
Trafalgar Square,
London, W.C.2

Dear Sybil,

I'm so looking forward to you coming home. I've spent the best part of the week cleaning and airing your room and changing your bedsheets. It looks lovely now and smells like a summer's day.

Not much has changed since you left. Bombing has been more on a tip-and-run basis, which doesn't mean there is no damage, but the destruction is less severe. Don't mention that to Mrs Myers whose daughter's house in Deptford took a hit and left her badly injured. As you know, the poor soul has already lost a son to the Jerries so she's living on her nerves.

Despite my protests, Blanche spends less time out and about and more time working on paintings here at home. Imagine, when you return there will be two artists hard at work on two easels set up on the other side of the living room.

Like me, Michelangelo is getting old. All he wants to do is sit on the windowsill and watch the world go by. When I turf him out, he wanders around to the front of the house where he stares at me with a look of utter disbelief until I relent and let him come back in.

I have recovered well from my fall and am now in the happy position of going out for walks on my own almost daily. For some reason the district nurse still calls, even though I tell her there's no need. Tomorrow, I will make it quite clear that her time would be better spent with less able patients.

Do let us know when you'll be home so we can have something special in for tea.

Your loving aunt,

Myrtle XX

Miss Blanche Northcutt,
78, Broxash Road,
Wandsworth,
London, S.W.11

Saturday, 15th January 1944

Mrs S. Paige,
c/o Miss J. Butterworth,
Personal Assistant to Sir Leonard Thwaites, CH KOB FB,
War Artists' Advisory Committee,
Ministry of Information,
The National Gallery,
Trafalgar Square,
London, W.C.2

Dear Sybil,

Thank you for your last letter. I'm pleased to know all is well with you and that you will soon be home.

I have no doubt Auntie Myrtle has written to tell you that everything is going splendidly with her, but I must warn you that is not the truth.

Her leg is ulcerated, and the district nurse is treating it with clean bandages and ointment every day. She's also been told she must keep it up on a stool, but she will not have it. I came home from the shops a few days ago to find her spring cleaning your bedroom, although I had made it quite clear that I would do it. She said she wanted to save me the trouble, which I do appreciate, but I told her it wouldn't have been any trouble at all and she must rest, but she looked at me as if I had just landed from a different planet.

More alarming to a certain extent, is that she's becoming a bit confused and forgetful. When I go out, I give her strict instructions to stay indoors until I return, but the other afternoon I came home to an empty house. You can imagine how frightened I was. After searching the streets and knocking on neighbours' doors, I found her wandering along the high road. It was pouring with rain, and she didn't have a coat or umbrella, for goodness' sake. By the time I got her home and in front of the fire, she was shivering and couldn't really remember why. Needless to say, I now spend as much time as possible at home. It's all terribly upsetting, and I must admit I'm perplexed by it as other times she's perfectly succinct and we have the same kinds of wonderful conversations we've always had.

Oh dear, reading back through this I can see that I might have alarmed you, but I feel it's my duty to let you know what's going on at home in advance of your return. On the bright side that Auntie Myrtle always looks for, she still cooks the most wonderful meals and the RBP continues to be interested in my work.

With love,

Blanche XX

Mrs S. Paige,
c/o Miss J. Butterworth,
Personal Assistant to Sir Leonard Thwaites, CH KOB FB,
War Artists' Advisory Committee,
Ministry of Information,
The National Gallery,
Trafalgar Square,
London, W.C. 2

Monday, 24th January 1944

7709567 Capt. Fortescue, I.G.,
2nd Battalion,
Royal Norfolk Regiment,
c/o APO England

Dear Ignatius,

I'm afraid I must dash off this letter as I'm packing up ready to leave my commission.

Two things that my time here has taught me are that I can be self-sufficient enough to feel quite alright on my own, which I suppose could be called resilience or self-confidence, but that I crave the company of others. Does that make sense?

I hear from Dame Lily that you will be thirty on the 18th of February. Very many congratulations on that milestone. Wherever we both happen to be on the day, please be assured that I will be thinking of you and raising a glass to your good health and happiness.

Sybil

MONDAY 24TH JANUARY 1944

SENT FROM CHARING CROSS POST OFFICE LONDON

PRIORITY MISS M ASHCROFT AND MISS B NORTHCUTT

78 BROXASH ROAD WANDSWORTH LONDON SW11

MRS S PAIGE HOME WEDNESDAY 26 JANUARY STOP PM STOP

22

January 1944

It was dark when Sybil rounded the corner into Broxash Road but nothing like as pitch as the hills and valleys of Blaenau Ffestiniog. She stopped for a moment to take in the details of number 78 – the house she'd learned to call home. She could make out the size and shape of the windows, blanketed with blackouts. Two milk bottles stood empty on the front porch and the luscious dark sloe fruits had been stripped from the blackthorn ready to make Auntie Myrtle's favourite gin.

Even though they would be waiting for her inside, she put down her case and stood for a moment. Her stomach churned with excitement, and she imagined spreading out her belongings in her room, setting up her easel, scratching Michelangelo's ear; but she'd dragged herself around when she'd packed her things to come home, finding it difficult at the last minute to think the little cottage would no longer be her sanctuary. Mrs Edwards and some of the men who guarded the artworks came to see her off and she was hit by a hammer of surprise when saying goodbye to them wrenched at something deep inside her – as if she were leaving behind the comfort of a family. As the car taking her to the station pulled away, she'd looked out of the rear window and tears had welled in her eyes.

Although she'd been headed home, pangs of grief stabbed at her on and off during the train journey, and she realised that no matter where she went or what she did, there would always be something or someone to miss.

With that thought in mind she ran towards the door, fumbling for her key. 'It's me,' she called out. 'Home again.'

Blanche hugged her close and kissed her cheeks. She wrestled her bag and art equipment from her and ushered her into the cosy living room, unchanged since the day she'd left.

Auntie Myrtle tried to struggle up from her armchair, but Sybil gently held her back with a hug. Ribs jutted from beneath her clothes, and the skin on her hands was so thin, Sybil was afraid it would shred beneath her touch.

When she took a step back to look at her adopted aunt, Sybil was shaken by what she saw. Fear passed through her like an electric shock that left her heart pounding. Auntie Myrtle was shrinking into the cushions propping her up. Her pink scalp shone through her thin hair, and the brown spots on her face were larger and darker. Through filmy eyes, she looked from one to the other of the younger women, but Sybil wasn't sure how much she could see or hear or understand. Tears threatened again and her stomach turned over.

'We have a lovely tea ready, don't we Auntie Myrtle?' Blanche enunciated each word.

For a beat, Auntie Myrtle looked confused, then it seemed as if a light bulb had been switched on in her head. Her face brightened and she sat up straighter. 'Yes, Sybil.' She spoke slowly through one side of her mouth. 'To welcome you home from wherever you've been. Where have you been?'

Sybil drew her finger over her lips and said, 'Hush, hush, Auntie Myrtle. You know that.'

Auntie Myrtle chuckled wickedly.

'I'll take my bags upstairs and have a quick wash,' Sybil said. 'Then we can have a lovely catch-up.'

Her room seemed smaller than it had before she went to Wales, but it was clean and aired and fresh towels were on the bed. Blanche and Auntie Myrtle were so good to her although they needn't be. She was no more than a cuckoo in a meadow pipit's nest, and now it was obvious that the time had come to take care of the unsuspecting bird that had taken her in.

Downstairs again, Blanche was walking Auntie Myrtle around the living room, one hand around her waist, the other holding her elbow. She cooed and coaxed her along by telling her to mind the rug and lift her feet. Sybil joined them, and together they eased Auntie Myrtle into the chair at the head of the table.

Auntie Myrtle didn't have much padding of her own, so Sybil asked if she should fetch some cushions for her to sit on.

'Thank you,' Blanche said. 'That's nice of Sybil, isn't it, Auntie Myrtle?'

'Sybil?' Auntie Myrtle looked straight at her. 'When is Sybil coming home?'

Grateful that her task involved looking down so the others couldn't see the tears that had gathered in her eyes, Sybil slid the cushions into place.

There were no-sausage rolls, chopped ham sandwiches, potato biscuits, corned beef fritters, rock buns, pickled beetroot and raw grated carrots and cabbage with homemade chutney and gallons of tea. They'd saved their rations and put on a wonderful spread for her, but every time she looked at Auntie Myrtle, the delicacies stuck in her throat.

The conversation jumped from subject to subject, with gaps when she or Blanche filled in details for Auntie Myrtle. Then there were times when they explained something in detail only to be met by the evidence of Auntie Myrtle's full understanding. 'I had a letter from Ellen last week,' Blanche said. 'She seems to have taken to her posting, although I'm sure it must be very dangerous.'

Auntie Myrtle's hand flew to her chest. 'Is Ellen in danger?' All colour drained from her face. 'We must fetch her home immediately.'

'I'm afraid we can't,' Blanche said patiently. 'She's been posted overseas. Besides, she wants to do her bit.'

'A bit of what?' Auntie Myrtle said. 'Cheese? Yes, please. That would be lovely. And where's Sybil?'

It was exhausting and Sybil realised that there was no hope of anything like a normal chat.

As soon as they'd finished, Blanche said they'd leave the kitchen until later and put Auntie Myrtle through her bedtime routine first. 'It's a bit too early,' Auntie Myrtle protested in a lucid moment. 'Look, it's not quite eight o'clock.'

'Alright, Auntie,' Blanche said. 'We'll just turn down your bed.'

As soon as they were alone in the hallway, Sybil grabbed Blanche's arm and said, 'I had no idea she was this poorly. What's to be done?'

'Nothing, I'm afraid,' Blanche whispered. Her voice cracked around the lump that must have gathered in her throat. 'The doctor decided she'd suffered a stroke when she fell down the stairs and there's no medication and no cure.'

'Has that affected her memory?'

'Possibly, or that could be a different condition. Either way, she's not going to get better. In fact ...'

Sybil waited, but Blanche was unable to carry on. They bumped down on the bottom stair, put their arms around each other and quietly sobbed.

'... the doctor says that the next one will be the last.'

Sybil nodded. Somewhere deep in her mind she'd known that the minute she'd seen Auntie Myrtle earlier that evening, but it was awful to hear it said out loud. 'Perhaps there won't be another and she'll remain like this for a very long time.'

'No, she'll have a second stroke any time now, I'm afraid. Besides, we wouldn't want to watch her in this state for years and years, would we? I wouldn't at least, for goodness' sake.'

'Nor would I,' Sybil agreed softly. 'How have you managed on your own?'

'The doctor calls once a week, and the district nurse comes in every morning, which gives me a chance to dart out on errands. And of course, when Ellen was here, she sat watch when her shifts allowed.'

'But how do you get time for your art?'

'Once she's up or in bed, there's not too much of a problem.' Blanche took off her spectacles and wiped her eyes. 'She's my dear aunt and she's no trouble.'

'And mine,' Sybil said. 'I'm here now, so I can help.'

Blanche patted Sybil's arm.

In that short space of time, Auntie Myrtle had forgotten she wanted to stay up and announced that she'd had a lovely day, but it was time for bed. Despite pronouncing she was able to sort herself out, Blanche and Sybil followed behind, ready to jump in if she suddenly forgot where she was or what she was doing, and when she was safely tucked up, they cracked open a bottle of sloe gin and helped themselves whilst they wrote up a care roster with breaking hearts.

After Sybil handed over the last of her notebooks to Sir Leonard, he said that for now she was free of a contract and could concentrate on whatever she chose, but he hoped she would present many more paintings to the WAAC. 'Can I please clarify that you still don't want me to turn any Manod mine sketches into paintings?'

'Not at this time, Mrs Paige. And I'm afraid that you're still bound by the Secrecy Act.'

Sybil was bewildered about what would become of that unique set of drawings but felt sure that Sir Leonard must have something in mind or he wouldn't have given her the long commission to catalogue them.

'Do you have to sign secrecy documents?' she asked Jane as they sat in a Corner House later that day.

'One after the other,' Jane said. 'You'd have thought one would be enough, but that's not the case. How's your aunt?'

Sybil carried on stirring her tea distractedly. 'Not well,' she said. 'It's most peculiar, but she seems to rally a number of times each day, then quickly reverts back to not knowing who we are or where she is.'

'I'm so sorry. That must be difficult to live with.'

'What about you? Any news from Cyril, the world's most reluctant Casanova?'

'Actually,' Jane leaned in closer, 'I think he might have proposed.'

Sybil could feel her eyes popping. '*Might* have proposed,' she echoed. She thought back to Graeme bending down on one knee in a puddly London Street after a night on the town. When she'd said yes and he stood up, his trouser legs were covered in streaks of dirty rainwater. He'd seemed completely devoted then, but now she wondered if he'd merely been fuelled by alcohol and fumbling hands and a starry sky. 'I'm intrigued by how he worded it to make you unsure of his intentions.'

'I've been waiting to get you on your own to ask your opinion.' Jane dived into her bag, brought out a one-page letter and handed it to Sybil.

She scanned the first couple of paragraphs filled with pleasantries about Jane's work, her mother and the dog. He wrote about rations and endless paperwork and how he missed home. Then from nowhere he said, '*When this ****** war is over, I think we should get married.*' That was it. No pleading for her to accept or lines telling her she was everything to him or promises to make her happy forever.

'Well.' Sybil folded the letter and handed it back. 'I think it is a proposal,' she said.

Jane's perfect red mouth formed a perfect circle. 'How very exciting, but on the other hand, not very exciting at all. I don't know whether to laugh with joy or cry with disappointment.'

Sybil reached across the table and held Jane's hand. 'You've always said he was a shy man.'

'Yes,' Jane snorted. 'But there's reticence and then there's taking someone for granted.'

'What will you do?' Sybil asked. 'Accept or turn him down.'

Jane looked thoughtful. 'If I turn him down, I doubt I'd get another chance with anyone else. Not at my age. I think I'm going to spin it out. You know, make him sweat a bit. It's not wrong to think he owes me a bit more than this lame proposal, is it?'

'No,' Sybil said. 'Not in the least. All I think about that is: good on you.'

Perhaps it was her imagination, but as she painted picture after picture in the changing light, the house seemed to shrink around her. In a much smaller version of the Manod mine, every room and hallway and surface was crowded with materials, canvases and artworks in the process of being completed.

Blanche produced idyllic paintings of forgotten corners of London – a dank alleyway that led to a hanging basket of lavish flowers swinging from the front of an antique shop or an enclave of daffodils standing guard along railings in a park. Ellen's sketches, no longer able to be stored in the basement of St Mary's, had found a home under a weight on the sideboard.

Sybil was lucky to have her room to herself, although that was crammed too. In a corner, she kept her self-portrait under an old towel and whenever she felt able, she would get it out and add to it. She was strict, and whenever she arrived at the point where she wanted to spoil it, she forced herself to hide it away until she could look at it again.

She gave a lot of thought to what life would be like if she found a place of her own, and more and more often, the idea filled her with feelings of liberation rather than dread.

Money was no longer a problem as she'd accumulated a nice sum from her paintings for the WAAC and she felt somewhat secure that her reputation would stand her career in good stead. She could find somewhere with an extra room for a studio and perhaps a bit of a garden for the dog or cat she would keep for company. Graeme wasn't coming back – she'd realised that in Wales when she'd released herself from the false hope the imagined last paragraph of his letter had given her. As for loneliness, that would be the price she had to pay for reaping the benefits of having her own space around her, something else she'd come to appreciate during the long nights in Blaenau Ffestiniog.

But there was Auntie Myrtle, and Blanche, and no question that she would stay put in Wandsworth for as long as she was needed by them. What would happen after that unhappy day would have to be put on hold until then.

Since her return from Wales, the WAAC had purchased three more of her compositions – the whistling man cleaning windows in Canterbury; the women in headscarves sweeping the ever-accumulating rubble off the station platforms in York; the bell from St Sidwell's Church nestled in a straw-lined box. She had so many sketches she could work from but she was eager to acquire up-to-the-minute ideas, so once a week she took herself off for the day to sketch new subjects, and a few days later, Blanche would do the same.

Although the air was heady with smoke and the industrial smells that came with clearing-up, Sybil would stand and take a deep breath, feasting on the anticipation of being outdoors for the entire day. Their stifling existence gave them little time to appreciate winter turning to spring and spring to summer. It hurt her to think it, but the house had started to feel stuffy and harbour unpleasant odours. It wasn't that she and Blanche didn't keep it clean, just the opposite was true. They scrubbed and swept and washed endlessly, but Auntie Myrtle was often cold, so the windows stayed closed and they kept as much of a fire going as possible. To save them having to change their aunt multiple times a day, they'd taken to tying a cloth around her neck to catch the spills when she ate, but a whiff of stale food lingered. The routine was claustrophobic, especially as Auntie Myrtle's coherent moments diminished until, one morning, she'd called for Sybil to help her remove the unrecognisable, bossy woman – Blanche – from her room. When things had calmed down, she found Blanche face down on her bed, crying her eyes out for the auntie who no longer knew who she was. That was when the unthinkable popped into her head, that they'd all be better off when ... she'd stopped herself there, but not before guilt engulfed her.

The same remorse hit her that morning when she leaned over to kiss Auntie Myrtle goodbye. 'I'll see you this evening,' she said. 'Don't get into any mischief whilst I'm gone.'

As if waking from a dream, Auntie Myrtle looked at her with clear eyes. 'Don't go, Sybil.' She clutched at her hand. 'The Jerries are out and about with their nasty V-1s.'

Sybil pulled back in alarm, barely able to believe what she'd heard. There had been a long discussion between her and Blanche the night before about the buzz bombs that were falling from the skies over the south of England. In between comments, they'd taken it in turns to coax Auntie Myrtle to eat, but she'd seemed far away, as if she couldn't see or hear or smell the root vegetable casserole they'd tempted her with. But that was obviously not the case.

Sybil signalled for Blanche to follow her into the kitchen. 'She heard every word we were saying last night,' she hissed. 'How often do you think that happens? And what if she understands when we're talking about her?'

'Oh dear.' Blanche blinked from behind her spectacles. 'I hate to think that's the case. I asked the doctor, and he said it's a fluke that she can repeat what she's seen or heard but not to be alarmed as it doesn't sink in very far.'

But Auntie Myrtle was unsettled and Sybil felt disturbed. 'Should I stay today as she's asked me to?'

Blanche shook her head. 'No, I'll make her a cup of tea and then she'll have a nap. When she wakes, she will have completely forgotten all about the Jerries and their V-1s. Go and have a break.'

Sybil slipped out of the door reluctantly and inhaled until the feeling that she was abandoning Blanche and Auntie Myrtle faded. On the Underground, she decided that unless she saw an outstanding example of the opposite, she would concentrate on uplifting sketches for the day. There was a woman sitting across from her whose red-rimmed eyes and blotchy skin gave her away as having experienced a recent bereavement. Every few seconds, she sniffed on a hiccough, which made Sybil's stomach twinge with pity. Any other day, she would have surreptitiously got out her materials and drawn the woman, whose hands wrung at a soggy handkerchief. But instead, she sketched a young mum with a toddler on her lap. They were looking through a picture book and the little chap repeated the words his mother pointed to out loud. Every item he wore was too small and his mother's clothes were too big. *Bombed out, poor things*, Sybil thought. And yet there they were, enjoying themselves and the cardboard book. The toddler reached up and placed his hand on his mother's cheek. When she pointed to a page and said, 'Pretty flowers', he echoed something quite unintelligible which sent the young woman into fits of laughter that were as catching as a flame from an incendiary. It was them she chose to immortalise in her sketchbook. When they hopped off at Holland Park, she gazed after them and quickly drew the way they held hands, the mother smiling down at her little son as he zoomed a tin spitfire through the air.

At the Palace of Westminster, she sketched a few scenes of unfazed workmen carrying out renovations in the aftermath of water damage. As usual, one of them asked her what she was up to and she produced her documentation much more confidently than she had three years ago.

The man, covered in masonry dust, studied her permits then shook his head. 'That's a strange job,' he said. 'How about sketching an unusual picture of me and me mates?'

A number of images of what he meant by 'unusual' passed through Sybil's mind, but she said she would give it a go. The man called to his colleagues, and they snaked their arms around each other's waists. On a command, they each lifted one trouser leg and posed like a chorus line of cancan dancers at the Moulin Rouge. Sybil threw back her head and laughed so loudly that it was almost impossible to complete the charcoal drawings. 'You've cheered me up no end,' she said as she tore off a sketch and handed it to the workman who'd initially noticed her.

'Thank you, my duck,' the man said. 'I'll pin this up in the changing hut so we can keep our sights on a possible new career after this bloody war finishes.'

Sybil laughed again. 'I don't think there'll be a lot of time for dancing,' she said. 'Clearing up the entire country will take the rest of our lives.'

A smoke-blackened, melancholic church stood half hidden behind bushes, and trying to stick to her decision to keep away from the heartrending, Sybil went to hurry by, but at that moment the doors opened and a bridal party emerged into the sunshine. The bride was lovely, her dark hair sitting in waves on her shoulders and the groom was proud in RAF uniform. Sybil ducked into the shadows and sketched as the scene unfolded. Following behind the family members were four firemen who looked as though they'd just stepped away from dousing an inferno. Their uniforms were streaked with ash, and as their helmets were in their hands, it was plain to see their hair sticking to their heads with sweat. Telling the story of this occasion would make a striking composition – the happiness in the eyes of the newlyweds, the exhaustion on the faces of the firemen.

A small band of local women had gathered near the iron railings and Sybil joined them as they chatted. One of them said the church had taken it so badly the night before, it was a miracle the wedding had been able to go ahead.

'Were the firemen involved in putting out the fire?' Sybil asked.

A woman with a feathery brooch on her grey coat turned to her. 'I bumped into the vicar this morning and he told me that the fire crew had saved the dome and the groom asked them to stay and watch them get married.'

'What a lovely thing to do,' Sybil said. 'But I expect they'd rather get their heads down for a kip.'

'I'm not sure about that. It's surprising how a nip from a hipflask of whiskey can cheer you up,' another woman quipped. 'I saw them handing it round a few minutes before the ceremony.'

Sybil finished a stick of charcoal and started another as the firemen formed a guard of honour. The young couple walked through it whilst their friends and relatives sprinkled a handful of rice at their feet. She was sure she wouldn't capture anything better – this was her picture for the day.

Although she drew a number of other quick sketches, that thought proved to be right. But she had a cup of tea in a café and enjoyed the outing. She hadn't been bothered by bombs, doodlebugs or otherwise, and as pale lemon and orange streaked the sky, she thought she should get back to Wandsworth.

The fresh air and feeling that she'd done her work well had invigorated her and she walked home from the station with a lighter step. If she hurried, Blanche might have time for a walk around the Common before the bedtime routine, and then they would look through the sketches Sybil had drawn that day. As for waiting an entire week before she could have another day out, that thought didn't seem too bad now. Auntie Myrtle had helped her when she was in dire straits, and she would continue to repay the kindness.

Michelangelo sat upright in the window when he saw Sybil approach the house, then he bolted and scrambled through her legs when she opened the door. She watched him race to the blackthorn tree and relieve himself in a deluge that the firemen at the wedding could have put to good use the night before. 'Only me,' she called out. 'I've had a very productive day. How's everyone here?'

Silence shouted at her.

'Hello,' she tried again as she eased out of her shoes. It was strange – Auntie Myrtle didn't always hear well, but that couldn't be an excuse for Blanche. Perhaps she'd ducked out for a pint of milk, and Auntie Myrtle was asleep in her chair. Sybil hung up her coat and called out that she'd put on the kettle, but when she walked into the living room it was empty. A frantic rumbling started in her stomach. She peered into the kitchen, checked the scullery and called up the stairs. Then amongst the artwork, paintbrushes and charcoals on the table, she saw a scrap of white paper that somehow looked more pallid than the others. She pounced on it.

S. Auntie M taken a funny turn. Come to Queen Mary's. B.

Even as she raced through the streets to the Underground, she could not have related how she found her way to the hospital. A policeman tried to stop her, but she showed him her permits and carried on. Breathless when she reached the reception desk, she asked for Miss Myrtle Ashcroft who had been brought in earlier that day, and a porter took her to the correct ward. There, a matron walked adeptly to meet her, and when she asked again to see her adopted aunt, she was shown instead to a bare room where she sat on a hard chair and fiddled with her wedding ring until her finger was inflamed.

Then the door opened unceremoniously, and Blanche stood in front of her, tears pouring down her face and clouding her spectacles. She put out her arms and Sybil caught her.

Later that night, they sat in the living room and Blanche told her the whole story yet again, but still it didn't seem real. She said the day had progressed as any other since Auntie Myrtle had become housebound except that when she'd fallen asleep, she hadn't woken up. Blanche had murmured her name, then shaken her and finally shouted but never got a response. Mrs Myers had called an ambulance from a telephone box, and they'd been taken to hospital. 'I didn't give up, Sybil,' Blanche said. 'Not for a minute. I truly believed that, once in Queen Mary's, she would rally. But they told me she'd gone in her sleep and there was nothing that could have been done.'

That didn't stop Sybil from regretting every minute she'd been out of the house that day. Talking to workmen, sketching a wedding, sipping tea and nibbling an iced bun whilst Auntie Myrtle was dying and Blanche was coping on her own. 'She warned us,' Sybil mumbled.

'Sorry. What was that?' Blanche asked.

'She didn't want me to go this morning. Do you remember? She was worried about the V-1s.'

Blanche nodded. 'Yes, I remember,' she said. 'But I'm not convinced that was a premonition. Although a funny thing happened not long before she nodded off. There was a loud noise from the high street. You know, where they're shoring up the Co-op. She sat bolt upright and said, as plain as day, "A V-1. Don't let it get Sybil."'

That started Sybil's tears yet again. 'She treated me like her own niece,' she said. 'And it was the same with Ellen. She always thought about us before she thought about herself.' She brought the palm of her hand down hard on the table. 'Oh, I feel so bad about not being here for both of you.'

Blanche reached over and touched her arm. 'There was

nothing you could have done except stopped me from running around in circles.'

'At least that would have been something,' Sybil said.

Ellen couldn't get leave, but she sent a telegram saying her heart was broken. There weren't many at the funeral – Blanche, Sybil, Mrs Myers and a few neighbours and friends. Despite the summer sun, the church was cold and Sybil shivered when she walked down the path, bordered on each side by gravestones. The creak of the door as the undertaker closed it behind them made Sybil's heart skip a beat, it sounded like someone's last croaky attempt at a few words.

Auntie Myrtle's last words had been, 'Don't let it get Sybil.' They should have been about Blanche or Ellen or herself – for once. No matter how she'd protested, Blanche insisted the vicar entwine that into his eulogy. She wanted him to use it as an example of Auntie Myrtle's selflessness, and Sybil couldn't bring herself to explain that, no matter how she tried to justify it, Auntie Myrtle's last sentiment made her feel guilty and undeserving.

They sang a hymn, listened to a reading and cried when they dared to look up at the coffin. As the vicar took to the podium, the heavy door rasped again and they couldn't help themselves, they had to turn for a moment and see who on earth had joined them. The neighbours glanced then swivelled back to the front. Blanche stared at the interloper then at Sybil with a confused look that creased her brow, and Sybil couldn't take her eyes off Ignatius as he tiptoed towards their pew on gleaming uniform shoes.

A rush of colour tinged Sybil's face bright red, and she felt a stinging sensation under her arms. Her hand, threaded through Blanche's arm, felt hot and sticky. She hadn't yet written to Ignatius about Auntie Myrtle, so she could only presume Dame Lily had passed on the information. He nodded once in their direction, then focused on the vicar. She didn't know how she felt about him being there uninvited. The thought flashed through her mind that it was noble and kind of him, but did he think that she, or they, couldn't manage on their own? Apart from that, he was distracting her from concentrating on the ceremony, and if she missed one word or failed to experience one emotion, she knew she would regret it.

Against her better judgement, her eyes flickered towards him at the same moment he peeked at her. They both snapped their attention back to the front of the church, but not before Sybil had taken in the bulk of his arms and the amber of his eyes. The vicar had reached the part of the tribute that involved Auntie Myrtle's last words and Sybil's face flushed again. She couldn't wait for the service to end and held on tight to Blanche as she tried hard to concentrate on her friend rather than herself.

They walked behind the coffin as it weaved through the cemetery to a fresh plot of turned-over earth. With deference, Ignatius placed himself last in the line of friends and Sybil didn't contradict his decision by calling him forward. The vicar recited the committal and as the coffin was lowered, Sybil and Blanche held onto each other for dear life. It didn't seem real that the roses they threw landed on a wooden box that contained the woman who had loved them so completely. When they knew they couldn't stay a moment longer, they filed towards the path with leaden steps. Ignatius was waiting for them at the gate, and for a moment, Sybil was surprised to see him. The realisation that she had given Auntie Myrtle her heart and soul and full attention for the last few minutes gave her some comfort.

'Ignatius.' Blanche kissed the young man on his cheek. 'How thoughtful of you to come along. You being here has made us very happy. Hasn't it, Sybil?'

'Of course.' Sybil felt her lips tremble with the effort of trying to sound convincing.

'Mama knew I would be passing through London on my way to— Sorry.' He drew his fingers along his mouth. 'I can't divulge that. She feels terrible that she couldn't be here herself and asked me to come along as her envoy.'

'I can't tell you how much that touches my heart,' Blanche said. 'Thank you. I insist you come back to the house for tea, gin and a bit of cake. Please say you will.'

'There's nothing I'd like more,' Ignatius said. 'But duty calls, I'm afraid.'

Relief flooded Sybil. She wanted to go home, serve refreshments to the neighbours and think about Auntie Myrtle rather than why Ignatius's intrusion made her feel embarrassed and clumsy.

A warm breeze swirled around their ankles and disturbed a pile of leaves into a momentary maelstrom. The heady scent of flowers came and went in waves. In the distance, the callous mechanical buzz of a doodlebug brought all conversation to a stop. A blast caused the air around them to wobble, and everyone reached for the wall or each other to hold themselves steady. Sybil's heart found its way to her throat, and from there it dropped back into position with a lurch. She and Blanche locked eyes, and Auntie Myrtle's last words screamed in her mind.

'That was close,' one of the neighbours said. Blanche turned to talk to them, and Sybil and Ignatius were left facing each other.

Although Ignatius looked dignified and able in his uniform, he clasped his hands behind his back as it was his turn to glow pink.

'I should have sent a telegram that I was coming,' he said. 'That way I wouldn't have made you feel uncomfortable.'

Sybil shrugged and wondered why she was so desperate to appear nonchalant. 'It would have helped to know you planned to attend.' The formality in her voice made her flinch inwardly.

Ignatius nodded. 'I'm sorry. I didn't know anything about it until the last minute.' They stood in silence for a few moments, then he sighed and continued. 'Something always seems to go wrong when we see each other, and to tell you the truth, I'm such a chump I can never figure out exactly what it is.'

Pity for him made her feel a fresh wave of guilt. He hadn't done anything wrong other than try to get her to take an interest in him. It wasn't his fault that she'd come to the conclusion that Graeme never loved her or that she'd made such an ungracious mess of her night with Hector. Yet, all she could say was, 'Yes, perhaps we get on better in our letters than we do face to face.'

The umber dots across Ignatius's cheeks faded as the colour drained from his face. He bowed towards her from the waist then, without another word, he shook her hand and marched towards the Underground station. Sybil closed her eyes, but the relief she'd hoped to feel at his departure failed to envelop her. When she looked again, he'd disappeared from view.

23

58223814, Staff Nurse, Hewitt, E.H.,
QAIMNS,
c/o British Military Hospital 133

Friday, 30th June 1944

Mrs S. Paige,
78, Broxash Road,
Wandsworth,
London, S.W.11

Dearest Sybil,

D-Day! The sweetest words in the English language – or any language for that matter. We received the news here on the same day as you did in dear old England, and I must say, I'm still reeling. You should have heard the cheers in the hospital. Do you remember Churchill's speech in 1942, I think it was, when he said it wasn't the beginning of the end? But now everyone here agrees it is exactly that. We are elated and excited and are starting to allow ourselves hope.

Your painting of the wedding with the firemen in attendance sounds exquisite, and I so like the sketches of Auntie Myrtle that you sent in your last letter. Might you create a composition of her funeral? It would make an excellent contrast if hung next to the one of the young couple leaving the church.

Every time I'm on the cusp of sleep, I half imagine and half dream about her. Sometimes she's standing at the door greeting us, other times she's making a pot of tea or stroking Michelangelo as he purrs on her lap. Then the image of her last day that I've cobbled together from Blanche's letters takes over and the tears begin. She was wonderful to us, wasn't she? And do you know, I'm so grateful for the way she passed away. I have seen lovely people on agonising deathbeds that you wouldn't wish on anyone. To go in her sleep was a blessing, believe me.

Do you think Blanche will keep the house on? I suppose it would be foolish of her to let it go and have to look for somewhere else to live, although I do realise that to stay there, in the place that was so indelibly marked as Auntie Myrtle's, might be unbearable for her. I'm so glad she's got you there.

With love and hope for an end in sight,

Ellen XXX

Mrs S. Paige,
78, Broxash Road,
Wandsworth,
London, S.W.11

Sunday, 16th July 1944

58223814, Staff Nurse, Hewitt, E.H.,
QAIMNS,
c/o British Military Hospital 133

Dearest Ellen,

Thank you for your lovely letter and like you, I'm hoping that we'll soon be able to sing 'I'll Be Seeing You' in earnest. But the vicious flying bombs have seen another exodus of young mums and children flee London, and their absence makes me think that the cycle of attack and retaliation will never be broken.

I hope my composition of the wedding lives up to your expectations. It's almost ready to present to the WAAC, and I'm hoping they might accept it. Still no sign of another commission from them, but I have accrued enough material to last me a lifetime so am content on that score for the time being.

Blanche hasn't discussed the subject of the house with me, and I, of course, wouldn't initiate the discussion. I know what you mean about there being too many memories for her here, or perhaps for any of us, but accommodation is priceless and no one can afford to be picky. In confidence, I had been musing over the idea of finding a place of my own, with some sort of studio attached, before Auntie Myrtle took a turn for the worse, but I wouldn't be able to leave Blanche on her own now.

All my love,

Sybil XX

Dame Lily Brampton, DBE RA ROI RWS,
Seagulls' Watch,
Cley-next-the-Sea,
Norfolk

Friday, 25th August 1944

Mrs S. Paige,
78, Broxash Road,
Wandsworth,
London, S.W.11

Dearest Sybil,

Paris is ours again! Isn't it wonderful? I'm sure the French would insist that their capital has been returned to France, but it feels like it belongs to us, too, and that the surrender was our victory as well. It's very heartening and makes us think that we're creeping ever closer to the end.

In my opinion, that calls for a celebration. I know I've asked before and Blanche hasn't felt up to travelling, but would you and she like to come here for a week or so? I'm thinking about the last week in September. The fresh air and change of scene would be a tonic for both of you. You could bring your materials and we can trek along the coast and sketch what we see, or you can use the light in the house to perfect whatever you're working on.

I haven't seen you for ages and my dear Geoffrey and I could use a bit of outside entertainment. Having said that, we appreciate that Blanche, in particular, needs a gentle approach which I can assure you she will get from us. After all, we're still stuck in no-man's land as far as mourning Dominic is concerned as I know you are with Graeme.

With much love,

Lily X

Mrs S. Paige,
78, Broxash Road,
Wandsworth,
London, S.W.11

Wednesday, 30th August 1944

Dame Lily Brampton, DBE RA ROI RWS,
Seagulls' Watch,
Cley-next-the-Sea,
Norfolk

Dear Dame Lily,

Thank you for your very kind invitation. I have spoken at length to Blanche about it, and she now says she's ready to make the trip and thinks it would do her the world of good. She asks me to thank you for your kindness.

We will both bring our artwork with us and hope to spend some pleasant days with you sketching the sea and the shoreline and the light as it filters through the clouds.

Everyone here is over the moon about Paris, and we're hoping it will be the start of a pack of cards momentum for Europe.

Apart from drawing and painting and presenting to the WAAC, the only other news is that Michelangelo has followed Auntie Myrtle. He wasn't the same after she passed away, and a couple of days ago, he didn't return from his daily constitutional. Blanche found him curled up under the blackthorn tree, so we dug up a bit of earth and buried him there.

With much love,

Sybil X

7709567 Capt. Fortescue, I.G.,
2nd Battalion,
Royal Norfolk Regiment,
c/o APO England

Wednesday, 30ᵗʰ August 1944

Mrs S. Paige,
78, Broxash Road,
Wandsworth,
London, S.W.11

Dear Sybil,

I'm sorry it has taken me such a long time to write, but I'm sure you can ascertain from the news that things have been very busy.

I do hope you and Blanche are well and able to carry on with your wonderful works of art. Mama continues to be busy with the WAAC, and Papa continues to work at his own pace in his studio as he always has. Nothing appears to faze him – except the situation with Dom – and I think he missed his calling in politics as he would have taken everything thrown at him in his stride.

The main reason for this letter is to inform you that I wrote to Mama about my upcoming leave, and she decided to invite you and Blanche during the same period of time. I'm so sorry. If I didn't know her better, I would almost suspect her of trying to set us up.

So, I am now in the position of asking whether I should cancel my leave or if you can bear to be in my proximity for a few days. I am in favour of the latter because, if you are to remain my mother's friend – and her heart would break if you weren't – our paths will cross more frequently as time goes on, and we must find a way of working around this.

For my part, I will give you as wide a berth as possible at Seagulls' Watch.

I look forward to your decision.

Iggy

Mrs S. Paige,
78, Broxash Road,
Wandsworth,
London, S.W.11

Wednesday, 13th September 1944

7709567 Capt. Fortescue, I.G.,
2nd Battalion,
Royal Norfolk Regiment,
c/o APO England

Dear Ignatius,

You must think me awfully churlish, which is definitely how I think of myself.

In answer to your question, Blanche and I have accepted Dame Lily's invitation to stay at Seagulls' Watch and we are looking forward to it. For my part, I wouldn't dream of distancing myself from your mother – she means so much to me, so I agree with you that we have to find a way to manage the situation.

I walked around the Common today with my head down and thought about all of this in great detail. Although I mentioned it in the previous paragraph, neither of us has ever spoken about what our situation involves, so I am going to be honest about it from my point of view. Both of us know life is too short to do otherwise, don't we?

I think you want more from me than friendship and I cannot deny that, if I allowed myself to get dragged in, that is what I would want too. But life is complicated, especially during this ****** war and I'm not in a position to let myself get involved. Apart from the obvious reason of still being married, things that I don't want to go into about that marriage and subsequent incidents have led me to lose my trust in others and in my own judgement. This is no reflection on you.

Let's be friends and enjoy each other's company when we meet up. I hope you will be comfortable with that.

With best wishes,

Sybil

7709567 Capt. Fortescue, I.G.,
2nd Battalion,
Royal Norfolk Regiment,
c/o APO England

Monday, 18th September 1944

Mrs S. Paige,
78, Broxash Road,
Wandsworth
London, S.W.11

Dear Sybil,

Thank you for being honest with me and for opening up an entirely new conversation. I admire you greatly for it.

Of course, your summation of my feelings is completely accurate, and I will admit that my plan has been to woo you from the minute I first met you. However, I respect your wish to keep me at arm's length, and with our friendship in mind, I am looking forward to seeing you in Norfolk. I also appreciate your need for privacy, but if you do want to talk to me in confidence about your experiences, I will listen without judgement and never betray your trust.

Yours,

Iggy

P.S. Mama told me about Michelangelo and I'm sorry to hear the news. At least he's happy now with Auntie Myrtle.

24

September 1944

Blanche was having the time of her life at Seagulls' Watch. She wore a cream satin blouse and black skirt for the first evening meal and jazzed the outfit up with a pair of clip-on earrings she'd found in the back of Auntie Myrtle's wardrobe.

They talked about the progress of the war and how it must surely be over soon what with Brussels being liberated soon after Paris. There was always a but, Sybil had learned that, and the ever-logical Sir Geoffrey reminded them not to forget the V-2s. Dame Lily waved the thought away with a dismissive hand. 'They're falling short of their mark time and again,' she said. 'Our cobbled-together barrage balloons are seeing off their huge, expensive, odious weapons. That's how fantastic we are.'

Sir Geoffrey replenished the wine glasses. 'But we mustn't forget how devastating they are when they do hit – whether it's on their intended target or not.'

That quietened the table. The first rocket had killed a woman in her sixties, a toddler and a sapper who was home on leave. And there had been many more.

'I know,' Dame Lily said. 'It's cruel beyond belief. I stopped going to London after the V-1s were launched because I couldn't deal with the noise.' She covered her ears with her hands and shuddered.

'We're lucky we can call Norfolk home,' Sir Geoffrey said.

He looked pointedly at Sybil and Blanche. 'Thousands have no choice but to stay put.'

'Yes,' Dame Lily conceded. 'I'm very grateful for that.'

'And we,' Blanche said as she raised her glass, 'are most appreciative that you've asked us to share the relative peace and tranquillity with you.' She blinked at each of them in turn.

'Do you mind if I …' Dame Lily produced her cigarette case and lit up before any of them had a chance to answer. 'I choose to believe though, despite the doodlebugs, that we are on the path to victory and what a relief it will be.' She looked into the distance. 'Up to a point.'

'I agree with you, Lily,' Sir Geoffrey said. 'And whatever the outcome for our Dom, the end of the bloody war will be a blessing for everyone.'

Dame Lily blew smoke out of her nostrils and smiled thinly in a show of unity first at her husband and then at Sybil.

'I hope I'm not speaking out of turn,' Blanche said. 'But where is Ignatius, has his leave been cancelled? If so, that might be a good sign.'

Sybil took a gulp of wine that she hoped would excuse her red face. She'd wanted to ask the same question but thought it might make her seem too eager to see him or disappointed that he wasn't there – both of which were too close to the surface of her emotions not to go undetected.

'He telegrammed,' Dame Lily said, 'to tell us that he won't be here until tomorrow evening. Give or take – I don't know – a few hours or days. He said he'd be in touch again if needs be. There was an underlying tension in the telegram which gave me another reason to think something big will happen soon. Although selfish, I don't want whatever it is to interfere with his leave.'

Sybil kept her eyes on her plate and concentrated on the smudge of gravy left around the edges. How she wished she had a Yorkshire pudding to mop it up. Like Dame Lily, she hoped Ignatius would make it home although she was also dreading it if he did.

'What say you, my dear Sybil?' Dame Lily asked, in a way that made Sybil feel as transparent as cellophane.

'I agree with you, Dame Lily. Although if his leave is deferred, I hope it's for a positive reason.'

Ida came in to gather their plates and Dame Lily asked her to serve the dessert. 'And the port that's left to go with it, please,' she added.

Sleep was hard to come by that night. Sybil breathed in and out with the ebb and flow of the waves and listened for the hoot of owls as they rummaged through the night. Perhaps Ignatius would make an appearance, perhaps he wouldn't. The war might end soon, but then again it might not. The port had been good, but the cheese rolled around in her stomach.

Before dawn, the seagulls started their choking call, and when she sensed that the day was breaking behind the blackouts, she dressed, gathered together a sketchbook and charcoals and quietly went downstairs. At the back door, she donned her overshoes and hoped the key wouldn't screech when she turned it in the lock. Then, from the kitchen, there was the scrape of a chair followed by a sleepy, 'Is that you, Mama?'

She stood still, her hand on the doorknob, and thought about whether to show herself or make a bolt for the beach. But that would only delay the inevitable, so she called softly, 'It's me, Ignatius.'

He looked exhausted but smiled at her when she peeked around the door. 'I should have gone straight up to bed when I came in, but one whiskey later, I was fast asleep with my head on the kitchen table.' He craned this way and that. 'My neck certainly knows all about it.'

'Well,' Sybil said. 'You did better than me tucked up in a luxurious bed. Do you think Ida would mind if I made us a cup of tea?'

Ignatius sat back down and shook his head. The little lines

around his eyes were deeper and there was a bit of grey in his hair that she either hadn't noticed before or perhaps had only recently appeared. The war had so much to answer for. 'Oh, Ida wouldn't mind, but tea wasn't what you were thinking about. Where were you sneaking off to?'

Sybil laughed. 'I wasn't being sly,' she said. 'I was just going to take advantage of the early morning light whilst I could.'

Ignatius studied her as if he wanted to say something but was worried about the reaction. 'May I join you or do you want to be by yourself?'

Now it was her turn to think for a few moments. She had been looking forward to time on her own, but this might be a good opportunity to break the ice with no one else around to monitor her awkwardness. 'Of course you can,' she said.

There was a chill in the air along with the fetid smell of rotting seaweed. Reeds swayed on either side of the beaten path that led down to the beach and Ignatius told her that last night, V-2s had been aimed at Ipswich and Norwich but had missed their targets.

'Oh no,' Sybil said. 'That's frightening. Dame Lily has avoided London because of those rockets. Now she'll think they've followed her here.'

'I won't mention it to her,' Ignatius said.

'Nor will I, but she's bound to hear about it somehow.'

'If I know Mama.'

They admired the pastel streaks of dawn and talked about how difficult it was to capture them without making the composition either too pale or too gaudy. Sybil said Ignatius's childhood must have been perfect what with the sea and the sand and the fresh air.

'It was, although we spent a good deal of time away at boarding school. Having two brothers to fight with during the holidays was idyllic. But now there's only …' He looked into the distance and his voice caught.

Sybil touched his arm, and when he half smiled at her, she was struck again by how he looked straight at her without guile. It was as if he wanted to know everything about her – her thoughts, feelings, ideas, ambitions, what made her laugh and what made her cry.

A weathered wooden boat lay on its side in the middle of a marsh as though it had been stranded by a low tide. They stopped to draw it from different angles, and Ignatius explained that it had been there for years and he'd often thought of rescuing it and making it seaworthy again but didn't know when he'd get the time and opportunity now.

'Never put off until tomorrow what you can do today,' Sybil chirped. A wave of strawberry blonde hair worked itself loose from her clip and whipped across her face.

'Do you truly believe that?' Ignatius stood still, his charcoal poised over his notebook. 'Surely it's better sometimes to step back and think logically about the outcome of what you want to say or do.'

Sybil smiled at him. Something about the fresh sea air, being where the war didn't seem as significant as it did in London and the flecks in his tawny eyes that mirrored the colours of the sea and sand made her feel light-headed and impetuous. 'I suppose you're right,' she conceded. 'But don't you sometimes want to be nothing more than carefree and spontaneous?'

Ignatius stared at her so intensely that she would never be able to accuse him of looking through her as Graeme had done. Then he threw down the things he was holding and kissed her hard on the lips.

Maybe she should have pushed him away or slapped him or fallen limp in his arms. But the truth was that she wanted him to carry on. Her limbs filled with electricity and her breathing came in gulps. A pulse tamped in Ignatius's throat and kept time with the hammering of her heart. It was shocking, not that he'd taken the initiative, but that she'd joined in so wholeheartedly.

He grabbed her hand and pulled her towards the abandoned

boat where he tore off her cardigan and struggled out of his pullover. She nestled against him and smelled the salt from his skin mingling with the brine of the sea. Then his frenzy slowed down and he asked her if she was sure, if she wanted to take things slower, if she wanted to tell him about her previous, unhappy experiences or if she wanted them to exchange promises.

'None of those,' she said softly. 'Not now.'

Under cover of *My Lovely Jean*, as the boat was called, Sybil was reckless enough to forget she was still married to a man who had probably never really loved her and to wonder if this man did. And when they lay, Sybil's head on Ignatius's chest, listening for the sounds of footsteps, he did make a promise to her. He said he would salvage the boat as soon as he could and rename it *My Lovely Sybil*. But he needn't have, Sybil thought. Even now, she wasn't going to allow herself to expect anything from him other than this moment they were experiencing together. It was more than enough for her and if she kept strictly to that way of thinking, it would save her from the agony of wondering if he meant what he said or misjudging his intentions or ruminating on how things could possibly work out between them. She had convinced herself in Wales that she could get used to the idea of living on her own – and probably thrive on it – now all she had to do was hold herself aloof and enjoy what Ignatius had to offer her whilst she could. With that thought in mind, she waited for whoever was walking their dog on the path to pass by, then pulled him to her again.

In the brighter light of full morning, Sybil wondered if the others, Dame Lily in particular, would pick up on how the relationship between her and Ignatius had shifted. Back at the house, she washed and dressed carefully and found everyone taking an informal breakfast in the dining room.

'I understand you've already managed to have time alone with my son whilst the rest of us had no idea he was home,' Dame Lily said.

Sybil silently cursed how easily she coloured and wished she could control it. 'Yes,' Sybil smiled. 'We managed to get some beautiful sketches of the beach in the morning light.'

'It was a very productive couple of hours,' Ignatius said, and Sybil was aware of his eyes roaming over her from head to feet.

'Do you want to rest, dear Iggy?' Dame Lily asked. 'Or would you like to ramble with us. I think Blanche is eager to get the countryside into her sketchbook.'

'Yes, I am,' Blanche said. 'But for goodness' sake, I don't want to have responsibility for the final say. I'm happy to go along with what everyone else wants to do.'

Sybil stabbed a slice of mushroom and ate it with a scoop of powdered egg whilst she waited for Ignatius's reply. If he said he was going to stop at home, could she possibly manipulate staying with him? A bed would be a luxury after the barbed marsh grass, and no one would bother them as Sir Geoffrey would be cut off in his studio at the bottom of the garden. She and Ignatius looked at each other briefly, but not before she saw the longing etched on his face. It was too risky, she knew that, and no matter what his decision, she would have to join the others. 'I'll go wherever you lead, Mama,' he said.

During the next few days, they found two occasions to be alone together in the house and they used them to their advantage. There was also one more dusk scramble next to the old boat before a telegram arrived commanding Ignatius to return to his post ahead of time. Dame Lily fussed around her son on the morning of his departure, making sure his bag was packed with clean underclothes and a freshly baked currant cake. Then she hugged him for such a long time that it was hard for anyone else to get a look in. He threw his arms around Blanche and Sir Geoffrey and when it came to Sybil, he held her close for what felt like a moment too long and a lifetime too short, and whispered in her ear, 'I promise.'

They sat in the drawing room with coffee after he left, each of them deep in their own thoughts. Dame Lily dried her face on her blue and magenta scarf and lit one cigarette after another.

'You can't go home tomorrow,' she demanded of Sybil and Blanche. 'I insist you stay another few days which will be much more cheerful for all of us.'

Blanche was delighted and Sybil wanted nothing more than to be distracted from the intrusion of reliving every minute she and Ignatius had been alone together, so she accepted graciously.

As promised by Dame Lily, the time in Norfolk had done them good. They were rejuvenated when they returned home and approached their artwork with renewed energy. The WAAC accepted Sybil's paintings of the wedding and the group of workmen at the Westminster Palace site, and Sir Leonard told her to keep at it, although no exhibitions would be planned until the end.

Vague, infrequent letters arrived from Ignatius, none of them expanding on the time they'd spent wrapped in each other's arms at Seagulls' Watch. The brief period when they hadn't been able to keep their hands off each other had clearly meant nothing more than that to him, and that outcome was fine with her. In her next letter to him, she wrote about the progression of her latest piece and how there was no conversation other than the end of the war. She said she'd enjoyed their time in Norfolk and that she was looking forward to seeing him again as a friend. When she reread the lines before she sealed the envelope, they sounded right. Now they could go about their lives without fear of one hurting the other, but out of curiosity – and nothing else – she wished she knew what he'd meant by the promise he'd made when they'd parted at Seagulls' Watch.

Blanche was working on a piece that depicted the George and Dragon pub sign in Cley. Sybil admired the way it made her feel as if she were standing on the ground, staring up at the board swaying in the breeze with clouds scudding behind it. Then Blanche put down her brush and gazed at the windowsill for a moment. 'Do you think we should get another cat?'

Sybil tried not to sigh out loud. The more she'd thought about getting her own place to live, the more she'd warmed to the idea and longed to get started on the quest. And whilst that life did encompass a pet, she couldn't very well have an opinion on a cat that Blanche would end up looking after on her own. But perhaps she should agree as she couldn't find the words or the courage to tell her friend she wanted to move out.

The letterbox rattled and Blanche said she'd go. 'One for you from Dame Lily and one for us from Ellen.'

Sybil said she'd put on the kettle for a break.

'Right,' Blanche said. 'Shall I go first?'

'Yes, please,' Sybil said. 'It seems like ages since we heard from Ellen.'

Ellen wouldn't be home for Christmas again this year.

'Poor girl,' Sybil said. 'And poor us, having to miss her for such a long time.'

'But what she does say is, "*All things being equal, and I know they're not always, I should be home for good soon after and when I'm back in dear old Blighty I don't think I'll ever leave again.*"'

That made Sybil laugh. 'She must mean she never wants to work in a field hospital again, and who could blame her?'

'She's not sure what she wants to do when the bloody war ends. She says nursing has been fantastic, but she never thought of it as a career, although it would be very sad not to use her skills in that area again.'

'That must be a dilemma for a lot of people.'

Blanche stopped for a moment and dipped a bit of dry flapjack into her tea before continuing to read aloud. '"*I'm not sure if I'll be able to make a go of it as an artist although having sketches accepted by the WAAC will hopefully help. Please don't ask me why, but I'm drawn to lithography, printmaking and textile design. Maybe it's because I've put my heart into nursing and there isn't enough of it left to depict people in a raw, emotional state. I think I'd be better off leaving that to you, Sybil.*" Oh, and she's still writing back and forwards to that chap Ian with the poorly arm. The one she nursed overseas. He's been medically discharged from the Services and is working in his brother-in-law's haulage firm.'

'There must be a lot of call for that,' Sybil said. 'Some people are very clever in their business dealings.'

Blanche nodded. 'Oh, for goodness' sake. She asks most diffidently if she can stay here when she gets home. Until she gets on her feet. As far as I'm concerned, there's no question that she must. But what do you think, Sybil?'

Sybil sat up straight. With Ellen on her way back to soften the blow, this might be the perfect opening in which to bring up the subject of moving. She wiped her hands on her skirt and took a deep breath. 'Blanche,' she started. 'You are very dear to me. You know that, don't you?'

Blanched nodded and blinked. 'Of course I do,' she said. 'We're closer than some families. You, me and Ellen. But what's that got to do with ...'

'I think it might be time for me to find my own flat. With room for a studio. Soon. Maybe not too soon. But to start thinking about it, at any rate.'

Blanche took off her spectacles and wiped them on her skirt. When she put them back on her eyes were cloudy. 'Aren't you happy here?' she asked. 'I know I'm not Auntie Myrtle, but I've tried to make you feel welcome and comfortable. This is your home, isn't it?'

Sybil reached over and grabbed Blanche's hands. 'I think,' she said gently, 'that this will always be my home. But maybe I'm too happy here, and if I stay indefinitely I might never leave. It has nothing to do with you or Auntie Myrtle or Ellen – it's to do with ... space and independence and making myself do something I never thought I could: get used to living by myself.'

'I could see it in you,' Blanche said. 'A restlessness. And then there's Graeme and Ignatius to consider.'

Shock coursed through her, and she pulled her hands away

from Blanche. 'Graeme, of course. There's still a chance he might come home. But Ignatius?'

'I wasn't born yesterday,' Blanche said as if she were sucking a slice of lemon. 'Anyone with eyes in their head could see there was something exciting going on between the two of you. Even an old spinster like me.' She stared at Sybil, daring her to tell her she was wrong.

That familiar flush crept up towards Sybil's hairline. She sat back in her chair and looked at Blanche. She cringed when she thought of Dame Lily and Sir Geoffrey and how she and Ignatius had probably failed to hoodwink them too. 'Does everyone know?' she asked in a feeble voice. 'How could I have been so naïve?'

'No one mentioned it when we were at Seagulls' Watch, but I saw Dame Lily and Sir Geoffrey look at each other and raise their eyebrows a couple of times. Not unkindly. It was more of an "I told you so" gesture.'

Sybil pressed her fingers to her mouth and tears started in her eyes. 'How humiliating.' She hung her head.

'I'm not being judgemental, although I will admit to feeling a touch envious. You mustn't feel bad about yourself. There's nothing wrong with having feelings for someone else. I think you've done marvellously well to carry a flame for Graeme all this time. You deserve your bit of happiness. No one begrudges you that.' Blanche sat on the arm of Sybil's chair. 'I'm sure Dame Lily and Sir Geoffrey are the height of discretion, but they might be worried, too. It's not uncomplicated, is it?'

Sybil wrung her hands and slipped her wedding ring over her knuckle and back. She looked at Blanche and tried hard to keep the blush from rising. 'No matter what people think, there is nothing between me and Ignatius,' she insisted. 'Just a few days of recklessness. Nothing more. Very foolish of me, I'm sure you'll agree and I ...'

'Well, you might be able to kid yourself,' Blanche said quietly. 'But you can't fool me.'

'I must insist there isn't, and to tell you the truth I don't believe there was ever anything true about Graeme's feelings for me, either. But if he does come home, that is something we will have to sort out one way or another.'

Blanche looked at her with pity and that made Sybil squirm. 'I had to get used to being on my own, too,' she said. 'Although I did have dear Auntie Myrtle. It was the Great War that did it for me, but it doesn't have to be that way for you.'

'I think it does and I have to plan for it,' Sybil said.

Blanche sighed. 'I do understand your wish to have a place of your own and a studio sounds spectacular. But there's enough room here for all of us if you do want to stay. After all, entire families are living in one room so finding anything like the space you're talking about could be difficult. We could spruce up Auntie Myrtle's old room and give that to Ellen, so we're in a better position than most.'

Sybil blew her nose and looked up at Blanche. 'For my career and for my future, I think I must head out on my own. Anyway, I think it will take me a long time to find the right place. That's why I wanted to talk to you about it sooner rather than later. Is it alright if I stay until it's all sorted out?'

'Oh, Sybil. This is as much your home as it is mine, and I will always love you with my whole heart.'

'Dear Blanche,' Sybil said. 'You are truly your aunt's niece.'

'Do you know, I think that's the loveliest compliment anyone's ever paid me.'

Blanche retrieved Ellen's letter and they both read the last paragraph in silence.

'Right, now let's hear from Dame Lily.'

'I'd forgotten about her letter.' Sybil picked up the envelope. 'Don't tell her, will you. She'd be mortified to think something else had distracted us from what she had to say.' Her fingers shook when she split the envelope. What if Dame Lily wanted to reprimand her for whatever it was she thought was going on with her son, or she accused her of being a brazen married hussy? Perhaps she'd told Ignatius she knew what they'd got up to at Seagulls' Watch, and when he'd said it was nothing more than a fling for both of them, Dame Lily hadn't been as liberal-minded as she appeared to be and accused them both of being promiscuous. Or maybe a neighbour had gossiped about how they'd spied on them when they'd abandoned their clothes to get at each other behind *My Lovely Jean*, and she blamed Sybil for ruining her family's reputation in Cley. But she'd never know until she took out the letter and read it.

Not wanting to embarrass herself in front of Blanche any further, she scanned the writing first and to her relief, other than one superficial sentence, Ignatius wasn't mentioned at all. What Dame Lily did say was that she was giving her and Blanche the head's up. Sir Leonard was planning a major touring exhibition for the end of the ****** war – which was not long now, she hoped – so they should work furiously and present as many paintings to the WAAC and RBP as possible.

'That's that then,' Blanche said. 'No more tea breaks for us.'

Sybil took the cups and plates to the kitchen and when she returned Blanche gave her a close hug. 'Everything will come right. Take my word for it.'

Then they picked up their brushes and started again where they'd left off.

That evening, after Sybil put away a few bits of laundry in her room, she stood and stared at the towel covering her self-portrait. She hadn't worked on it for a while, but she knew where she needed to pick up. She thought about the ifs and buts and implications the conversation with Blanche had brought up and her stomach clenched. When she'd received the telegram years ago, she was hysterical that her husband of a few months might never come home – now she was distraught when she thought he might.

She peeled back the covering and peered at the half of herself she'd completed. Anger rose again from a wound deep in her chest, and she wanted to slash the canvas with a pair of scissors or throw it out the window to rot beneath the bushes. Then she looked at it again and saw the same spot of fortitude and daring that had been in the female stoker's eyes. She knew then that the portrait was about so much more than the crumpled telegram she held in her painted hand. It was about that last letter from Graeme and the paragraph she'd made up to rewrite the narrative. It was about the WAAC and RBP, the waitress in York, the young woman with the empty pram, the angry man in Stoke and the bride in the incinerated church. It was about Ignatius and Dominic, isolated nights in Wales and choking, smoke-filled days in London. It represented the horrors of sleeping in the Underground and living on rations and the eerie noise of the doodlebugs with a list of names written on their underbellies. Not least, it was about Blanche missing her chance because of the Great War and Ellen working tirelessly at a job she never intended to do.

Her legs buckled beneath her and she bumped to the floor. What would she do with it if she did finish it? Perhaps she could hang it in her own home as a reminder that the war had provided her with a break into the art world. But no, she shook her head. It wouldn't do to glamourise that fact. She would give up all she'd accomplished if it meant the war had never started in the first place. All along she'd wondered if she would have the nerve to exhibit it, but if she couldn't expose herself to that extent, then she would have to decide what she was painting it for, and now she knew. The depiction of agony and mettle was for everyone living through it with her. She took a deep breath, picked up her brush and added a little bit more to the slip of bad news in her hand.

The Home Guard was stood down and Christmas came and went. At the end of January, they reeled from the details they heard on the news about the liberation of Auschwitz.

'It hardly seems possible,' Blanche said. 'We knew all along that Hitler and his mob were heinous, but how could they have done such dreadful things?'

'It beggars belief,' Sybil shook her head. 'Children, too. I can't find words to say how vile it is. And I expect there's worse to come. I know the war isn't over yet, but it seems to be a given, so I feel justified in saying it would have been a waking nightmare if they'd won.'

'No matter what, I don't think Churchill would have let us give in.'

A few photos had filtered through, making the atrocities more stark than their imaginations ever could. 'Do you think the WAAC has sent anyone to the scene?' Blanche asked.

'Men, no doubt,' Sybil huffed. 'Our constitutions wouldn't be able to bear it. We'd end up fainting or something worse. Crying about messy hair or a laddered stocking.'

Blanche laughed. 'I know we haven't seen battle close-up ...'

'Don't forget those dog fights in the sky,' Sybil interrupted.

'That's true. And the immediate effect of so many bombing raids. But,' she stood back and gazed at the canvas of a bus stop that was resting on her easel, 'I don't think I could draw the aftermath at a concentration camp,' she said. 'Could you?'

Sybil added a swathe of grey to the damp coat worn by a woman hurrying away from a queue outside a butcher's shop. She grasped a small boy's hand, and another teetered beside her with a shopping bag of his own. The woman looked the viewer in the eye as if she were wondering why they didn't have anything better to do than stare at her. 'I think I could,' Sybil said at last. 'Because their stories most definitely need to be told and, as we've said before, women bring a different perspective to their pieces.'

For months they trudged backwards and forwards to the WAAC with their compositions where all of Sybil's were purchased immediately along with most of Blanche's, but as Sir Leonard had said would happen, none of them were put on display yet. Whenever they were there, they held onto each other and gawked at the picture of the month hanging in splendid isolation, not unlike Sybil when she'd been alone in Wales. Whilst they were admiring *Christ Driving the Traders from the Temple* by El Greco, it almost slipped out that she'd seen it on the walls of a bunker deep in the mines, but luckily she bit her tongue in time.

'It must have been well taken care of, wherever it was. It doesn't look dirty or chipped at all.'

'No, it looks as though it's been treated lovingly. And I'm sure we don't know the half of it,' she said, although she was privileged to know the whole story. 'Shall we look in on Jane?'

Jane lifted her perfectly arched eyebrows and smiled when she saw them. 'I'm about to take coffee to Sir Leonard then we can have a cuppa and a chat.'

Whilst she was gone, Sybil whispered to Blanche, 'If she doesn't bring it up herself, I'm going to ask how things have proceeded with Cyril.'

'Alright,' Blanche hissed back. 'And I won't let on that you told me all about it.'

'I think that might be best,' Sybil said.

'I'm so glad you popped in,' Jane said. She was carrying a tray and kicked the door closed behind her. 'It's been ages since I've seen you. Wonderful news about the end, isn't it?'

Sybil winced. 'I know that's all everyone is talking about, but I don't want to get overexcited. Not until we hear it officially.'

'Well, I'm allowing myself to be elated,' Jane said. She handed around a plate of rich tea biscuits. 'If you've read about Dresden or Iwo Jima or the conference that met in Yalta, how could you be otherwise?'

Sybil looked out of the small window above Jane's head. Despite the dimout, the blackouts hung limply on their rail in case an alert sounded and they had to revert to a full ban on light again. That was enough for her not to get too carried away by the momentum, although it was hard to stay sceptical in the face of everyone else's optimism.

Jane sat up straight and fluffed her hair with her red fingernails. 'Have a look at these.' She produced a stash of letters from her bag. 'Do you think I should let Cyril off the hook or make him hang on a bit longer. Read them aloud, please, they make me feel triumphant.'

Sybil and Blanche took it in turns to read the letters from Cyril which changed in tone from rather arrogant and flippant to worried, then to downright degraded. '"*And so, my beautiful, sophisticated Jane,*"' Sybil read. '"*If I were with you, I would hand you a huge bouquet and let you feel my thumping heart. I can't think about coming home from this ****** war without knowing you have consented to become my fiancée. I agree to all your stipulations from allowing the dog to sleep on our bed to your mother living with us. Please put me out of my misery and say yes. As soon as I'm demobbed, we can shop for a ring and set the date.*"'

Blanche giggled and Sybil could see the funny side of it, but felt a twist of sympathy for Cyril, too. Jane had got exactly what she wanted, now she thought it was time for her to stop rubbing his nose in it. 'Poor bugger,' she said. 'And if he takes a hit now at the last minute, it will be poor you as you'll never forgive yourself.'

Jane tapped her nails on the desk until they were a blur of red. 'You're right.' She nodded. 'Of course you are. Will you both come to the wedding?' she asked.

They smiled and agreed, but Sybil wondered why what she'd said had made her think of Ignatius when she had so many more important things – a place of her own, an art career and whether Graeme would return or not – to dwell on.

They lost each other in the crowds on V-E Day and Sybil worried that the crush might make Blanche anxious. She should have known better. Finally, she spotted her in Oxford Circus, her lips firmly glued to the mouth of a man in a shiny suit, and wondered how many years had passed since Blanche had been kissed like that. From a distance, she watched until she, too, was whirled around and pressed to a soldier's face. He smelled of sweaty beer and cigarettes and they both laughed out loud when they parted.

When Blanche's chap moved on, Sybil grabbed her friend's elbow and guided her back into the slipstream of revellers.

'I've lost my sketchbook,' Blanche slurred.

Sybil laughed again. She knew Blanche liked a gin or two, but she'd never seen her worse for wear. 'Let's try and find it,' she said. 'Or the amount you've had to drink won't be the only thing you regret in the morning. Can you remember where you last had it?'

Blanche peered through her spectacles and turned in a circle. 'In a pub,' she said.

'That one?' Sybil pointed across the road.

'I don't think so. But we could give it a try. Have another little one whilst we're there?' Blanche framed her fingers into a measure.

'Maybe later, to celebrate if we find your sketchbook. Can you remember what the pub was called?'

A look of deep concentration made Blanche scrunch her features. 'Something to do with music,' she said.

They wandered about, getting caught up in hugs and hokey-cokeys and the froth slopped from pints of beer. 'Maybe it was that one,' Sybil said as she pointed to The Lyric.

There was a crush inside and someone in a group shouted, 'You're back!' when they saw Blanche. The sketchbook was being used as a beer mat on the table near them, and when they called for the same all around, Sybil found herself with a double Gin & It in hand and thought she too would soon be garbling her words.

The landlord, a pint in each hand, told everyone to be quiet whilst he got Churchill on the wireless. A cheer went up when the

Prime Minister spoke about the unconditional surrender signed by the Germans, the ceasefire that sounded all along the Front and how the dear Channel Islands had been freed. Then when he said, '*We may allow ourselves a brief period of rejoicing, but let us not forget for a moment the toil and efforts that lie ahead,*' the landlord switched off the radio and yelled, 'Bugger that!'

More drinks were called for and they joined a snaking conga that found itself a minute too late for Churchill's appearance on the balcony of the Ministry of Health building. That made Blanche bawl and blather and repeat at least ten times that she had so wanted to see the great man. One more drink and a few more kisses, then Sybil guided Blanche towards home before she had to carry her the whole way.

25

June 1945

The sun struggled behind a sheet of grey sky on the day the official letter dropped on the mat. Sybil sat and traced the black edging with her fingers whilst she watched Blanche's cat, Constable, stalk a leaf under the blackthorn tree. Opening the envelope would rip apart the sticking plasters holding her old wounds together, and she knew what it would say, so it hardly seemed necessary.

She looked towards the kitchen furtively and thought about hiding it until she could tear it to pieces or throw it on the fire when next it was lit, but Blanche poked her head around the door. 'Anything for me?' she asked. 'Oh.' She put her hand on her heart. 'Shall I sit with you whilst you open it?'

'Yes, please,' Sybil said in a dull voice. She made room for Blanche in the armchair, took a deep breath and opened out the one sheet of paper. Graeme James Paige was pronounced dead whilst on active duty presumably at the time and in the place where he was reported missing in action. The authorities regretted having to tell her this news. They sent their condolences and wanted Sybil to know that they were most grateful for his service.

One tear escaped her eye and made its way down to her chin where Blanche wiped it away. 'I'm alright,' she said. 'It was expected.'

'But to see it written down is another thing.' Blanche sounded choked up.

'Yes,' Sybil said. 'After years of being in limbo, I suppose I'm officially a widow.' She slipped her wedding ring over her knuckle.

'I don't think you have to do that just yet,' Blanche said. 'Many widows wear their rings for the rest of their lives.'

She hesitated, the tiny gold circle dangling from the tip of her finger. Although a deep sadness wrapped itself around her, she felt lighter without it. 'I know,' she said. 'But I don't think I want to do that.'

'Can I get you anything? Shall we have a cup of tea?'

'Thank you,' Sybil said. 'That would be lovely. I'll just go and put this upstairs for safe keeping.'

'Right you are,' Blanche said. She put her hand on Sybil's arm. 'It's perfectly alright to cry. Either on your own or down here with me or anywhere you feel you must.'

Sybil nodded and felt something catch in her throat.

In her room, she stood and gazed out of the window. A couple of neighbours were gossiping over their fence, and in the distance, a crane swung its load over a building site, a cloud of dust dancing around it. Far beyond where she could see, Graeme might be lying under newly planted crops or beneath a rebuilt road, or perhaps his body had been picked up, gently and lovingly, by another woman who'd also lost a husband, and placed in a grave with others who'd taken it that day.

She burrowed her ring in the envelope and nestled it in with their wedding certificate and her other important documents. Then she lay on the bed and thought about how they'd met and how much Graeme had seemed to love her then. Enough, at least, for him to ask her to marry him. She'd been so happy. Or thought she had been. But she knew now that he'd represented nothing more for her than a way out of her loneliness – another body in the flat, someone to sleep with, cook for, a reason to come home. Just as she was a diversion for him from whatever had happened with Heather.

She turned on her side and hugged her knees to her chest. The tea was probably ready, and the smell of toast drifted towards her from the kitchen. Up to a point, he'd been good to her and for her. He'd come along at a time when she needed someone, and he'd filled that void. Although she was sure they wouldn't have stayed together, he certainly didn't deserve the end he'd met.

Tears came then, and she heaved from an empty stomach. It wasn't fair that the war had taken away his future but given her the break into the art world she'd longed for. She snubbed her running nose on the sleeve of her cardigan and told herself that the best thing she could do was continue to paint the stories of the countless numbers who'd experienced the war for as long as the world wanted to see them.

The tea and toast revived them, and Blanche asked if she still wanted to look at flats that afternoon. They'd viewed three to date, none of which were quite right, and Sybil thought Blanche enjoyed the process more than she did.

'Yes,' Sybil said. 'I think we should go ahead. But first I must write a letter to Dame Lily and tell her about Graeme. I imagine she'll soon get news about Dominic, if she hasn't done already.'

She wanted to stay reasonably close to Wandsworth as it seemed a big enough step to be moving out, let alone to the other side of London. That being the case, it was a miracle there were two more places to look at when so many properties were beyond habitable.

They were met by the landlord at the first flat which was in Putney. Sybil wondered about the landlords and how they had accrued the money to buy up houses when almost everyone else was living hand to mouth. Then she cringed when it struck her that she'd accumulated quite a tidy sum herself, and if she wanted to be altruistic, she could buy property and rent it out inexpensively to people in dire need. But she wasn't a businessperson, she was an artist, and she wasn't making her money from increasing rents needlessly. Still, guilt crept over her. 'Perhaps,' she said to the landlord as he showed them around. 'It would be better to rent this to a family who's been bombed out.'

As the man straightened his necktie, a wristwatch glinted from under the cuff of his shirt. 'Not many families could afford it,' he said.

That flat wasn't right either, but had it been perfect, Sybil was sure she wouldn't have given him a penny of her money.

The next address was above a parade of shops in Tooting. Despite the dull day, light flooded into a room that overlooked the Commons. 'This would make a wonderful studio.' Blanche clapped her hands together.

There was also a living space, a small kitchen, a bathroom and bedroom, but it was difficult to see them properly as they were crammed with knick-knacks, clothes, books, papers and crockery. They looked at the pieces of art on the walls, and Sybil thought whoever had lived there had a good eye. She asked the same question of the young landlady that she'd asked the previous landlord.

The woman wrung her hands. 'This was my Nana's flat and I'm not very good at being a landlady,' she said. 'Nana loved it here.' She looked around the living room as if she hoped to find her grandmother tucked up amongst the paraphernalia of her life. 'She was staying with her sister in Finchley when they took a hit and I'm afraid ...' She swallowed loudly.

'It's alright.' Blanche clasped the woman's hand. 'We've lost people, too. Haven't we, Sybil?'

'We all have,' Sybil said softly. 'Can we sit?' She pointed to the sofa.

'I told Mum I'd take care of this as she can't face it, but I'm not sure I can either,' the woman continued. 'We would have gladly rented it to a family, but we're quite precious about it so thought a single person or a couple would be a bit easier on the walls and doors and carpets. Is it just the two of you?'

'Me on my own,' Sybil said. 'With a lot of art materials.'

'Oh,' the young woman said. 'Nana loved art.' She swept her hand around the room. 'As you can see.'

They both nodded and Blanche looked at Sybil, encouraging her on with raised eyebrows.

'Would you allow a pet,' she asked. 'A cat or small dog?'

The landlady closed her eyes and didn't open them until she'd smiled sadly and said, 'Nana loved animals, too.'

'Then may I please take it,' Sybil said.

The landlady reached across and shook Sybil's hand with both of hers. 'I'm so glad,' she said. 'And Mum will think you're the perfect tenant.'

They agreed on rent and then the landlady muttered the inevitable word. 'But – must you vacate your place immediately?'

'No, she must not.' The lines around Blanche's mouth turned into the strings of a pulled purse. 'She's lived in my house for quite a while and can stay as long as she likes.'

That probably confused the young woman. Not many people decided to leave adequate accommodation at the moment, but she kept her thoughts to herself and said they needed about a month or so to sort out her nana's belongings. 'Would you like any of the furniture?' she asked.

Sybil hadn't given that a thought, but now that she did it made sense to keep some pieces as a good start. They went through the flat and the landlady wrote a list of what Sybil wanted. When they talked about a lovely old table and chairs, the young woman started to sniffle. 'We sat around this so many times for tea and games of cards.' She stroked the wood with the tip of her finger.

'Would you rather it didn't stay?' Sybil asked.

'None of us has room for it, so it would have to go to the WVS. I'd much rather it was here. I'm sure you'll take good care of it.'

Sybil said she always did her best with the things she owned, but she racked her brain to think of any of her possessions, other than her art materials, that were precious to her. No one had left her anything and she'd always lived in furnished places so had nothing to cling onto. But she had people she loved and admired, she told herself, and she tried to hold onto them although some slipped away.

'You'll keep these, won't you?' Blanche was caressing the long, dark, velvet curtains in what would be the studio. 'They must have cost a fortune, and they'll break the bank to replace.'

Sybil pulled them as far back as they would go, and dappled light spotted the room. 'I don't think so,' she said. 'We grumbled about the lack of light for so many years, now all I want to do is bathe in it.'

'But what about if you want to paint at night?'

'I could use streetlamps. Or the moon and stars. There's candles and electricity, too. And no more blackouts, so I wouldn't have to worry about the light attracting wardens or bombers.' She raised her arms and spun around the room like a child in a playground. 'We're free from all that at last.'

Blanche pushed her spectacles up on her nose and laughed. 'And the good thing is, I don't think this room is overlooked from any angle.'

'No, it isn't.' The landlady joined them at the window. 'Nana used to say she could walk around here in the nude, and no one would be any the wiser.'

'That,' Sybil said, 'would make quite a picture.' She wondered if their newfound freedom from the war would give her the chance to try something in that direction. It would be quite different from anything she'd done before. Or she could turn her hand to horses in fields. Or children hop-picking or museum attendants or waiters. The list of possibilities made her dizzy with excitement.

Dame Lily had received a letter about Dominic and said she and Sir Geoffrey had taken a few quiet days to themselves. Aloysius had come home, and she'd unashamedly followed him around so closely that she was sure he was pleased to return to his duties. Sir Leonard had been in touch to say a final WAAC exhibition was being arranged for the beginning of November at Burlington House. Had she had notification? She had a meeting with him on Wednesday the 11th of July to discuss it, and Sybil was invited to meet her afterwards for lunch at the Ritz. She'd be there from noon.

Sybil had never been to the Ritz, and the thought of walking through the doors held open by a man in uniform had her scuttling to look her best. She pinned up her waves and held them in place with sugar water, made sure her eyebrows were even and wore a fawn-coloured dress with a dark green jacket. Blanche asked her if she wanted to borrow Auntie Myrtle's earrings and when she tried them on, they caught the light like chips of glass on the beach.

She knew the grand hotel had taken it nine times and the restaurant had been closed twice due to bomb damage, but no one would have known. As she was swept into a hushed world, she was easily fooled into believing nothing as distasteful as a war had ever touched it. The carpets were so dense she bounced when she walked on them, and subdued lighting bathed the marble in a soft glow. There was an abundance of artwork hanging on the walls and standing on plinths, and she wondered if it had all been stored deep in the basement during the bombing.

She gave her name to the maître d' at the front desk, and with his hands behind his back, he ushered her towards Dame Lily's table. Gawping at the bronze figures and ceiling of pink clouds on a blue sky, she didn't see Ignatius sitting with his back to her until it was too late to turn and run. He obviously had no idea she was joining them either, because he jumped when Dame Lily said, 'Sybil, how lovely to see you, my dear. You look wonderful, as always.'

She and Sybil exchanged kisses and when Ignatius offered nothing more than his hand for her to shake, Dame Lily's eyes widened in surprise.

'I hope you don't mind Iggy joining us?' Dame Lily threw her silver and lilac scarf over her shoulder. 'He was in town for an interview at the Royal Free, and I want to spend every possible minute with him now that I can. Champagne?'

'Yes, please, Dame Lily,' Sybil said. The trembling she'd felt when she'd unexpectedly seen Ignatius had stopped, and she smiled at him with her mouth closed. It was inevitable that their paths would cross at some stage, and that time might as well be now. 'Did you get the place?' she directed the question at Ignatius.

He cleared his throat and ran a finger around his collar. 'I'm afraid I don't know yet,' he said. 'They're going to inform me.'

'But you've been demobbed already?'

He shook his head. 'Not yet, but if I'm selected to read medicine, I'll jump the queue.'

The waiter presented Ignatius with the label on the bottle of champagne, and when he nodded his approval, Sybil thought about the strange custom. No doubt Dame Lily would pay for the meal but her son, a soon-to-be student, was given the privilege of accepting or rejecting what was poured into their glasses. *It's all for propriety and appearances*, she thought, and a sudden weariness came over her. How she wished that wasn't the case and they could all be more open with each other. Life would be so much easier that way.

'I was so sorry to hear about Dominic,' she addressed mother and son.

'As we were to find out about Graeme,' Dame Lily said.

Ignatius murmured his condolences and when he caught sight

of Sybil's bare wedding ring finger, he paled and looked away quickly.

'Although the outcome was what we thought it would be deep in our hearts, it's still a shock.'

'We're going to have a memorial service for Dominic in the near future.' Dame Lily lit a cigarette and blew the smoke towards the puffs of painted clouds above them. 'I know you never had the privilege of meeting each other, but we want to invite you and Blanche as you are like family to us.'

The pallor of Ignatius's skin changed to crimson. Sybil knew how that made her feel, so she averted her gaze until he gathered himself together. 'Thank you, Dame Lily,' she said. 'Blanche and I would be honoured.'

They tucked into braised kidneys, veal sweetbreads, carrots and peas. Dame Lily ordered wine and when Ignatius mopped up the juices on his plate with a slice of fluffy white bread, Sybil followed suit. There was no point in wasting the most delicious food she'd ever tasted. Dame Lily laughed. 'You two were meant for ...'

This time it was Sybil who felt hot colour rising from the neckline of her best dress.

'What are you working on, Sybil dear?' Dame Lily seamlessly changed the subject.

Sybil thought about the self-portrait under the cloak of the old towel. When she'd received the definitive letter about Graeme, she'd thought she wouldn't be able to finish it, but slowly she began to feel she could stand back and view it from a distance. Since then, she'd hardly worked on anything else. She knew she was the same woman in the picture, but she felt so different now. The thought of taking it – raw and incomplete – to her new beginnings in the flat was unbearable. It needed to be inconclusively finished when she moved, so the momentum to complete it had escalated into a near frenzy.

She could have told all of that to Dame Lily, but she didn't feel ready to do so. Instead, she described her idea of painting a young soldier greeting his wife and little girl outside a terraced house in Latimer Road. She'd come across the scene on one of her jaunts, and the sight of the man scooping up his wife and spinning his child around had made warmth spread through her.

'Do you still use your permits?' Ignatius asked.

'Oh, yes,' Sybil answered. 'No one's asked for them back, and they allow me much better access to situations than I would have as a mere nosy member of the public.'

'Yes,' Ignatius said, 'I can imagine.'

'Did you know that Iggy is going to exhibit at Burlington, Sybil dear?'

'Are you?' Sybil was surprised. 'That's marvellous. Studies from your active duty?'

'I hope so. And one portrait.' Ignatius held her gaze as he referred to the painting of Dom he'd trusted her to know about. 'If I get them finished and if the Committee accepts them.'

'I don't see any reason why those things won't happen,' Dame Lily said.

'Blanche will definitely be exhibiting.' Sybil dabbed her mouth with a corner of the snowy serviette. 'And Ellen has had a couple of paintings accepted by the WAAC, but she intends to work on others when she gets home.'

Dame Lily straightened her scarf. 'I'm sure both Iggy and Ellen will be successful.'

Their plates were taken away and tiny meringues topped with swirled cream and a slice of strawberry were put on the table. The sweet treats melted on Sybil's tongue, and she wished they'd been served in big slices. They had coffee and squares of chocolate, then Dame Lily put her serviette on her plate and excused herself abruptly. 'I'm so sorry, I forgot to tell you that I promised Catherine and Desmond I'd be with them in Chelsea at a quarter past two on the dot.'

'But, Mama.' Ignatius rose from his seat. 'I insist you let me take you.'

'No, I insist you don't. I shall have a cab hailed. Ask the maître d' to put everything on my bill.' She kissed and hugged each of them, and then she was gone in a slipstream of shimmering lilac and silver.

They sat back down and stared at each other.

'It's so unlike Dame Lily to leave without rounding off the meal with a cigarette at least,' Sybil said.

'Nothing about Mama surprises me.'

The silence between them was so absolute Sybil could hear her own pulse in her ears. She watched Ignatius stir half a teaspoon of sugar into his coffee. 'Mama tells me you're moving into a flat of your own,' he said at last. 'That's very brave of you.'

'Yes,' she said. 'It's lovely. Light and spacious. With a wonderful outlook. You must come and ...'

'Perhaps,' he said. 'But we can't keep doing this forever.'

'Doing what?'

'This strange dance.'

'We tried dancing once,' she said with a smile. 'Do you remember?'

'Of course. Then you ran away. Like you always do.'

Sybil was taken aback, and without giving the statement much thought, came to her own defence. 'I'm quite sure I don't know what you're driving at.'

Ignatius studied her openly, then leaned back and lit a cigarette of his own. 'I think you must do,' he said steadily. 'But I'll give you the benefit of the doubt and explain. I've given you advance warning that Mama has invited us to Seagulls' Watch at the same time, and I've offered to bow out if you want me to, but you always assure me it will be fine because, if we are to be friends, then we must get used to being in each other's company.' He took a breath and waited for her response.

'Yes, that's right. And I stand by that. We're bound to come across each other on occasions, so we have to behave like the friends we are.'

He looked down, flaring his nostrils until the rims were white.

'But then you allow me to think you want to be more than that and bang! You pull away again.'

The tops of her ears were throbbing with a deep red blush. 'I'm sorry if I've been giving you the wrong impression. I suppose I was trying to sort out my feelings.'

Ignatius nodded then looked away. 'I have feelings, too, which I need to sort out. And,' his eyes bored into hers again, 'I've made them quite plain to you. I like you very much, Sybil. In fact, I would go so far as to say I'm in love with you.' His voice cracked when he put that into words. 'And you seemed very keen yourself when we were last together at Seagulls' Watch.'

'Nothing was said between us, so I thought those few days were a short, sweet diversion from reality. For each of us.'

'Sybil.' He leaned forward. 'You are my reality. Or could be. And if you remember, I offered to exchange promises, but you said you didn't want any and I respected that. Then when we wrote to each other afterwards, you used some fancy footwork to skip backwards again and said we should revert to friendship, nothing else.'

A waiter appeared soundlessly at the table and asked if they required anything else. Ignatius ordered a whiskey and soda and Sybil a Gin & It.

'It seemed easier that way,' Sybil said. 'What with Graeme, and you starting medical school, and my career and new flat to think about.'

'You're not very open, are you,' Ignatius said.

That gave Sybil a jolt. An hour or so ago she'd been decrying British society for that buttoned-up trait which she thought they'd all be better off abandoning.

'And I haven't wanted to pry. But I know something happened in your marriage and it hurt you …'

'Not just that.' Sybil squirmed inwardly. 'I'm not a very good judge of character. Or of people's intentions,' she said. 'Let alone my own.'

The little lines around Ignatius's eyes softened when he

heard that, and he reached for her hand. 'I also said at Seagulls' Watch that you could tell me all about it, but again you demurred.'

She started to protest, but he held up his hand. 'Never mind that now. I still I think we can make each other happy, but I can't and won't wait forever. I have to watch out for myself too. So, if you think we have a chance, or would at least like to try, can you please let me know?'

She opened her mouth to answer, but he drained his glass and cut her off. 'Not here.' He looked around the room as if suddenly aware of where he was. 'Let's stay away from each other completely, no letters or telegrams or meeting up until … I don't know … the end of October? Just before the exhibition.'

Three months, Sybil thought. That was long enough to give them both enough time to cool off. And by then, when she told him without any doubt that all she could offer was friendship, he'd be used to the idea and wouldn't take it so badly. 'I think that's a very good plan,' she said.

'Can we shake on it?' he asked.

With an overwhelming feeling of relief, Sybil giggled and offered him her hand. They shook and then pulled apart, but not before they both held on for a beat too long.

He folded his napkin and stood. 'I'll clear the bill at the desk,' he said.

'Thank you, Iggy. But one more thing. What was your promise when we said goodbye at Seagulls' Watch?'

He looked at her sadly. 'Not now,' he said, echoing her own words to him when she turned down his offer of assurances before they'd scrambled for each other behind *My Lovely Jean*.

She sat and watched him walk away, the heads of a few other diners turning to follow his smart retreat. Exhausted, she gave him a few minutes to make his getaway and followed after him at a much less purposeful pace. When she passed the bar on the way out, she caught a glimpse of him sitting on a stool, nursing another whiskey. His shoulders were hunched over, and he looked miserable. She thought about going to him, but they'd made a pact, and she was determined it was best to stick to it – for both of them.

She felt like a wrung-out cloth when she got home, but she had a cup of tea with Blanche and answered all her questions about dining at the Ritz. 'After I get settled into the new flat, I'll take you there for a high tea. Ellen, too.'

'My goodness,' Blanche said. 'That would be a treat, but I couldn't possibly. I wouldn't know how to conduct myself appropriately.'

That made Sybil laugh. 'You've never had any problems on that score,' she said. 'You always know exactly how to behave. Well, except for V-E Day but that was an exception.'

She made her excuses and went to her room where she could have flopped on the bed, gone over the days' events and slipped, hopefully, into an untroubled sleep. But there was the old towel in the corner and under it, the self-portrait that needed nothing more but a touch here and there to complete it. She rummaged under her bed and dragged out an easel, set it up and lifted the canvas on to it. Without ceremony, she took off the cover and stood back to look objectively at the composition as she'd trained herself to do. But she couldn't maintain that point of view this time and tears took over once again. She cried for herself as she had been and for the thousands of others who'd experienced the same heartbreaking situation she had. And also because, against all the odds and false starts and shattered emotions, she had been able to finish the piece, and what felt like a huge chunk of fallen masonry lifted from her shoulders. Now all she had to do was decide what to do with it.

When Ellen came through the door, none of them could say a thing. All they could do was throw their arms around each other and hold on tight. Then once they started talking, none of them could stop.

'You look wonderful,' Sybil said.

'So do you. There were times I thought I'd never see you again. Look – there are paintings everywhere.'

'Your sketches are here, too. All in a pile. You'll have to get started on them soon for the exhibition at Burlington House. How was your journey?'

'Endless,' Ellen said. 'But nothing's truly that, so here I am.'

'Are you still in touch with the haulage chap?'

'Yes. He'll be in London next week as he and his brother are trying to set up a branch here. It's been so long since I've seen him that I've honestly forgotten what he looks like. And Iggy?'

Sybil shook her head. 'We're nothing more than friends,' she said. She turned in time to catch Blanche as she lifted her eyes to the ceiling for Ellen's benefit and she felt small, like a child who didn't know her own mind. But she had her career, she had her flat, she'd learned to be on her own. There didn't seem to be any room – or need – for Ignatius.

Then Ellen looked at Auntie Myrtle's empty chair and the bare place on the windowsill and the tears came again. It was all new and raw for her.

'Oh dear.' Blanche rubbed Ellen's arms. 'Sybil and I have had a chance to get somewhat used to missing both of them,' she said. 'And I'm afraid we've put you in Auntie Myrtle's room, but we can easily swap. It wouldn't be a problem.'

'No.' Ellen was adamant. 'I'll be absolutely fine. The stark reality was a bit of a shock, that's all. And I am so grateful to be home.'

'We've smartened the room up for you,' Sybil said. 'And moved the furniture around. Shall we go up and see it?'

They all trundled upstairs with Ellen's things and settled her into the room. The breeze that fluttered the curtains felt like the touch of a warm cloak. 'I like the view from here,' Ellen said. 'I've missed the city.'

'Wait until you see the outlook from the windows in Sybil's flat,' Blanche said. 'I'll be over there every day painting the changing scene.'

'It's very exciting for you.' Ellen turned towards her. 'But please tell me you're not moving out because I'm moving in.'

Sybil laughed. 'You make it sound like a French farce. And no, of course not. But I'm glad we have a week together before I go. Come on.' She grabbed Ellen's hand. 'You must see what we've got for tea. Let's get it out from under wraps and tuck in.'

Ellen explained that she hadn't left the nursing service but would return to her position at St Mary's after a few days' leave. She picked up a tongue sandwich and nibbled at a bit of gelatine hanging over the crust. 'I don't know what I want to do, so I thought I'd stay on for now.'

'I'm sure you're still needed,' Sybil said.

'Desperately.'

'What about pursuing lithography and textile design?' Blanche asked. 'I thought that sounded fantastic.'

'I'm still interested,' Ellen said, but without commitment. 'Oh, I don't know. There's so much to think about now. So many of the things we dreamed of and yearned for before the war have changed or don't exist or no longer seem important. Time's moved on and circumstances have taken us in different directions. I suppose we're all starting over from a different perspective – good or bad.'

'I'm afraid you can't have one of those without the other.' Blanche blinked a few times. 'That's what Auntie Myrtle would have said.'

During the following week, Sybil and Blanche painted and Ellen joined in when she didn't have a shift. They tripped over easels and canvases and boxes of brushes and each other. Sybil's lovely dusty-pink blouse was smeared with black oil paint when she got too close to Ellen as she brandished a brush, and Constable's tail was trodden on a number of times.

The night before she moved, a sadness came over Sybil as Blanche helped her pack her things and said she would miss her and that she must come back whenever she wanted to.

'I'm going to miss you and Ellen, too,' Sybil said. 'But I won't be far away, and we'll be back and forth all the time. Don't forget I want you to paint the changing seasons from the window. Actually, I would love four compositions of just that to go on the left-hand wall. Can I please commission you?'

'What a wonderful idea,' Blanche said. 'You have such an eye for the potential. I'll start with *Winter* right after the exhibition.' The plan made them feel they were keeping a tight hold on the closeness that had grown between them.

The three of them made two trips backwards and forwards the next morning, laughing about what others on the number 16 bus thought about the motley collection of bags and boxes they were carrying. Sybil had tied string around the towelling cover over the self-portrait and she hugged it tight against her chest.

'What's that one?' Blanche tried to take a peek. 'For goodness' sake, you're protecting it as if it's an old masterpiece.'

It felt more important than that to Sybil. She'd sweated and cried and been through a whole orbit of emotions to bring it to life and she couldn't chance hurting it now. She wanted to see that tiny light of bravura in her eyes and have it speak to her of where she'd been then and where she was now. And if it was exhibited, perhaps next to *Woman Stoker*, she hoped it would show other women their own courage and strength and determination. 'Oh, don't undo it,' she said.

'You've tied it so tightly, I couldn't if I tried,' Blanche said. 'Is it something we haven't seen?'

'Yes.' Sybil nodded reluctantly. 'I've been working on it in my room for quite a while.'

'Mysterious,' said Ellen. 'Can we see it when we get to your flat?'

'I don't think so,' Sybil said slowly. 'I'm keeping it under wraps for now.' She could feel Blanche studying her closely.

'Are you saving it for a grand unveiling at Burlington House?'

'I haven't decided what I'm saving it for.'

Ellen pulled the cord for the next stop.

'I understand that it might be especially poignant for you,'

Blanche said. 'We all have pieces of work like that. But knowing you, I dare say this speaks for and to many people and therefore shouldn't be kept under lock and key.' She patted the top of the wrapped canvas. 'And after everything the war has put us through, I think we deserve to see an image that would help us.'

They unpacked Sybil's bags and boxes and put as many things away as they could. Sybil treated them to a fish and chip supper, then they hugged, and Blanche said she would pop over in the morning to check everything was alright. Sybil found it hard to swallow as she watched them walk away arm in arm, but when she closed the door and stood in the flat all alone, she felt as if she were shedding an old skin for one that was fresh and new underneath.

The weeks took on a shape, with the three of them going between the house in Wandsworth and the flat in Tooting and it helped, knowing they were close by and that their friendship hadn't suffered because she'd pulled herself away. So it didn't take long for Sybil to settle down and feel as content as she'd done during the long, starlit nights in Blaenau Ffestiniog.

Very early one morning, she woke up refreshed and knew that the changes that had burgeoned in Wales were complete. She saw clearly that she hadn't really wanted Graeme or Hector. She'd merely wanted someone – anyone – when all she'd needed was herself. Now she felt she was self-reliant and self-sufficient, and if left entirely on her own, she knew she would be alright. That was when an ache for Ignatius started in the depths of her stomach and wouldn't go away. It seemed as if her newfound independence had opened a tiny chink that she thought she'd tightly sealed against him.

But they'd agreed on a plan and Sybil was glad of it. It gave her a bit more time to think and decide and form the words to say she agreed with him: perhaps they could bring each other happiness.

Besides, there was the exhibition to think about. The WAAC bought one after another of her paintings, and Sir Leonard said they would choose which to display at Burlington House and on the subsequent tour. During one of their meetings, he asked her confidentially if she would be interested in one last commission.

'Another?' She was taken by surprise. 'I thought the WAAC was going to be stood down.'

'Quite right.' Sir Leonard smoothed the front of his jacket. 'But this is a commission that must be fulfilled, and the Committee has agreed that you would be the best artist to bring the subjects to life. We need someone who is both highly professional and who will see right into the hearts and souls of those involved and lay them bare for all to see.'

Sybil thought she might cry. If, years before she was recognised, she could have chosen words to describe how she wished to be known as an artist, she would have used those that Sir Leonard had spoken. She felt humbled. 'Thank you, Sir Leonard,' she said quietly.

'Watch the post for a letter from me,' he said. 'And we can take it from there.'

Then, from out of the blue, Sybil asked if she could show a composition at the exhibition that he or the Committee hadn't previously viewed.

'That would be most unconventional,' he said. 'May I ask why you don't want us to view it first?'

'I know it sounds strange.' She shifted in her chair. 'But it's deeply personal and I keep wavering between letting it go or keeping it to myself. I don't think I'll be able to make up my mind until the very last minute.'

Sir Leonard studied her closely then said, 'If it wasn't for your remarkable reputation, I would say no. Categorically. But in this instance, I will make an exception. I do hope you'll decide in our favour, I am most intrigued to view it.'

'Thank you, Sir Leonard. For being so kind.'

Burnt orange and crimson leaves hung like gems on the trees as Sybil walked to the Underground. She took a deep breath and thought how lovely it was to look at them without fear of a bomb or incendiary spoiling the view. It didn't seem possible that she'd lived through the last five years. A woman pushing a pram emerged from a building that looked as if it had vital parts missing from it. She stopped to pick up a pint of milk from the doorstep and tucked it in next to the baby. There was still so much rebuilding to do – of their hearts and minds as well as their homes and offices, shops, pavements and factories – but for today all she had to worry about was what to say to Ignatius when and if he got in touch and whether or not to exhibit her self-portrait. After six long years of war, it was a wonderful position to be in.

26

War Artists' Advisory Committee,
Ministry of Information,
The National Gallery,
Trafalgar Square,
London, W.C.2

Wednesday, 3rd October 1945

Mrs S. Paige,
38, Garrad's Road,
Tooting Bec,
London, S.W.16

Dear Mrs Paige – Sybil,

I trust you are well.

Further to your discussion with Sir Leonard, the Committee is now in a position to offer you what will probably be the final contract commissioned by the WAAC. They are asking you to attend the Nuremberg Trials which are due to start in Germany on the 20th of November 1945.

None of the commissions you fulfilled for the WAAC during the war were easy, and this one will be no exception. Sir Leonard and the Committee can only imagine that it will be harrowing to observe, but if you decide to accept, they have no doubt you will present them with remarkable, haunting works of art to mark what will surely be the culmination of a terrible period of time.

During the years that Sir Leonard has known you, he has come to learn that you have a remarkable capacity for portraying emotions and inducing empathy, and he and the Committee sincerely hope that you will put your skills and talents to good use for this final, most important, commission.

The Committee would appreciate it if you would inform them of your decision directly.

Yours sincerely,

Miss J. Butterworth – Jane,
Personal Assistant to Sir Leonard Thwaites, CH KOB FB

Mrs S. Paige,
38, Garrad's Road,
Tooting Bec,
London, S.W.16

Saturday, 6ᵗʰ October 1945

Miss J. Butterworth,
Personal Assistant to Sir Leonard Thwaites, CH KOB FB,
War Artists' Advisory Committee,
Ministry of Information,
The National Gallery,
Trafalgar Square,
London, W.C.2

Dear Miss Butterworth – Jane,

Thank you for details of the commission the Committee has requested I undertake.

It is an honour for me to say that I would very much like to accept the commission and ask that you please thank the Committee on my behalf for trusting me with this unprecedented task. As always, I will do my utmost not to give any of them a reason to regret their decision.

I would appreciate you informing Sir Leonard that, with regard to the matter of the painting that I was unsure whether to exhibit, I have decided that I would like it to be hung at Burlington House and in the touring exhibition. However, I request that it remain in my personal collection.

Please inform me of when you would like me to come to your offices to sign the contract for the commission. At such time, I will bring the painting with me.

Yours sincerely,

Mrs S. Paige – Sybil

Ignatius Fortescue,
The Royal Free Hospital,
Grays Inn Road,
London, W.C.1

Thursday, 25th October 1945

Mrs S. Paige,
38, Garrad's Road,
Tooting Bec,
London, S.W.16

Dear Sybil,

I hope you are well and enjoying life in your flat.

As you can see from the above, I have been accepted to read medicine at the Royal Free, and so far, it certainly hasn't been an easy option as getting used to studying again is quite hard. But I'm not complaining, as I'm also finding the whole process very worthwhile.

Please find enclosed a photograph which Al took of me on the marshes in Cley. Mama and Papa would have made a better job of it, but they would have asked too many questions, whilst Al is still the younger brother who does exactly what I ask him to do. It was a windy day and that is why my hair is so ruffled – I can't get used to having it a little bit longer yet. In case you can't make it out, I'm kneeling by our boat and the name on the keel has been changed to *My Lovely Sybil* – I always keep my promises.

Iggy X

Mrs S. Paige,
38, Garrad's Road,
Tooting Bec,
London, S.W.16

Monday, 29th October 1945

Ignatius Fortescue,
The Royal Free Hospital,
Grays Inn Road,
London, W.C.1

Dear Iggy,

Thank you for the photograph. I am going to keep it close to my heart at all times.

I look forward to seeing you at Burlington House.

With love,

Sybil X

27

November 1945

When Sybil came into view of Burlington House, all she could do was stop and stare. Despite the relentless rain, the queue for the exhibition was longer than any she'd seen for sausages or milk or a dab of butter during the war. She skirted around the throng and was about to slip into the exhibitors' entrance when in the distance she caught sight of Dame Lily, grappling with a black umbrella.

'Dame Lily.' Sybil hurried towards her. 'Is that the same umbrella you had an argument with when I bumped into you outside the Central all those years ago?'

'My dear.' Dame Lily offered Sybil her cheek to kiss. 'It might as well be. Each of the bloody contraptions I buy ends up in a tangled mess – like this.'

'Never mind that now.' She took Dame Lily's arm. 'Let's get inside and sort it out later.'

She guided Dame Lily towards the door and closed it behind them.

'Oh.' Dame Lily shuddered. 'It's colder back here than it is outside. They could have given us a nicer way in.'

'We couldn't have used the main entrance. Have you seen the queue?' Sybil asked. 'It's unbelievably long. It's made me feel quite jittery about this.'

'People have been starved of culture.' Dame Lily took a

deep breath and closed her eyes. 'We're heading back towards civilisation. I'll soon be exhibiting my seascapes again.'

'Hopefully, Dame Lily. But for now, we must tidy ourselves ready for the off.'

They walked through what Sybil would have thought was a rabbits' warren before she'd worked at Manod mine for six months. Following the yellow arrows this way and that, they found the cloakroom and joined the other artists exhibiting that day.

Every time the door opened, Sybil strained to see if Blanche or Ellen had arrived until at last, there they stood, framing the doorway together. They didn't immediately run and throw their arms around each other, but smiled softly and pointedly, enjoying a moment of deep understanding. Then as one, they met in a huddle. Dame Lily joined them, and they murmured their congratulations and thank goodnesses and well dones. There was mascara to be wiped away after that. Blanche cleaned her spectacles; Ellen swept her hair up in two combs; Dame Lily rearranged her scarf, lit a cigarette and blew the smoke towards the ceiling. And with her back to the others, Sybil patted the photo from Ignatius that was cosseted in her vest. Then it was time to make their way to the gallery.

Once the doors were opened, Sybil doubted there would be any time to think, but she wondered if the others, like her, were dwelling on how they had made it to this point. So many things could have stopped them in their tracks – not least of all a world war which had arbitrarily taken the lives of millions of others but had somehow left them to start anew. The thought made tears prod the backs of her eyes and when she glanced at Ellen, she had welled up, too.

Some of the artists standing next to their works lifted their hands or nodded towards her. She scanned the room for Ignatius and when she couldn't see him her heart seemed to plummet, but then he appeared from behind a panel in the furthest corner of the hall and she smiled, her heart back where it should be. He stood still as if immortalised in a timeless portrait and looked at her, his face a bright puce.

Jane Butterworth, immaculate in a navy two-piece suit and heels to match, asked for quiet and announced that Sir Leonard would like a quick word.

'Ladies and gentlemen,' Sir Leonard said. 'This a monumental occasion and you should all be rightly proud of yourselves, as I am of each and every one of you. Thank you all for your contributions over the years, which I am sure the crowds today and the generations to come will appreciate as immensely valuable. As you are aware, the WAAC will be dissolved next month so I, along with the Committee, would like to wish you the very best with your careers.

Now, before the public beats down the doors, you are allowed a few minutes to admire your own and others' compositions before I declare this exhibition open.'

Sybil took a deep breath and gazed at Blanche's groundsman maintaining a football pitch for the lads clutching a ball and Ellen's patient hooked up to a line of lifesaving medicine. Then she stared in disbelief at her compositions of the angry man in Canterbury; the beautiful firewatching sisters in St Ives; the ragged Union Jack clinging with all its might to a razed terrace of houses; the courting couple in their bombed-out hideaway; the soldier spinning his little girl in Ladbroke Grove. And of course, the female stoker in Darlington, hanging next to the younger woman Sybil had been, collapsed in a chair with her head thrown back, mouth wide open in anguished torment, a crumpled telegram hanging limply from her hand. No one else had viewed it until she'd handed it over to Sir Leonard, and now he was by her side, a crowd gathered behind them.

Not a sound could be heard until there was one long collective intake of breath. She had wondered if the tiny glints of diamond-bright temerity in both their eyes would be discernible in the space of a gallery, but they were there in all their shocking intensity. Sir Leonard started to clap quietly, and the others joined in.

'Congratulations, my dear.' Dame Lily touched her shoulder. 'These are extraordinary. Together they will undoubtedly be two of the war's most significant and poignant paintings.'

'Thank you, Dame Lily,' she said. She looked again for Ignatius and found him, staring first at the self-portrait, then at her. She tried to excuse herself to get to him, but viewers began to file in, and he returned to his station to mingle with them. She stood on tiptoes to take in his exhibits and could make out three of military scenes that were overshadowed by a stunning portrait of Dom. The grave yet innocent face was beautiful, and tears gathered in her eyes when Dame Lily wavered slightly as her gaze followed Sybil's.

Sybil answered question after question about her work and her career as a war artist. Whenever she turned, her self-portrait had attracted quite a group, and she was aware that the public found it compelling. She thought back to the number of times she'd started it, then left her attempts torn or crumpled or for ashes in a fireplace. It seemed then that she'd been trying to put her whole being into the piece and leave it there to rot. It wasn't until she was thriving on her own that she realised she could put her heart into the painting and walk away with it intact and able to beat in a new direction. Walking past, she glimpsed the self-portrait over the heads of the crowd and saw again the smallest flash of pluck she'd captured in her own eyes. Perhaps people thought it shone with the belief that her husband would eventually come home, but she knew it was a glint of spirit for ultimate acceptance of herself and her situation.

Her other paintings garnered a lot of attention, too, and a man in a dark coat approached her with a notebook in his hand. 'Mrs Paige, the artist?' he asked.

'Yes,' Sybil said. 'That's me.'

He nodded. 'I'm Desmond Phipps, Arts Editor at *The Illustrated London News*. May I have an interview, please?'

Those familiar feelings of flattery, and having done nothing to deserve it, washed over her again. She looked around for guidance, but everyone was in deep conversation with other people.

'And my photographer will be along in a few minutes to take a snap of you with one or two of your remarkable paintings.' Then he carried on as if she'd given her permission, and she didn't stop him.

'Would it be possible to have your age and a few of your details? Place of residence, place of birth, where you studied, etc.?'

'I'm thirty-three, I was born and live in London and studied at the Central under Dame Lily Brampton.' She indicated her mentor with a quick look in her direction.

'Ah, yes,' Desmond said. 'I hope to get an interview with Dame Lily, too. What were your commissions for the WAAC?'

'I was lucky enough to get a number. My first was to catalogue the part women were playing on the Home Front up and down the country.'

'Is that where you found the inspiration for *Woman Stoker* and *Firewatching Sisters*?'

Sybil thought about that. Of course she knew what he meant, but the word inspiration made it sound as if the idea for the composition had popped into her head from nowhere. 'Yes,' she said. 'I was sketching in the North Road Locomotive Works and saw the female stoker from the corner of my eye, then spent a little while drawing her at work. But ...' She wondered if she should go into it with the reporter or leave her thoughts where they were.

'Please go on,' he said. 'Our readers will be interested in anything insightful you have to offer.'

'Well, I'm not sure if inspiration is the right word. It sounds too vague and ephemeral. As if the ideas came to me in dreams with very little input from the subjects, when in fact what I hoped to achieve was the gritty reality of each person's life. Whether I had an actual concrete conversation with the subjects or not, each of them shouted to have their story told and I was no more than the means to do that. It was as if they became a part of me and guided my hands to reflect the reality of their situation at that particular time on that given day.' She thought she might be rambling, so asked Desmond if any of that made sense.

'Absolutely,' he said, looking at her with curiosity. 'I can tick off a number of my questions all at once. And your next commission?'

'I was contracted to travel to each of the Baedeker-raided cities and draw the clear-up efforts. That's where I met this bereaved gentleman.' She pointed to *The Angry Man*. 'I will never forget him. Or any of the others I met, subjects or not.'

'That must be very hard for you.'

'I suppose now their stories are a part of mine. As you're probably aware from the press release, my following commission was six months in the Manod mines where I was tasked with sketching how the treasures from the National were being kept safe.'

'I was going to ask about that. What an experience that must have been.'

'In so many ways.' Sybil remembered the labyrinth of tunnels, backed up with masterpieces, the walks amongst the hills, the nights she'd spent wrestling with her own thoughts whilst she looked up at the night sky. 'It was humbling to see the genius of Sir Leonard and Professor Hazelmere at work.'

'I believe we'll all benefit from the addition of monitored air conditioning after the National is redesigned. As will other galleries around the world. But why are none of those drawings on view?'

'I believe that some are in the vaults, but the vast majority were given to the workers in Blaenau Ffestiniog who manned the mines during the war.'

'I see. I have a feeling my editor will be sending me on a jolly to Wales next. Can you talk me through this one, please? *The Telegram*. It's both harrowing and hopeful.'

They walked towards the painting and gazed at it along with a number of other people. This was the first time she'd had to talk about the composition that had wrung her inside out for years. She took a deep breath and said, 'It's a self-portrait. Early on in the war, well before I'd had a commission from the WAAC, I lived alone in a bedsit. There was a knock at the door and when I opened it, I was greeted by the sight of a telegram boy who handed me a black-trimmed envelope. "I'm sorry, Miss," he said. All I remember is opening it with quaking fingers, reading it through to find out that my husband was missing in action, and collapsing into the nearest chair. I closed my eyes to shut everything out and when I opened them again, the world was a different place.'

'May I be so bold as to ask if he's ...'

Sybil answered that she'd had an official confirmation that Graeme would not be coming home.

'I'm sorry for your loss,' Desmond said.

Talking about her paintings was one thing, but opening up about her private life was another. 'Thank you,' she said. And left it at that.

'And it's extremely poignant hanging next to *Woman Stoker*.' He looked from one to the other of the paintings several times. 'What is it that draws the two together. I can't quite ...'

Sybil waited to see if he would be able to discern the one similarity.

'Oh, how remarkable,' he said. 'The eyes. Or the glint in them.'

He stared at her, then scribbled furiously in his notebook.

Sybil didn't want to elaborate, she thought it much more meaningful to let the portraits speak for themselves.

Desmond cleared his throat and continued. 'You haven't used many colours,' he said. 'Do you prefer to draw and paint in black, white, grey and a touch of sanguine?'

All traces of diffidence gone, Sybil answered with confidence. 'Initially, it was the lack of light during the blackout that attracted me to draw in chimerical shades, then as time and the war marched on, I realised that we were all living in shadows and my work should represent that.'

Sybil had given her full attention to the reporter for some time, so was surprised when she looked up and saw a number of people milling about, listening to her interview. She turned, and behind her she caught a glimpse of Dame Lily talking to a woman whose back was to her. Blanche was chatting with Ellen and another couple, and when she became aware of Ignatius, looking at her from afar, a visceral reaction to his closeness ran through her.

'Will that be alright, Mrs Paige?'

'I beg your pardon,' Sybil said. 'Would you repeat that, please?'

'I know I'm taking up a lot of your time, but can you please tell me about any other commissions entrusted to you by the WAAC?'

'There is one other,' she said. 'It starts next month. I've been asked to be the official war artist at the Nuremberg Trials.'

Desmond's mouth hung agape. 'My goodness,' he said. 'That's quite a ...'

'Privilege,' Sybil finished for him. 'Although I'm well aware that listening to the evidence will be excruciating.'

'How are you preparing for it?' he asked. 'I mean, can you somehow harden yourself against it?'

'I wouldn't want to do that,' she said. 'As much as possible I want to experience all of it as the victims themselves had to.'

A young man with a camera and flash bulb tapped Desmond on the shoulder and she was asked to stand between two of her paintings and pose for a photograph. She didn't know how to arrange her face. To smile seemed almost sacrilegious in light of the subject matter next to her, but if she didn't, she thought she would seem too solemn for an end of war exhibition. At that moment, she glimpsed Ignatius, his hands behind his back and his dark auburn hair aflame as it caught the light. She touched the hidden photo of him next to their boat and he must have thought she was touching her heart – which perhaps she was – because, as the flash popped, he reddened and smiled. The photographer said the pose was perfect and her shoulders relaxed.

'What next, Mrs Paige,' Desmond asked. 'I mean, after the Trials. Will you start to paint in colour?'

'Oh,' Sybil said. 'I hadn't thought of that, but perhaps I will experiment in that direction. I'm also thinking of composing nudes.'

'That will certainly be different.'

'Or concentrate on what will surely be a long period of rebuilding. Whatever happens after Nuremberg, I will continue to try, at least, to speak for people through my art. People and what they tell us through their eyes and expressions will remain at the essence of what I do.'

'Thank you for your time, Mrs Paige.' Desmond held out his hand. 'This spread will be in Saturday's edition. Now, I must go and find Dame Lily.'

He wandered off and Sybil tried to push her way through to get to Ignatius, but she was stopped by questions being thrown at her, and it wouldn't do to ignore them. She began answering as many as she could and when next she looked up, Ignatius was leaving by the main door.

By the time the exhibition closed, Sybil's voice was dry and she was in dire need of a drink. Dame Lily twirled her bright peach-coloured scarf around her neck and declared that she was glad they didn't have to be present for the entire run.

'Oh, I agree with that,' Blanche said. She sat on a bench facing one of her pieces and rubbed at her swollen ankles.

'It was rather invigorating though,' Ellen said. 'I mean, some of the questions really made me think about how I'd achieved what I had.'

'That's right,' said Dame Lily. 'But I'm wary of too much analysis. It can take the magic out of the process.'

'Some of the questions were downright silly, for goodness' sake,' Blanche complained. 'I wish I had a pound for every person who asked me if I was happy that the war was over. Really! I don't think any person on earth would say no to that.'

'Perhaps they meant in terms of no more commissions from the WAAC and RBP which leaves us in the position of having to find other subject matter now.'

'Yes, I suppose so,' Blanche conceded. 'But nothing would make me unhappy that the war has ended.'

Dame Lily wandered over to Dom's portrait and stood for a few moments taking in every detail. Then she kissed the tips of her fingers and laid them on his painted face. When she turned, tears were in her eyes, but she commanded, 'Coats, umbrellas, the pub.' With that in mind, they quickened their steps to the changing rooms then filed out into the squally weather.

Dame Lily tucked her arm through Sybil's and snuggled close. 'Part of me is envious of your final commission, but mostly I'm so glad it's not me having to experience the war through the eyes and words of the victims. You will take care of yourself, my dear, won't you?'

Sybil smiled at Dame Lily. 'You've always watched out for me, Dame Lily. Thank you.'

Dame Lily squeezed her arm. 'I couldn't let a talent like you go unnoticed and then ... well, you know how much I think of you. Now, of course, we've been through a lot that holds us together. Your Graeme, my Dom.' The name of her son gathered in her throat, and it took her a few moments to press him back down towards her heart. 'And then there's ...'

'... Iggy,' Sybil finished for her. But she wouldn't say anything more to Dame Lily before she'd had time on her own with Ignatius.

'Have you heard from any societies?' Dame Lily was adept at changing the subject yet again.

'Yes, the Royal Institute of Oil Painters and the Society of

Women Artists. Of course, I've replied and said I would be honoured to join.'

'Good, good. Nothing from the Royal Academy?'

Sybil shook her head. 'But I'm quite alright with that. Please, no canvassing on my behalf. This is me clicking my fingers at you. Something I've longed to do for ages.'

Dame Lily laughed. 'Oh dear,' she said. 'What goes around, comes around.'

The rain stopped and Sybil looked behind to make sure Blanche and Ellen were following. Ellen was smiling, and Blanche shook her head in mock disappointment at what her younger friend had said. It was good to see that some things never changed.

'Where are you taking us?' Sybil asked. 'I thought we'd be going to The Marquis. Our usual.'

'We're on our way to the Queen's Larder,' Dame Lily said. 'We're almost there now.'

'I haven't been there for years,' Sybil said. 'Not since …'

'All that time ago when we met again quite by chance. The war was just beginning.'

'And we had to hurry to get to shelter before the blackout and the bombing. Little did we know then what was to come.'

'Thank goodness for our ignorance.'

Dame Lily stepped through the door Sybil held open for her, and they waited for the others to catch up. A corner of the lounge bar must have been caught up in a raid because it had been inexpertly shorn up, waiting for a more permanent repair. Sybil thought she might like to sketch the shoddy wall, regulars harbouring against it with pints in their hands – but not now. This evening was for celebration, not for work.

They found a table, and Sybil and Blanche said they would go to the bar with the order of four double Gin and Its.

She looked around whilst they waited and thought that the pub wasn't as much of a curiosity as it had been. Gone were the candles along the bar and the detested blackouts had given way to lighter, flowery curtains which remained open to let the glow of streetlamps in and the blaze of electric light out. *How strange it will be*, she thought, *to try to explain all of this to the generations who hadn't experienced it.* But the paintings they left behind would make that easier.

At the table, Dame Lily was telling Ellen that she would be returning to Cley within the next day or two and that she was welcome to visit at any time. She took her glass from Sybil and said, 'It's quiet, except when we host a party. But the light and the views are magnificent. I'm sure Sybil and Blanche have told you as much.'

'They have,' Ellen said. 'It sounds like a beautiful place. But Ian's parents have invited me to stay with them in Hertfordshire for a week or so and I'll have to do that before I accept any other invitations.'

'How is he doing now, poor boy.' Dame Lily lit a cigarette and inhaled deeply.

Ellen laughed. 'Please don't feel too sorry for him,' she said. 'In comparison to some of the sights I've seen, he got off lightly. And his business is doing well. It would, though, in this environment, wouldn't it?'

'And what do his parents think about having an artist in the family?' Sybil asked.

'We're not quite at that stage yet,' Ellen said. 'But—'

'Oh,' Blanche chipped in. 'You'll soon be like Edith Hopkins rushing out of Morgan Langley's room with curlers in her hair.'

'I can assure you that Ian is nothing like the odious Morgan Langley.' Ellen pretended to be insulted. 'And I, as you can clearly see, have no need for hair curlers.'

'For goodness' sake.' Blanche sniffed. 'You've always been so proud of that hair. I remember when you wore a ribbon in it every day as an affectation. You were privy to that, weren't you Sybil?'

Sybil tried not to giggle, but it was hard. 'Yes,' she said. 'I was.'

She controlled herself and added that the style had been very fetching.

'Who are those two characters?' Dame Lily asked. 'You're making them sound less than attractive.'

Blanche sketchily described Morgan Langley and Edith Hopkins, and Dame Lily said Langley sounded like the worst kind of art snob.

'Did they marry?' Ellen asked.

Blanche put her hand over her mouth and her eyes widened. 'What with everything else, I must have forgotten to tell you. Edith took to going to London at weekends, and eventually she failed to return. Not long after, Mr Merton received a resignation letter from her in which she asked him to tell Langley she'd married an old flame and was very happy.'

There was stunned silence around the table. Then they burst out laughing as if that news was the funniest thing they'd ever heard.

'Langley is all yours then,' Ellen said.

'Please.' Blanche held up her hand. 'I wouldn't dream of standing in your way.'

'Oh, my dears.' Dame Lily wiped her eyes. 'You are a splendid double act. I insist you visit Seagulls' Watch together. In fact, I am banning each of you without the other. Iggy.' She raised her hand in greeting. 'We're over here.'

Her back to the door, Sybil could feel her face colouring. She longed to see Ignatius again, there was no doubt about that, but she wanted them to be on their own in a quiet café, or the corner of a restaurant, or sitting on a park bench in the shade of a tree. She wanted them to say what needed to be said without anyone else listening or changing the conversation or watching for their reactions. And she needed to see his face and the light in his eyes and make sure that what he said was the truth about his feelings for her.

Dame Lily introduced him to Ellen and said, 'Blanche and

Sybil you know, of course. Sybil quite well by now, I would have thought. What with all the letters and visits that used to go backwards and forwards between you.'

Ellen and Blanche looked from Ignatius to Sybil but didn't say a word.

'Gin and Its all around, please, Iggy. Doubles and whatever you want.'

Ellen looked at her quizzically, but Sybil changed the subject by asking how many people they thought had passed through the exhibition that day.

'Hundreds, my dear,' Dame Lily said. 'Jane will have a more accurate number and she'll keep me informed.

'I thought she might have joined us today,' Ellen said.

'Yes, I did ask, and she still might, I suppose. But I think she wanted to get home to the dog, her mother and her fiancé.'

'I can't believe it.' Sybil looked at something far away and her voice was small. 'So many terrible things have happened, but we've come through as the lucky ones. We have our lives and we've made a jump start into our art careers.'

There were murmurs of agreement and Sybil thought about Jenny, the waitress, the female stoker who had given her so much, Gertie and Harriet and their flag, the angry man, the women of the WI and the young woman with the empty pram. Then with all her heart she silently wished them well.

Ignatius avoided Sybil's eyes as he handed a drink to each of them.

'Here's to us,' Ellen said as she held out her glass for a toast.

When it came to touching her glass to Ignatius's, Sybil and he looked directly at each other, and a shadow of a smile crossed both their faces. 'To us,' he mouthed and raised his drink with a nod.

'Iggy.' Dame Lily held an unlit cigarette between her fingers. 'Grab a chair from that table and sit here.' She shifted closer to Blanche.

'It's quite alright, Mama,' Ignatius said. He walked around the table to Sybil and tentatively placed his hand on her shoulder. 'I'm happy here.'

Sybil covered his hand with hers and left it where it was. She would show him her flat and perhaps he would sit at the table, his medical books spread out around him, whilst she painted in the soft light that filtered through the window. There would be walks and cups of tea and drinks in pubs. She would tell him about Graeme and why the female stoker meant so much to her. They would chat and laugh and discuss paintings they viewed at the National. They would go to Seagulls' Watch where she would help him varnish their boat and the salt in the air would sting their faces.

But before any of that, she would sketch the trials at Nuremberg and let the paintings speak for each and every one of the victims – and hope that the entire world would look and listen and learn.

Acknowledgements

A big thank you to my agent, Kiran Kataria at Keane Kataria Literary Agency, for her support and advice.

My thanks go my editors, Bianca Gillam, Holly Humphreys, Tania Doney, Lottie Hayes, Lydia Mason and the entire team at Aria Fiction/Head of Zeus/Bloomsbury Publishing.

For the lovely cover, I would like to thank the designer, Simon Michele.

Colette Paul, my fantastic tutor on the MA Creative Writing course at Anglia Ruskin University and The National Centre for Writing in Norwich have given me invaluable support for which I am very grateful.

I would like to thank my beautiful grandchildren for keeping me busy and out of mischief.

A huge thank you goes to Don Gilchrist, Kelly Collinwood-Erdinc, Liam Collinwood, Ozzie Erdinc, Arie Collinwood and to all my family and friends who give me their very much appreciated support and encouragement.

Author's Note

With the publication of my fifth novel, I think it would be fair to say that the chance mention of an event that happened during World War 2 - the rebuilding of Waterloo Bridge by women - was the catalyst that led to me becoming an author of novels set in that era. As well as learning so much about the courage, adaptability, and resilience displayed by women and men during the war, I have also come to understand that the experiences people had during that time, in terms of the human condition, are still being experienced now. The details may differ but human beings, and the ways in which they act and react, don't change. Writing about that era is a wonderful opportunity to explore universal emotions, ambitions, love, loss, parenting and a whole list of other life events. My novels explore the many ways in which ordinary people are affected by extraordinary events and how they cope during times of adversity. I'm also interested in highlighting the similarities, as opposed to the differences, between people and the way that shared experiences and emotions bind them together.

About the Author

JAN CASEY was born in London but spent her childhood in Southern California where a love of books and literature was instilled in her by bookworm parents and regular trips to the library. For many years, she was a teacher of English and Drama and she worked, until recently, as a Learning Supervisor at a college of further education.

Now that her lifelong dream of becoming a published author has come true, she spends her time writing, reading, swimming, walking, cooking, practising yoga and enjoying her grandchildren.